A
PRIDE
OF
HEALERS

A PRIDE OF HEALERS

Richard Clark Hirschhorn

WILLIAM MORROW AND COMPANY, INC.

NEW YORK   1977

Printed in the United States of America.

1   2   3   4   5   6   7   8   9   10

Library of Congress Cataloging in Publication Data

Hirschhorn, Richard Clark.
   A pride of healers.

   I. Title.
PZ4.H67234Pr [PS3558.I675]   813'.5'4   76-48130
ISBN 0-688-03128-5

BOOK DESIGN   CARL WEISS

. . . TO MY FATHER,
who taught his son that in exercise of the intellect
does Man share in the Act of Creation, and

. . . TO MY MOTHER,
who made such arrogance bearable.

That I may find him, and with secret gaze
Or open admiration him behold
On whom the great Creator hath bestow'd
Worlds, and on whom hath all these graces pour'd;
That both in him and all things, as is meet,
The Universal Maker we may praise;
Who justly hath driv'n out his Rebel Foes
To deepest Hell, and to repair that loss
Created this new happy race of Men
To serve him better: wise are all his ways.
  So spake the false dissembler unperceiv'd;
For neither Man nor Angel can discern
Hypocrisy, except to God alone,
By his permissive will, through Heav'n and Earth:
And oft though wisdom wake, suspicion sleeps
At wisdom's Gate, and to simplicity
Resigns her charge, while goodness thinks no ill
Where no ill seems: Which now for one beguil'd
Uriel, though Regent of the Sun, and held
The sharpest-sighted Spirit of all in Heav'n . . .

PARADISE LOST, Book III
JOHN MILTON

A
PRIDE
OF
HEALERS

Chapter / **ONE**

HAD FRANCIS HÉBERT LIVED THIS WARM, SUNLIT APRIL DAY, HE might have recalled the wave of languorous peace evoked by fifteen milligrams of morphine sulfate injected into his left buttock. To those who received his pain-wracked body from the ambulance, it seemed only that the excruciating agony that had torn and lacerated his abdomen was abating. With a grateful sigh, the patient lay back upon the stretcher and uncoiled from his tortured fetal position.

Even as the intern scanned the old hospital record for some clue as to why the patient in front of him was dying, and the nurse isolated a vein into which to run saline, and the laboratory technician drew from the collapsed vessel a sample of blood for cross-matching fresh plasma to reinfuse life, and the orderly inserted a flexible rubber catheter into the penis to monitor the urine production from the failing kidneys, Dr. Lansing Prout's telephone answering service was trying to reach the perpetually elusive doctor. Somehow, Cromwell's most prominent physician held the strong conviction that patients and their diseases should respect a lifetime's labor, and reserve dire calamities for weekdays between the hours of nine and five. Saturday afternoons were sacred, as were Wednesday afternoons and Sundays. The inconsiderate intrusions into those hallowed times of such manifestations of human frailty as incipient death were to be scorned and looked at askance.

By the time Prout's white Mercedes pulled up into the No Parking Fire Lane outside the Mercy Hospital Emergency Ward entrance, it was obvious to those pumping blood into the unconscious patient that life, an always mercurial commodity in these chambers, was fleeing the sinking hulk before them.

Prout sought out the intern. "What's happened to Hébert here?" he inquired, with just the slightest tinge of apprehension staining his calm.

The people clustered around the stretcher moved back like the Red Sea parting before Moses. The tall, regal physician moved closer to the prone figure. Prout soberly scanned the comatose patient whose limbs were writhing and face grimacing in response to some inner mortal struggle.

The dying patient was about sixty years of age, grossly obese with rolls of fat crowding the confines of the narrow stretcher. He had long since stopped breathing on his own. His round bald head and fat face were punctured by a long black corrugated rubber tube inserted into his windpipe and connected directly to a thumping mechanical lung. Four thin wire electrodes fastened his arms and his legs to an EKG machine from which flowed smooth rivers of white paper with cryptic etchings. Two bottles of blood were pouring simultaneously through separate plastic tubes into both wrists, oblivious to the fact that with every beat of the weakened heart, a torrent of the same vital fluid was escaping from a crack in the ruptured wall of the aorta, that singular great artery through which must pass all the freshly oxygenated blood of the body.

The patient heaved spasmodically, his limbs convulsing and flinging out to mark his subconscious fight against the inevitable ascendancy of death.

The intern was no more than twenty-five or -six years old, short, slight, with smooth cheeks, blue eyes, and blond hair cut in an old-fashioned crew cut. A panicked expression marred his young face. He could not respond to the interrogator's rapid-fire questions. His hands minueted ineffectually over the surface of the patient without ever stopping to accomplish anything tangible, the constant motion a vain attempt to obscure his patent impotence.

Turning away from the young doctor with a disgusted shrug, Prout looked impatiently for Bea Wharton. As he expected, the tall, thin head nurse was calm and unruffled. In her early sixties, devoid of bosom or buttock, packaged in a rigid starched white uniform, she seemed designed strictly for function. Her rimless glasses were perched on the end of an angular pinched nose. Her face was pale, the skin smooth and set off by clusters of tight gray curls surrounding the precariously situated nurse's cap.

After thirty years of experience in the Mercy Emergency Ward, Bea was inured to the repetitive mortal skirmishes. She had long been a constant and attentive spectator in this test arena where Cromwell's physicians were ruthlessly challenged and exposed in their attempts to salvage impending disasters.

She knew Prout well. In his early seventies, handsome and distinguished, he walked proudly, shoulders back, head erect and covered with snowy white hair, his face lean, expression stern, eyes still clear and piercing. She was deeply aware, however, that Prout's sage demeanor, his measured speech and careful assured movements were all false external symbols of a once-enviable medical wisdom and skill. How he had deceived the people of Cromwell for the past ten years, she would never know. But, trap him in an emergency, present him with a critical problem that demanded instant action, and he was worthless.

Countless times she had seen his veneer crack as the flaw of his own incompetency surfaced. Ironically, despite insults and tragedies that would have stunted a lesser individual, his reputation never suffered, but was mysteriously augmented. Bea had often observed what almost amounted to an article of faith among the dim-witted of Cromwell—that to die at the hands of Dr. Lansing Prout was an act of grace.

She reached out and gently drew the patrician figure away from the crowded table. With deliberate tact and practiced humility, she offered the patient's old hospital record to her captive.

"Dr. Prout," she whispered, "I thought you might like to review the old chart." She continued in a casual tone, implying that the physician was no doubt in full possession of the facts without her assistance. "You had Mr. Hébert in here about two years ago, when his diabetes was out of control."

She handed the chart over to Prout. He took it and riffled through the pages, his eyes blinking back and forth from the paper to the heaving prostrate form before him.

"I think," Bea said, taking the chart from his hands, "if you check back to the Discharge Summary on that last admission, he was signed out as having an aortic aneurysm." She opened the folder to the place at which she had earlier bent down the corner. "You listed the diagnosis right here."

Prout reluctantly glanced at the page to confirm the tragedy she was pressing upon him. He chewed his lower lip in a nervous gesture. He did not really have to see what she held before him. He knew well what lethal process was destroying his patient's life. He did not need Bea Wharton to remind him. Certainly Hébert had an aneurysm. Now, it had ruptured, letting escape the rushing stream of warm blood that had kept this fat Canuck alive.

He remembered, as if it were only yesterday, the difficult time two years before when the life-threatening condition had first been discovered. Hébert's son and daughter had asked him whether their father should be operated upon then, to remove the frayed rotting tube and replace it with a woven Dacron vessel graft. He had been compelled to tell them that although the operation carried a high risk in an obese diabetic with coronary artery disease, the chances for survival were greater if the surgery was carried out electively at that time, rather than waiting until the vessel totally disintegrated and the patient went into shock from hemorrhage.

If he had told them the truth, why wasn't the patient operated upon? He wondered if he could have swayed the children not to sign the Operative Permit? Could he have subtly suggested that their father might live years longer without the aneurysm ever causing any trouble?

Prout caught the stern expression of the nurse by his side. He lowered his eyes to the chart again. The final decision had been a deceitful one. Now, like a biblical revenge, retribution was reaching across the years, branding him with guilt.

His eyes traveled over the patient's swollen abdomen, tense and turgid with quarts of sequestered fresh blood distending it and compressing the intestines trapped within. He knew very well why he had subverted the proper course of therapy. Up until fifteen years ago, all such vascular cases in Cromwell were sent into Boston for surgery. Then Carl Lash had come onto the staff, fully trained to do complicated blood vessel reconstruction. Prout clenched his fists, a wave of hostility and unrepressed resentment spilling over him—Lash insisting that these cases could be operated upon at Mercy, and successfully too, but only by those with board certification in vascular surgery. Yes, the secretive maneuvers by Lash and the rest of those young upstarts to restrict surgical privileges at Mercy had started it, the slow rot that was still infesting Cromwell, *his* Cromwell, *his* hospital.

The memory of that bitter fight remained sharp and clear. The battle must have taught Carl a lesson or two. Did Lash and his carpetbagger friends think that Mercy would move against a Prout, who had practiced there for forty-two years, and his father and grandfather before him? A century of Prouts in Cromwell.

He was one of the old school, not a fancy specialist—even the word tasted sour on his tongue—like Lash and Halpern and Crowther who were pecking away at him and his colleagues, curtailing their rights in the hospital until someday, if they weren't resolute and vigilant, they would be reduced to simple triage officers like trained nurses—or worse.

Well, he concluded with silent pride, he had survived their meanest tricks. But there lying in front of him like Lazarus, only coming from the living to join the dead, was Hébert, testing him, mocking him. What should he have done two years ago? When he had suggested sending the patient to Boston for surgery, the family countered, why Boston, when that new Dr. Lash could do the same thing right in Mercy Hospital? Should he have turned the patient over to that outsider? No, he was convinced he had acted properly to recommend against surgery. After all, the man *did* live two years, perfectly well. Was the loathesome mass of dying flesh blocking his vision this Saturday afternoon a sign that he had been wrong?

He shook his head to free it from the cloud of conflicting thoughts. It was too late to send Hébert to Boston. Should he call in Lash? Bile rose in the back of his throat at the thought of that tall cocky bastard asking the family why the aneurysm had not been treated two years ago.

Damn it! Prout had skinned his own skunks for over forty years. It would not be the first time he would perform an operation he had never done before. Every surgeon faced that unforeseen eventuality some day.

He turned to face the waiting nurse with the patina of carefully cultivated condescension, his particular hallmark in Cromwell.

"Bea, you had better get the Operating Room ready. I am going to have to go in. Please take care of the blood and the prepping."

Turning to the intern, he asked, with an exaggerated air of concern, "Is the family in the waiting room? I had better talk with them."

As he moved away from the scene, it is unlikely that anyone in the room realized that never once had the haughty physician touched the sinking human form in front of him. Now Lansing Prout had only one thought: to convince Hébert's son and daughter that their father, in some perverse way, had reappeared for the sole purpose of causing him unnecessary and unwarranted discomfiture, something, at his age, after what he had done for Cromwell, he positively *did not deserve.*

Chapter / TWO

LIKE SPREADING RIPPLES FROM A STONE THROWN INTO A TRANQUIL pond, Dr. Lansing Prout's decision to operate on Francis Hébert triggered off a series of reflex actions whose ramifications were to involve an increasing number of persons that afternoon. No sooner had the surgeon left the Emergency Room, when Bea Wharton picked up the telephone and dialed the switchboard operator. Within seconds, the loud nasal message, "Mrs. Hollis . . . Mrs. Marjorie Hollis," was bleating from loudspeakers in every corridor and department of the vast hospital.

The nursing supervisor had just placed her weary and overly

ample posterior onto a less than ample stool in the coffee shop for her eighth cup of coffee of the day, when the raucous call came piercing through the noisy background. With a muffled curse, heard only by the empty seats next to her, she barged her way through the crowd at the gift counter to reach for the telephone secured on the wall behind it.

Marjorie was a physically formidable lady in her early fifties, a widow for almost ten years. After her husband's sudden death, she had returned to nursing with a passion and zeal calculated to tire her mind and body so that she had neither the time nor energy to think of the too few years of her happy marriage. Weekends, night duty, Christmas, and holiday shifts, she took them all. No children. Few friends. Mercy was now her entire life. It gave her purpose, satisfied her craving to be productive, to be needed, and, most of all, voided that desperate cry of why she was the one to be stricken with loneliness after only five short wonderful years of marriage, which had come to her too late in life for a family.

"Marge?" Bea's concerned tone was almost frightening in intensity. "Prout's going to do an aneurysm. The patient's in shock."

"Prout?" Marjorie's incredulous voice echoed the Emergency Ward nurse's dismay. "Has he ever . . . ever done one? Bea, listen," she grasped for words, "listen, I've seen Lash struggle for hours over one of them. And he's good." She paused, half-hoping that it was all a big joke, that she had not heard correctly.

"Marge. You heard. Don't ask me why. Not now. You know Lansing. It's his patient. There is nothing you or I can do about it. You had better get things rolling." She stopped for just a minute, her voice breaking with fear. "The man is in real bad shape. And, Marge—pray."

As soon as she had broken the connection with the Emergency Ward, Mrs. Hollis reached into her bulging pocket. She took out a small battered spiral notebook and ran her finger down the numbers listed inside the back cover. She dialed the Valley Telecommunications Company office.

"Beep nine-oh-seven and six-one-five. The usual. Emergency!"

She banged the receiver in place and moved back to the counter. Still standing, she pushed her steel-rimmed glasses high up into her dyed red hair, gulped down the lukewarm cup of coffee that now tasted rancid and bitter. She moved ponderously toward the door, her normally placid face now twisted with worry.

Bea Wharton had not replaced the telephone, but kept hefting the receiver in her hand, her brow knitted in thought. Spinning the dial, she swiftly consummated the remainder of the necessary preparations for surgery.

It seemed forever until the Blood Bank answered. "We have a patient going to surgery. You had better send someone stat to the E.W. for another blood sample. It's an aneurysm and he's bleeding badly. You've set up six units already. We are just running in the fifth. Cross-match eight more." Knowing the desultory pace of her listener, she snarled, "Move on it!"

The Orderly Room answered promptly with a courteous greeting.

"Arthur," she snapped, "we need a prep. Nipple to crotch. Total abdominal-perineal." As she was issuing the instructions, she visualized a cardiac arrest on the table, requiring the necessity of slashing open the thorax to get at the heart. She considered the possibility for a moment. "You had better do the whole chest, too, just in case. And, Arthur—fast!"

The Biochemistry Laboratory got the rapid-fire orders: "Full profile, liver chems, bleeding studies, kidney tests. On the double!"

The EKG technician was not in the Cardiology Laboratory. Bea dialed the switchboard operator to page her for the E.W. She knew that an official EKG tracing had better be procured for the record in the event the patient died unexpectedly.

To Radiology, she ordered, "A portable chest film. Patient's name is Hébert. In the E.W. Tell Linda to move her fanny, the patient's going to surgery."

Intensive Care Unit. "Helen," recognizing Mrs. Winner's voice, "get ready for a big one. Prout's going in on a dissecting aneurysm."

She could sense the shock. "The man's name is Francis Hébert. Helen, tell Admitting that the patient will probably be going to you, if he lives, and to put him on the danger list. Thanks, pal."

She hung up, not waiting for a reply. The whole process had consumed less than two minutes. Through the glass panel in the door, she could see the agitated activity coursing around the dying patient she had just left. Jesus Christ! If it was already like this before the afternoon had even started, what would it be once the bars had closed at midnight? Always on *her* Saturdays on. Why for once couldn't she have a simple straightforward weekend like everybody else, with colds, sore backs, peanuts in the ear, and foreskins in the zipper? With a shrug of resignation for come what may, she threw back her shoulders and reentered the arena.

Chapter / THREE

"THAT'S RIGHT, MOTHER. JUST RELAX," THE PORTLY BALDING anesthesiologist reassured the pale young woman sitting hunched on the side of the Delivery Room table, her legs dangling loosely over the edge. The refugee Cuban doctor could see her trembling in the cool damp room. Her head was bent down, shoulders fallen forward, her naked body nestling limply, fully supported by the upright frame and rigid arms of the stocky nurse standing in front of her.

"Just . . . relax . . . no trouble . . . easy does it . . . that's the girl . . ." The physician's thick padded fingers ran firmly up and down her curved spine trying to identify the bony landmarks. The fingertips made patterned dark brown smudges on the skin where the powdered starch on the outside of the gloves reacted chemically with the still-wet alcohol and iodine solution. He pressed the spinal vertebrae separately in turn, then slid into the slight depression below each one before continuing on down the line to the next one. The girl intermittently winced and groaned from the severe labor contractions that trapped her abdomen in a crushing vise. Suddenly she let out a shrill cry and snapped back, straightening her spine and ruining the doctor's count.

He stopped and patiently caressed her back, urging her again to assume the forward bending position. He spread his two hands on both sides of her hips to feel the top edge of her pelvic bone just below the belt line. He drew an imaginary line to connect the two iliac crests. He placed the index finger of his left hand where the line crossed the spinal column, noting the faint pit in the interspace between the fourth and fifth lumbar vertebrae.

He pivoted around to the sterile table by his right side and, removing a thin plastic syringe, injected a small raised bleb of one-percent novocaine solution in the skin at this point.

Replacing the syringe, he picked up a long thin needle, approximately three and a half inches long. With slow pressure he pushed it through the interspace to pierce the overlying skin and muscle. He met a faint resistance as the needle abutted against the thick ligamentum flavum protecting the spinal canal and its delicate bundle of nerve fibers. Suddenly, he felt a loud "pop" as the point entered the spinal column. He removed the thin wire stylet that had plugged up the fine channel in the center of the needle. He looked up at the nurse, a pleased smile on his swarthy dark-shaven face, as he monitored the steady drip-drip-drip of the clear spinal fluid that flowed out of the hollow center core of the metal needle.

"Easy . . . easy . . . everything . . . is fine . . ." he purred as he reached back to the side table, this time for a large glass syringe that had been filled in advance with two tenths of a millimeter of one to one thousandth epinephrine solution, five milligrams of one-percent solution of tetracaine, and one-half millimeter of ten-percent dextrose solution. He attached the end of the syringe to the project-ing tip of the needle and slowly sucked back from the spinal canal into the syringe one-half centimeter of the transparent spinal fluid to reassure himself of the patency of the connection.

He paused and watched the patient for the end of the present contraction. Just before the onset of the next labor pain he injected the full content of the syringe. The instant the last drop had entered the spinal canal, he pulled out the needle and rubbed his index finger roughly over the puncture site to seal it. He stood up and began to lower the patient back on the narrow metal table. She started to strain to help herself move. "No. No. Let *us* do the work. You just relax," he cautioned as he and the nurse positioned her to await the ten minutes for paralysis to occur.

The anesthesiologist checked the intravenous bottle. It was flow-ing well. The needle was still in place in the arm and had not been dislodged by the patient's movements. He pumped up the blood pressure cuff and let the air slowly out to check the vital signs. He tested the valves on the oxygen and nitrous oxide tanks on the inhalation machine by his seat. He shifted his stool to the head of the table and bent down to whisper in the patient's ear.

"Everything . . . is . . . fine. Everything is fine. Pretty soon . . . maybe . . . you will have your boy." He rubbed his hand on her cheek. She glanced up at him about to thank him, a wan smile on her bloodless lips, when the next crushing spasm drove out her last scream.

The nurse tapped lightly on the closed door to the Obstetricians' Locker Room. No answer. She knocked again. Then, tucking sev-eral straggly wisps of blonde hair back in place under her cap she straightened her tight creased gown, which clung in corrugations to her full frame, and pushed the door open a crack. She could see Dr. Joseph Brandon sprawled out, asleep on the worn green leather sofa in the corner of the dark drab room. He had already changed into the required starched baby-pink cotton scrub pants and shirt. His own clothes lay scattered around the room where he had dropped them. His breathing was slow and labored. He was in a deep sleep although he had collapsed in a twisted position no more than five minutes before.

She hesitated to wake him. God knows he needed the rest. He had been up delivering almost every night this month, with no letup, no respite. Rounds every morning. Office hours in the afternoon. The free maternity clinics twice a week, and with no help. Her stern expression softened a little as she watched him breathe. His lower jaw hung loose as the relaxed facial muscles lost the harsh lines of fatigue. He tossed restlessly in his sleep as if fighting some nocturnal battle.

Everyone knew Dr. Joe Brandon. How many years had his father, a prominent insurance agent, boasted that his son would return to Cromwell a doctor? How proud he was when Joe was accepted to Tufts Medical School. Then, Obstetrics-Gynecology training at the Boston Lying-In Hospital and Free Hospital for Women. Vietnam, plus a year in Guam delivering babies for the navy wives. Finally, back home, bringing with him his medical school roommate, Brian Terris, whose sister Alice he had married. Their new office on High Street. What could be better? An obstetrician and a pediatrician. How high the hopes of the two young doctors.

Then it started, subtly, insidiously. The pressure. The blackmail. They were being strangled. There was nothing either of them could do, nor anyone else for that matter. The town could only sit on the sidelines, on its hands, and watch the slaughter.

"Dr. Brandon." She shook his shoulder. He groaned once or twice and then rolled over away from her. "Dr. Brandon, Mrs. Gary's spinal is in. You'd better come." He responded to her vigorous shaking, rolling his head erratically during the last minute before consciousness reasserted itself. He looked up at her, dazed, slowly bringing her short thick profile into sharp view.

"Yes . . . yes . . . Grace. Thank you. I'll be right there." She watched him, refusing to move until she was certain that he was on both feet and headed toward the door. She remembered only too well a week ago when she had awakened him and left, only to find him back asleep on the couch and baby's head crowning. He almost had a third-degree laceration into the rectum that time. He was damn lucky she returned when she finally did. She held the door open for him, watching his lean, wiry form shuffle down the corridor, trying to put on his cap and mask with one hand and his paper booties with his other hand, stumbling, hopping awkwardly until he almost careened into the large double door that led into the Delivery Suite.

Grace knew that lately there had been many disturbing rumors about his professional competence. She had refused to accept them and had continued to cast aspersion on those who propagated the evil tales. It couldn't be. Not Oscar Brandon's son. Quarterback at Holy Cross. With his nice young wife and three children. But, what if the rumors were true and not just more filth spread by Flaherty and his Ob-Gyn partners trying to drive him out of town?

Still, she *had* noticed a change. And not only the leaden weariness that dampened his physical movements and clouded his clinical judgment. Small, perhaps unimportant, but there was now a definite tenseness. A callous, almost hostile streak that surfaced without his noticing when he was in a particularly stressful situation. At such times, she could almost swear that there was another, a more hateful man fighting for ascendancy.

As she entered the Delivery Room, she could see Brandon talking to the anesthesiologist, checking the patient's progress in labor, then scrubbing before being helped into his sterile gown and gloves, once more the thorough physician. She drove the evil thoughts deep into her subconscious, and, with an expression of sympathy for Ralph Flaherty's young competitor, entered the room to receive Mrs. Gary's fourth child—hopefully this time a boy.

Mrs. Helen Gary had come to Dr. Joe Brandon during her last

((29))

trimester when she and her husband moved to Cromwell. The obstetrics records transferred from Framingham indicated that she had been an ideal patient there during her first three pregnancies. No reported complications. No hypertension. No diabetic tendency. No kidney or bladder infections. She had exercised religiously and kept her total weight gain each time to no more than twelve or thirteen pounds.

The husband, whom Joe had met only once, impressed him as a clean-cut responsible young man. He had moved to Cromwell to take a job with the Pratt Paper Company. At his last job there had been a strike for six months. When the strike was over, the workers found that the company had very quietly folded its tents and moved all its production to its other plant in Puerto Rico, leaving them not only without jobs, but also with lapsed medical insurance. Peter Gary was apologetic. His new job at the Pratt Paper Company in Cromwell did not provide maternity coverage until he had worked there ten months.

"I can assure you, Dr. Brandon, that we pay our bills," he told the obstetrician. "You can trust me." Somehow, Joe felt that he could. He also promised that he would arrange for Peter to have a vasectomy by Sam Halpern, the urologist in town. He apologized that because Mercy was a Catholic hospital he could not tie his wife's tubes after the delivery. The husband was agreeable. He wanted a son. But, if the fourth was a girl, they had decided that was it.

Dr. Brandon stationed himself on the stool at the foot of the operating table. The patient's two legs were elevated and spread wide apart, securely strapped to the cold steel Birhoff stirrups. Joe wore the infant stethoscope belted around his forehead like a coal miner's lamp. He pressed the conelike tip against the heaving abdomen. The baby's heartbeat was rapid, fluttering like bird's wings, but strong and steady. God, he thought, people think these little creatures are weak. Just listen to that. One hundred and sixty beats a minute, racing to beat hell. The head, overly large, preparing to batter a bloody passage like a wedge of steel-helmeted guards going over for a one-yard touchdown. Never again in a human being's whole life would his body be subjected to the brutal trauma of wrenching its way into the world in order to take its first powerful breath.

He leaned back to watch. It was the part that still thrilled him after all these years, after thousands of babies. He could still remember his professor's lecture at the Lying-In during his residency. "Doctors, this is the best part of all. Don't rush it. Wait. Watch. Enjoy it. This is the beginning of life. You alone can see Creation as it must have been. Remember that babies have been born for many years without your skill. Sit back and observe—and marvel."

Joe was aware that this dictum was not just an idle philosophical whim, but instead a cleverly concealed medical admonition. Joe knew well all the dangers, the paralysis, the dislocations, the lacerations, the hemorrhages, if the physician became overzealous and began to precipitate the arrival of the infant, to force, to pull, to tug, to press, to rupture, to mutilate. He had trained himself at this point to take several deep breaths, to lean back and pretend that he was just a curious spectator.

With each contraction the perineum began to bulge as the baby's head, caught and compacted between the pubic bone and the back of the spine, spun upon itself in response to a mysterious command. Slowly, surely, the head magically rotated on its own axis to present the narrowest possible dimension to the already inhumanely stretched pelvic structures.

He could see the large head fracturing the few layers of tissue remaining to block its passage. He held out his hand for the scalpel and swiftly cut open the vaginal ring, creating a wider orifice for the skull to penetrate. Then with each contraction, he swept back and tucked away from the encroaching cranium the clitoris and labial folds still obstructing the child's descent.

The propulsive convulsions came faster and faster, until before his eyes he could see the dark, slimy mixture of hair and scalp.

Then, a face. A strange, disembodied head staring down at the floor, the eyes closed, the skin color a dark dusky red. He watched as the baby's chest, still trapped inside the mother, was compressed by the next contraction. He could see draining from its nose the amniotic fluid and mucus squeezed out of the child's wet lungs so that those patiently waiting chambers in its chest would be dry and empty to fill with God's air.

Joe depressed the head down toward the floor to facilitate delivery of the child's right shoulder. He gently lifted the head to extricate the left shoulder. How much easier it was to deliver a third or fourth child than a first. He smiled to himself. It was certainly easier to *make* the third or fourth than the first one, thinking for a moment of the long fretful time he and Alice had wondered if they were sterile before their three came in the space of three years.

He could hear Grace Molling preparing the surgical instruments for him to repair the episiotomy once the rest of the baby was delivered. He looked up at the Cuban who was beaming with his thumb pointing up in the air, signifying that at his end all was well with the anesthesia. Joe bent forward and pressed the stethoscope funnel against the lower abdomen. He could still hear the strong beats of the young heart announcing its staying power.

He now had both his hands around the half-child, nestling and supporting its head and shoulder, arms, and chest. Only a few seconds more. Another six inches. Gently . . . gently. The child began to slither out. Faster and faster. Now in a desperate rush to join the race of mortals who had made themselves in the image of their Lord.

Suddenly, the extracted life fell into his arms. His hands grasped the warm slippery body. He bent closer to examine the still motionless form. He gave an involuntary gasp that echoed softly around the silent white-tiled room. When he finally raised his head, there was horror in his eyes.

Chapter / FOUR

THE EIGHTY-FOOT STEEL TOWER SOARING HIGH ABOVE THE BARREN summit of Mount Eliot functioned without benefit of human hand. Within minutes of Marjorie Hollis's telephone call to the Valley Telecommunications' office, her specific requests were being relayed by leased cable to the waiting transmitter overlooking the city of Cromwell. Upon command, powerful electromagnetic waves were sent beaming in all directions to ensnare the unsuspecting victims.

Nine-oh-seven had not gotten beeped all day. Even now, the small brushed aluminum and embossed black vinyl receiver lay hidden on the chair seat under a loosely piled heap of clothes that had been shed only minutes before. Her short, lithesome body was stark naked, with streams of long blonde hair scattered on the white sheets. Two large blue eyes gazed down at the moving head of brown curly hair pressed to her breasts. Her hands stroked the back of his neck as she spread her legs to encourage the clever fingers lightly caressing her thighs. She lay there, twisting with growing arousal.

Nine-oh-seven had made love only six times before. By now, the pain of penetration no longer scared her. The initial soreness, the shock, the sudden violation and deep wounding were all faint memories. All she could think of was the pleasure the rigid penis could evoke alive inside her even as her partner discharged each time like an uncontrolled animal. Why had she been so frightened of men up until then? And why had she finally chosen to love this particularly chubby one?

She shifted underneath the young stocky male. He could feel her smooth fingers tighten on his back, pressing into his flesh. He began to push forward, to insert his swollen organ through the still-raw hymeneal ring. He tried to hold back to refrain from forcing too hard, but a desperate pressure kept shredding his considerate resolve and drove him forward. Oh, how he loved this small warm body responding to his touch. Please, dear God, he found himself begging, no pain for her this time.

With the constant motion, the slippery erotic friction, his sexual tension rapidly mounted. He moaned. His muscles tightened. His breaths came out in short gasps. "I can't wait . . . oh, I am sorry . . ." he cried out as he prepared to lunge forward and climax his commanding frustration. When suddenly the pile of clothes by the side of the bed began to beep!

By the time Connie Mercier had jumped out of bed and managed to find the receiver to turn it off, Dr. Brian Terris was no longer the same man. Lighter in weight by two tablespoons of vital white fluid, Cromwell's newest pediatrician stared up at her, his hands around a subsiding erection, his mouth open and panting, as the involuntary convulsive shudders slowly subsided. When he finally focused on her still-unrequited desire and removed his sticky hands from around the flaccid impotence, all he could say weakly, half-crying, half-laughing, was "I'm sorry . . . I'm sorry . . ." Then he ducked as she threw two pillows at his head and leaped on the bed to pound him playfully with sincere unhappiness.

Chapter / FIVE

Marjorie Hollis had just entered the Emergency Ward when Connie's call reached her. She wondered about the reason for the strange detachment in the young nurse's tone. Marge had assumed an almost maternal protective role since the daughter of her college roommate had decided to become a nurse. The older woman had followed the young girl's career in Cromwell with both passive pride and active help since Connie's mother had died. Marjorie knew that her ward's physical attributes belied an ambitious drive. For the past six months Connie had been Operating Room supervisor at Mercy and ran a tight ship. Unlike the sour-faced nun whom she replaced, the young girl managed to command respect not only from the women working under her, but also from the many surgeons, those demanding prima donnas technically her superiors, with all somehow functioning smoothly and efficiently, a goal never before achieved in the hospital despite the overwhelming piety of her predecessors.

Marge repressed her curiosity for the moment. "Connie, Bea is sending over a dissecting aneurysm, Prout's doing it. I know. I know," she offered to the stunned silence. "You had better get in an extra scrub . . . or two . . . or three—there's going to be trouble. And, Con," she asked, her voice soft and caring, "tomorrow night. Dinner with me? Six-thirty. No excuses. Good-bye, my child. And please try to see that Lansing stays out of trouble."

Connie looked over at the short chunky doctor. He looked so helpless without his clothes on. His skin was soft and pink with smudges of brown hair on his chest and between his legs. The freckles on his pleasant square face continued to sprinkle over his body like seasoning. His hands were large and firm as they reached out to pull her back onto the bed.

"No, Brian. I've got to go. That damn beeper! I'm sorry I jumped out of bed so fast. Please, darling. Tonight, if I get home." Her face tightened in a worried scowl.

Noticing her sudden change of mood, he asked, "Why? What's the matter? What was the call?"

"That was Marjorie Hollis. Lansing Prout has a dissecting aneurysm he's going in on. Now!" She looked at her watch and pulled herself away from his grasp after giving him a sisterly kiss on his forehead. With much reluctance, the pediatrician rose from the bed and started to put on his clothes.

"I'll drive you to Mercy. I have rounds to make anyway, and I can take you home when the case is over." He moved close to her and gave her a long, affectionate embrace. Connie stopped her rushed dressing for a moment and clung to him, pressing her pelvis firmly up against his. When she shifted, she could feel his rising potency and pulled herself away.

"Tonight," she consoled, "and this time I won't have the beeper."

Before putting on the rest of her clothes, Connie located her pocketbook and pulled out the mimeographed schedule of the April Operating Room roster. Running her finger down the list until she reached this Saturday, she dialed Valley Telecommunications. Silent waves reached out to summons lightly, but imperiously, six-six-six, one-eight-four, and one-eight-five, who, at the moment of invisible electronic contact, were watching the Yankees play Cleveland on TV, trying on a pair of blue jeans in Sears, and about to shampoo her hair for a blind date that evening.

During the long drive from Terris's apartment on the outskirts of Cromwell, Connie sat content in the front seat of Brian's five-year-old red MG as he dodged the heavy Saturday afternoon traffic clogging the roads leading into town. She leaned over and gave him a kiss on his cheek and then rubbed her hand on his thigh. He looked up, startled for a minute, and blew her a kiss.

Was it fate that had put her on duty the night one of his patients had required emergency surgery? She remembered the case well. The baby no more than six weeks old, a scrawny, almost emaciated black boy, with pyloric stenosis. Since birth, he had suffered with horrible recurrent abdominal pain and persistent vomiting, which the family pediatrician, Arnold Best, had repeatedly diagnosed over the telephone as colic. In desperation, the mother had brought the child to the Emergency Ward where the intern immediately called Terris.

The younger pediatrician made the diagnosis within one minute. How could anyone have missed it? With the diaper off, everyone in the room could feel through the cachectic abdominal wall the small olive-shaped bulge of tissue. A little barium dye to swallow, and the discrete but deadly congenital obstruction at the exit of the stomach where it joined the intestine showed up in black and white on X-ray.

It took the surgeon, Dr. Crane, even less time to confirm the diagnosis and schedule the child for an emergency Ramstadt Procedure, to remove the blockage and allow the child to feed once again.

Brian had accompanied the baby to the Operating Room, but insisted on delaying surgery until the results of the blood tests he had ordered were back. He had sat there at her desk, waiting patiently, doodling on the paper pad, until the laboratory called with the data that the child was anemic and needed a blood transfusion. When he finally got up to leave, he gave her one of the small cellophane-wrapped lollipops he kept in the pockets of his shapeless Harris tweed jacket for his patients.

What had made her blush and tease him by saying that all her pediatricians used to give her pistachio-flavored lollipops? What had made him look at her bashful bluster and remain there while the case was going on and then ask her for a date before he left?

Connie soon learned to love this gruff, awkward doctor who could get down on the floor and play with his patients, burp them on his shoulder, wiping up the spit and curdled milk deposited on his clothes with a shrug. Who never got angry, had a good word for everybody, and never minded being called whatever the time of day or night. He was a lovable grown-up teddy bear.

Brian was content. Each time Connie nuzzled close to him, he could feel a faint rush of blood to his groin. He blushed at the memory of that first night they had decided to make love. How they laughed at their initial clumsiness. How she bit her tongue, trying hard to hold back the tears as he ripped through her innocence. She cried for fear that her pain and tightness was going to frustrate him. He assured her that they had a whole lifetime to learn how to please one another. How, each time, their pleasure increased until they could in all honesty proclaim graduation to the proud state of living in sin.

It had been a spontaneous and almost immediate decision that they would be married in the fall if, he quickly thought with a bitter feeling of discouragement sweeping over him, he had a practice to support a wife.

Now Connie caught that fleeting look of concern and saw his jaw muscles clench. The instant change of mood alarmed her. She knew what he was thinking. Everyone at Mercy knew. Tears welled up in her eyes. Brian was such a good doctor. Parents and children loved him. Why should he and his brother-in-law be the victims of a plot to drive them from Cromwell? How two such incompetent bastards like Best and Flaherty could even have had the brains to sit down and think it up amazed her. They certainly never demonstrated any such perspicacity in their treatment of patients.

It was so simple. Flaherty and his partners did over ninety percent of the deliveries at Mercy. At least fifteen hundred a year. It was no problem for them. They rotated on call among themselves. Even if one was up all night, he was off duty the next two. Not so for Joe Brandon, whose only choice was to give up trying to stay awake long enough to compete with them and crawl out of town, or worse, to commit some blunder from numbing fatigue. Physical and mental exhaustion would eventually dull his clinical judgment with tragic results. It had to happen sooner or later. And then? They would crucify him!

In the meanwhile, what did they do? They gave all the new baby examinations in the Nursery to Best. How all the doctors laughed when Arnold Best incorporated with his partners and chose the name, "The Best Baby Doctors, Inc." But it was no joke. Fifteen hundred times forty dollars. Sixty thousand dollars a year, cold cash, to the "Best Baby Doctors" just for checking the belly button and slicing off some foreskins. And not a single cent for Terris or any other pediatrician who might dare to enter Cromwell and defy them.

That was only the beginning. Every one of those fifteen hundred mothers continued to take their fifteen hundred newborns to the friendly pediatrician who first came to see them in the Delivery Room and arranged for the baby's immunization afterward. And the mother brought not only *those* fifteen hundred, but also all their brothers and sisters at home, so that the whole family could have all their shots at the same time.

Where did that leave Dr. Terris? Out in the cold. Sure, he got his brother-in-law's deliveries and some transients whom the Emergency Ward sent over to his office, but what kind of a full and satisfying practice could he ever build up?

The payoff! That was the height of hypocrisy. Flaherty and Best jerking each other off in the Executive Committee. Each blocking applications from competitors to the other. A motion to table and an automatic second from each in turn. Who on that committee of hyenas would go against *both* men, chiefs of two of the biggest departments in the whole hospital?

It was all so sweet. It was so bitter, too. Connie stared through the windshield at the busy stream of traffic rushing past the small low car as if to trample it should it not stand aside. Her body was taut, consumed with hatred and love as she saw loom up before her the heavy mass of Mercy, suddenly no longer a sanctuary from disease, but a vast gray mechanism to swallow up the dreams and hopes of people like her and Dr. Brian Terris.

Chapter / SIX

Lansing Prout glanced around the Operating Room as he
had done daily for too many years to recollect. No matter how
many times he had tried to convince himself otherwise, he could
never quite repress the instinctive feeling that the sterile, harshly
lit, white-tiled chamber was a more appropriate setting for death,
a morgue, an autopsy room, than a fight waged by dedicated human
beings to preserve life. Even the actors in this hermetic aseptic pit
seemed especially lifeless, garbed in shapeless, sexless, shroudlike
outer garments of identical gray-blue covering all four extremities,
both arms tapering to brown rubber gloves outlining ten plastic

fingers. Faces blotted out to conceal any vestige of humanity. Only the eyes, quickly darting, signaling in sensitive semaphore messages to indicate the spark of human life hidden somewhere behind the helmetlike casings of cotton caps and masks.

The pervading heavy, almost dank silence, wet and labored, with the wheezing staccato rasping of the lung machine to mark the patient's still human presence. The rhythmic squeak-ping of the cardiac monitor mechanically chiming each contraction of his arhythmic failing heart. The patient himself, almost unwanted, mercifully unidentifiable like an obscene afterthought, a lump of flesh, carefully draped under yards of antiseptic gray-blue sheeting with only a dark amber slash of iodine-stained skin showing through the slit in the sheets.

The hush, the suppressed hesitant eagerness, all unwillingly poised, waiting for that initial puncture to violate the pristine artificiality of the tableau. To humble it to mortal dimensions by mapping its boundaries with drops, then rivulets, later rivers of thick adhesive red blood that would stain the skin, the drapes, the gloves, the gowns, the walls, the floors, caps, masks, finally reducing this immaculate abattoir to a gore-soaked pit of man against the treachery of human disease.

The operation was a nightmare. The incision had barely been made when massive quantities of blood squirted out of the bloated abdomen. The partially congealed red pasty material camouflaged the entire operating field, drenching the front of Prout's gown and splattering him on his forehead, which was wiped clean by the circulating nurse. The surgeon worked to staunch the turbulent flow of blood obscuring his view, to isolate the ruptured vessel that with each pulse of the heart poured out a torrent of blood, this same liquid that only seconds before had been pumped into Francis Hébert's collapsing veins.

Prout tried to place a stainless-steel clamp around the aorta, to occlude the broken conduit and allow time to replace it with a new woven textile tube. With a blind thrust, he managed to insert one of the two blades of the Satinsky clamp in back of the fragile vessel, only to have the other blunt blade crunch through the brittle wall, totally shattering it. With that ill-advised maneuver, the entire blood volume of the patient suddenly welled up in front of him, converting the open abdomen into an overflowing cauldron of churning warm scarlet liquid in which floated twisted loops of dying white intestine.

Prout shook with terror, shocked at the sight of the ebbing life in his hands. Cold sweat beaded on his face, between his thighs, and under his arms. He shivered, trembling, and rocked back and forth on his soles. He feverishly threw every towel and gauze pack he could lay his hands on into the open cavity, packing it with linen strips, to hide the opaque flood exsanguinating the patient gutted by his deed. Then, magically, the river of blood stopped. He looked up, elated, about to say to his frightened assistant, "See, everything will be all right," when he heard the anesthesiologist warn him, too calmly, and perhaps with a weary sigh of relief to the termination of the unequal and tragic battle he had been witnessing.

"Doctor, the patient's heart has stopped. I can't get any blood pressure or pulse." He looked over at the aged surgeon who stood frozen and immobile, unsure of what to do next.

"Dr. Prout!" His voice rose in timbre, trying to arouse the physician still half-paralyzed with fear and indecision, "Dr. Prout!"

The physician looked up. "More blood," he pleaded, unable to offer anything else to counter the catastrophe that had overwhelmed him.

"Dr. Prout," the intern asked, "should I open the chest?"

The older man did not reply. The surgeon's increasing apathy inspired the intern with an initiative he had not displayed up to that time. Quickly, he slashed the left diaphragm. Reaching his hand through the incision, he started to knead the exhausted heart while watching the EKG screen where the dancing pattern had given way to an ominous straight line indicating imminent death.

Over the next hour, nothing helped. Not the cardiac stimulants injected directly into the still flaccid cardiac muscle. Not the tiring manual massage of the dead human pump. Not the avalanche of fresh blood flowing unabated into the veins. Not the fervent prayers silently uttered by the surgeon who remained leaning against the table, staring into the wound, only half-conscious of his surroundings. It seemed almost a blissful act when the anesthesiologist shut off the inhalation machine, ending the thumping of the rubber lung and the high-pitched hissing of the oxygen tank.

He looked at the mute surgeon, and with long overdue resignation offered, "His pupils are fixed and dilated, Dr. Prout. The EKG pattern hasn't changed in an hour. I think it's useless to continue."

The surgeon shrugged his shoulders in assent and walked out of the amphitheater, slightly stooped, his eyes red and watery, his step tremulous, unable to defend, even to himself, the debacle he had allowed.

He did not see the intern sew up the abdominal incision with slow cosmetic stitches, as if the patient would have a lifetime to admire the delicate workmanship. Nor did the intern observe the knowing look on the anesthesiologist's face as Dr. Martin Abels disassembled his machine, checking the valves on the gas cylinders, and retrieving the endotracheal tube that up until an hour ago had supplied oxygen to the living patient. Only once did Dr. Abels glance over the screen at the meticulous work of the young intern. He did not have the heart to tell him that his effort was all wasted, for within hours the incision would be ripped open and the patient's body torn apart.

The anesthesiologist looked at the cadaver lying in the exact center of the room. The silent form was rapidly cooling as the warmth of life fled like smoky mist off a warm pond chilling in a spring twilight. Already he could smell the sweet musky chemical ester and aldehyde scent of dead flesh decomposing back into the dust of its inorganic origin. The skin, without its infusion of oxygenated blood, was now a translucent yellow. The face was waxlike, the mouth carved open, the eyes wide and staring without a single blink to indicate its communality with the fraternity of living mortals.

Abels shook his head, a half-smile on his lips. Through the door he could see Prout slowly being helped out of his blood-soaked sweat-drenched gown. He remembered, as no one else in the room had thought to, that Francis Hébert would receive an exhaustive autopsy at the hands of Simon Pirie, the hospital pathologist. According to the laws of the Commonwealth of Massachusetts, any patient who expired within twenty-four hours of admission to a hospital was automatically a coroner's case. As Abels watched the bent figure move slowly out of range of sight, he was unable to suppress the commingling feelings of pity and hatred for the aged man who only moments before had futilely let a body's life flow out between his fingers as casually as if it were only an ordinary crimson liquid instead of a unique human soul.

Chapter / SEVEN

MARJORIE HOLLIS PUSHED THROUGH THE SWINGING DOUBLE DOORS
to the Emergency Ward, letting them slam behind her, as if she
was fleeing the devil. The afternoon had been hell! It seemed as if
the paging system knew only her name. She was tired. Her feet
hurt, notwithstanding her clumsy-looking contour shoes. Her leg
muscles cramped despite the high groin-length elastic stockings
worn to frustrate her varicose veins. Her back ached through the
Velcro-lashed elasticized back support. Colicky waves of pain
streamed across her low spine to radiate down the back of her
thighs from the sacroiliac joint to her knees. Even her heavy, sag-

ging breasts were sore and defied the textile superstructure designed to support their tugging mass. For the first time in months she was aware of a burning sensation between her chafing buttocks, a recurrence of her hemorrhoid problem aggravated by increasingly troublesome constipation over the past few weeks.

"Bea," she said, with a disgusted toss of her head, "I am falling apart. My arches. My veins, My back. My goddamn piles." Looking with envy at the tall, thin Emergency Ward nurse, fifteen years her elder and still trim and immaculate, she asked, "How do you do it, Bea? Goddamn it! You don't even have a hair out of place. I'm out of breath and ready for the trash bin."

Her friend smiled at her, cognizant of the excessive weight, the face florid with beads of perspiration, and finally, the constant hacking smoker's cough.

"Marjorie," she reached out her hand and led her to the tiny Nurses On-Call Room in the far corner of the Emergency Annex, "sit down, relax. You look as if you've had quite a day." Pointing to the steaming coffee urn, "Black?" she hinted.

Mrs. Hollis opened a metal folding chair in front of her and lifted both beefy legs on to it. "You are an angel." Holding out her hand for the cup, "Four sugars and lots of cream . . ." she ordered with a sheepish expression. "I know, I know. Tomorrow for sure, *black*! You'll see. But, not now."

Bea took her own cup black and sat down, her legs primly tucked underneath her.

"Did you hear about Prout's aneurysm?" Marjorie asked, after taking several noisy slurps of coffee.

"News gets around fast. Arthur brought the glad tidings," Bea added sarcastically. Suddenly sober and thoughtful, "What will happen now?"

"What do you expect?" Marge retorted. "Nothing! Nothing at all. It's not the first time, and it won't be the last. Listen, Bea, if you are Lansing Prout . . ." Her voice dwindled off as she turned her attention to the more productive effort of finishing her coffee and giving the cup to Bea for a refill. "Thanks. Thanks, pal. I'm so bushed, I don't think I could make it to the can if I had to."

The two women sat quietly in the relative tranquillity of the hidden cul-de-sac. Nobody came in to bother them. That was one of Bea's rules. Unless it was a case of life or death, this was her sanctum sanctorum, and its threshold inviolate for her and her friends. Years ago, Bea had thoughtfully disconnected the squawk box outside the alcove and nothing but smothering silence could penetrate the shielded room.

Bea Wharton had never married. She was a parsimonious woman, thrifty in speech and manner to match her frugal physical endowments. In every case but one she was similarly guarded and selective in her close companions. For some strange reason, which no one in the hospital could fathom, she had become intimate with the gregarious younger woman, as if seeking from the worldly widow some vicarious element missing in her own spartan life.

Bea held her coffee cup and saucer neatly on her flat lap. For a long time she said nothing. A faint hint of a smile skirted her face, making her stern visage suddenly soft and warm and oddly attractive. In a low, almost sensual tone of voice, she began to speak as if reciting to herself.

"Oh, I remember years ago when Lansing Prout first came to Cromwell. That was before your time, Marge." She observed the interested expression on Marge's face.

"He was tall and very good-looking. His father, Marshall Prout, looked very much like Lansing does today. Every inch the aristocrat. Lansing was the most eligible bachelor in Cromwell. How everyone tried to snare him." She turned away to hide an evanescent blush. "Even me, Marge, the virgin Wharton. You didn't know. Hardly anyone here today remembers, but Lansing and I . . ." She glanced up, a look of half-shame, half-pride on her face. "I know what everyone thinks of me. An old parched prune. I don't deny it, Marge. It doesn't bother me anymore. I'm too old now for it to matter. But, I know differently. Lansing Prout and I . . ."

Her voice drifted off, consumed in stoking the embers of a long-dead passion.

Mrs. Hollis gazed at her friend, shaking her head in amazement. Bea and Lansing Prout! Well, why not? Take off forty years. From both. A handsome young doctor in town. A tall, thin, attractive student nurse. Why in the world not?

She thought of her own circumstances. She and Harry marrying at the age of forty. Both huffing and puffing their way through middle age. She was no prize. Neither was Harry, overweight and pretty nearly bald. She shifted in her seat as a twinge of annoyance flushed her groin. Goddamn it! Even now she shivered a little bit at the memory of both of them in bed making love like two smooth-skinned hippopotamuses. With a sneer of contempt she dismissed the ridiculous notion it seemed all young people had that only nubile young maidens and lean handsome men could have orgasms. God was smarter than those whippersnappers. It had nothing to do with looks, or spare tires around the middle, if you really loved somebody.

By the time Marge had finished her third cup of coffee, Bea had shed her mood of reverie. "Marge, I've heard rumors that Lash is out gunning for Lansing. If that is true, God help Prout after today."

Both women knew that the talented, successful new Chief of the Department of Surgery was trying to upgrade the caliber of surgery carried out at the hospital. So far, he had been thwarted by Prout, Flaherty, and several other old-timers who had passed their prime after the Second World War and were refusing to fade into the background and allow the younger, better-trained men to assume their place in the medical fraternity.

"I have heard them too, but if I had to bet any money, I'd stick with Lansing. That old fox," Marge said, with a sigh of admiration, "has more lives than the proverbial cat."

"It's always been like that, hasn't it, Marge?" Bea did not expect or wait for an answer. "Look around you. You have been here long enough. Look at them. Like a jungle full of wild beasts. At each other's throats, but not for food, only for the sheer pleasure of the kill."

Marge looked puzzled. "I don't know what you mean, Bea."

"Just look around you. There are the doctors like Lansing Prout and Ralph Flaherty and Arnold Best, all the old guard. Holding on at the top for dear life, clutching the cream of Cromwell for their practices. All the landed money in Cromwell buttoned up in their back pockets. Then there's the next tier. Those who came here after the Second World War, Samuel Halpern, Crowther, Carl Lash, Craig, Brad Gill. How young and fresh and enthusiastic they were—once. How they struggled to make it to the top. And you know they are almost there. One or two good leaps and they will be at the peak. Even now, they run the committees in the hospital. Look at the new Medical Arts Building they own, with their private offices next door to the hospital. How they got to build that on Mercy land I will never know. They even have a restrictive covenant in the building. It's nothing illegal—this is confidential, Marge—but no physician is allowed to have an office there unless every tenant agrees. Can you imagine Lash ever letting in another general surgeon, or Halpern a urologist, or Craig an orthopod?"

Bea took in the astonished look on Mrs. Hollis's face. "Why do you think that there is so much bitterness among the younger men at Mercy, the ones who have come here since the Korean War or Vietnam? Good men like Brandon and Terris. God, Marge, they are so young, even with their silly moustaches and sideburns. But look at them, too, trying in their turn to climb. How far have they gotten? Take Brandon. He was trained to use those exotic new drugs to cure sterility. He gave a lecture to the student nurses. I heard it. On how many hysterectomies were done needlessly and could have been prevented by proper hormone control. Do you wonder why Flaherty and his partners are trying to drive him out? They refuse to cover for him. Joe Brandon has been on duty every day

((53))

and night since he came here two years ago. He can't even take a day off, an hour, in case one of his patients goes into labor. He hasn't had a night's sleep in God knows how long. I don't know how much more he can take before he cracks."

"Did you hear about the close call he had in the Delivery Room?" Marge asked.

"Yes, I know all about the Delivery Room." She shook her head bitterly. "But what else can he do? He tried to bring in a partner. Some nice young fellow. I think his name was Kline, Jules Kline. Flaherty blocked his application for privileges in the Executive Committee month after month until the poor man was forced to withdraw his application and go to Fall River. And Terris? Arnold Best has a stranglehold on him that nobody can break. Marge, I bite my tongue when I see what goes on here. Look at Leonard Paillard," the older woman continued. "How can he survive when Craig won't let him on the Emergency Room roster. Seventy-five percent of an orthopedic surgeon's practice comes in right through here. I see it all. Trauma, accidents. Craig has kept him off the rotating schedule, starving, on one trumped-up excuse or another for three years now."

Marge could only nod her head affirmatively at each accusation, angry at the cruel tactics of the doctors she had been taught to revere and help. Each charge silently reinforced her own indictment of the very physicians with whom she worked every day, whose patients she sweated over, growing old and tired in the travail.

"It's one big ladder, Marge. With people like Prout on the top. Lash and his buddies in the middle. Brandon and his crowd on the first steps. All of them, straining, pushing, crowding, to struggle up the rungs, not caring on whose hands they step, whose fingers they crush. And don't tell me the ones at the bottom are any different from the ones at the top." She saw Marge's gesture of denial. "Just give them a chance. They are *all* bastards." She pointed at the door. "There they are. Cannibals. For what? By the time they make it to the top, they are so worn out and old, they can't even hold on. They fall off. Nobody cares or notices. That's the trouble. All those saviors in white are so interested in climbing high that they never bother to look *down,* to see the cluster of mangled bodies piled up at the foot of the ladder, maimed or dead, ignored by everyone in the mad scramble up the greased pole."

She paused to formulate some profundity. "You know, Marge, what they really need? They need an eye in the middle of their butt to see behind them, to look down at the ground, at their colleagues who made it to the summit long before them, only to drop like rotten apples in a fall wind."

Marge laughed, the soft throaty sound breaking the tension. "An eye in their butt. That's not such a bad idea, Bea. I think that's where most of them have their brains anyway." She raised her cup to her friend's, both women toasting the misdeeds of the medical fraternity in a gesture of female consanguinity.

There was a timid tap on the door. It cautiously opened and the new ward secretary poked her head through the crack. Acknowledging Bea's instant stony glare of disapproval, she apologized for her necessary transgression.

"Mrs. . . . Mrs. Hollis. They are paging you. Another emergency case for surgery. Also, please call Delivery. Dr. Brandon is waiting there. Something about a newborn baby." She glanced down at the scribbled note in her hand. "He also asked whether Doctors Terris, Halpern, Crowther, Paillard, or Crane were possibly down here."

The two nurses looked at each other, startled by her inquiry. Their eyes made momentary contact, the same question forming on both their lips at the same time. What grotesque new inhabitant for God's Kingdom could Dr. Joseph Brandon have just delivered that would simultaneously require the emergency services of a pediatrician, urologist, neurosurgeon, orthopedic surgeon, and Cromwell's only female general surgeon on this sun-drenched Saturday afternoon?

Chapter / EIGHT

THE OBSTETRICS RECOVERY ROOM WAS DARKENED TO A SUBDUED half-glow. Like members of a discordant chorus, the recumbent figures on the narrow high-castered stretchers would stir and moan, each responding to the cumulative effects of hours of harrowing pain, blood loss, and physical exhaustion. They were all in the semi-stuporous state of recovery from anesthesia. Some were more obtunded than others by the many drugs and narcotic agents that had yet to be metabolized and excreted from the body. They shifted and moved. Some reflexly spread their legs apart and grunted hoarse groans, unaware that the effort was no longer needed. They would scowl or grin, or even smile as a particularly happy thought pierced the twilight state of consciousness.

No matter what the agony, it was all over. If they were happy, it was from the inner knowledge that they were part of the endless chain of life from the beginning of time. If, through the amorphous cloud of thoughts that dampened acute perception, there could have been one consolation to redeem the months of physical deformity and emotional strain, it was that they now possessed to love for a lifetime that tangible product of their labor. If Mrs. Helen Gary shared their silent belief, it was a cruel jest. For this patient mother, there was to be no Redemption.

Joe Brandon sat alone in the dictating booth in the far corner of the Recovery Room. The small brass student's lamp cast a blot of white light on the pitted writing surface in front of him. The harsh glare reflecting off the pad of paper made him blink as he bent to his task. The rustle of the dry sheets crackled sharply in the still air. In rotation, rubber-shoed nurses would quietly move to his side and then turn away to their labors without a word.

He looked up only when the heavy-set anesthesiologist shuffled over to him, one bootie half off and scuffing the floor as he walked. He put his hand lightly on Joe's shoulder. He tried to find words to communicate the depth of his compassion to the obstetrician. He knew in advance that the attempt would fail and wisely retreated behind instinctive ritual.

"She's asleep, Joe. I gave her an extra fifty of Demerol. Her vital signs are good. I don't think she will need any blood. She's not spotting very much. I told Grace to let you know if she awakens." He paused, searching out the seated figure's weary, lined face. "I ordered ten of Valium every six hours, if that's OK with you."

He hesitated, unwilling to proceed. He swallowed hard. "Joe, the father, Mr. Gary." God! It was hard to think of what had to come. "He's outside. In the waiting room." He could not continue.

Brandon nodded. He clasped his hand over the Cuban doctor's in a token of thanks for his help. He did not even look up when the outer door opened, fracturing the gloom with a sudden blade of cold fluorescent light from the floodlit hallway, as the anesthesiologist left the room.

What does one usually say to excuse such a situation? It's just one of those things? How could anyone write a love song with such a title? What were the odds? One in fifty thousand? In a hundred thousand? In a million? Jesus Christ! Did it really make any difference to the Garys? Could a statistic explain away their horror when he would eventually have to show them their fourth child? That was the *real* reason the nurses hesitated to break the barrier they had erected between themselves and him, afraid lest they inadvertently be committed to assist in that too-horrible-to-contemplate act.

What could he have done? He stretched to view the crowded room, seeking out the somnolent, blissfully ignorant mother. The lamplight caught his profile and accentuated his narrow face with its deeply etched lines, too old for a young man of thirty-two. His eyebrows, strong and prominent, arched forward, overhanging the darkly sunken eyes, hidden back under their sheltering bushy cliffs. The hollows under his cheekbones gashed inward with black smudges, as did the deep cleft in his chin. He ran his hand through the locks of black hair that fell forward to cover his forehead.

What *could* he have done? He could recall every minute of the past hour as if he were unrolling a silent reel of movie film for the thousandth time.

His fingers had known that something was wrong even before his eyes, that most sophisticated sense of all, could communicate with his brain. His right hand had curved quickly under the falling child to prevent it from dropping. He tightened his grip to overcome the slipperiness of the natural lubrication coating the warm, soft body. He could feel the strong muscular shoulders, but there, where the base of the spine should disappear between trim, tiny-formed buttocks, was the crime—the hard, shiny, round smooth mass—which jutted obscenely out.

((59))

There was a gasp of horror from Grace Molling as she sucked in her breath and looked at the obstetrician, ashamed at her outburst. Joe could hear the stool scrape on the tiled floor as the anesthesiologist stood up and leaned over the screen to see what had caused the cry of alarm. His eyes locked with the obstetrician's in a gesture of knowledge, regrettably shared.

"A meningomyelocele?"

Joe nodded his head as he ran his fingers gently over the swollen protuberance that contained the destroyed, malformed spinal column, the countless dead nerves that would never, and only God knew the reason why, allow this helpless child to crawl, to climb, to walk, like every other of heaven's creatures since they emerged from the trees, or from the Garden, as you will.

Nerve fibers that, in some other child, could render it continent of urine and feces.

Nerve fibers that in some other baby destined to be a murderer, a rapist, a thief, would enable it to participate itself in the act of procreation.

But, no. His fingers traced the large distended fluid-and-tissue-filled swelling that branded this child a cripple, paralyzed from the waist down, to live in its own uncontrollable excrement until the day of its death.

Joe looked down at his hands. His fingers were rhythmically outlining a swollen circle on the paper in front of him. What had happened at that point, he wondered back? It seemed as if a curtain had suddenly descended between him and the fact of the child's congenital mutilation, and, transiently, mercifully, blotted out acute perception of the frightful and irrevocable defect.

He had returned to the waiting job of completing the interrupted delivery. He lowered the child below the level of the mother to allow the blood in the placenta to drain into the living baby. He felt the umbilical cord, still turgid and warm, pulsating with rushing blood. His eyes were riveted upon that last cordlike link between the generations, the scar of which the individual would bear upon its abdomen until the day of its death. If he had the irrational urge to occlude that lifeline before the child had yet taken its first breath to establish its claim to mammalian air, he savagely repressed the sinful thought.

Gradually the cord narrowed on its own, became pulseless, and collapsed. Joe cut it, separating the baby from its maternal root. He tied the stump close to the baby's skin with a short piece of sterile string.

He inserted a soft rubber bulb into the baby's mouth and nostrils to suck out any remaining vestiges of the warm fluid that had cushioned it for nine months. The poking and probing must have irritated the child. It started to make small erratic movements. Joe watched the increasing signs of irritability as the baby, deprived of its mother's lungs as a substitute for its own, experienced, for the first time in its nine months of life, a cruel lack of oxygen.

Far back in the base of the brain, hidden deep in the medulla, a small group of quiescent cells mysteriously began to stir. No more than a tenth of an inch in diameter, the tiny gland sensed the strange change occurring in the blood that bathed it. The rapid buildup of deadly carbon dioxide. The precipitous drop in the life-demanding oxygen tension. The cells suddenly became unstable, agitated, frantic. In spite, or in anger, one would never know, they retaliated by triggering a harsh electrical storm, firing off thousands upon thousands of waiting nerve fibers to course and twist their predestined way to the silent motionless chest of the baby, compelling it against its will to contract—to twitch—to gasp—to breathe!

With a cry, an unexpected loud, shrill, hateful shriek, the baby sucked in its first breath. It sputtered it out just as fast, unhappy with the taste of God's atmosphere. But, it was *addicted*! It could not help itself. It took in another and another and another and another. Dr. Brandon cried to himself at the miraculous sight. The mutilation now lived to challenge him for its own primacy.

He swallowed hard. Any thought of murder or acquiescence in

the witting or unwitting destruction of the child was gone. Once more the compleat physician, he broke open a wax vial of two-percent silver nitrate solution and instilled a drop into each eye. He immediately washed out with saline this potentially scarifying chemical solution whose transient touch had paradoxically prevented blindness.

Grace Molling reached out for the child, nestling it in the pre-warmed sterile blankets. Joe turned his attention to the mother. He sat and waited several minutes for the spontaneous separation of the placenta from the uterus. He slowly sewed up the episiotomy with careful stitches of number-one chromic catgut, approximating the severed tissues so that the bruised and traumatized delivery channel could at least have this slight token of attention and consideration. He worked meticulously, trying in a subconscious manner to delay the child's examination, which had to be done to document the tragic findings.

Grace Molling had cleaned off the baby and placed it in the draped portable crib. Joe turned the baby on its stomach. The mass was still there, the pale blue color imparted by the dusky fluid swirling within, even more prominent than before by contrast with the now pink skin.

He continued his inspection. He spread the tiny lean buttocks. He gave a start. With mounting concern, he forced them further apart. The child gave out a loud cry from the pain of the wrenching separation. Nothing! Nothing! Only a dimple where the child's rectum should be. As if the child had not been cursed by his Maker with enough sorrow.

Afraid of what other gross anomalies might be present, he flipped the baby over onto its back, taking care not to bruise the meningomyelocele. The abdomen was smooth, the muscles firm. He had forgotten the most important thing of all, the first question the father would ask. Is it a boy or girl? He bent down to look at the genitalia. More! Why not, he thought bitterly? The poor bastard has everything else wrong. There it was. A total anomaly of the sexual organs. In a textbook fashion, as if he were back in medical school listing physical signs for his professor, he inventoried the cruel disfigurement.

No vagina. No scrotum. Only two fleshy folds on each side of the groin. Were they to be female labia? Or were they each half of a nonfused male sac?

Where were the testicles? Were they hidden behind those skin flaps, only waiting for some clever surgeon to attach the folds together and insert the masculine appendages inside them? Or were the two reproductive organs concealed deep within the abdomen where they must be painstakingly sought out? And, when found, would they turn out instead to be ovaries?

And what was that little protuberance sitting between the folds? Red, smooth, and diminutive. A penis? Far too small for this symbol of male pride. Yet, if a clitoris, far too large for such a tender little girl. Which one? Neither, or both?

He wrinkled his brow. This was a human life. Not a wax dummy. Yet, his clinical detachment was gratefully welcomed. It somehow served as a fuzzy screen to block the pathos of the creature, allowing him to function as he had been trained. The dispassionate physician.

The child's legs hung lax and loose, at an odd angle. He seized both upper legs and rotated the paralyzed limbs. Were the thighs oddly placed? What difference if it was born with both hips congenitally dislocated? The child would never walk anyway.

Then, the worst tragedy of all, the cruelest irony. Why was it always like this? The rest of the child was perfect. Incredibly beautiful. Perfectly formed. The head, large and well molded, with clear eyes, fine lips and ears. He inserted an index finger into the mouth and could feel the intact palate. His hands caressed the skull, palpating the two empty fontanels where the bones of the skull casing had parted to allow the brain room to expand as the child would age with wisdom. Just under the thin layer of skin, he stroked the firm, vibrant brain, healthy and growing. If *only* the fontanels had been closed. The skull sealed and rigid. The brain hard and shrunken or monstrous and hydrocephalic. If the child had been a cretin, or mongoloid, or any other kind of mental defective, then maybe one could have condoned the evil thoughts that flooded his mind.

But no. The child had a fine head. A fine brain, and would grow up to plumb and fathom to the fullest the unchartable depths of human despair and hate and pain—whenever it gazed below its umbilicus.

No, the baby would live. Whatever it was. Monster. Saint. Angel. Devil. Boy. Or girl. It would survive. That, if nothing else, he knew for sure.

Meningomyelocele. Hypospadias. Undescended testicles. Bifid scrotum. Chordee. Urethral agenesis. Imperforate anus. But, can we ever make it walk? Have an erection? Have a baby? Stand up to urinate? Control its bowel movements? Ever . . . ever . . . make it think for a single moment that it was a whole human being? No. Better to let it die. To kill it!

Then, just as quickly, the evanescent wish to cleanse by death passed. He was a doctor, not a murderer. To emphasize his commitment Dr. Joseph Brandon picked up the pad of consultation requests. Tearing off the yellow-tinted paper sheets one by one, he wrote out the formal orders, irrevocably setting in motion the myriad human skills and talents that would forever insure this unhappy creature's survival. Enshrine his intelligence in a flawed garment. But, most of all, exorcise from the deliverer's mind and conscience the possibility of a future change of heart.

Chapter / NINE

TO THE SIXTY-FIVE THOUSAND GOOD CITIZENS OF CROMWELL, IT was as if God Himself had ordained a geological basis for class distinction in the weary New England industrial community. Lying sprawled along the Quabbin River were the Flats, mile upon mile of monotonous blocks of worn tenements hugging the grimy mills distinguishable from their neighbors only by their saw-toothed window roofs, just as black this century as the flat tar tops of the adjacent human dwellings. Crisscrossing the mass of concrete and brick were three sinuous murky canals. In their primal past, these sluggish channels contained the rushing torrents of water that pow-

((65))

ered the ancient textile mill town, but now served only to frustrate attempts at urban renewal.

Rising steeply from the river, the land suddenly took a severe upward tilt to the commercial shopping and professional section of the city, where, on this clear April afternoon, light, white and brilliant, ricocheted off the broad shiny storefront windows to bounce back to the sun-drenched sky. Finally, making one quick vast leap to the verdant hills overlooking the oxbow of the river as it turned upon itself to enclose the industrial slum, were the Highlands, where one- and two-family houses, each with a private border of green, punctuated the fertile rolling landscape.

It was to the high bluffs overlooking Cromwell that the rusting, wheezing 1967 Volkswagen aspired this late Saturday. It paused for a moment at the southern entrance to the city, only to reject the multitudinous signs hustling the business area. Instead, it made a sharp left turn and aimed for the high ground, grinding in lower and lower gear to protect the tenuous life remaining in its over-worked engine. At the first scenic turnout, the car pulled over and stopped. Its occupant emerged, unfolding his frame like a car-penter's yellow wooden ruler until he stood erect, towering over the diminutive vehicle.

He was tall, that dimension overwhelming his other features. The light blond hair fell in shaggy locks down his neck and ears, over his forehead and collar. His expression was open and ingenu-ous, yet, with an unexpected harsh set to the jaw. He was close-shaven, and, when he smiled, deep lines broke the smooth facial contour. He wore a black turtleneck shirt under a well-worn dark brown tweed jacket, which lit up by contrast his fair complexion and sun-bleached hair. His neatly pressed tan flannel trousers were marred by deep-set wrinkles radiating out in all directions from his groin after the long hours of driving in the cramped automobile.

He stretched and flexed his legs and arms, doing several deep knee bends to restore the circulation in his feet. He could feel the pleasant rhythmic tingling of his muscles. He sucked in deep lungfuls of the fresh spring warmth. Limber once again, the stranger moved close to the edge of the metal pipe railing to take in the panorama below. He nodded at the plush plots of green dotted by swimming pools and massive houses, all homes of the mill owners and their heirs, the factory managers, and mobile professional classes. His eyes lowered down to the nondescript Flats where black and gray pigments were dominant with never a tint of green to disgrace their dark homogeneity.

He scanned the Flats carefully until he saw what he had come all these many miles to find, a new shopping center still bleeding raw earth from the vicious machines that had torn down the long-since abandoned Bell Mills and excavated the broad clearing. It appeared to be in the exact center of the Flats.

Then, scanning to the left and to the right, he searched the Flats in vain for another large set of buildings. Having never been to Cromwell before this day, he could not know that the city's primary institution of healing was located in the Highlands, close to the wealthy families that had managed its conception, endowed its maturity, and insisted on its transfer far from the majority of the citizens who required its services. Had he been able to locate Mercy Hospital, its illogical site would have occasioned a wry smile, for the callous placement vindicated certain of his long-cherished personal beliefs.

Annoyed at his patent failure to pinpoint the medical complex, he returned to his car and telescoped himself into the front seat. Carefully maneuvering the car into the rushing stream of vehicles, he retraced his way back to the original entrance to Cromwell. This time he turned right, to penetrate deep into the heart of the Flats.

There he found an exquisitely rigid geometry of city blocks, the much-admired hallmark of this nineteenth-century planned tenement community. The streets were dirty, the sidewalks crowding the curbs untroubled by a tree belt to entice the groups of children

((67))

out of the way of threatening traffic. The nondescript facades of yellow and red brick were adorned with rusting fire escapes and high cement front stoops. An occasional window air-conditioner precariously overhung the sidewalk. Plywood patches pockmarked buildings in the process of being condemned for tax arrearage or housing code violation.

The sight of the garish chrome and glass shopping center presented a welcome change. The stranger parked his car on the outer fringe of the vast lot and walked slowly around the perimeter until he located the spot he had traveled over eight hundred miles to find. The store was vacant, the windows soaped around a large "For Rent" sign. Trying to look inside, he peered through the crack between the soap and cardboard placard.

"Doc? Dr. Amen? Dr. Christopher Amen?"

Chris straightened up to see a short, dapper middle-aged man approaching him. His skin was swarthy, the close-shaven beard still black and rough. His face was round with a perpetual grin. He seemed to be bouncing with energy even while standing still. He held out one hand to Chris.

"Mr. Cardano?" Chris asked, though certain that the bright yellow shirt, green pimpled tie, and double-knit white and brown plaid suit belonged to Alex Cardano, Cromwell's most successful real-estate developer whose recent acquisition of the derelict Bell Alpaca Mills had once again proved his perspicacity by swiftly accomplishing their demolition. He alone had seen the true value in the deserted buildings, their geographic location within the most densely populated section of Cromwell, a strategic nucleus surrounded by a captive population of thirty thousand within four square miles.

Inside the empty store, Amen's eyes accommodated to the cavernous space that, devoid of any inner walls or partitions, resembled an abandoned warehouse.

Cardano was sensitive to his potential tenant's blanching enthusiasm.

"You are real lucky, Doc. Yes, real lucky. The last tenant, Kiddie-Land, took everything with them. You can plan the rooms exactly the way you want without having to spend good money to tear down what he left. Believe me, remodeling costs are bad enough, without having first to undo somebody else's mess. But," he moved back and beamed at Amen, "I can really help you out there, when you are ready."

Amen was slowly pacing the twelve-thousand-square-foot space, visualizing the dream he held sequestered deep in his heart. He could see the patient waiting area, the treatment rooms, the laboratory and X-ray facilities, the medical and surgical consulting rooms, pharmacy, social service, and minor operating theaters. As he walked, the space became peopled with children, adolescents, the elderly; clothed with walls and carpets, furniture; noisy with the wonderful bustle of patients and nurses and doctors. It was the smile on Christopher's face that told Cardano his Millsite Shopping Center was soon to have a new tenant.

Amen returned to the waiting figure, his body dwarfing the little man. He shook his hand. "It will be fine, Mr. Cardano. You already have the contracts from Washington. I will call them Monday morning and tell them to go ahead with the lease. Thank you for showing it to me today." He stared at the businessman but his eyes focused again on the fruition of a vision long pursued and now soon to be culminated.

"It is my pleasure, Doc." Cardano shook his head wistfully. "I never would have thought of using a shopping center. Goddamn it! Kiddie-Land yet."

He looked at Chris with a sigh of admiration. "Do you have any idea how many customers the clinic will attract to the Plaza? Just think of it." He gave a happy nod. "And, if you keep the patients waiting for hours like those bastards in the Highlands do," raising his eyes up toward the hills overlooking the Flats, "they can always come outside and shop around."

He glanced at Amen, afraid that his blunt comment about physicians in Cromwell might have offended this young doctor. Amen just gazed back, a half-smile on his lips as he lilted the words to himself like a playful Scottish jingle—bastards in the Highlands. . . .

"Thank you, Mr. Cardano. I like that phrase. Yes, very much. Thank you."

The two men shook hands in parting. Cardano was hard pressed to explain the bitter expression that fleetingly crossed the face of his affable new tenant. This young doctor "seemed" different from those "bastards" in the Highlands, but, until he knew him better, he had better keep his guard up.

As he watched the retreating figure shoehorn himself into his yellow car, he had an intuitive feeling that this storefront facility of his was to attract more than those in need of medical grace and succor in the long hot summer months to come.

Chapter / TEN

Simon Pirie was on his way home to surprise his wife, an undertaking unique in his married life. Not only was his premature arrival home from a Pathology Conference in Columbus, Ohio, unexpected, but also his enthusiasm, a decidedly infrequent state for this bland restrained physician.

Simon was drab in appearance without any redeeming fact or fancy—average height, thinning gray hair neatly combed and parted to one side, large eyes behind gold-rimmed glasses, a high, slanted forehead with receding hairline and light-shaven cheeks. Even the nose was a trifle too large and the chin too small. He was neatly dressed in a tight blue and white seersucker suit relieved by an expensive Florentine gold key chain with a Phi Beta Kappa key dangling beneath his early paunch.

Simon belonged to that silent unseen corps of doctors whose empiric work never sees the light of day. As Chief of the Pathology Department at Mercy, he oversaw a vast empire that, like an inverted cornucopia, received each day the infinite outpourings of blood, feces, urine, sweat, pus, spit, menstrual blood, gonorrheal discharges, syphilitic skin scrapings, and all the other odoriferous debris and excreta of that wonderful creature who had made himself in the image of his Lord.

Collecting all the flotsam and jetsam of human disease, he and his workers matched and mismatched, cut, sliced, froze, dried, stained, boiled, sifted, siphoned, and then analyzed by computer, microscope, and chemical reaction until, reduced to arabic numerals on a white sheet of paper, or to black letters on a yellow chart, the magic symbols were returned to the original donor who, had he been aware of this modern-day alchemy, was no longer a manufacturer of feces, urine, tears, or blood, but, instead, of specific gravities, cell counts, protein levels, and milli-equivalents.

Simon loved his work. He never bothered to respond to the jibes about his few patients, iced and rigid, who would never bleed or cry out during the long, meticulous autopsies for which he was noted. He never envied the larger incomes of his colleagues in private practice. His world was infinite in satisfaction, though finite in scope and confined to the sub-basement of Mercy Hospital, where he and his loyal staff toiled like Sisyphus under the avalanche of human detritus that figuratively and literally poured down on their heads each day.

Love, had it ever been present in his marriage, had disappeared in the rush of years. Sex had never existed, other than the infrequent ejaculations that oddly enough produced in early rapid succession three children, as an unexpected by-product, like green stamps given when shopping in a store one would never again enter. And now, what to do with those little impressive pieces of paper, which one can never bring oneself to throw out, yet never augment into a viable commodity? One boy and two girls, all away in boarding school. Children whose sporadic homecomings could never evoke the pungent memory of human conception. To Simon, the only compulsion was to escape eagerly each morning into the bowels of the earth with the effluvia of the bowels of the patients.

Sixteen years of married life for the lovely and accommodating Abigail Pirie had not dried up that ever-nascent hope that life should be more than the homely virtues her name might have connoted to others. She had married young, at eighteen, to her husband's thirty. Now thirty-four, she resented his forty-six, as if his age was a thick rope dangling above her, suspended into the present from the future like an Indian rope trick. An upward climb she was driven to pursue. Each night, the figure who snored loudly in bed by her side reminded her of her own mortality, and it was the inevitability of ending her days with this meek attentive man who fleshed her world with cloistering detumescence that finally aroused her to action.

She had never finished college, but left after one year to marry the shy, retiring, yet promising medical resident who proudly paid court to her prominent sexual allures. Allures that, at the time he was too dazzled to realize, were amply provided to compensate for a dearth of any other faculties.

As Simon was a good provider, she never had an incentive to develop any skills, intellectual pursuits, artistic proclivities, or merchandisable talents. She discovered, to her dismay, that her mind had become a rusty tool. Only in her reflection did Abigail realize that she possessed, intact, a ripe commodity.

Each day, when the house was quiet and empty, she would take off all her clothes and stand before the full-length mirror in her bedroom, inventorying her assets. She would take down her hair and let the long black cords spill over her naked body. The glistening strands crested around her head, then swiftly descended to frame her face, where the skin was unblemished, smooth and pink, with large hazel eyes, high cheekbones and full red lips. The locks flowed lower to tickle erect nipples, still jutting outward and up, on large milky breasts, somehow spared the ugly blue veins of parturition. Then, descended even further to hide the slightly protuberant pubis balanced solidly on top of the dark inverted triangle of tight shiny black curls. Finally, the jet curtain ended at her thighs, which briefly touched and privately kissed.

She would stride back and forth in front of her reflected image, twitching her hips, jutting out her buttocks, clad only in high heels, pushing up her breasts with both hands until they overflowed her palms like succulent offerings. Testing, enticing, a provocative sneer on her lips. With a careful appraisal of these highly personal resources and a modest delineation of her desired goals, Abigail commenced her private excursion into the world.

Despite her philosophical decision to be unfaithful, Abigail was a pragmatist. She enjoyed sex, not as a surrogate for love, but as a substitute for masturbation, actual intercourse with Simon being such a seldom event. She never asked her partners for hypocritical protestations of affection. If they used her, she did the reverse. Her affairs lasted anywhere from several weeks to several months and never left any bitter feelings upon termination. In fact, she would often laugh, it was *she,* and not her physician husband, who had the largest referral practice in the family.

The only caveat that Abigail insisted upon was that Simon be protected from knowledge of her dalliance. She was not a cruel or senseless person. She was perceptive enough to realize that the older she grew, the more valid became the material reasons for which she had married her husband. Thus, Abigail, for her own reasons, conspired to protect Simon Pirie from the sharp horns of his cuckolding, a placid, self-sustaining scheme of events that, this warm April day, was to be irrevocably shattered.

Simon had just been elected president of the American Histological Association, a position that carried with it a two-month all-expense-paid tour of Europe for himself and his wife to the various international meetings. Although Simon had never evinced an interest in traveling, he knew that Abigail had long been consumed by romantic raptures of visiting Europe. Then, this dream too, as so many others, had been flushed from her life like the monthly menstrual discharge that marked the relentless passage of time—and youth.

Arriving home a day early to share his good fortune, his face beaming with anticipation, he boasted to himself, Abigail will never believe it. Europe in the fall, with all expenses paid. He strained forward in the seat, exasperated with the slow pace of the traffic. It was with heightened expectation that he turned into Woodside Glen and traversed the maze of shaded streets that curved to show off lawns still sodden from the heavy spring rains. At last, he pulled into the driveway of his hidden home. For the briefest second, he was tempted to blow the horn, but such an act would have been too radical a gesture, even on such a day as this. His hand merely rested, mute, on the steering wheel. Suddenly, he slammed on the brakes, almost crashing into the silver-blue Lincoln Continental, which he knew even without reading the MD-12 license plate could belong only to Carl Lash.

In keeping with Simon's trusting nature, his first thought was something untoward had happened to his wife. Had he persisted long in that innocent tack, he would have been forced to conclude that only a very unusual circumstance could entice the philandering divorced Carl Lash into a house call, anywhere, for any reason whatsoever. His second thought was that he would now have *two* people with whom to share his personal triumph. It was not every day that Simon could top Cromwell's suave, handsome general surgeon.

If achieving that physical status was a feat that Simon had never experienced, it was one Abigail was savoring to the fullest at that very moment. Full dedication to their blissful pursuits insulated the pair from the loud opening of the front door and prevented them from hearing the hearty greeting that Simon offered while crossing through the empty hallway and living room. Neither were they alerted to his taking rapid inventory of the other deserted rooms on the first floor, nor even of his quick search of the outside patio. They were not cognizant of his movements, now much quieter, if not outright suspicious, as he started up the stairs.

The door to the master bedroom was partly opened. As Simon reached the first landing, he saw what was to haunt him for weeks to come. Lash was lying sprawled on his back, his legs wide apart. The dark hair that sheathed his body gathered in a dense patch where the long limbs joined his trunk. Abigail was kneeling astride his lean pelvis, moving rhythmically up and down as she moaned indistinct sounds.

Her long black hair streamed like a torn curtain with white streaks of skin glinting through the dark strands. Her head jerked spasmodically as she moved in the relentless sexual momentum. Carl's hands were moving up and down her body, fondling aimlessly, as he thrust back and forth to meet her rocking pace, groaning coarse guttural noises.

Faster and faster they moved, until with one final convulsion they locked together, pelvis frozen against pelvis. White droplets splashed out and snowed on the dark hair of his thighs. Then the slow uncoupling. Pirie saw the fierce grasp of Lash's hand on her buttocks, clutching her close to him, and when he removed his fingers, ugly red blotches remained on white skin.

Above all, the balls. Those large round testicles, which slowly relaxed their anchor high in the groin and lowered until they hung loose, heavy in the bed, thick, hairy pouches of flesh and skin like objects with no owner.

As Simon tiptoed back down the stairs that last sight was charred in his subconscious. Those two coarse black organs. He drove blindly for as many long hours as remained of the afternoon and far into the darkening gloom of dusk, until at long last, exhausted, he found refuge in a cheap motel.

During those long, bitter hours, he tossed in the too-soft unfamiliar bed, covered with sweat, his heart racing fast, his expression fixed and angry. He stared at the fractured plaster ceiling, seeing only the two loathsome sperm-laden appendages, which had raped his gentle soul and left behind a new life conceived in filth and hate. Once born, a virile violent bastard that would never stop or rest until it had delivered retribution for the accident of its birth.

Chapter / **ELEVEN**

THIRTY MILES TO THE NORTHEAST OF CROMWELL, THE LAND mass ended abruptly in a giant-sized ribbon of jagged boulders. The seas were no more than two to three feet. The gentle waves licked and tickled the harsh granite rocks. Although it was late afternoon, the sun was still high. The sky was a cerulean blue, a deeply pigmented crystalline curtain that stretched to the east across the smooth horizon. As far as one could see, only one white sail marred the exquisite junction of heaven and water.

The wind had not changed direction since noon. The solitary occupant of the nineteen-foot sloop looked up at the telltale on the shroud, pleased at the constancy of the southwest wind. The tide had turned. Strong sea breezes skimmed over the heavy fathoms, trying in some futile way to compel them to reverse direction and accompany the moving air back in its flight to the land.

The sailor took in a deep breath, held it a long time, and let it out slowly. The wet, salty fragrance rasped her nostrils and made them sting. She was a tall, willowy woman, in her early thirties, her long tawny blonde hair gathered in a single tie from which it streamed out in the wind behind her head like a golden pennant.

Her face was large and plain, but pleasant, and redeemed by enormous blue eyes and even white teeth. She wore no makeup. The sun and wind had bronzed the skin in dark hues of copper. Her neck was long and sinuous, her arms and legs smooth and brown.

She sat stretched back against the gunwale, her bare feet resting on the empty seat opposite, her head and shoulders flung back to catch the breeze. Her head was aimed straight to the sky, eyes closed against the molten fiery ball of light.

If only she could stay here forever and not return to her life on land. Perhaps if Barry had liked sailing, or skiing, or, if she was truly being fair, she in her turn had liked the symphony or his family, maybe things would have worked out differently. She knew those were just sham excuses. The flaw ran much deeper than a disagreement over recreation.

God knows it wasn't money that caused their marriage to founder. Both of them had more than enough, thanks to rich and generous parents. Perhaps it was sex. But, how could she ever know? Barry was only the second man she had ever made love to, and that only months before their marriage while he was at Harvard Law School and she at the Medical School on the other side of Boston.

When the years of training were finally over and Barry was taken on as junior partner in his father's law firm and she opened her small office to practice in Wellesley Hills near their new home, the fabric of their marriage began to fray and tear. She did not know why Barry was so adamant at first, and later so bitter, when she told him she did not want to have any children until her practice was established. Barry seemed to have forgotten that they had, after all, agreed to defer a family until they were both set.

He suddenly demanded a child. She had refused. Her practice was just barely growing. It was difficult enough being a woman in a man's specialty. It would have been easy if she had been a pediatrician, or an allergist. But, a surgeon. That was different. Even after one year on the staff of the Newton General Hospital her colleagues seemed to entertain the half-hope that she was some sort of unhappy apparition, a misplaced gremlin, who, if you left well enough alone and did nothing to encourage, would disappear.

Children. That was only the first argument. As her practice grew and she was called to the hospital nights and weekends, there were more fights. How much time did she formally owe her husband? Was there some magical number that would satisfy all the claimants in a marriage like the defendants in one of her husband's tort cases? What was so unfair was the one-sidedness of it all. She was not expected to complain when he went on a business trip. But, if she had an emergency appendectomy and was gone for the evening, she could expect an explosion upon her return.

The wind shifted slightly. Stephanie pulled the tiller toward her, turning the boat into a broad reach, heeling over at an angle of fifteen degrees. The boat was now perfectly balanced. How few things in her life were in such perfect harmony.

Perhaps Barry was right, she was frigid. At the beginning he would boast after a marathon evening of sex that she was the best partner he had ever had. Had she really changed toward the end, as he had insisted?

He became cold, unfriendly, blaming her for his increasingly poor performance. Then it got worse. They would lie there at night, naked, sweating and panting with frustration and even rage. Finally, the nights he did not come home. When she confronted

((81))

him with his infidelity, he did not hide it or even try to excuse it.

"Goddamn it, Stephanie. Why in hell should you care where I go to get laid? Don't try to fool me. That operating room of yours gives you a bigger orgasm than I ever could give. No penis in the world can ever match the one you hold in your hand with a scalpel blade at the end. No, Stephanie. It's no good. No good at all."

The separation was painless. No children. Separate trust funds. Each able to earn a good living. All she insisted upon was the house on Greenings Island, off Brewster Port, and the boat.

Stephanie ran her eyes along the glistening bright work, the deep ruddy glow of varnished mahogany contrasting with the dull gray-yellow teak cockpit sole under her bare feet. They had found it one summer in Camden, a derelict hull, and had it towed to Greenings Island. It cost them more to have the Hodgdon father and son restore it than to have built an entirely new one from scratch, but she did not care. An authentic Herreshaft design, it was destined for scrap timber, an abandoned orphan, until they—she—resurrected it. Now it skipped like an impatient bird on the water.

Did it take the place of her baby, as Barry had accused her?

All she knew was that now, when she had nobody, and her only memories were those of personal failure, somehow the boat and the water were all she had left.

Stephanie's fingers rested lightly on the tiller. She kept them there from habit, aware that the boat was running true on course. The curved wood rod was smooth and stiff. She ran her fingers up and down the slippery polished shaft. Her hand curved around the swollen ball carved at the very end. She closed her palm over the round protuberance, caressing the warm wooden head with her skin. Her fingers then returned to the shaft. She stroked her fingers back and forth along the length of the tiller aimlessly.

Her body bent forward as the action became more intense. She spread her legs. The cool air penetrated the sudden wetness in her groin. Her left hand let go of the line and dropped to her lap. The fingers began to rub gently, pressing in a deepening swirl.

((82))

Faster . . . and faster. Harder . . . and harder. Until, with a spastic thrill, she hurled out a shrill cry of relief, which soared high above the running boat, to defy the gods who had ordained her solitude and misery.

Her body jerked upright, her legs rigid as she squeezed out the last spasm of pleasure. The quick motion spun the tiller from her hand. The boat lurched to starboard, twisting the stern of the boat directly in front of the wind. The strong air caught the end of the boom and violently flung it over the cockpit to the other side, jibbing the craft in a dangerous thrust. The young woman threw off her languorous state, now aroused to the peril. The boat shivered as the boom hit the shrouds and ricocheted off them, bouncing against the tense steel wires as if to break these vital cables that held the mast upright.

Stephanie sought the telltale. Holding the tiller firmly, she eased the boat back on a beam reach and hauled in on the lax, outstretched mainsheet. The boat responded to her careful maneuver. Within minutes, the vessel was stable and back on its original course. But now the sailor was sitting tense on the edge of the seat. Whatever the pleasure self-stimulation had produced was now gone. She thought of what Barry had warned her. Perhaps the decay of their marriage *was* her fault.

She suddenly heard a loud boom echoing in the distance. Then another and another. She looked up to see graceful crescendoes of smoky-tailed flares crisscross the sky as they fell back to earth. Young Hodgdon was signaling her special emergency call.

Reluctantly, Dr. Stephanie Crane reset the sails to beat the new course. The starboard tack brought the wharf at Greenings Island into view. Without her being able to stop them, warm tears fell from her eyes, to mix their salty content with the dry spray already crusted there from the ocean she loved so much.

Chapter / TWELVE

JOE BRANDON ROSE FROM THE COUCH IN RESPONSE TO THE KNOCK
on the door. He greeted with heartfelt warmth the two figures
who entered the small Obstetrics Conference Room. His eyes told
his pleasure and relief in seeing Stephanie and Brian respond so
quickly to his urgent request.

"Stephanie, thanks for coming."

Turning to his brother-in-law, he shook his hand. "Brian," he
warned, "we've got trouble. Fourth child. Three normal girls. This
one," he said, fixing them both in a dead stare, "meningomyelocele." He caught the gasp of horror. "Not only that. Intersex. I

just don't know. Bifid scrotum? Hypospadias? Cryptorchidism?" Registering the silent shock on their faces, he rushed to conclude, "There's more. Imperforate anus. Bilateral dislocated hips." His hands fell to his sides in a gesture of futility. "Other than that, a beautiful child!"

Mute for a moment, and then almost in unison Brian and Stephanie said, "We'd better not waste time. Let us see the child, Joe." They left for the Nursery, leaving Brandon to complete his paperwork.

The examination was carried out swiftly. Their fingers poked and probed, percussed and stretched, pressed and caressed, twisting limbs, bending the neck, and testing for reflexes present and those forever tragically missing. Grace Molling stood by the dressing table to pin the diaper back on again when they had finished. She could see the hands and arms, weaving back and forth, almost obscuring the tiny life they were reducing to long Latin terms. She could see them catch each other's eye, to silently concur on the long list of anomalies.

Upon their return to the obstetrician, they found him half-somnolent, head fallen on his arms over the desk.

"Joe." Brian gently nudged him. "We finished with the Gary baby." Then, in an attempt to lighten his brother-in-law's mood, he teased, "For a baby-catcher, you're not a bad doctor. You even remember your second-year medical school." Joe smiled at the vain effort to relieve his anxiety. His head slumped down again, weighed by the burdens of emotional stress and sheer physical fatigue. Brian took in Joe's exhaustion. His sister Alice was right. If Joe didn't get some relief, and soon . . .

"Joe," he placed his hand on his shoulder, "I'll take over." Brandon raised his head to cast a thankful smile at the pediatrician. "Have you told the father . . . or anybody else in the family yet?" Brian asked.

"No. I wanted you to see the child first." Joe turned to Stephanie. "Steph, what do you think?"

"What can I say? It's a shame. A waste. Otherwise, it is a perfectly healthy baby—*from the waist up*." She gave a wry laugh. "I wonder if somewhere, at this very moment, there are three healers of magic like us," sarcastically mouthing the words, "sitting around a table, and some other general surgeon like me is saying brightly, 'Such a healthy child—*from the waist down*'?" She shook her head sadly. "I wonder what God had in mind when he cursed this helpless little thing?"

Then she straightened up, once more the clinician. "The child weighs only four pounds, eleven ounces. It's too small to jump right in to do a primary repair of the rectum. Unless Brian has some contra-indication, we had better do a colostomy—immediately —or the child will be vomiting to death by morning." She looked at the short pudgy pediatrician for his approval. Joe pointed to him. "It's *your* ball, Brian."

Dr. Terris did not answer immediately. The other two could see his brow knitted in thought. Finally, he said, "Stephanie's right. The kid has to have an opening for his bowel movements to come out of, even if it's into a bag on his abdomen. Later on, when the child is bigger, she can do a rectal pull-through to make a new anus and close the colostomy. But, right now, let's get the colostomy done."

The surgeon nodded her approval.

Brian continued, "We can ask Crowther when he wants to close the meningomyelocele. It's been so long since I've seen one of these that I can't remember exactly when the neurosurgeons like to repair the spinal defect and push the nerve fibers back inside. I would guess they would carry out the surgery in a week or two before the mass gets infected from rubbing on the sheets and soiled diapers. Sam Halpern can do an I.V.P. and make sure that the kidneys are OK and the kid can piddle. I'll start the Barr body count and chromosome analysis to see if it is a boy or girl. Once we know for sure, you, Stephanie, and Sam can decide how and what you want to do to straighten out the sex mess. That's the least of the child's problems. It's not going to be using its little pecker or hole, as the case may be, for at least another ten to fifteen years, if . . . if it lives that long."

"Brian," Joe interrupted, "you and I know that sexual identity isn't a medical emergency. But you have one hell of an anxious father waiting right outside there who is going to ask you in exactly two minutes whether he has a son or a daughter. What are you going to tell him?"

The pediatrician's mouth hung open. "Joe. You . . . you haven't told him?"

"I was waiting for you to check my diagnosis. Anyway, the father will have to give the operating permission for Stephanie to unblock the intestines. The mother is still snowed by narcotics."

"Jesus . . . Christ!" Dr. Terris let the words escape in a loud hiss. "Well," moving close to his two companions for moral support, "we had better get it over with."

Chapter / **THIRTEEN**

GRACE MOLLING USHERED THE THIN YOUNG FATHER INTO THE
conference room. She introduced the pale, apprehensive man to
the three physicians seated around the oval walnut table, the dark,
dusty blackboard on the back wall providing an ominous background. He stood awkwardly in front of them, aware that their
combined presence boded ill for his wife, or child, or both. He
searched their impassive faces for some clue. The tension eased
slightly when Joe Brandon got up and urged him to a chair.

"Peter," he said, "I have asked Dr. Crane and Dr. Terris here
because of some problems we have wi——" He stopped at the

sudden look of alarm that crossed Gary's face. The young man started from the chair.

"No, Peter," Joe said, "Helen is fine—just fine. And, the baby —doing well. They are both sleeping. Don't worry. Please." He waited until the young father had relaxed once more.

"Then, what is the problem?" Gary asked, and not waiting for an answer, added, "what have I got? A boy or another girl?"

"That is the problem, Pete. We don't know."

"What do you mean, you don't know?" He glanced around the room, accusing each physician in turn. "I asked you a simple question. Is it a boy or a girl? You know . . . a prick or a cunt!"

They did not respond to the insult but stared at him with pity. Better to let him get rid of his anger now. Let him berate. Soon enough he would have reason to curse the God of his religion.

"Well?" he demanded, bewildered by their odd silence. "What is it?" Then, just as suddenly his bravado was gone and was replaced by a leaden fear, an increasing dread of what these waiting devils were too scared to tell him.

"Mr. Gary," Brian's voice was matter-of-fact, "your child was born with a rare anomaly. I am sorry. I didn't mean to use such big words. An anomaly is something that went wrong with the development of the child as an embryo, while it was still inside the uterus. We don't know why most of them occur. Sometimes, if the mother had German measles or was on some new untested drug during the first three months of pregnancy, the child will come out deformed, missing some extremity, or deaf, or blind, or with a defective heart, or harelip, or something like that.

"As far as we know, your wife was not exposed to any of those things. Nevertheless, the baby was born with a defect in his genitals. There is no penis. No true penis. Only some tissue that looks like a penis. The scrotum, the sac to you, is not completely developed. And the testicles, if it is a boy, are high inside the body and must be brought down. All I can tell you," he said, staring straight into the father's eyes, "is to trust me. We can fix Nature's mistake so that you will have a child with either male sex organs or female sex organs."

Gary listened patiently to the explanation. Once or twice he started to ask something, but refrained. When he heard the pediatrician's assurance he breathed easily again and leaned back in his chair.

"Making a penis or a vagina is not an insurmountable problem, Pete," Terris continued, "but first we must know if the child was intended to be a boy or a girl. Once we know that, then we can start to patch up where Nature didn't do a very good job. We will run some tests and will have the answer for you before the baby goes home."

"OK . . . OK . . . Dr. Terris. If that is what must be, OK." Gary hurried, impatient to end the scene. "Can I see my wife?" To his surprise, nobody stirred, but remained fixed in place.

"In a minute, Pete," Joe said softly. "There is another problem."

The earlier look of panic quickly flashed across Gary's face.

"Mr. Gary." Brian took over once more. "Whenever Nature makes a mistake, unfortunately it makes more than one. I am afraid that your baby was born with something wrong at the end of its intestinal tract. It has no rectum."

"No rectum?" Peter Gary could not believe what this fat young doctor was telling him. "But how? Where does it take a crap from? Jesus, it has to have an asshole!"

"It doesn't," Brian said. "That is just the trouble." Seeing the man's abject puzzlement, he added, "And if the food can't get out, the baby can't eat, or it will blow up and vomit."

Stephanie responded. "Mr. Gary, that is my job. What I have to do now is to make an artificial opening on the baby's abdomen for the bowel movements to come out." She could see the father shudder at the thought of that obscenity. "But, it will only be for a short time. Just as soon as the baby gains some weight, then I will open up the blocked anus and close the colostomy. The baby will be fine." Seeing the continuing look of disbelief, she fell back impotently on the magic phrase. "Trust me, Mr. Gary. I am not lying to you."

The father did not fight anymore. His mind mercifully blotted out acute perception of his child's disfigurement. Could he now be released to see his wife? Why weren't the doctors getting up to leave, like him, and at least offering him congratulations on his new baby?

He cringed back in his chair. He clutched the arms of his chair until his knuckles grew white and the bony outlines almost pierced the blanched skin.

"Pete," Brian said, "there is one more thing. One last thing."

The father bent forward, aroused, angry. He demanded, "Tell me, Dr. Terris, what else is wrong?"

"Your baby has what we call a meningomyelocele. It means that there is a defect at the base of the spine." Receiving no response from the tensed father, he plunged on: "For some unknown reason, the bones of the spinal column did not fuse, but are spread apart, and many of the nerve fibers from the spinal column are all twisted in this large swelling on the baby's back." Still no response. "I have asked Dr. Crowther to see the baby. He is a fine neurosurgeon. He can remove the mass, straighten out all the nerves, and put them back into the spinal canal where they belong. The baby will look fine." He stopped to take in a deep breath. His eyes locked with the father's in a gesture of commiseration as he stabbed him with the last of the poisoned darts. "But the baby will not be *entirely* normal. It can never have any control over its bowel movements . . . or its urinating . . . or . . ." he lowered his eyes to the floor, unable to protect his composure, "its legs. It will be paralyzed for life."

Dr. Terris looked at Peter Gary. Why didn't the man say something? Now was the time for him to rise up, to scream, to rail, to challenge the dictate of his child's affliction. But the man's face remained rigid and masklike. He just sat there, mute. Hadn't he heard? Brian started to repeat his sad message. The father held out his hand to stop him. He stared coldly at the three physicians.

"If I don't give my permission," he said, "for her to make this hole, or for your fine Dr. Crowther to cut up my baby or for any of these other fancy tests, then what will happen?"

"The baby will die," the three uttered almost in unison. Then Brandon said, "The baby is otherwise completely normal. It is a beautiful healthy baby and, if the surgery is carried out successfully, it can live a reasonably normal life."

Even before the words were out, the father had leaped to his feet. "Normal! Normal! Paralyzed, living in shit and piss. Not even able to fuck or to be fucked. Normal! If it was you, would you believe you were leading a reasonably normal life?" He started for the door, then stopped and held out his hands in front of him, to ward off their entreaties. "Don't give me any of your fancy words. Not anymore. Don't try to fool me. How normal could *it* ever be?" He defiantly opened the door to leave. He turned and shook his head with resolute conviction. "No, gentlemen. You are all wrong. You forgot one thing. It is my child, and I, this thing's father, believe that IT would be better off dead!"

Chapter / FOURTEEN

SAMUEL HALPERN STOOD BEFORE THE OPEN MIRRORED DOORS OF his liquor cabinet and scanned the bottles, then, almost as quickly, closed the doors. The movement was not lost on his seated observer who shook his head with just the slightest hint of disgust.

"Goddamn it, Dad," the young man said, "take a drink. What in hell do you think is going to happen? You are still afraid of your own shadow."

His father turned and looked for a long time at his son. They had played out this verbal hand many times and it had always ended in a frustrating stalemate for both.

"Stephen . . . Stephen . . ." he said, "you just don't understand. I don't think you ever will."

The speaker was sixty-five years old and of medium height. He stood erect, rotating his pelvis forward in an effort to partially hide the thickening waist. His head was covered with thinning gray hair carefully parted on the left, and, despite its paucity, cut short on the sides where the color whitened. His rounded face was delineated by horn-rimmed glasses, thick lips, and eyes sunk far back into their sockets from a lifetime of myopia. His forehead was lined with furrows that were echoed by the vertical creases in each side of his cheeks. He wore a gray herringbone suit with a vest, black wing-tip shoes, but most striking of all, a somber carriage of work and responsibility with little place for levity or relaxation.

His son vindicated the old saw of genes skipping a generation. At least six feet two inches, lean and lanky, he had long dark brown hair that curled over his forehead, ears, and neck. He was not myopic. Clear hazel eyes looked out from under dark lean eyebrows. His features were chiseled and handsome, but he too had his father's thick lips and slightly hooked nose.

He slouched in the chair, with one leg dangling in constant motion over the armrest. Without any discernible provocation, a close squint of concern tightened his eyes and a nervous twitch agitated his lips.

"Understand what?" he retorted. "This is 1976. One drink isn't going to make you a drunkard."

"Stephen, you, if anybody, should know that I have never taken liquor when I have been on call. You want to practice in this community?" The words hung momentarily in the air, more a rhetorical statement of fact than a question seeking an answer. "Then, remember, this is a small town in many ways and you can't be too careful."

"Jesus Christ! You still act like the poor little Jewish doctor who crawled into Cromwell thirty years ago." He rose to his feet and strode over to his father. He glared down at him. "Goddamn it! You are still running scared. That has always been your trouble."

"Your trouble, my son, is that you have never had to run for anything in your whole damn life!"

"And whose fault is that?" The words boomeranged back with vicious strength. "You have carried me on your back for thirty-one years. And you won't let go." He clenched his teeth. "You—you—enjoy your burden!"

Samuel shook his head sadly. "For you, Stephen, coming back here will be harder—because of me. You did not earn the legacy of trust I bequeath you. I can afford to abuse the community now, if I wanted to. I have thirty years of hard-earned chits to call in." He shook his finger at his son to warn him. "But, not you. You inherit a community without even lifting a finger. Yours is the crueler burden, the more fragile responsibility."

"I never asked for it."

"I am giving it to you anyway. You are my son!"

Stephen's expression was ugly, his face red. "That is the goddamn point. Maybe I want to earn my own legacy. What if I don't want your gift? With your conditions? It is your dream, not mine. I don't want it to turn out to be my nightmare."

Samuel turned on him, his voice strident with contempt and disbelief. "When have you ever earned your own way? You may be my flesh and blood, Stephen, but I don't fool myself. You are coming back here because I am giving you a ready-made practice. You don't have to lift a finger."

His son almost shouted, "Maybe that is what I need to do."

"What for? I have already done it for you."

"Then . . . don't begrudge me."

"Begrudge?" A condescending smile flickered across his lips. "You are the one who objects."

Stephen moved closer, his face menacing, when his father held his finger up to his lips to warn him, as Mrs. Halpern entered the library.

The short, heavy woman moved slowly. Her face was round, the smooth skin etched with a fine tracery of creases and lines that radiated out from all corners. Her eyes were hidden behind small steel-rimmed glasses perched far down on her thin nose. Her hair was a blend of white and gray, worn in a large bun. Her dress was simple, black, relieved by a single strand of Oriental pearls.

She looked up at Stephen and kissed him in a motherly fashion on his forehead. He reached over to return the kiss, but she had already moved on to her husband, with a speed surprising for her size. She repeated the same gesture for him, but he did not reciprocate. He was still lost in thought, pondering the exchange of just a few minutes before with his only heir.

The room was silent, no one daring to shatter the fragile peace. Stephen elected to abort the emotional scene with his father. Kissing his mother on the cheek, he strode out of the room to seek his wife.

Sylvia Halpern turned to her husband. "What were you and Stephen arguing about?"

"We weren't arguing," her husband protested.

"Well, then, talking about? Please don't get into a fight with him this weekend. It's hard to believe—three more months and Stephen will be practicing with you."

"You know, Sylvia," he placed his arm around her shoulder and hugged her close, "we have grown old, and our children are still young."

Sylvia pulled away. "Answer my question, Sam. What were you and Stephen talking about?"

"Oh, it is the same old thing." If nothing else, his wife was tenacious in her curiosity. "He doesn't understand Cromwell." His voice became stern. "He was telling me that it's OK to go into the hospital and take care of my patients with liquor on my breath."

"Couldn't you? I mean, people have cocktails on Saturday afternoon. It is no crime."

Surprised at her lack of sympathy, he said, "Sylvia. Sylvia. *I know these people!* I know this city. I have spent thirty years walking on eggshells. I have never given anyone the slightest chance to say anything suspect about me. Isn't that right?"

"Yes, Sam. That is what you have done." Even before the next words left her mouth, her eyes were already asking the question, "But, was it all really necessary? Where else would the patients go? Forty-five miles to Boston to be treated? You are too good a doctor for them to go elsewhere. People come to you now, even from outside of Cromwell. Why do you still worry? Thirty years of good work are not going to disappear like morning mist. You are not going to fail or starve. Not anymore."

Her husband was visibly disturbed. "Why did I come to this pesthole in the first place?" he asked. "You know the answer as well as I. When I was discharged from the army in 1947, the only medical school I could get into was the University of Milan, in Italy, on my GI Bill of Rights. A poor Jewish GI from parents who still talked Yiddish, thirty years after they landed in New York City, living on Avenue C on the East Side, and buying from the pushcarts in the streets. They didn't have any pull like the rich Jews in Scarsdale and Shaker Heights. If I had been a genius, I could have got into an American medical school in the five-percent quota for Jewish geniuses. But I was a B student. A Jewish B student! A goy with a C could get into an American medical school, but not a Jew with a B, and a poor one at that," he said with scorn.

"When I came back to the United States and tried to get a residency in Cardiology, who wanted an Italian medical school graduate?"

Sylvia put out her hands to calm him. Many times she had heard this litany and had always been helpless to mitigate its painful memories.

"But, the Soldiers' Home in Boston looked the other way. They needed a scut boy to take care of the paraplegics, the amputees, to treat their bed sores, their rotting limbs, to wipe up their shit and piss. And, I was cheaper than a nurse!"

His voice became thin and scratchy. The words issued forth in resurrected anger to mock him. He paced back and forth, agitated, his steps thumping hard on the antique Ispahan beneath his feet.

"So, for five years I did their dirty work. And they threw in a free residency in Urology. When I finished, they gave me a license to practice in the state."

His words were calculated to make the old wounds fester again as if the momentary pain would perversely cancel out the old hurt.

"Maybe you don't remember anymore, but I do. Thirty years ago, Cromwell was a medical wasteland. One dying fifty-bed hospital without even a doctor to give anesthesia. Anyone who was anybody went into Boston for treatment. Only the dregs stayed behind, the leavings. And this was where I came to spend the rest of my life." His body gave an involuntary shudder as the long-repressed memory surfaced to sear him.

"It is different now. All the people who left Boston when the blacks and Puerto Ricans came in, fled out here. Nice, clean, rich VIPs with money, big houses, expensive tastes." His tone turned sarcastic. "They even have expensive tastes in hospitals. So all of a sudden Mercy Hospital, which had only poor virginal nuns to run it, now has a gold-plated board of bankers, contractors, State Street lawyers, all with money and lots of it. Now we have a beautiful new hospital. Why? To cater to the rich bastards who are too lazy to travel into Boston to get their hemorrhoids fixed or their prostates reamed out.

"So, something finally went right for Samuel Halpern. At last little Sammie got a crumb, a big rich crumb. But, remember, Sylvia, without Route 128 for the WASPs to come back here each night to sleep with their horsey wives, Sammie Halpern would still be sucking around the fringes."

His wife watched him pace back and forth. She knew well the full dimensions of that canker still ulcerating his ego. His recent success had never been able to dilute the misery of those early years. To his wife, who had lived and relived the dregs of that time, life was a continuum, not an accumulation. The past was important, but only as a movement toward the present and then on to the future.

She lived content, from day to day, not from a lack of sensitivity or callousness to the past, but with a naïve optimism that the present was sufficient reward for those fortunate enough to be alive to possess it, and she had long ago resigned herself to his opinion of her as a shallow, superficial person.

"Sam, Mercy is a good institution. The thirty years are over and you are a somebody. How many doctors from Cromwell go to Boston to teach two afternoons a week? Sam, the years have been good to you. Even more important, those years have been good for you. You succeeded by your own efforts without anyone to help you. You have no reason to be the frightened little boy in the ghetto. But you act as if you were. Sam, you are still scared. I think that Stephen is right. You have not changed."

Her manner softened, maternal in spirit. "Leave Stephen alone. Let him make his own way, his own decisions. Even his own mistakes. He will do all right."

"Sylvia. Sylvia," Sam said, exasperated, "you are so blind. You think because there is a big hospital with marble in the lobby that this community has changed? It is still the same hostile anti-Semitic jungle it always has been. Do you think Abe Kupperman is a trustee at the hospital because he teaches at Tufts?" He shrugged his shoulders, deprecating the suggestion. "Heh. He never went beyond the sixth grade. Because he is a great golfer? They still won't let him into the Cromwell Country Club. No, when they needed a new wing ten years ago, where did they go for the money? Cromwell has a lot of Jews today. Rich ones, who commute to Boston just like the rich Protestants and Catholics. They have money—gelt." He rubbed his thumb and index finger together. "That is why they made Abbie Kupperman a trustee."

He paused a minute before continuing, his face flushed and damp.

"Sure, in 1976, Samuel Halpern is suddenly a success. Because I am a good doctor? Oh, no. It is not all that simple. Not that clean. Thirty years ago, Cromwell was the end of the road. No decent doctor would settle here. I did. Now I am in the driver's seat. The trustees, the bankers, the other doctors, all the big shots in town are my patients. I have my finger up every important rear end in town and I keep it there."

He gave his wife a contemptuous look and continued. "Haven't you ever wondered why there has never been another urologist to compete with me in Cromwell?" he asked, disgusted by her lack of insight. "Since the new Mercy building went up ten years ago, and the rich commuters settled in West Cromwell, this city has been a magnet for specialists trying to get a piece of the golden goose."

"Why, Sam?" she asked.

"Because I play asshole politics to keep them out. So that my son, Stephen, can have my practice, my city, intact, unspoiled. Sure I am a success," he boasted bitterly. "A little luck. Some breaks. But, remember, I sweated for it. Kissed asses for it. I still do. And, I don't drink liquor on Saturday afternoon."

He stood erect, his shoulders held back, his voice firm and assertive.

"Sylvia, the thirty years were worth it. It is my dream, all for Stephen. No one will ever take any of that away."

"Sam," his wife argued, "thirty years has to mean something more than just living for each night, to dream for a son. God help you, Sam, if it doesn't turn out the way you have planned."

Samuel Halpern brushed away the disconcerting doubts. "He is my son. Thirty years was the painful price of my dream. I paid off the mortgage on Stephen's future with my sweat and tears, my honor, my youth. I am worn out now, Sylvia, but the future is his —all free and clear. It is my final gift to him—my dream."

He stared out through the French doors, welcoming a future that only he could see distant over the horizon. An aroused God of Wrath, he intoned, "And he will possess it—*on my terms!*"

Chapter / **FIFTEEN**

A JACKSON POLLOCK DRIBBLE OF BRIGHT CHROME YELLOW, THE small Volkswagen crisscrossed the fabric, trickling into each corner, puddling in the Flats near the Millsite Shopping Center, sneaking up and quickly touching Mercy Hospital, hesitatingly entering the Highlands, boldly traversing the mills, the factories, the commercial shopping area. Always moving, until its shiny yellow trail seemed a slashing gridwork, binding together the diverse areas and elements of the Cromwell landscape as over the next month Christopher Amen probed into the substance of Cromwell. He saw the rigid dichotomy between the Flats, whose laboring families fueled and supported the businesses controlled by the elite denizens of the Highlands. To his discerning eye, it became apparent that the steep rise to the elevated regions personified not only geologic tilt, but also money and social rank. This glaring disparity, accepted out of inertia by the lower classes along the riverbanks and perpetuated by the upper classes commanding the dominant strategic heights, was, for his peculiar purpose, a rich and fertile seedbed.

Each day he would spend hours pacing the empty space of the soaped-windowed store, its "For Rent" sign now proudly absent, one or more eager salesmen at his side, their shoes clattering in the cavernous high-ceilinged clinic-to-be.

The Cromwell medical fraternity was little cognizant of the bustling activity, preoccupied each day with their heavy load of patients, commuting from their homes in the Highlands to their offices in the Highlands, to Mercy Hospital, highest of all. Who would have expected these good doctors to recognize the two stern-faced officious young men with bulging brown leather briefcases who arrived from Washington, D.C., one afternoon? Met by Amen at the nearby airport, they were taken on a whirlwind tour of the city, now familiar territory to their peripatetic host.

It was in the shopping center that their manners and formality dropped, their voices rose loud and excited, their gestures animated. They carefully examined the blueprints, the charts, the meticulously tabulated demographic figures, the tables of economic and social statistics that their host had culled both from personal observation and from the caseloads of documents the local Chamber of Commerce had obligingly supplied. They left, trailing behind them a thick cloud of enthusiasm and free money. No. Why should anyone in Cromwell have recognized those two strangers, or for that matter the pioneering tall blond Volkswagen owner himself?

But the other visitor to explore the Millsite premises, that unexpected guest. Not a tradesman, not a sightseer, his frequent presence certainly should have registered on someone serendipitously passing through Millsite. Shorter than Amen by at least two or

three inches, his facial features less refined and darker by comparison, his attitude slightly more hesitant, unsure. Certainly a patient
or friend of his family should have wondered why the tall handsome
stranger in the unseemly battered car with an out-of-state MD license
plate would, of all places in the world, have been seriously con-
versing in a deserted children's toy store with Samuel Halpern's son
and only heir.

Chapter / **SIXTEEN**

Samuel Halpern looked forward to the weekend visits of his son and daughter-in-law, extrapolating the too-brief times into his son's final settling in Cromwell, come July. Recently, however, it seemed that Stephen was avoiding contact with his father. Samuel began to experience an increasing uneasiness, though for what reason he still was not certain. This Friday night, Stephen seemed more on edge than usual. If his father had been more perceptive, he would have detected a faint glimmer of apprehension, or even more unexpected, one of guilt. But no one at the dinner table, not even Sylvia, seemed alerted to Stephen's withdrawn behavior.

Sylvia Halpern's long, laborious Friday night dinner, weighty with family tradition and religious ritual, had finally drawn to a close. Both she and her daughter-in-law started up from the table to clear the dishes and bring in coffee and dessert. Seeing Ann rise, Mrs. Halpern stretched out her hand to restrain her. "Sit down, Ann," she urged. "Please. This weekend you are a guest," knowing that both the request and its polite rejection were the habitual pas de deux.

"Dad," Stephen broke his unaccustomed silence, "do you remember my mentioning a Christopher Amen?" His father shook his head.

"Chris was in my class in medical school. He graduated with me."

"What kind of a doctor is he?" his mother asked.

"He is a family physician."

His father nodded at his wife. "That means a GP, Sylvia."

"No," Stephen retorted, "that is unfair. Many good hospitals have long residencies for this kind of doctor. He doesn't just hang out a shingle after medical school."

"Like I said, a GP. So he read a few more books. So what?"

"Chris is planning to come to Cromwell. He wants to open up a family clinic here. He has great plans. We will hit this community like a bolt of lightning."

Only his father caught the "we" and its implication. "Cromwell isn't a community that likes to be hit with a bolt of lightning. What do you mean, 'we,' Stephen? You had better explain."

"Chris spent two years in the Peace Corps in Chile after finishing his residency. He then ran a hospital in New Mexico. While in the United States Health Service, he made valuable contacts in Washington with the government agencies who are funding community medical centers."

The silence that greeted his words was more the preamble to a deadly skirmish than tacit approval.

"Chris wants to open a clinic here in Cromwell. If it succeeds, Chris has already planned a whole chain of satellite clinics in the surrounding county."

"Please, Stephen," Samuel pleaded, "not so fast. I am not as young as you."

"Dad," Stephen ignored the hostility in his father's tone, "it is an exciting concept. Until the clinic gets off the ground, Washington will back it with grants from different agencies."

"Sure," his father rebutted, "but how long will the government keep this utopia afloat?"

"That is just the point." Stephen savored the puzzled expression on his father's face. "When Congress passes its medical insurance act, all Chris has to do is to convert his clinic into a prepaid plan and he will be all set." He looked around the room, pleased. "Think of it. A total comprehensive health-care package all set to go and five years ahead of anybody in the state."

Samuel replied sharply, "When you get as old as I am, my son, you don't get excited over celestial visions. Tell me, where does all this leave the rest of us, who in our own inadequate fumbling way just happen to have been taking care of all the living and dying in this town for the last hundred years—without any government handouts?"

"Any doctor who wants to join is welcome. If he agrees to certain rules."

"Rules? Of course, I forgot. Why not? All virtuous enterprises have to have rules. Gives them respectability. What are they?"

"First, he must give up his private practice. Second, he can still see all his old patients, but they will belong to the clinic. Third, the physician must practice within the confines of the clinic's physical plant."

His father led him on, playing out his questions like a line to a hooked fish. "Who is going to run this colossus?"

"Everyone. The physicians in the group, along with representatives from the local unions, the school board, the churches, and, of course, Chris."

"Of course, Chris," his father parroted.

"Chris most of all. He is the link between the clinic and Washington."

"Link?" Samuel countered. "You mean he is the bagman with all the free loot?"

"Without him, the clinic couldn't get off the ground," Stephen argued. "We need him!"

Samuel Halpern's face twisted with anger. "We need him? *I* don't need him! You don't need him, nor his goddamn clinic. You are coming with me this July."

"Dad, that is something I have to talk to you about. It is no longer simply a matter of finishing residency and going into practice with you. I have a decision to make," Stephen started in, hesitant and apologetic, half-hoping to entice his father into an easy acquiescence.

"A decision. A decision! What decision?" Samuel stood in front of his son, his face red and flushed with anger. "You are set to come in with me this July. There is no decision. You come to me and talk about a choice, as if the past never existed. Mature people do not do things like that. Not my son!" His voice eased. "A choice? What kind of a choice? To grab a union card from a lunatic who has barely finished medical school. The great hero who took care of some starving Chilean peasants, some tuberculous Navajos. You want to punch a time clock for some unregistered saint with a Social Security card who is coming to Cromwell to show us, the unwashed pagans, the Holy Grail of Medicine. His Holy Grail?"

He shook his head. "What kind of a moron are you, Stephen? Chris, I understand. I have lived longer than you. I have seen lots of Messiahs in my lifetime. Many, many. It makes no difference what their goals were, or, for that matter, what their gods were. All of them had some kind of dream. To change—to make better —to help mankind. You know what happened to them? What always happens to Messiahs? If we were lucky and found them out in time, we crucified them. If we weren't fast enough—or smart enough—they crucified US!"

"That is not fair, Dad. Not fair at all."

"Fair, Stephen?" his father shot back. "What has fairness got to do with this? What gilt-edged equity do you deserve? You dare to tell me that you have a decision. You presume to discuss my dream, to dispose of my future—with an apology—all because you follow some crusader for free Pap smears."

Livid with rage, Samuel shouted, "Never! Never! Don't talk to me of decisions. You are trying to walk before you have crawled in this life. Warm shit still ferments in your diapers." His nose wrinkled with derision. "It smells up this room. Clean yourself, my son. In my house you will learn to stand up and walk straight before you talk to your father. I am your father, Stephen. I love you, but I am not a loving father. Don't disobey me."

The older physician turned on his heel and left the room without even a backward glance. His words lingered behind, a dank vapor to smother his victim and choke off any vestige of resistance.

Stephen, his wife, and mother watched the retreating figure, stunned by the vehemence of his reaction. They looked at each other in turn, seeking something to erase the bitter scene and break the oppressive silence.

Sylvia spoke first. "Stephen, that wasn't right, springing this on your father. Never even a little hint. You knew about it long before this evening. Why didn't you say something earlier? You could have told *me*. Why so sudden? Your father is right, Stephen. It isn't fair at all." Her words were full of reproach.

"Mother, you are right. I know. I know. But . . . but I just didn't know how to tell Dad before this. He has been so set on my going into practice with him that I couldn't talk to him before."

"Was this way any easier?" she retorted. "Better for you or for him?"

"No—but—I—Ann and I just couldn't . . ."

"No, Stephen," Ann said. "Don't bring me into this. You were the one. I told you earlier at least not to be so positive about coming into practice with him in July. You, you couldn't stand up to your father. So you hurt him—very badly. I feel sorry for him."

The slight dark-haired young woman continued, her hands folded in her lap between her legs. "You know your father better than I do. Perhaps some day he will accept what you have done. After all, you are his flesh and blood and you will be practicing in his community." Her voice wavered. "Is he the kind of man who will accept half a loaf rather than no loaf at all? I hope so, for your sake." She shook her head. "He hates Chris, his ideas, what he stands for. He despises you for accepting them. Will he give in and accept you —on your terms?" She looked at the closed door and shivered just a bit as if a frigid shaft of chilled air had pierced her flesh. "Even if he does, he will *never* forget that you wounded him and then asked for his blessing."

Ann got up and walked over to her mother-in-law. She placed her hands on her shoulders, squeezing them in a gesture of solidarity.

"Stephen, you owe your father a lot more than just asking him to bless your new venture, to condone your treachery, because he is your father. You praise the clinic. You extol Chris. His federal grants. But, what did you say about your father's shattered dreams? His plans? His goals? His hopes? Stephen, your father is not some clinic patient. Treat him with the love he has for you."

"Ann is right," his mother said, her face reflecting the compassion radiating from her daughter-in-law. "Go . . . go . . . to your father. Don't discuss Chris. Ask his forgiveness. You and Ann are going to be living in this town with him the rest of your life. Give him some consideration. He deserves it. If not as your father, then at least as a fellow physician. Go, Stephen. Go to your father."

Stephen rocked back and forth on the balls of his feet for several seconds, his turbulent thoughts trying to coalesce around some appropriate response. Finally, he held out his hand to Ann, a plea for support. "Come," he begged.

His wife rejected the proffered pact. She edged back, closer to Mrs. Halpern. Ann was oddly defiant, resolute. Her stance was guarded. There was no smile on her soft mouth.

"No, Stephen. I am not going to hold your hand. He is *your* father."

She helped her mother-in-law up from the chair and clasped her arm in her own.

"Come, Mother," she offered. "We must empty the dishwasher." And without even a cursory backward look, the two of them left the room, shunning the impotent entreaty of Stephen Halpern, son and husband.

Chapter / **SEVENTEEN**

THE COLD BODY OF THE ELDERLY NUN WAS PAST CARING ABOUT the frantic activity of the four women scurrying around it. In turn, they would sneak a hasty look at the large round clock on the wall and return to their distasteful task. Dr. Martin Abels had already wheeled his anesthesia machine out of the room and was busy replacing the gas reservoirs in the Anesthesia Supply Room at the other end of the hall with fresh ones in anticipation of another emergency.

Connie Mercier stopped her cleaning for a moment and straightened up, both hands on her hips. She reached up and swept back a lock of hair that had escaped the tight confines of her cap and fallen over her forehead. "What a pigpen!" she said, as she knelt down again to resume checking one by one the dozens of blood-soaked sponges and gauze pads that had been used by Dr. William Crowther no more than an hour before. As she picked each one up, she carefully examined it to make certain no surgical steel items were buried in the sticky red folds, before tossing the cloth strips into a large plastic bag for delivery to the incinerator.

Each of the 211 neurosurgical metal instruments were separately washed and placed in large stainless-steel trays to be taken back to Central Supply for sterilization by autoclaving. The room was then inventoried and a separate punched card made out for all sutures, medicines, and disposable material consumed by the patient. Finally, the floor, walls, tables, and stools scrubbed with disinfectant.

Grudgingly, the battle-stricken area was restored to a semblance of normalcy. The four women stopped and looked around them with pride. Connie knew that they had all worked hard.

"OK, girls," she offered kindly. "You might as well leave. I will take care of her." She pointed to the cadaver resting on the operating stretcher.

There were a few ineffectual gestures of protestation, which she graciously refused, shooing them outside. Their faces beaming, they fled through the door with scarcely a backward glance.

"Noblesse oblige," the head of the Operating Room softly hurled after them.

Connie walked over to the built-in cupboard and opened the glass doors. She reached way back on the lower shelf for a sealed package. There was only one left. Christ! There had been five there yesterday morning and nobody else had died in the OR since then. She sighed. Another damn thing to come down on the girls. Pulling out the remaining disposable pack, she tore off the tough plastic covering and exposed the sterile contents.

It contained one large folded three- by six-foot white vinyl drape to cover the recumbent body, a second one-foot-square sheet for the head, four three-foot-long pieces of twine to secure the two plastic coverings in place, and last, but not least, a manila paper bag to fasten to the patient's big toe with her Christian name, age, and hospital Addressograph plate number.

Connie slowly wrapped the corpse, tucking in the loose corners with care. She shaped the head covering and completed filling out the label. Giving one last glance to the room and its white-enveloped mummy, she turned off the overhead lights and closed the door behind her.

She sat quietly at her desk while waiting for the orderly to answer his page. For the moment, the trauma of the operation was repressed. She even dismissed the horror of the silent occupant waiting in the adjacent room for transport down the service elevator to the morgue. Mercifully, only one crazy thought kept running through her mind. Prynne! How in the world did the Administrator expect her to keep track of every goddamn tweezer and nail file when she couldn't even stop her girls from stealing the shroud packs to use as tablecloths for their weekend picnics now that summer had come?

The Operating Room Suite was deserted and gloomy. The small lamp on Connie's desk cast long bizarre shadows on the floor and walls. She could hear the slow mechanical whirring of the electric clock above her head. She glanced anxiously at the door. Why didn't the damn orderly come for the body so that she could lock up and leave with Brian? Maybe they could still have time for dinner before the meeting at Millsite.

She shuddered just a bit, suddenly cold, and immediately felt silly. Long ago she thought she had given up the fear of working with death. It was too common an occurrence in these ten, now lifeless, operating rooms off the darkened central corridor. Yes, oddly, she felt frightened of the corpse lying no more than ten feet away from her on the other side of the door.

She gave a slight scream when the door to the suite flung open. With a sigh of relief, she relaxed at the sight of her fiancé. Brian barely gave her time to rise from her chair when he swept her up in a strong, clumsy embrace, squeezing her in a choking bear hug. She could feel the hard swelling expand against her crotch. It was not difficult to read his mind.

"*After* we get back from the meeting," she said, laughing at his crestfallen expression.

Brian looked at his watch and gave her a mischievous grin. "We've got lots of time," he coaxed, "especially if we skip supper. You have been hinting that I should go on a diet. You know, they say sex burns up more calories than tennis."

"Brian, you're impossible." Connie could not help smiling at his sheepish pout. "I've been sitting here for twenty minutes waiting for Arthur to take the damn body down."

"What have you got?"

"An intracerebral hemorrhage. A patient of Dr. Crowther's. A nun. She ran the electroencephalogram lab. It is ironic. There she was, doing EEG's on everybody else's patients while a cancer was growing in her own frontal lobe and that very test might have diagnosed her own tumor in time to save her life."

"Didn't anybody suspect anything?" Brian's clinical curiosity had finally succeeded in overcoming his aroused libido.

Connie made a deprecating sneer. "All that anyone could notice was a slight change in mood. She became forgetful. Her memory began to fade. She would mix up instructions with patients. One day, they found her sitting on the bench outside the Mother House, waiting for a bus to take her downtown shopping. She sat there for hours and let a dozen buses go by and never bothered to get on any of them. One of the parking lot security guards became suspicious and reported her to Prynne's office. Do you know what they did?"

Brian shrugged his shoulders.

"They sent her to see Larry Fels, the psychiatrist. He told the Mother Superior that she was just getting a little senile and he put her on all sorts of drugs. Apparently he kept changing them every week because nothing helped. I heard Crowther tell all this to his assistant during the case. Then, this morning they found her unconscious at Vespers. She had ruptured a blood vessel deep inside the invading cancer. There wasn't anything Crowther could do. He tried to evacuate the clot to decompress the brain tissue. But it was a very vascular tumor. I think he said a glioblastoma, and he couldn't get control of the artery. So . . ." Her voice faded as her gaze turned toward the corpse resting quietly on the other side of the partition.

"But," seeing his morose expression, "let's talk about something more cheerful. Is everything still set for tonight?"

"It's all systems go. Chris and Steve have lined up almost everybody in town that we can use. Everybody except . . ." He looked upward. "The big shots, of course."

"Is Joe coming?"

"I talked with Alice again this afternoon. I don't know how she managed to persuade him, considering how tired and testy he has been lately."

"They still haven't let up, have they, Brian?"

"No, I'm afraid not, Connie. It's getting worse for Joe all the time. I just hope that Millsite works—even more for his sake than for mine."

"What do you mean?"

"Joe is determined to show Flaherty and his partners that they can't drive him out of town. I think for Joe to stay in Cromwell and fight back means more than just winning a practice. For him it is almost a test of his manhood."

"Brian," Connie asked, "don't you think that Joe is doing the right thing?"

The young doctor did not answer for a minute. He stared at her, aware of how much effort this young nurse had invested in his and Joe's fight for medical survival in Cromwell. He had an instinctive feeling that she would not approve of his stance. "That's just it, Connie. It may be the right thing for him, but not for me. I grew up never wanting to be anything else but a doctor. I was lucky. I was accepted at medical school even though I wasn't the brightest boy in my class in college. They took me and rejected classmates who wanted to be doctors with a passion far exceeding mine. And they were brighter, too. Maybe even more dedicated. I still don't understand why I was chosen and they were not. And, when I entered residency, I decided to become a pediatrician. Maybe because I am just a big baby at heart myself." He blushed shamedly at the confession. "Anyway, that is it . . . all of it."

He searched Connie's face in vain for the glimmer of understanding he hoped would be present.

"Don't you see, Connie. All I want is just to take care of little kids. It doesn't make any difference to me where I practice or how much money I make, or whether I work in a fancy new building or in an old battered one. I don't give a damn if I never get on any Executive Committee or Credentials Committee or if my commands never cause people to tremble with fear. That is not why I became a doctor. Let the others do the politicking and have the internecine feuds and all the battles, and get the honors and trophies."

"But Brian . . ."

He held her silent, determined to get it all out, once and for all. "If for some reason I cannot get a practice going in Cromwell, with Millsite or without, I will just go elsewhere. There are plenty of other places in the country that need a pediatrician. Places where the hospital isn't quite as nice and pretty, but then again, maybe the town wouldn't be rich enough to attract all the specialists to come in and slit each other's throats."

To his surprise, Connie did not rise to echo his sentiments. She gave him a long, quizzical look, then leaned forward. "But, Brian, doesn't being a physician obligate you with a responsibility to do more than lower fevers and dry up runny noses? When the medical school made you a doctor, did it expect you to blind yourself only to eyes and ears and throats, and not to the souls of your fellow physicians? Did the curriculum specifically forbid you from sharing the burden of improving your chosen profession, cleansing its wrongs, and expunging the malefactors? Isn't that part of medicine, too?"

"Connie, I am not a politician. I am not a Flaherty, or a Best, or a Lash, or a Prout. I can't play their dirty games. I don't know how and I don't want to know how." He spread his hands out in a futile gesture to deny her claim. "I am not a doctor like them. I just want to do a good job practicing medicine."

"And let those bastards dishonor your profession?"

The question hung heavy between them. He could not answer.

"Remember, Brian, the angels may have graced the medical profession, but it is the doctors who have disgraced it, and not only the polluters like our great men in Mercy, but, even more, well-meaning doctors who plead dedication and purity as their excuse for washing their hands like Pilate."

Connie registered the pained expression on her lover's face. She felt guilty to have posed her feelings so vehemently to this warm-hearted physician, especially for condemning those very faults for which she loved him. If Brian changed from the naïve, altruistic doctor into some kind of a fighter, would he not lose those qualities that endeared him to patient and friend alike?

Maybe he was right. All doctors were *not* cut from the same cloth. Some were the bastards. Some were the crusaders. And some, like Brian, were the honest considerate plodders who made that magical mystical love-affair between man and his healer endure through the centuries.

She was confident deep inside that she was right in her conviction. She also knew for a certainty Brian would never change. Perhaps, though, the Joe Brandons of the world should be the ones to do the fighting.

She heard Arthur's desultory pace approach the swinging doors. With a broad smile on her face, she hooked her hand around Brian's arm. With a devilish smirk on her face she said, "Let's go burn a couple of calories together instead of supper."

Chapter / **EIGHTEEN**

WHY STEPHEN THOUGHT THAT BRINGING HIS FATHER FACE-TO-face with his nemesis would mitigate the son's deceit, it is hard to say. Perhaps he entertained some mystical but forlorn belief that reason would temper his father's anger, or that Christopher Amen possessed magical powers of persuasion. What was certain only was that the elder urologist's reluctant appearance at the first Millsite meeting was doomed to fail from the beginning. By the time the father had left, his determination to expunge the contagion was, if anything, reinforced.

In contrast with the other physicians gathered in the dimly lit store, Samuel Halpern was tense, his hostility poorly concealed. He barely responded to the respectful greetings of the younger doctors who had come in response to his son's and Chris's invitation.

Stephen knew most of the physicians assembled in the room. He stood up to introduce Chris who stood quietly waiting to be heard. This was the first time Samuel had seen Amen and as much as he was prepared to dislike the stranger, he could not help but be impressed by his quiet, thoughtful appearance, his calm, relaxed air of confidence. As for his son, the father took in Stephen's naïve gestures, the vicarious pride, the youthful enthusiasm. He wondered how he could extricate Stephen from his false gods without causing irrevocable consequences for the Halpern family?

Christopher Amen surveyed the roomful of Cromwell medical have-nots. Then his glance took in the somber figure of Stephen's father. He saw there the face of the enemy.

The young doctor began to speak. His voice was low and soft. He told of his own background, his interest in the concept of community health facilities, his liaison with those funding government agencies willing to commit money and support for his project. Finally, his decision to come to Cromwell, thanks to his classmate, Stephen Halpern.

As he talked, his manner grew more animated. He strode back and forth before them, drawing in broad imaginative sweeps, to be pigmented in their minds by their own ambition and desire, the bricks and mortar, the flesh and blood of a new medical establishment of their very own. A complete center, replete with the most modern equipment and personnel. A clinic, backed by the government and endowed with a financial lock on half of the population by virtue of ironclad contracts with Cromwell's largest industrial concerns.

But, when he insisted that Millsite must be founded on a truly cooperative enterprise, he could see the sudden concern sour their exuberance.

"But what about our private practices?" a voice objected from the back of the room.

Chris could not make out who the speaker was, but it did not matter. He knew that the others there echoed the same doubt. This was the moment of truth for all of them. For Millsite to succeed, it was critical that he bury forever their clutching hold on the fee-for-service solo-practice concept rigidly ingrained in their pattern of behavior and demand in its place total subordination to the collective goal of an integrated system of medical care.

"What have all your individual and solitary efforts in Cromwell these many years brought you up to now?" He sought out Terris and Brandon and Paillard and the others whose faces he knew only briefly. "Only heartache and disappointment, or you would not be sitting here tonight listening to a stranger."

Their tacit assent was all Chris needed to know that they would hear out his dream. But . . . would they accept it without any caveat?

A dream. His dream. Sure, Millsite would be twelve thousand square feet of test tubes and syringes and men and women with medical diplomas on the walls. A shiny new complex in which to diagnose and treat diseases of the mind and flesh. But so were the other tens of thousands of similar offices spread across the country. Millsite was all of this, but yet so much more.

How could he explain it? He looked over the audience, his forehead wrinkled. How to communicate to those before him his crucial belief so alien to their way of thinking, yet the bedrock of his faith.

He began quietly. "As physicians, we spend a lifetime fighting microscopic vectors of infection. Have any of you ever stopped to consider which are the most successful of the microbes that have afflicted mankind over the millennia? As physicians, it would be instinctive to award such a prize on the basis of virulence. Think of that most deadly enemy of man, the Pasturella bacillus of bubonic plague, which struck without warning and decimated a continent.

"But, what if we were to judge the contest, not from our customary stance as doctors, but instead through the eyes of the disease? Consider carefully that a parasite, by definition, cannot fend for itself. It must rely totally upon another's helpless body for its food and shelter, warmth and protection. What does it avail such a microbe if it successfully ravages its host, shatters its defenses, and murders without mercy? What then the fate of the poor parasite when its victim finally succumbs? If it compulsively burns itself out of home and larder, it must rapidly seek another host, and failing that, perish itself as tragically as did its unfortunate victim.

"How much luckier the parasite that does *not* kill its host. Ignore as stupid and blindly self-destructive those well-publicized mortal vectors as smallpox, yellow fever, viral meningitis whose total victory would produce their simultaneous extinction. Think instead of the quiet little bacillus of leprosy. Sluggish, demure, protected by an unattractive thick greasy coat of wax, this reticent bacterium takes years before it heralds its presence. Then, once entrenched, it wisely refuses to kill the carrier, preferring instead to remain in a kind of humble symbiotic relationship with it. The human being lives out his or her entire normal span of days. The bacillus happily enjoys its own fourscore and ten of peaceful life, wanting neither for food nor shelter, never obliged to leave its familiar comfortable domicile to seek another alien lodging, content to coexist as an unobtrusive boarder until the host succumbs of natural causes.

"What then is the answer to our original question? To man, the wiser most successfully evolved parasite must obviously be the deadliest. But, to the parasite, it is quite the reverse, the meekest. The paradox is in the eyes of the beholder.

"I did not come here tonight at Stephen's invitation to lecture to you on the life cycles of human diseases, but only to illustrate how easy it is to become parochial and narrow-sighted in our vision. For all of us in this room, medicine as we know it is so much a habit that, without our knowledge, we have lost the vital perspective to see our actions as others outside our immediate caste might view them. Like the seven blind men and the elephant, we can no longer step back and encompass the full scope of our deeds.

"Examine now, through the eyes of the patient, how medicine has been practiced in the United States over the past two centuries. One cannot help but be struck by the odd fact that in our society, the physician is rewarded only for the misfortune of his patient. Years ago, the rich Chinese would pay the doctor when he was healthy and deny him remuneration when illness occasioned. In other cases, the doctor was even punished when the patient was in ill temper or demised.

"Ours is truly a race of men among men which prospers only by the pain and suffering and misery of our fellowmen. Eliminate the gall and kidney stones, the swollen prostates and tonsils, the shrunken wombs and cataracts, trauma, infections, heart attacks, cure strokes, congenital anomalies, cancer, and our modern-day witch doctor would wither on the vine and starve. Is there not here a unique economic advantage of illness that inures solely to our benefit?"

He held his hands out in mock seriousness, to defend himself from the sharp looks that crossed the faccs of those nearest him. He hastened a sympathetic laugh as he apologized.

"No, I am not suggesting that physicians deliberately aspire to perpetuate the ill health of their patients or prolong their suffering or agony for private gain. But if you keep an unprejudiced mind, where is that overwhelming dictate for our profession to keep the lay public healthy? Where is our Categorical Imperative to avoid unnecessary medications and surgery, X-ray and laboratory tests? To the patient, are we doctors not coexisting happily in incestuous consort with the diseases of the world? Do we not, like them, fasten upon the patient and gain sustenance from the injured body as do the vectors of disease? Is not medicine today, in actuality, predicated upon monetary reward when the patient is sick and punishment in terms of financial deprivation when the patient is well?"

There was a hush in the room as each of the young men and women in turn was struck by the logic of Amen's thesis. Their defenses had been lulled by his opening verbal ploy. They were not prepared for the sharp cerebral thrust that unexpectedly challenged their long-held beliefs.

Chris moved quickly to anticipate the rebuttal of any dissenters. "Some of you may claim, with some validity, that to remove the goal of personal gain defies human nature. At least now, if the doctor gets rich, the patient gets healed. Perhaps, until that time as man ceases to function as an upright animal forced against his baser instincts to live in communal habitation, we must acknowledge and respect such primal urges as private aggrandizement at the expense of another's sufferings. But . . . but . . . what if we should reverse the incentive for compensation? What if it should become financially attractive to our healers not merely to treat sickness, but instead to keep the patient well? What if doctors have as their primary aim to maintain health and reduce the cost of care, rather than to tolerate and hypocritically thrive on its abuses? Do not execute the doctor if the patient becomes ill as did the Assyrians. But, neither reward him with payment only when the patient is sick. Dissever, once and for all, the patient-physician relationship from a standard of gold."

Chris stood motionless before them. His towering shadow climbed high on the walls of the store. He held his hands straight before him, as he pleaded for their support.

"In Millsite, the physician must care for human beings in health as well as in sickness, without financial reward contingent upon personal affliction. Every person, each family, shall pay a fixed fee per month, the same whether they are healthy or sick. The doctor will be paid a fixed amount per month, commensurate with his skills and training, and proportional to his hours of duty. If he reduces the cost of medical care, let him share in the savings. Millsite will not penalize the patient with catastrophic medical expenses at a time when he is least able to tolerate the crushing burden. But, conversely, neither shall the doctor be rewarded only when the patient is prostrate and out of work. Let the physician of the future learn that a patient long-lived and healthy is more profitable than one acutely ill. This is the medicine that I bring you. Only this . . . and no other."

Chris stopped. His audience was silent. He held his breath, unsure of their reaction. He could see their faces as they absorbed his message, carefully tested his hypothesis, then savored the conclusion that he was right. For an instant, they looked at each other, nodding, whatever their private motivation, elated to accept his dream and make it their own. Suddenly they rose from their seats as if a single soul, to shake his hand and clasp him on the back. They gathered at the head of the room as a group, crowding impatiently around the charts and blueprints spread out before them as Chris commenced the pragmatic exploitation of their philosophical commitment.

All during this time Samuel Halpern had seemed almost detached. Only when he heard Amen inform the group that the AFL-CIO was negotiating a contract with the Millsite Clinic for the Kupperman assembly plant in South Cromwell did he give a start and prick up his ears. Samuel leaned forward to hear what possible connection his close friend and patient, Abraham Kupperman, could have with this Christian carpetbagger.

Chris noticed the older doctor's aroused interest. "Yes, Dr. Halpern, with Kupperman's employees in the fold, we will have the necessary volume to attract and support a full complement of specialists. Even more," he informed the group, "the Teamsters Pension Fund has voted to put up the extra cash for working capital."

Chris could see the dismay on the older man's face.

"For years," Chris explained, "the unions in Cromwell have tried to get a foot in the door of Mercy Hospital. Why shouldn't they? After all, ninety percent of the patients in Cromwell are industrial laborers without any voice as to how medicine is practiced. Their only function is to provide Cromwell doctors with warm bodies and cold cash and nothing else. Now, with two men on the board of the clinic and control over the source of patients for Mercy, they will finally have some clout in the delivery of medical care in the community."

Samuel could no longer restrain himself. He rose to his feet, ignoring the fervent plea of his son not to make a scene. "How can you . . . you . . . a total stranger . . . come into this community and use us as a laboratory for your schemes?" he demanded of Amen, his tone belligerent and harsh.

"You are right, Dr. Halpern. It *is* a laboratory. I couldn't have chosen a better word myself to describe it. This *is* an experiment to provide a different kind of medical care for large groups of people. My father died when I was twelve. We couldn't get a doctor to come to the poor section of town where we lived. Even if we could have gotten one, and somehow managed to pay him, we wouldn't have been able to buy the medicines he would have prescribed." He shook his head to dispel the bitter memories of his childhood. "So . . . he died."

Chris was now oblivious to the other people in the room. His eyes were fixed on the urologist, seeing there an opponent dressed in ancient armor of intolerance and arrogance.

"I know that you have a visceral loathing for me and my goals. Most of the physicians I have talked to feel the same way. Ironically, it is not solely because of the clinic. The roots lie far deeper than that. I represent 'change.' That is what scares you and your kind.

"You and I and everyone in this room alike spend many painful years learning knowledge by rote, laying it up as if it were a catechism. We genuflect before the guardians of medical tradition, sacred and inviolate. We tread gingerly in the footsteps of those who have gone before us, taking care never to miss a single step, to keep along the same prescribed pathway. To vary a millimeter is forbidden and replete with tragic consequences. We inherit the awe of the community. We cloak ourselves in an immutable mantle of unchanging divinity.

"How can we who exist as a continuum of our medical heritage suddenly challenge and hold up to scrutiny those hallowed and enshrined rituals of the past, let alone tamper, transmute, or experiment with this immortal past. Hell! That would be heresy. And you know the punishment for such transgressions against the gods." His voice became softer and gentle. "I don't blame you, Dr. Halpern, any more than any other physician. How can I expect you to change when you are afraid even to question the need for such a change?"

"OK. OK," Samuel said, "but can't you experiment within the system, with the doctors already there?"

"Come on now, Dr. Halpern, do you honestly expect the Establishment to condone challenge, to allow heretics like me to post bulls on their door? I cannot believe that you are that naïve. I am certainly not that sanguine over the abundance of human charity. You seem to have an invincible faith in the goodness of your fellow physicians. Why?" he asked rhetorically. "Are you yourself that virtuous? Damn! Every one of them will fight to break me—and others like me. Even you when the chips are really down. You know that."

Samuel could not counter the accusation. What Chris divined had the ring of validity. Was he, Samuel Halpern, so pure of heart to condone tampering with a system in which he had labored hard to achieve final success? No, whatever else his other vices might be, he was not a hypocrite. He kept silent, unwilling either to confess his culpability or to acquiesce in Amen's degrading charges.

What Christopher Amen could not know was that the father's instinctive rejection of Millsite stemmed from a far more fundamental human emotion than fear of competition. It was not the clinic, nor even change so eloquently indicted. It was the father fighting for his son. For his immortality. Samuel Halpern's son was his alone. There was no room for sharing. The blond alien, like the blemish of Hawthorne's "Sorcerer," had to be cast out in toto.

Resolute in his conviction, Samuel turned to leave. He motioned to Stephen to come with him, but his son averted his eyes. His head held high, Samuel Halpern abruptly left the store. Even as he traversed the broad area he could hear Chris's closing words echoing behind him.

"I may not succeed here or anywhere else. But, it won't be from lack of money or patients, or even devoted doctors like yourselves. If I fail, if all of us fail, it will be because of men like Dr. Halpern and what medicine means to him."

Chapter / NINETEEN

To Joe Brandon, the metamorphosis taking place before his eyes in the deserted storefront facility was a dream come true. He would not have admitted it, except in his darkest moment of despair and then only to Alice, but he had been beaten by Flaherty and his partners. It was something they never taught you in medical school—that incompetence and prejudice could triumph over skill and devotion. The great medical profession! A bunch of greedy hypocrites. He stopped short, angry at himself, stung by the irony. He was one of them, for better or worse. The only difference was that he was on the outside looking in and not on the inside keeping everyone else out.

Goddamn it! He would not leave. Not as long as he could keep his two eyes open and put one foot in front of the other. He took in a long deep breath and attempted to get his emotions under control.

Sitting next to him in the storefront, Alice could feel his inner tension. Connie and Brian had told her of the many times Joe had come close to making a blunder in the course of his working day. So far he had been lucky, but he risked certain disaster if he persisted without coverage or a partner.

For the past year he and Brian had received attractive offers from doctor-poor areas. She had urged him to leave Cromwell before some terrible tragedy would occur. Anything, she pleaded, was better than seeing him consumed each day with hate and ground down by fatigue and fear. To Alice, the prospect of moving was a welcomed blessing.

But, not to Joe Brandon. His pride. That was the real rub. It would be one thing to give up because he faced competition and there were too few patients to go around. To be licked fair and square. But, to be defeated by Flaherty and Best, doctors who thrived by virtue of perverted ethics! That was the burr that kept him in town, laboring against the stacked odds.

Listening to Chris, Alice quickly grasped the potential of the Millsite Clinic to provide what she knew her husband really wanted, the chance for a clinical practice on parity with his competitors. She glanced out of the corner of her eye to see him absorbed in the presentation.

Joe leaned forward to listen more closely, now attentive to every word. He sucked in the statistics, the legal and bureaucratic jargon. The risks and rewards. He held his breath, scarcely daring to believe what Chris was saying. It was almost too good to be true. There was no question but he would accept Millsite on Chris's own terms. What other viable alternative did he have? But, even more, if Amen was right, and if Millsite could deliver on its promise, then . . . then . . . maybe he and not Flaherty would end up on the inside after all.

Stephanie had said nothing the entire evening. She sat silent against the naked cinder-block wall in the back of the barren space, next to a pile of gypsum board, her white cashmere sweater resting in her lap. She felt little community of interest with the young doctors there, struggling for ascendancy in the medical pyramid. Had it not been for Joe's personal request, realizing the fledgling clinic's urgent need for a general surgeon, it is unlikely she would have been present.

Those horrible days after the divorce. Thank God she could no longer taste the disappointment and despair that were her only companions during those unhappy months. Then Joe Brandon had reappeared in her life. He had attended a county medical meeting in her hospital. Seeing him again made it seem like only yesterday they were interns together at the Pratt. He had suggested she come to Cromwell, that what she needed was a change. But had Cromwell really been any different, any better, for her these past two years? Her practice was slowly growing. The community was as pleasant as one could have expected. But something was missing.

Barry was wrong. She knew that now for a certainty. The operating room did not give her that super orgasm, which he had accused her of substituting for warm flesh. The scalpel was no substitute for the sweet, painful thrust of a potent male stabbing out a release in her eager body. She pressed her thighs together to crush out the wave of frustration that invaded her groin.

Chris had noticed Stephanie's arrival with Joe Brandon and his brother-in-law and had been struck by the lovely blonde woman. Toward the end of the meeting, when Stephen took over answering the cogent questions the eager young physicians raised about the logistics of the clinic, he found himself staring at the silent woman. He wondered what the reason was for her agitated state, that inner turmoil expressing itself in short, quick movements and involuntary facial gestures. Once or twice, he caught himself locking glances with her, embarrassed that he was the one who had to break the communion first.

When the meeting was over, most of the invited doctors began to leave except for a few who remained behind to talk to Stephen. Chris noticed that Stephanie had not left. He was not at all displeased when she walked over to him and said, "Dr. Amen, I will be very happy to help in any way you can use me in the Millsite Clinic."

"Thank you, Stephanie. Joe and Stephen told me how much they hoped you would join us." He gave an embarrassed half-laugh. "I'm sure they also told you that we will need all the help we can get before all this really gets off the ground."

As Stephanie turned to leave the room, Christopher's eyes were fastened upon her. There was some mystery about this woman that intrigued him. She seemed imprisoned in a wizard's bottle and if he could find the magic incantation she might spring free from whatever evil spell possessed her.

Chapter / **TWENTY**

SAMUEL HALPERN AND HIS SON WERE TALKING IN THE LIBRARY after the Millsite meeting. Their conversation was heated.

"Stephen, *this* is going to be your life? Your future?"

Stephen's eyes blazed with anger.

"Damn it and damn you, Dad. You know Chris was right and what he wants to do in Cromwell is good also. You don't wish to join us? OK. But my decision is made." He paced back and forth, quivering with fury.

"I won't keep silent, Stephen. You—and this radical—" He raised his voice. "Stephen, you don't know what you are doing. Believe me."

There was another long silence in the room as each man tried to avoid shredding any further what remained of the umbilical tie still holding them together. When Samuel spoke again his words were casual, as if nothing untoward had transpired between the two of them.

"Did you have your interviews with Carl Lash and Bradford Gill?"

"Yes," Stephen replied, suspicious of this new tack. His father rarely surrendered the field of combat without at least some token bloodying of his opponent. "I saw them this morning. They sent you their regards and wished me luck this July."

"Why not? They all know you are Samuel Halpern's son." The father's manner was one of silent stealth. "Who else did you see for your application for staff privileges at Mercy?"

"I saw Mr. Prynne, the Administrator, and a Dr. Martin Abels, the Chairman of the Department of Anesthesiology. They were all very friendly."

"Heh," Samuel snorted. "They shouldn't be? You are not just some jerk coming down the road. You are my son. Don't you ever forget that." Then, as some inconsequential afterthought, he inquired, in a bland, disarming fashion, "Did you tell them you were going into this clinic thing with Dr. Amen?"

"No, I didn't."

"Why?"

"Chris said that I shouldn't say anything about it."

His father's manner iced. "You let those men on the Executive Committee think that you are going to go into practice with me this July?"

"Yes," Stephen said, puzzled. "What difference does it make?"

His father coldly appraised his son's naïveté. "Tell me," he asked, "did Chris have his interviews? He must also get on the Mercy staff by July if he is going to take care of his clinic patients."

"He saw the men yesterday. Why?" Stephen envisioned himself a fly caught in a silken web.

"Did he say anything to you afterward?" A definite flush was now reddening his father's pallid cheeks.

"No, just that he had made the required ritual sacrifice before the 'elders of the temple.' That was all. Why do you ask?"

A smile flicked at the corners of his father's mouth, annoying the stern set of his mouth. All he would allow was a noncommittal "Hm . . . hm . . . hm . . ."

Suddenly Samuel straightened up and threw his shoulders back as if relieved of some heavy burden. Even more unusual, he opened the bar and poured himself a quarter glass of liquor. He raised the Scotch to his lips in a silent toast. Stephen watched this pantomime, becoming increasingly apprehensive.

"Son, I like that phrase. Yes," noticing his son's bewilderment, "that phrase of your friend's. 'Elders of the temple.' Are you sure that Amen didn't say 'money-changers in the temple'? That is more his style. But, anyway, it really doesn't make any difference."

He smiled and placed one hand on his son's shoulder, in a solicitous manner. "Stephen, I have a feeling, call it a gut feeling, that everything is going to be just fine. Yes. I think that everything is going to work out perfectly well. For you and for me." Then, with a bounce to his step, Samuel Halpern left the library, leaving his son in an enveloping web of perplexity.

Chapter / TWENTY-ONE

ALTHOUGH ABIGAIL AND SIMON PIRIE WERE BASICALLY WELL-
meaning people, they were insensitive to each other's emotional
needs. It was not that Simon ever alluded to witnessing Abigail's
wanton debauchery, or that his wife had abandoned her clandestine
extramarital gestures, but coincident with that episode, an evanescent chance for reconciliation was within their grasp and they
failed to seize it. When Simon revealed the trip to Europe in the
fall, Abigail was ecstatic. As she read and reread the travel books
and Baedekers, it was with Simon that she gazed at the pigeons in
St. Mark's Square, rode horseback in the Bois de Boulogne, entered

the turnstile at Tivoli after dinner at l'Angleterre in Copenhagen.

Simon did not recognize this sign when his wife tried to express her appreciation in the only currency she was familiar with. Night after night, when Abigail would stroke his soggy, flaccid discontent, trying subtly and then flagrantly to arouse his receptivity, he would just lie there recalcitrant.

He misinterpreted her increased sexual maneuvering as a soiled symptom of her infidelity, some clitoral hypersensitivity, produced as a by-product of her sordid encounters with Carl Lash. When, briefly, the rising genital tension would cloud his forced belligerency, and he would follow her down the tantalizing path of sexual excitement, the vision of bloated hairy excrescences would float before him and he would force her hand away and turn over to sleep.

So it was that the Piries lived in the same house, slept in the same bed, side by side, each unable to communicate to the other the landmarks of their unhappiness. Simon, ignorant of both his wife's superficial frustrations and her need for him. Abigail, unable to fathom this sudden hardening of his fundamental laissez-faire attitude. Together they stripped the calendar of days, only to throw each crumbled unused leaf into the wastebasket of time.

Samuel Halpern and his wife, Sylvia, too had moved apart during this period. If one could plot marriage partners on a graph, such a linear concept would have appealed greatly to Samuel, who felt most comfortable when human beings were reduced to dry dimensions. Happiness, he knew intuitively, was a pair of parallel lines that, by definition, would merge to oneness and touch only at some far distant point in infinity. But never in this world.

He had long since given up any hope of Sylvia's understanding the weevil boring in his soul, that unrequited hatred he harbored for the traumatic days of his early life in Cromwell.

Thus she could not sympathize with her spouse who dealt with life as with an unworthy opponent, girding up his loins each day, to sally forth and wage battle. To Sylvia, the less sophisticated, life was a neuter and should not be dignified with confrontation. To Samuel, the committed, life was a person, masculine, to struggle with, as Jacob and the angel—to the death.

Chapter / **TWENTY-TWO**

WHATEVER THE WELLSPRINGS OF THEIR PRIVATE DISCONTENT, Cromwell's only urologist and chief pathologist hurried to Mercy Hospital this gray overcast day, the ground steaming, the air boggy with sodden wetness and charged with potential lightning. Mercy received them with open arms, as she did each day to 42 other physicians, 438 patients, 1011 employees, including 117 nurses, 6 elevator operators, 3 assistant administrators, 4 cooks, and 7 maintenance men.

The hospital itself, sitting on prized ground overlooking the city high on the west bluffs of the Quabbin, was ugly. Neither the spectacular setting that caused Alex Cardano acute envy each time he raised his eyes heavenward from the Flats, nor the daily ministrations of the gaggle of immaculate virgin wives of Christ who softly pattered through the halls, nor even the curious architectural design could alleviate the massive somber gravity-laden heaviness of the building.

Designed in the shape of a cross, one side arm contained the special services: X-ray, blood bank, pathology, operating rooms, rehabilitation. The opposite limb, a mirror-image, with housekeeping, boiler shops, laundry, cafeteria, purchasing, stockrooms, and the other support auxiliaries of this vast organism. The long stem of the building held the five floors of patient beds. Finally, the head of the cross was occupied by administration, teaching and conference rooms, nursing department, billing, transcription and record rooms—nicknamed the "paper annex."

If the architecture was intentionally uninspired, the interior design was intentionally inspiring. Replete with redundant symbolism, the institution screamed out to the nonbeliever, those eternally damned, with ritual cries honed over two thousand years, that *this* was a Roman Catholic property, a far-flung outpost of God's Child's inheritance in the New World. The mosaic crucifixion in the lobby, exalting the bloody spiking of a Jew with rough-hewn nails to rough-hewn boards where his extremities writhed decorously in ceramic chips. The plaster statues of the same Jesus comforting children, mothers, fathers, aunts, uncles, and probably now, Samuel commented to himself while waiting for an elevator, unwed mothers and Methadone addicts. The ever-present metal receptacles of holy water, used by the irreverent as ashtrays. The ubiquitous crosses made of mahogany, beech, ash, pine, metal, plaster, plastic, silvered, gilded, dusted and dusty, tall, short, thick, small, all with voodoo-sized figures of the same Jesus again, with the same decorous folds that had never slipped in over two thousand years, his limbs somehow still as graceful and fresh as restless pristine curves, despite two millennia of agonal ecstasy.

In the Surgeons' Locker Room, where Samuel repaired late for his eight-o'clock case, was the final irrevocable evidence that this was no ordinary shrine for civilian habit, no pedestrian antechamber for God's healers, but an oasis of the Vicar of Christ. The irrefutable placard: "The Code of Medical Ethics for Catholic Hospitals—Reproductive Organs and Functions, Principles II: Use of the Sex Faculty." Sealed in glass and bronze and bolted staunchly to the wall above the daily operating schedule. Proclaiming that man had decided it was against God's law to save a mother at the expense of the ripening seed in her womb. But, most important of all, masturbation was not productive of hairy palms and blindness in old age, but a violation of the Eternal Deity's Will, as was a condom without a pinhole in the end.

Samuel took off his clothes and placed them neatly in the locker with his nameplate on it. He pulled on the gray-blue scrub pants and shirt. He took off his watch and placed it in his right sock over his ankle. His wallet was secured in a similar fashion in the other sock. Despite the forbidding Christ surveying the locker room, the deified admonition against self-abuse, and the omnipotent holy water, watches and wallets had a curious way of disappearing from the lockers. Finally, he covered his shoes with conductive booties, grabbed a paper mesh mask and cap, and hurried to the Cystoscopy Suite for the first of his morning's scheduled cases.

As Samuel entered the small lead-shielded room, the first of his five cases that morning was already asleep on the table. Having glimpsed the urologist entering the locker room, Martin Abels had initiated anesthesia. Even now he was balancing the nitrous oxide and oxygen flowing through the black mask with the sodium pentothal dripping into the vein. He nodded to Samuel and handed him the patient's chart.

Samuel knew the patient well. Eighty-two years old, Stanley Misiaszek had never seen a doctor in his entire life until one week ago. Had he not awakened one morning with his legs totally paralyzed, it is unlikely even then he would have sought medical aid.

How had he lived those months with the cancer of the prostate growing, spreading, filling every bone in his thin wizened body? The tumor pressing and pinching the millions of nerves, excoriating his flesh with lancinating pain. The rich bone marrow no longer available to manufacture hemoglobin, the cancer having displaced this unique matrix from its osseous chambers. The gradual and insidious anemia until his heart was racing three times normal in order to circulate to his organs, the too-few red blood cells carrying vital oxygen. The blood itself, a thin, tasteless, watery insipid bouillon, rather than the thick, gaudy, rich syrup of life. Until that day when the once-rigid spinal vertebrae, infiltrated with puttylike cancer, were no longer able to support his wasted frame and collapsed upon themselves, crushing all the nerves that radiated out from them to his bladder, his rectum, and his legs.

Paralyzed, incontinent of urine and feces, anemic, cachectic, he lay there two days, in torment, until his next-door neighbor forced open the door. Even then, Stanley said not a word, but waited for death to take him. What did he think of the frantic activity centering on his person, on the fourth floor of Mercy Hospital? Intravenous feedings with bottle after bottle of blood transfusions to puff up his parched frame. Narcotics to ease his pain. A catheter in the bladder to empty the waste products of his kidneys. Clean starched sheets and fresh pajamas to shame, by contrast, his disintegrating human habitus.

It did not take Samuel Halpern long to make the diagnosis. A quick rectal exam diagnosed for him with a ninety-percent accuracy a cancer of the prostate, that silent masculine gland residing at the base of the bladder. Even more lethal for this elderly bachelor, the cells of the gland were no longer content to aggrandize locally, but had already started to invade the lymphatic system, the arteries, and the veins that coursed through their substance. Into each and every minuscule microscopic channel, small clumps of virulent cancer cells had broken off to swim freely in the rapid stream to whatever site the current would lead—the brain, chest, ribs, spine, lungs, pelvic bones, arms, legs. There they ended their silent voyage and fastened themselves in their new locations, like barnacles finally finding a home.

Though Stanley Misiaszek did not know it, colonies of this aberrant tumor were now thriving in his left leg, destroying the twelve vertebrae of his spine, crowding behind and displacing forward his left eyeball, stippling the back of his skull, and eroding and corroding every other location where commingling streams of blood and lymph could drain. All this Samuel knew from one glance at the bone X-rays and from the rocky hard coarse surface of the prostate that he felt at the tip of his right index finger when inserted into Stanley's rectum. But, most incontrovertibly of all, by the dispassionate, exquisitely precise arabic numerals reported by Simon Pirie's subterranean workshop.

Each colony of prostate cancer, as it invades, produces an infinitesimal fraction of a strange and rare chemical called acid phosphatase. An elevated level of this unique substance in the bloodstream of a male over forty is the irrefutable fingerprint of spreading prostate cancer, even though its colonies may yet be too small to manifest with symptoms, too pale to show up on X-ray, too few to be discernible on bone biopsy, too recent to suspect from a digital examination. In Stanley, the level of this harbinger of death was sixteen times normal, a level exceeding the maximum capacity of Simon's forty-thousand-dollar autoplasma analyzer.

Stanley did not know any of this as he lay asleep on his back on the cold metal table, his legs up in stirrups. The penis and testicles, stained dark brown from the iodinated antiseptic solution, were suspended loosely in air, pathetically abandoned as their muscular bond lost its grasping tone to the pervading anesthesia. Samuel introduced into the penis the long metal cystoscope, that cleverly contrived cylinder of hollow metal, through which passed thousands of hairlike glass fibers, each mysteriously capable of bending powerful light rays around corners to illuminate the most secret inner recesses of the bladder. Packed alongside this bundle of cold light were hundreds of small spherical lenses that enabled the urologist to peer deeply into the hollow of Stanley's pelvis. Samuel gave an involuntary gasp as he saw for himself the deadly white gritty cancer.

Samuel withdrew the wet blood-tinged instrument and put his left index finger deep into the patient's rectum. He could feel the granite-hard cobblestone substance of the cancer defying his rough touch. With his right hand, he inserted a hollow biopsy needle into the rectum, guiding it alongside the left finger until the barbed metal tip rested against the most prominent ridge of cancer. The tissue was solid and resisted the razor-sharp instrument. He forced the needle forward a fraction of an inch at a time, fearful of piercing into the bladder itself.

The needle crunched into the lethal nest of cancer cells. Samuel removed a thin metal wire blocking the center of the needle and replaced it with a tiny forceps, armed at one end with diminutive biting teeth that seized a microscopic fragment of the cancerous tissue. He twisted the forceps, compelling the jaws to tear off their prize, and then withdrew the whole apparatus from the rectum, which was now slowly oozing a thin film of brown feces and bright red blood.

He demonstrated the slender piece of Stanley Misiaszek to the circulating nurse and dropped it into a waiting bottle of Formalin for transport to Simon Pirie's laboratory. He repeated the process, taking three separate scattered cores of cancer from random areas of the prostate. Satisfied, he nodded to the anesthesiologist that he was finished. He took off his gloves and left the room.

That the biopsy would turn out to be cancer, he had little doubt. In anticipation, he scheduled Stanley for surgery in one week. As soon as Pirie had confirmed the tissue diagnosis, the patient would be castrated to gain weeks, possibly months of pain-free life, though removal of his testicles seeming almost a sin for this slight man who had so little human flesh to begin with.

The clever observation that cancer of the prostate thrives under a steady barrage of the male sex hormone had gained one observant urologist the Nobel Prize, and thousands of human beings a renewal of life long thought expired. Remove the testicles, deprive the cancer of testosterone, and miraculously, the malignant cells would retreat, regress, and shrink. The patient's pain would disappear. His blood cells regrow. His appetite return. His bones knit together. Until that eventual day when new independent cancer cells would mutate and resume their rapacious activity. Even more dramatic, the salutary effect of the castration could be prolonged by the daily ingestion of one pill of estrogen, the same female hormone imbibed by postmenopausal American women to render succulent and moist their parched and chafed vaginas.

As Samuel Halpern wrote the postoperative orders to accompany the still-sleeping man back to the Recovery Room, he felt a sense of satisfaction. If only for a short time, he could give life by the simple act of removing two useless appendages and prescribing a small tablet each morning. He was pleased. It was not often that he could stay the Angel of Death so facilely as with this emaciated pain-wracked patient.

Chapter / **TWENTY-THREE**

DEEP IN THE BOWELS OF MERCY HOSPITAL, SIMON PIRIE WAITED
to receive those faint slivers of tissue now washing so lightly in the
dilute formaldehyde solution. Simon had been alerted to Stanley's
existence two mornings before when his chief chemistry technician
reported that the hospital's prize Technicomp Sequential Multiple
Serum Analyzer 12 had glared and screamed its sudden violation
when Stanley's serum came coursing through its complex mechanism.

The seven cubic centimeters of fluid previously decanted from
the patient's thin blood had flowed through the miles of tubing,

meeting and coupling with the dozens of chemicals, reagents, and enzymes, marrying and spawning hundreds of catalytic and colori-metric dyes. Slowly the liquid was transmitted from the original, almost clear, faintly pale yellow human ichor, to an empiric arith-metic crescendo, a rising progression of numbers on a graph, quan-titating the level of sugar, urea, cholesterol, phosphate, calcium, bile, albumin, uric acid, lactic dehydrogenase, alkaline phosphatase, serum glutamic oxalacetic transaminase, and in the case of all male patients, acid phosphatase.

The incredibly high level of this latter substance had completely overwhelmed the capability of the machine. It ashamedly signaled its dismal ineptitude to subdue the chemical by a violent ringing of bells and flashing of multicolored lights. By Simon's direct order, a technician had been dispatched back to the patient's room to draw a second sample of blood, this time the acid phosphatase determination carried out through a laborious time-consuming hand method. The result was undeniable.

The pathologist sat there, long minutes, with the analysis in his hands, scarcely looking up at the technician who had brought him the final figure. It is doubtful the young man ever would have guessed why his superior was so preoccupied, any more than the nurse who, ordered to obtain yet another sample from the pa-tient, wondered why the Pathology Department needed so much blood from a patient who had so little to begin with. How could the bench chemist have explained the strange fact that his last specimen was not processed, but quickly seized and carried away by the head of the department himself, to be lodged in the farthest recesses of the bacteriology refrigerator, marked with the innocent gummed label, "Save Serum, Dr. Pirie."

The plasma safely sequestered, Simon now waited for the biopsy specimen that he knew would not be long in forthcoming. But it was to be five long days before he could hold in his hands that precious cellular structure. During this anxious time, the thin slivers were to be macerated, tortured, and metamorphosed beyond their physical limitations.

After its initial bath in Formalin, each core of tissue was washed in tap water to remove the evil-smelling preservative. The residual clinging water was dehydrated chemically by a bath of absolute alcohol. A quick dip in Xylol and the tissue was deposited in a small vat of hot liquid paraffin that slowly impregnated this once-human substance. When the wax was cooled and hard, an electric microtome reduced half the cube of slippery paraffin to a pile of slices, each only six microns thick and containing a small sequential leaf of the initial sliver.

Each wafer was carefully floated onto a glass slide where a thin wash of egg albumin glued it to the transparent bed. The wax was dissolved away. Only then did the truly critical process commence, that long, clever task of changing the pale, watery, ghostlike silhouette of the prostatic cells to sharp, bold, colorful pictures necessary for accurate microscopic recognition.

With split-second timing, the slide was soaked in two separate Xylol solutions, one wash of one-hundred-percent-pure absolute alcohol, five total baptisms in distilled water, and finally submerged in dark violet hematoxylin solution, which attacked the basic molecular structure of the cells, rendering them a vivid blue.

The excess hematoxylin was washed off by tap water. The slide rinsed with one-percent acid alcohol that chemically extracted from the cytoplasm of each cell the recently lodged hematoxylin, leaving only the nucleus still resplendent in purple.

The entire slide was now soaked in one-percent eosin, which selectively permeated the now colorless cytoplasm, lighting it up with an eerie pink glow. Four more successive washes in dehydrating alcohol cleared away any of the residual Xylol. The now stained, hydrated, dehydrated, pickled and unpickled, acidified and alkalinized, colored and decolorized six-micron remnant of Stanley Misiaszek came to its final well-deserved rest. With its companions, it was stacked in a cardboard folder, alongside Simon Pirie's two-thousand-dollar Zeiss microscope, next to the voice-actuated dictating system, to await the pathologist's identification.

Simon placed one slide on the movable substage. He slowly rotated the vernier focusing knob. The brilliant blue and red pattern leaped to his retina. The field was covered with neat rosettes of identical plump cells, regimented rows of similar rational structures, the glands and channels of the normal prostate.

Then, as he moved the slide, millimeters at a time, he could see the sudden violent intrusion into this placid scene of sharp, thrusting daggers of wild, irrational cells, streaking out in all directions, knifing through the tissue. Bizarre asymmetric cells, with scant red cytoplasm and large, heavily pigmented blue nuclei, each as different from the other as snowflakes in a blizzard. A tidal wave of Huns, Tartars, Goths, Mongols, surrounding, invading, overwhelming, subverting, disrupting, crowding, disorganizing the normal routinized matrix of civilized cells, impressing upon the staid architecture of normal prostate a cacophony of unpatterned haste and schizophrenic assemblage.

As he moved the lens deeper, the massive sheet of cancer cells spilled out in all directions, uneducated, wild, heathen, unprincipled, until Simon would have been hard put to draw their lineal heritage had he not seen that brief margin, that fleeting visual junction where the alien cells still pressed up against benign tissue, soon to succumb to their barbaric vigor and insolence and to perish beneath their pagan strength.

To Simon Pirie, the diagnosis was unequivocal. He finished the rapid dictation that forever labeled the malignancy and replaced the slides in their cardboard carrier. But not before jotting down the file number of the specimen.

Late that afternoon, when the laboratory was silent and abandoned, Simon remained behind, alone in his office. It was after seven o'clock when he finally left his desk and entered the histology file room. Checking the number he opened the correct cabinet drawer and extracted the remaining half of the original wax block. He wrapped the reduced square in a sheet of tissue paper and replaced the purloined original with a dummy approximately the same size. He secreted the removed specimen in the back of his top desk drawer and locked it securely.

He turned out the light and fastened the door behind him. He walked up the two flights of stairs to the parking lot. Simon did not usually hum. Tonight he half-hummed, half-sang some totally unrecognizable tune. Simon Pirie rarely smiled. Tonight there was the suggestion of a bold grin on his face. Simon Pirie's usual state was one of cerebral agitation. Tonight, the mentation was along a decidedly unusual pathway.

As he crossed the parking lot the image of a caveman flashed through his consciousness. A hunched figure covered with vermin, saturated with filth slowly chipping away at a flint. Was it the atavistic sensation of the cave, its cold, empty hostility? The family sequestered in the dense shadow. The mate cowering at his side. The unseen assailant. The known enemy, the cave intruder. The mate violator. The hunt—the attack—the kill!

The motor leaped to power with a coarse throaty roar. The car surged forward. The jostling springs, the rocking asynchrony, the rough vibrations tingled his buttocks and perineum. He felt an erection emerging from between his legs, beneath his paunch.

He was suddenly overwhelmed by the driving urge to demonstrate the power of his protection and possession. Later that night, not even the recurrent vision of Carl Lash's testicles, soon to be excised forever, nor Abigail's bewilderment at her husband's unheralded and miraculously resurrected raw libido, could deny the convulsive thrill as he thrust his turgid penis over and over into the receptacle that was his and his alone to violate.

Chapter / **TWENTY-FOUR**

"HOW HAS THE BABY BEEN FEEDING, GRACE?" JOE BRANDON asked, unable to look away from his exacting task to the nurse who was holding the screaming, struggling infant steady for him. The thin twenty-three-gauge needle had penetrated the skin, but each time the doctor moved the sharp point to perforate the slippery blue vein in the child's scalp, the tortuous vessel retreated away from the metal edge as if it had a will of its own.

"Damn!" he said under his breath, shifting his position to ease the cramp in his back. "One more try and then I give up." Even as he voiced his impatience, the tapered tip punctured through the thin wall and bright red blood started flowing out the polyethylene tube attached to the end of the hollow needle. Brandon straightened up and gave the nurse a grin.

"Well, I guess we scared it," he said as he collected the blood in two separate glass tubes for biochemical analysis.

"I'm sorry, Grace," he apologized. "If you answered, I didn't hear you. How has the child's weight been doing?"

"It's fine, Dr. Brandon. The little one has already made up its initial loss. The colostomy is working well. The baby had its first formed b.m. this morning. Dr. Crane was in to check the stoma earlier. She told Mrs. Gary that if everything continues as nicely as it has been doing, she will plan the second stage in about three weeks and close the colostomy."

Brandon handed the two tubes to the nurse, grunting his approval of what she was telling him. He picked up the hospital chart and rapidly thumbed through it. He noted the satisfactory vital signs and steady weight gain. He read the neurosurgical consultation from William Crowther. It was short, crisp, and to the point. No unnecessary lapses into the long-term emotional or social ramifications of the baby's incontinence or paralysis. Just a brief, "Agree—meningomyelocele. Will close two weeks. W. Crowther."

Sam Halpern's consultations, on the other hand, usually read like a textbook lecture, as if the man was building a case to convince some doubting peer. Joe could never understand why Cromwell's only urologist should have to try so hard. But, there it was, a page and a half, describing in exact detail every intersex and kidney anomaly known to Western man.

He rapidly skipped the labored erudition, to locate the summary in the last paragraph. He breathed a sigh of relief. The kidneys were fine. Halpern, like Brian, was awaiting the results of the sex chromatin tests. If male, the urologist would make definite plans for eventual genital reconstruction. The note ended with the guarded optimism that a sexually cosmetic male could eventually be fashioned. Joe pursed his lips. What good would a pretty penis be if the nerves to make it erect and ejaculate were dead strands floating in a cyst on the child's back?

He looked up as Grace Molling returned from the Nursery. She waited until the obstetrician had finished reviewing the chart and then said, "Can I speak to you for a minute?"

"What is it, Grace?"

"It's Mr. Gary. He hasn't seen the baby once since the night it was born. You remember," she added, "the night you and Dr. Crane and Dr. Terris took him into the conference room and told him about the baby. After you left he made me show it to him. He looked at it all over through the window. He never said a word, except to thank me." She shook her head at the unpleasant memory. "He has never asked to see the child again. One night, when he came to visit his wife, I asked him if he would like to see the baby. I thought he was going to hit me." Her voice became thin and reedy. "Another time he came into his wife's room when she was nursing. He turned around, walked out, and sat smoking in the waiting room until his wife was finished. He told me to let him know when the baby had gone."

She looked at the young doctor, tears crowding her eyes, unable to speak for a minute. She choked a bit. "And . . . Dr. Brandon . . . there is more. . . ."

"All right, Grace. Sit down and tell me," he urged as he took her by the hands and led her to the chair by the writing desk. "Tell me everything."

His face tightened in a worried expression. He should have expected this reaction, especially after it became evident that night that no amount of entreaty could persuade the embittered father to sign the Operative Permit. Stephanie had to delay the surgery until the middle of the morning when the narcotic had worn off Mrs. Gary.

What a cruel responsibility to have forced on the helpless mother, just hours after the trauma and blood loss of delivery, still drugged and in pain. How brutal to have shocked and bludgeoned her at that tragic instant with the horrors of her just-delivered birth. They almost cried when she agreed to the colostomy, without a protest. Even excusing her husband for his callous attitude. She was quite a woman. It was her pain and labor. She would have to stay at home and take care of the child. Bathing it and feeding it every day. She would be the one to change its soiled diapers and carry it from place to place whenever it wanted to move. And, not just for a few months, or years, but forever.

Still, if it had happened to his own family. . . . Suppose he had been out of work for almost a year, with debts and three young healthy children at home to raise on a salary that was barely adequate to keep them clothed and fed? Would he want a defective, a cripple, to be a perpetual parasite on the family's sustenance, sucking dry its limited strength and hopes? He swallowed hard. What kind of decision would he have made? He looked again at the anxious face of the young nurse who continued to twist the hem of her pink smock with her nervous fingers. "What else has happened, Grace?"

"Mr. Gary visits his wife every night, religiously. When he leaves, she is in tears. Once she was crying so hysterically I had to give her Demerol to calm her down. I don't know exactly what goes on in there, but one time I heard it out in the hall. Everyone heard, it was so loud. He was screaming at her that she should have let the baby die. She should have killed it." The nurse broke down, unable to continue.

Joe Brandon sat next to the young girl, his thoughts vague flashes of lifeboats and deformed monsters and crying hateful mothers and fathers.

Why, he thought, when we see the suffering and afflictions of others do we suddenly feel pious and pray? Why, when it is ourselves who are afflicted, do we rail and curse at God? The irony stung his conscience like an evil devil, which nowhere in his catechism could he find the appropriate magic formula to cast out. It was Grace Molling who lifted her head to catch his page over the loudspeaker. She picked up the telephone to take the message.

"Dr. Brandon, it is Ward Six. They have an urgent consultation on a patient up there for you." She looked up, puzzled. "It is a patient of Dr. Flaherty's." She caught his astonished expression, which mirrored her own. Working on the delivery floor, she knew well the personal antagonism between the two obstetricians. "The nurse said that you are not to see the patient until you speak with Dr. Halpern. He is making rounds in the house and would like you to page him when you are ready. He will be waiting for you. That was all."

The obstetrician stared at the nurse for an instant, about to ask her to elaborate. He realized how silly that would have been. She knew no more than he did. With an ambivalent sense of curiosity and dread, the tired physician rose from his seat and left to answer the strange summons.

Chapter / TWENTY-FIVE

"JOE. THANKS FOR ANSWERING SO QUICKLY." SAMUEL HALPERN walked over to greet Dr. Brandon as he emerged from the crowded elevator into the marble-lined lobby. He took Brandon's arm to lead him away. "I think we'd better find some quiet place to talk."

They entered the chart-piled transcription room. "What's the problem, Sam? All I know is that I was to call you before seeing some patient of Ralph's."

Sam stared at the young man, not sure where to start. He let out his breath, reluctant to commence what was obviously a distasteful task.

((165))

"The patient's name is Dearing. Laurie Dearing. Thirty-five. Mother of four. Nice young woman. Her husband is Frederick Dearing." He looked into his listener's eyes, to see if the name meant anything. He could see the faint squinting as Brandon tried to match the name with some distant recollection in his memory. "Yes, Frederick Dearing—of Dearing, Dearing, and Rhodes." He observed Joe's quickened interest at the mention of one of Cromwell's most prominent legal firms. "It's his wife," Sam added unhappily. "She is a sick cookie, Joe. She may die."

Brandon had an uneasy feeling that he was about to become privy to some secret that transcended clinical considerations. Halpern's reticence to cut to the heart of the matter, his defensive posture, could only mean trouble, and not necessarily for Mrs. Dearing alone. A patient's death did not customarily evoke such a guarded stance on the part of a consulting physician. Joe leaned forward, his curiosity aroused by the older man's labored foreplay.

"Four days ago," Samuel Halpern continued, "she was hit by a car in the Millsite Center parking lot. Apparently she was coming out of the A and P with an armful of groceries when a car backed out and pinned her against a parked truck." The urologist's manner became more confident as he lapsed into unemotional medical chronology.

"Bea said that she was in shock when the ambulance brought her into the Emergency Ward. Her left femur was fractured. The pelvis crushed. Four ribs cracked. Thank God Carl Lash was in the house. He tapped her belly. It was full of blood." He looked up with admiration. "Carl had her on the table and opened within twenty minutes. He did an emergency laparotomy and took out a ruptured spleen. Probably saved her life—at least that's what we thought at the time."

Joe stirred in his seat and Samuel hurried his pace. "After the spleen was removed, the patient still did not come out of shock. Carl looked further and found a huge expanding retroperitoneal hematoma, which completely filled the left gutter." He swallowed hard. "She had totally crushed her left kidney."

Joe started up to say something, but Samuel interrupted him. "They put in an emergency call for me. By the time I got to the O.R., the kidney was already out." He anticipated the question. "Carl did the right thing, Joe. I inspected the specimen on the table. The kidney was shattered. Just pulp. I saw the pathology report from Simon. It wasn't salvageable."

Brandon thought for a minute. "Did you get an I.V.P. before surgery?"

"Are you kidding? The patient was in shock. The dye wouldn't have gotten into the kidneys to show them up on X-ray, even if there had been enough time for the study before surgery. Besides," he reiterated, "the kidney could not be repaired. It had to be removed or the patient would have bled to death on the operating table. Before Carl closed the abdomen, he palpated the other side and felt the right kidney. I asked him about it later. Things were touch-and-go so he didn't spend hours playing with it but, according to him, it felt like a decent organ.

"Paillard patched up the broken bones after Carl had finished. We sent the patient to the Intensive Care Unit. As far as we knew, Laurie Dearing was a healthy woman. Carl had never seen her before, but the emergency lab tests and the EKG showed nothing out of whack." His expression suddenly turned grave. "Then she began to go downhill. She didn't put out any urine." Brandon looked startled. "Not a drop in the first twenty-four hours. At first we thought she possibly had some prerenal azotemia and her surviving right kidney wasn't working right away from the shock, the enormous loss of blood volume. We even considered such rare birds as the crush syndrome with hemoglobin molecules blocking the kidney tubules so that they couldn't make any urine. We ran tests . . . and tests . . . and tests. . . . No, Joe. It wasn't any of those things."

For the first time, Brandon noticed the large wide brown envelope of X-rays that the urologist had carried into the room and placed on the table in front of him. Samuel took out the films and clipped them in sequential order on the X-ray viewing box hung on the wall. The harsh white glare gave their faces a white waxy cast as they bent closer to look at the negatives.

"Here." Samuel pointed to the renal angiogram the Chief of Radiology had done. "Walter put some dye in the right renal artery. The vasculature was perfect. All the blood vessels leading to the kidney were open, perfect. However, despite the fact that the kidney was intact, we still could not see any evidence of urine coming out of it."

He took the films down and replaced them with a second series. "Last night I became worried and took the patient to cystoscopy. I tried to put a catheter up into the right kidney from inside the bladder. Look, here, at these pictures." He pointed to the dark films.

Brandon bent closer. He could see the shadow of the metal cystoscope in the bladder. Emerging from the tip of the long hollow metal instrument was a fine catheter about the thickness of a pencil lead. He could see the catheter start up the right ureter, that long tube that led from Mrs. Dearing's remaining kidney down to the bladder.

"No matter how much I forced it, I couldn't get it to go any further than two inches. I injected some dye. See . . . here . . ." indicating the large collection of white contrast material that remained puddled around the tip of the ureteral catheter. "It wouldn't go up any higher. The ureter was totally occluded at that point. That explains why the right kidney wasn't putting out any urine." He concluded soberly, "Before the accident, Mrs. Dearing must have been living on her left kidney alone. And when it was shattered, she had nothing to keep her alive."

"How is she doing now?"

"What would you expect? It's been four days. The B.U.N. has

climbed. It's going up the usual thirty to forty points a day. This morning it was one fifteen and we've started dialyzing her on the artificial kidney to bring it down."

Samuel began to put the films back in the envelope. Joe got up to help him. "Sam," he commented, still uncertain of the motive behind the urologist's presentation, "it certainly is a fascinating case. You have your problems. I don't envy you. But," he searched the older man's face for the answer to the question that still persisted in nagging him, "what does all this have to do with me?"

"Mrs. Dearing had a vaginal hysterectomy by Ralph four months ago. She had severe endometriosis. I read Flaherty's dictated operative note. Apparently, Ralph had trouble during the case. There was a lot of bleeding and . . ."

He did not have to finish. Brandon's face was suddenly alive. His eyes blinked with excitement. "So Ralph tied off the right ureter. Didn't he? Is that what he sent you up here to tell me?" A cruel smile twisted his lips. "But, I don't understand. If Ralph destroyed her right kidney, why are you telling all this to me?" he asked suspiciously. "I would have expected you and Carl to bury the patient as quickly as possible to cover up for that bastard." He could not understand why he had been allowed in on this lethal secret, a potential weapon to use against his tormentor.

What other kind of reaction could Sam have expected from Brandon? He knew what Flaherty and Best had been doing to Joe and his brother-in-law. You wipe my ass and I'll wipe yours was the coin of the realm among doctors everywhere. Samuel concluded to himself that Ralph Flaherty was about to reap the bitter harvest of his seeds of hate from his young victim.

"Joe, we don't know for sure if Ralph tied off the ureter. Maybe . . . maybe . . . there were . . . adhesions from the hysterectomy. You know that can happen." He got no further as Brandon cut him off.

"Don't give me any of that bullshit, Sam. I'm not one of Ralph's lackeys. Tell me. Have you ever seen an adhesion cause such a discrete segmental block at the pelvic brim, only four months after a hysterectomy, on one side only? Come on, now. Have you?"

Samuel lowered his eyes to the floor, the futile gesture providing Brandon with the loaded answer he sought.

"So, Sam, what are you going to do? You can't give her back her left kidney."

"I have her booked for surgery Friday. I am going to explore the right kidney and remove the obstruction, whatever," he stressed the word, "it may be, and reestablish continuity of the ureter."

"Well," Joe allowed with a sarcastic shrug, "that ought to get Ralph off the hook. He doesn't deserve a break like that."

Joe seethed inside at the apparent ease with which Flaherty was able to escape retribution for his incompetence. What he could not understand was why Halpern did not get up and heave a sigh of satisfaction for his crony's narrow escape, and leave.

"Joe," Dr. Halpern's tone was didactic, "a kidney that has been totally obstructed for four months—*may never recover its function.*"

Brandon stared at him, shocked. He was struck simultaneously by a shiver of elation that his predatory foe was now possibly the helpless prey and by the sudden realization that such a situation would automatically consign the luckless patient to certain death.

"I am going to put a nephrostomy tube into the kidney to decompress it and let out the urine, if it will make any," Samuel continued.

"That poor woman. What are her chances?"

"I don't know. There have been a few reported cases of a kidney surviving complete obstruction after several months, but they are extremely rare. I really don't know. We will just have to put in the tube and hope that urine comes out. It might take days, or weeks, or months, or *never*." His voice lowered as if resigned to failure.

Samuel anticipated Joe's next statement. "Ralph put out a consultation for you but it wasn't his idea. You know that." Brandon gritted his teeth in assent. "It was the husband's. Mr. Dearing demanded that another gynecologist review the case officially, now, for the hospital record." Samuel gripped the table in front of him. He turned his head away from the seated figure's hostile eyes. "Joe, Mr. Dearing is a very worried man. He has every right to be. Even more, he is angry, bitter. He wants revenge. To strike out, to hurt, even as his wife has been hurt. And, Joe, if . . . if . . . God forbid . . . his wife dies . . . he is apt to demand a life for a life."

With that, Samuel rose and touched the obstetrician on the arm to thank him for his time. He picked up the X-ray folder and tucked it under his arm. As he walked across the room to the door, he turned to take one last look at the young doctor. He gave an involuntary shudder at what he saw. God help Ralph, he thought. Then, ashamed, he quickly added, God help Mrs. Dearing.

Chapter / **TWENTY-SIX**

STEPHANIE CRANE LEANED HARD AGAINST THE RAILING OF THE
wooden deck jutting out from her house. The upper part of her
body was suspended like a bird against the empty space below.
She could see stretched out before her the inky carpet of Cromwell,
salt and peppered with car and street lights. The May air was warm
and heavy with moisture rising from the wetlands along the riverbanks. An occasional invisible stream of wind would make the
arduous ascent to the modern house cantilevered over the rocky
face of the cliff high above the city. The breeze would pause to
brush by her cheek and settle in her hair. She would take in a deep
breath and savor the sudden coolness.

Inside the house, through the wall of glass, she could see the tall blond man admiring the black Oaxacan pottery on the broad granite mantel. He gazed around the large open room, its lofty ceiling soaring like a cathedral to the second story and higher, carrying with it the massive boulders that straddled the central hearth to rise majestically like a stone tree through the middle of the room.

He tried to peer through the glass door to the other side but his vision was obscured by the double and triple reflections of the room's contents piling up on the shiny refractile surfaces. All he could see was the golden sheen of the young woman's hair. The rest of her body was lost somewhere in the mirrored image of the rusty carpet that poured out from where he stood to vanish into the black of the Cromwell night. He moved closer to the patio door, but hesitated to slide it open, preferring to stand only feet behind the woman, barred as finitely from her by the glass partition as by her personal conflict.

It had been almost a month since Christopher Amen had met Stephanie. He had come to Cromwell to fulfill the dream he had held in his heart since deciding to become a doctor years ago. Now, just days away from seizing the reality of that success, he had found someone to share it with, to love.

At this very moment he could sense a rush of blood to his pelvis. He shifted his weight and pressed his hand harshly over his genitalia to milk out the blood, unhappy at the heightened sense of anticipatory lust which that innocent action paradoxically precipitated.

No, it was not just wanting to have Stephanie crushed under him, though God knows he wanted that so badly his groin ached. Anyone who said that sex, pure and simple, was not a part of love, was an ass. But, love had to be more than genital friction. He opened the door to step out into the still night air.

Stephanie took his hand and gave him a broad smile of pleasure. She was a little surprised to see his unexpected look of concern.

"Look, Chris," pointing to the constellation hovering in the southwest, "there is Orion. I can always make out the three stars in his belt." She shifted her position and searched the sky directly overhead. "And the big dipper." She grew embarrassed. "That's all I know. My great sum of two constellations. But Barry, he knew lots of . . ." She stopped short and saw the look of worry flash again.

"I'm sorry, Chris. I know. I promised that I would not talk about Barry anymore, but I . . ."

Chris took her two hands in his own. "He is your jinx, isn't he? Something he did or said really has you climbing those steps of Purgatory. Isn't that true?" He pulled her closer, hurting her wrists in a tight grasp. "Say it, Stephanie," he ordered. "Get it out!" he pleaded. "Tell me, Stephanie."

She stared at him for a minute, wondering how the lines in his face could grow so rigid and cruel. She started to speak, then tore herself free. She moved to the other side of the redwood deck and wrapped her arms around herself.

He let her go—this time. Sooner or later it would have to come out. What was her problem? he puzzled. Nothing he could put his fingers on with certainty. She was a damn good surgeon. Considerate to her patients. Her inherited wealth had insulated her from the dirty politics and money-grubbing of her peers. Her only discernible flaw, if you could call it that, was her seeming detachment from the mundane vicissitudes of life.

Surely it was not a physical problem. She was an extremely desirable woman, and even now, after she had rejected his advances, he could still be bothered by that persistent perineal demand that would have to be satisfied some night, some time.

A lesbian? He shuddered at the thought. He had met such women doctors. They stated their sexual proclivity with honest conviction and then went on to be perfectly pleasant and competent professional colleagues as if what stimulated their clitoris was their private business and of no concern to someone who wished them to regulate diabetes or digitalis.

No. That was not her problem. It was more than just his big

masculine ego telling him that she desired sex as much as he. Yet, each time he tried to become affectionate, she would take fright like a wounded bird and withdraw, afraid of what that intimacy might lead to. What was she scared of?

He moved to her side and placed his arms around her. She gave an involuntary shiver that he met by increasing the pressure of his contact.

"You are cold, Stephanie." He felt the spasmodic trembling of her body. "What are you frightened of? Is it me?" he implored.

She twisted around to kiss his cheek. "Don't be silly. It's not you, Chris . . . and maybe . . . in a way . . . it is. Oh, don't ask me to explain." She fled away from him again into the protective warmth of the house. She stood in the center of the living room, locking and unlocking the fingers of her hands at her waist, in a nervous gesture. She was pale. He could see the pulsations of the carotid arteries in her neck signaling the swift pacing of her heart.

"Stephanie," he called softly to her. "Do not be afraid." He sat down on the floor by her feet. He reached up with his hand and urged her to sit down next to him. Almost in a trance, she lowered herself to his side.

"Stephanie." His voice was soft and soothing. "I am not going to hurt you." He looked into her eyes. "I love you. Don't ask me why. I don't know. Tell yourself you must trust me. There is a devil deep inside you. If I only knew how, I would rid you of it. But you won't . . . or can't, tell me. It doesn't matter. It will leave soon enough. Devils cannot tolerate human love, and they flee. Just trust, Stephanie, for once in your life. Don't be so afraid of falling in love again that it paralyzes you from ever seeking happiness."

As he was talking, Chris lay back on the soft thick carpet. He pulled the fearful woman down next to him, where she waited, tense and rigid. He stroked her hair, fingering the strands to trace their path over her cheeks and bosom. His hands, warm and moist, caressed her face, touched and lingered over her neck and arms. He could feel her breasts swell to meet his inquiring fingers. The nipples stood sharp and tumescent. With delicate erotic motions, he teased their tips.

She did not resist. Her lips grew dry and she licked them with her tongue, spreading saliva over the edges and in the corners. Their lean tanned bodies pressed together like two streams of molten copper fusing within a single casting. She could feel his potent masculine arousal. It felt good . . . so good. How long had it been since she had let a man entice her into sexual desire? Her features relaxed and her expression grew soft and dazed. She stood up with an eager smile and discarded her blouse and skirt. Then her underclothing. Until, naked, she stood over him, legs slightly apart.

He raised himself to his knees and hugged her around her thighs, his face buried in her pubic hair. He bent her down to the floor. She leaned over to nibble at his ear and licked around his chin and eyes. She ran her hand down his chest, then reached below to contact his swollen organ. He stood up to shed his clothes. She could see him silhouetted against the wall, his tallness exaggerated by the table lamp, his phallic shadow jutting out ahead of him.

"Stephanie," he said, "I love you so much."

Her words in turn echoed his as she clasped him to her breasts. His hand crept down in between her thighs, which opened ahead of his light touch. She lay back now, almost unaware of his rhythmic manipulation. She began to move her hips to urge him on faster.

"Oh, Chris," she called out through the thickening screen of sexual desire. "I want so much to love . . . to love . . ."

Suddenly, with a shriek, she pushed him away. She escaped into the corner of the room where she lay, huddled up, her body tightened into an embryonic ball.

Chris could not think of his unbearable frustration. He crawled over to where she lay and pulled her into his arms. "Don't, Stephanie," he said. "Don't be afraid. It will be all right." He stroked her hair, unable to break through her private agony. "Time . . . Stephanie . . . time. That is all that you . . . we . . . need. I am not going to leave you—ever."

Not until the first rays of sunlight broke through the plate-glass window to warm the naked flesh of the two huddled figures did Chris cease his gentle ministrations. He carried the now quiet woman to the sofa and covered her with the fur afghan folded in the corner. He collected his clothes and dressed, promising himself that this was one battle he had to win. He opened the sliding door to the deck. Confident of his future with this provocative golden-haired woman, he walked outside and sucked in deep lungfuls of the cool crisp morning air, as the dawn rolled back the night to reveal his future home.

Chapter / **TWENTY-SEVEN**

SAMUEL HALPERN BACKED CAREFULLY INTO THE OPERATING
Theater, pushing the swinging door open with his shoulder. He held
his dripping hands up in the air to protect their antiseptic scrub
from contamination. The two waiting nurses, both concealed within
their neuterlike surgical garments, hastened over to him. One
handed him a towel to dry his hands. The other helped him into
his sterile gown, holding out the drawstring to twirl around him
before knotting it across his waist. Each nurse took one rubber
glove and, opening it wide, held it immobile so that he could
thrust his fingers deep into the flexible brown latex skin. He wiped

the powder off the outside of the gloves with a moist towel, which he dropped into the bucket in the corner of the room. He turned to inspect the anesthetized patient.

Mrs. Dearing was lying on her right side. The narrow operating table had been cranked up in the center. Her body was contorted with her head and feet lowered at each end and her midriff forced up high into the air at an extreme unnatural angle. She was a thin pale woman and her ribs protruded under the tensed stretched skin like raised linear welts.

Samuel nodded to the orderly his approval of the patient's positioning. He picked up the sponge stick to paint the dark brown iodine solution on the body. With short pressing strokes he swabbed the bacteriocidal chemical over the chest and abdomen, swirling the pattern in an ever-expanding spiral that grew wider and wider as he worked out toward the periphery of the field.

When he had finished, he held his hands out for the four drapes that he used to frame the area of contemplated surgery. The nurse gave him a short needle to mark the ribs. He glanced at the illuminated viewing box on the wall. It held the X-ray films he had sorted out and placed there prior to his scrubbing. He pressed his fingers over the ribs, counting from the bottom up. Twelve, eleven, ten, nine. Over each one he scratched a light mark that penetrated the superficial layer of the skin. As he worked, a thin beading of blood oozed through the lines. He stood back to check. The patient's flank looked as if someone had scratched her with the tines of a giant pitchfork. He went over to the X-rays to confirm his original decision on where to make the incision. Yes, he nodded to himself, it would be an eleventh-rib exposure. Returning to the right side of the table, he held out his hand for the scalpel.

His assistant had said nothing during these preparations. In his own practice, Ralph Flaherty did not often act in a subordinate role. Usually it was he who did the surgery, with his two junior partners helping him. However, he commiserated to himself, there was no possible way for him to have avoided accepting Samuel Halpern's request to scrub on Mrs. Dearing's case. If the urologist could not isolate and remove the ureteral obstruction, or if, having done that, the kidney did not recover, the patient would die. Sure, he considered the option, she could live hooked up the rest of her natural life to an artificial kidney, but was that really any different than dying? As for giving her a kidney transplant, it would be years before she could get on the waiting list at any of the medical centers in the country that were doing that still-uncertain procedure.

And what about her husband? What pound of flesh would he extract? The aging obstetrician-gynecologist gave an involuntary shiver as with reluctant steps and a feeling of trepidation he approached the patient.

Samuel looked up as the bulky shape moved into his visual field on the side of the table facing him. For a moment, he could not repress a sense of pity for the man. Ralph had always been an extroverted, gregarious Irishman with a joke for everybody. How he got away with his raw, earthy humor, Sam never knew. Over the years, he even had the nuns laughing at his off-color jokes. Perhaps it was his round jovial face, always florid and smiling, framed by his white hair. Or his clear, innocent blue eyes. Or his huge girth, which bounced in front of him like the swellings of his maternal practice. He always had the habit of hugging his patients to his side when giving them a loud, boisterous greeting. He remembered everyone's name, birthdays, anniversaries and invariably had a good word to say no matter how unfortunate the situation.

Observing the man's face, now obliterated by the cap and mask, Samuel realized how much of Flaherty was a facade, just as easily extinguished as his expression was by a thin layer of pressed cellulose. Sam knew of his vendetta against Brandon, but for the first time seriously wondered if this newest competition for Flaherty and his partners would succumb to the pressure. In his recent dealings with Joe over Mrs. Dearing, Samuel had detected a determination that was every bit the equal of his persecutor's.

Halpern's daydreaming was suddenly interrupted by the stinging slap of the scalpel on his outstretched palm. With that smarting sensation, Samuel cast from his mind any thought other than the job in front of him. Within minutes he would know for certain what path Ralph Flaherty would be treading in the days to come.

"Ralph," Samuel informed his assistant as the knife blade cut through the overlying skin and fascia, "I am going to do an eleventh-rib exposure." Even as he talked, the field was obscured by the crisscross motion of glinting metal clamps being transferred from hand to hand to skin to pumping blood vessels. The flashing of steel would stop intermittently so that a blood-spattered hand could wipe a clean white gauze pad across the gaping incision to soak up the congealing red fluid and allow the surgeon to inspect the severed tissues. The saturated pad was then tossed on the floor where it added to a growing pile like a crimson stalagmite.

The scalpel blade finally stopped as it hit the underlying rib. Samuel pressed the knife edge deep into the bone, to split the tough periosteal fibers that covered it like a tight skin.

"Alexander," he ordered, his eyes not straying from the field. The periosteal elevator was smacked into his hand. He scraped the dense adherent white tissue off the rib, sweeping it to the sides.

"Doyan." By means of this hooked stainless-steel probe, Samuel managed to free the periosteum off the underbody of the rib where the Alexander could not approach because of its size.

"Guillotine." The heavy bone-crunching jaws cracked through the middle of the rib, severing it from the half still attached to the spine.

"Rongeur." Samuel smoothed off the spicules and burrs on the severed end of the rib left behind.

Samuel straightened up from the crouched position he had assumed over the rib cage and stretched. He then bent again to his cramped stance. The three muscle layers of the abdominal wall were divided. The external oblique. The internal oblique. The transversus abdominus. Each in turn serving to support the trunk like layers of plywood. These strong muscle bellies contained fierce arteries coursing through them, and once or twice, when Flaherty was not fast enough with the clamp, a thin jet of red would squirt high into the air and drench the front of their gowns. When the blood would land on Samuel's glasses, he would stop and allow the circulating nurse to remove them and wipe the lenses clean again before continuing his dissection.

"The easy part is over," Samuel commented as he prepared to penetrate through the few remaining structures that protected the kidney from violation.

The transversalis fascia, a translucent sheet of parchmentlike tissue, surrendered to a fresh scalpel blade.

Gerota's Fascia, named by an observant physician for the investing fibrous envelope around the kidney itself, tore easily under probing fingers.

Finally, the kidney itself, cushioned within thick gobs of yellow fat. Samuel peeled off the greasy layer, ignoring the infiltrating network of small arteries and veins that ripped and bled as he dissected. Flaherty tried to clamp the bleeders, but Samuel nudged away his feeble efforts. "It's not necessary, Ralph. They'll stop by themselves. Leave them alone or we will be here all day." Packing the bleeding fat under the pressure of a damp folded gauze pad, he leaned closer to inspect the target of his exploration.

As the last curtain of fat was removed, Samuel let out a short exclamation. Instead of a firm red organ, engorged with life-giving blood and tumescent from the vital pressure of the heart, what lay before his eyes was a pale, flabby, almost lifeless replica. For an instant, he had the fleeting thought that this worthless structure was some other tissue and that he had not yet located the true kidney.

He lifted the anemic organ and held it between his hands. He stroked the smooth shiny surface and pressed firmly to indent its substance, testing how much tissue remained. He cursed his inability to tell for certain. God, he prayed, let there be something left.

((183))

He lowered the kidney back in the wound and looked for the ureter. This two-foot-long tube, which conducted the urine manufactured by the kidney to the bladder, would normally be thin and spaghettilike. Now it was thick and distended, grossly swollen to four to five times its usual diameter and engorged with trapped stagnant urine unable to get past some distal obstruction into the bladder.

Samuel repositioned the gauze packs in the sides of the incision to provide him with greater exposure. He signaled to the second nurse to come around to his side of the table. He asked for the Finichetto. He inserted the large heavy ratcheting retractor in the field and cranked open the rib cage to enlarge the field of vision.

"Deaver. Large," he ordered. He placed the broad blade of the hand retractor into the wound, hooking it on the edge of the muscle layers.

"All right, my dear," he urged the nurse by his side. "Pull. Gently," he demonstrated, "but firmly."

Flaherty had not said a word this whole time. What Samuel could see of his assistant's face was white, with large beads of perspiration standing out on his forehead. Ralph held a clamp in one hand in anticipation of another bleeding vessel. Samuel could see the metal instrument tremble.

Halpern murmured in a soft voice so that the nurses could not hear. "I know. It doesn't look too good, Ralph, but you can never tell. Let's see what is going on down below."

Samuel asked for the skin scalpel and extended the initial incision still farther down to the level of the patient's pubis, slicing open the length of the abdomen with broad slashing sweeps of the knife. It seemed that he was moving more rapidly now, trying to accelerate the pace of the case, as if driven by the compulsion to finish and thus rid himself of the tragedy he was uncovering.

As he dissected deeper into the patient's body, he kept the ureter before his eyes, tracing its meandering course. He looped his left thumb and index finger around the conduit as he slid his hand down farther until it was deep in the pelvis where he could barely see it. He stopped, startled, and stared into Flaherty's eyes. Flaherty shivered for an instant as both men were suddenly locked in the knowledge of some yet unsaid, unseen, but detected horror.

"The ureter's stuck, Ralph," Samuel said in a soft, stricken tone. He asked again for the skin scalpel. With one final cut he laid open the patient's entire pelvis. This last extension of the incision was all that was needed. Whether it was the tension of the patient stretched out on the distorted table or the fact that the previous hysterectomy had removed the overlying uterus from obstructing the view, but there, exposed for all to see, was the ureter, snaking its way into a dense white block of coarse gritty material that surrounded it and was choking its hollow lumen as if to crush out its very existence.

Flaherty could not stop himself. He reached his hand down into the wound. His fingers palpated the obliterative mass, that alien mound of disease that lay like a knife pressed to his jugular. He felt the tissue over and over, rubbing it as if that impotent action would somehow make it vanish. He looked up, guilty, and withdrew his hand from the field, surrendering the destiny of the patient once again to his friend.

"Metzenbaum." Samuel took the fine scissors and with small snips teased the overlying mass from off the trapped ureter. It seemed hours while he worked to remove the fibrosis without injuring the delicate tube buried somewhere within the hard white tissue. The room was quiet except for the persistent hiss of the anesthesia machine and the slushing noise of the suction tube that Flaherty constantly employed to keep the field of dissection free of blood for the urologist.

Samuel raised his head to hand a piece of the removed tissue to the nurse.

"Send it down to Pathology for a frozen section.

"Just in case it is cancer," he said to his partner. The nurse placed the specimen in a labeled polyethylene bag and left the room.

Flaherty straightened up a bit at the lethal possibility. If it *was* cancer, then the obstruction could not be his fault. Mrs. Dearing's death would be just one of those accidental sets of circumstances. But, if it was not cancer. If the specimen did not harbor tumor cells, but something more benign, like catgut sutures that had accidentally snared a ureter in a hysterectomy, then . . .

Against his wish, he found himself possessing the desperate hope that Pirie's report would tell of some horrible, invasive, incurable malignancy. He glanced up to see Samuel staring at him with a puzzled frown. Ashamed, Flaherty bent his head down again and busied himself in the field aspirating the incision free of encrusted blood.

It seemed forever before Samuel had freed the entire course of the ureter. It now lay there, delivered safely, released of any blockage, smooth, patent, unencumbered from kidney to bladder.

Samuel attacked the remainder of the fibrosis. The scirrhous tissue was tenaciously plastered on the back wall of the abdomen. It reluctantly yielded to his sharp dissection. The nurse gathered the segments of tissue to transport down to the Pathology Department for the permanent sections.

Samuel pointed to the bottles. "It will take a week, Ralph, before we have the answer. I guess Simon must be having trouble with the frozen section. Sometimes it is damn difficult to differentiate retroperitoneal fibrosis from inflammatory tumors."

Samuel stepped back from the table and allowed the circulating nurse to wipe his forehead with a cool damp cloth. He checked the clock on the wall. They had been operating for over four hours. He threw back his shoulders to stretch out the cramp that had lodged between his shoulder blades. He sighed with fatigue. He was getting old. Thank God, another month and Stephen would . . . He stopped and rid from his mind the disconcerting thought. He could not afford the luxury of personal problems in the operating room, especially with this case. He turned again to the patient to complete the last stage of the procedure.

The nurse held out for him to inspect a series of long rubber tubes. He selected one red catheter about fourteen inches long and the thickness of his little finger. He picked up the kidney and slowly punctured its lower pole with a sharp clamp. There was a slow gush of clear fluid, which he caught in a sterile tube.

"For culture and sensitivity," he ordered, as he capped the glass vial and gave it back to the nurse.

With the Metzenbaum, he snipped off a raw piece of kidney hanging from the edge of the incision.

"Also, let's send this down to Pathology," he said to Flaherty. "While we are here, we might as well see what Simon says about the kidney. Sometimes, the microscopic can tell us if the kidney is irrevocably dead, or just arrested. If there are still viable tubules and cells, maybe in time, the kidney will work. You know, as I was telling Joe . . ." he stammered, embarrassed, "sometimes the kidney will come back." He continued: "It is possible, Ralph. It is possible. We just have to pray."

He threaded the tube through the rent in the kidney deep into the organ until the tip came to rest in the very heart to collect there whatever urine the organ might eventually make. He shifted the tube back and forth a fraction of an inch at a time, until he was satisfied with its placement. He sutured it securely in place with widely spaced bites of the needle through the capsule of the kidney.

Samuel checked the length of the wound to make certain that all was in order. No sponges left in the field. All open blood vessels clamped off. The retractor blades removed gently to avoid trauma to the adjacent tissues. He held out his hand to commence closing the incision.

As he worked, he became conscious of a new presence by his side. A shadow. A strange intruder into his tight little world. He turned, his hand frozen with the needle still in the patient's skin, astonished to see the figure of Joe Brandon next to him.

He could not tell how long he had been standing there. The man had not scrubbed, but stood silently in back of the urologist, his hand holding an untied mask over his face. He was standing on a low metal stool and his body was bent forward to see over Samuel's shoulder into the wound.

"Joe!" Samuel sputtered, unsure of what else to say. Had he been able to pierce through the shielding mask, he was certain he would have seen a mocking grin.

The young obstetrician nodded to Samuel and followed with an unctuous gesture to Ralph. "Sam," he said in a voice loud enough for all in the room to hear, "when you finish with Mrs. Dearing, there's a message waiting for you at the desk. It is a request for both of you to report to the reception lounge in the lobby. Mrs. Dearing's husband is waiting anxiously to see you. And, gentlemen," he warned, "I would recommend that you don't keep him waiting."

Chapter / **TWENTY-EIGHT**

MARTIN ABELS WAS WEARY. THE THIN MIDDLE-AGED PHYSICIAN pushed himself away from the file-cluttered desk. The uncomfortable metal chair scratched as the glideless third leg caught on the pocked linoleum covering the dingy floor of the Mercy Hospital Record Room. The harsh overhead fluorescent light ricocheted off his thick horn-rimmed glasses, causing him to blink. He stood up and stretched several times. He sucked in deep breaths and yawned once or twice to caress the thyroid gland into pumping more stimulating hormone into his fatigued body. He looked up at the clock. Nine-thirty. Another night's supper missed with his family. He walked around the room, his crepe rubber soles squashing on the slick floor as he touched, in turn, the dozen now empty desks, each with a silent IBM typewriter and sessile earphones, looking for all the world like a succession of rejected halos.

He turned back to the desk, to gather up his sheath of yellow, lined legal pad sheets. He gave a sigh of satisfaction as he looked at the calender on the wall. In three weeks, the June Executive Committee meeting would take place. The tedious travail would be worth it when the travesties of Cromwell's most famous surgeon would finally be exposed for all to see.

It had not been difficult to pursue the errant physician. As Chief of the Department of Anesthesiology, Martin had access to the Daily Journal of the Mercy Operating Room Suite, in which was recorded every surgical case carried out since the Sisters began their first medical mission on Canal Street in the Flats, in the late 1880s. However, Martin Abels was not interested in the historical legacy of Cromwell surgery. He confined his task to reviewing the last ten years of Lansing Prout's tenure on the surgical staff.

Starting with the ledger for January 1966 and continuing on through to December 1975, Martin reviewed the data sheets, recording on his pad each case of Prout's by date, patient name, age, hospital number, diagnosis, and surgical procedure. Next, he reported to Sister Margaret Immaculata, the white-haired matron of the Record Room and transcription pool. This congenial epileptic nun who had graduated from twenty years of cutting Host to her present responsibility, was effusive in her appreciation for Dr. Martin Abels's attention. Never before had one of the staff physicians ever solicited her aid in preparing a survey of Mercy Hospital's contribution to surgical progress over the past decade in the Greater Cromwell Community.

Not once did she question the massive number of charts that she extracted each day from the subterranean archives. Neither did she complain about the need for voluminous Photostats of records preserved on microfilm *fiches*. At no time did she wonder why Dr.

Lansing Prout should be singled out so prominently for his illustrious contributions to the medical health of the city, except possibly as a deserved tribute from such younger, less-renowned men as Dr. Abels, himself a product of the Bronx, in southern New York, the City.

Alone each night in the quiet, deserted room, a brass gooseneck lamp to light his solitary patch of activity when the harsh hot white ceiling lights became too oppressive, Martin studied each hospital chart. He scanned the pages, skimming the dusty records for the critical information he sought. Only when he placed the eviscerated record on the table behind him, and took another fresh one from the decreasing pile in front of him, would he stop to appraise his thickening stack of notes, that irrefutable mountain of evidence he was forging against Prout. At those times, a sense of purpose seemed to shake off his weariness and suffuse his body with a quickening of pulse and a bitter determination to continue.

As Abels worked and sifted and matched, he could see a definite pattern emerge from the rows of figures and statistics. Had his task not been colored by years of watching Prout's disintegrating talent injure his unsuspecting patients, he might have admitted that the evidence was of a more sorrowful than vengeful nature. Prout had been a reasonably competent surgeon—at one time. Ten years ago his diagnoses were, for the most part, well founded. Each disease was worked up thoroughly, with appropriate clinical and laboratory tests and X-ray procedures. The patient, carefully examined on several occasions with detailed thought-out notes in the chart chronicling the clinical case. The surgery itself adequately consummated.

Then the slow change. So subtle that, at any one time, it would have been imperceptible to the perpetrator himself, let alone to an outsider. The deterioration, a growing fungus hidden away in the dark. A strain slowly spreading each day, until the fabric was irrevocably damaged. The razor-sharp edge of his diagnostic acumen dulled, pitted, tarnished. His surgical prowess now erratic, inconsistent, inadequate. His clinical competence—no more!

As Martin Abels watched shape and form coalesce from the mass of data, he could not avoid a curt gesture of sympathy for the physician, a there-but-for-the-grace-of-God-go-I to the man whose healing skills were leaking away like liquid sand. But then, when he would examine one particularly tragic case, he would shake his head to shoo away those sympathetic thoughts.

The charts, those paper tombstones, were *not* merely cellulose tableaux, but living human beings. People who had gone to Prout with full expectation of receiving competent medical care. It was to him that they surrendered their bodies, their shame, their modesty, their privacy, health, limbs, lives, money. Did they not expect, should they have not received, the maximum that was theirs to obtain? The truth dulled his sympathy and, with a sigh of regret, he would move on to the next chart.

Abels was quick to note that in the early years of the decade the abdominal catastrophes were worked up well, the diagnosis swiftly made and surgery carried out at the appropriate time. The patient with the inflamed gall bladder, the infected appendix, the perforating ulcer. The results, ten years ago, were excellent.

Then, the change. There could be no denying it. The appendices. Either operated on too late when they had already ruptured and spilled caches of pus into the abdomen, purveying potential death from peritonitis. Or, even worse, patients without appendicitis were explored needlessly when all they suffered from was indigestion, constipation, or even menstrual cramps.

The same pattern held for other diseases. Either the surgery unwisely postponed, the sharp decision required to operate absent, the patient victim of unconscionable procrastination. Or else, the operation too precipitously performed, with innocent gall bladders, pristine stomachs, content ovaries and uteri, all removed for naught, while the pancreatic cancer, the kidney stones, the rectal cancer ignored—until too late.

Then, almost as if Prout himself had been in the room five years ago to anticipate Abels's unpleasant task, something mysterious happened. It was not that the insidious pattern was abandoned, but rather the complexion of Prout's practice began to change. The number of extirpative surgical procedures gradually dropped off. Abels knew, as Prout certainly did, according to hospital regulations, all tissue removed from a patient was sent to Simon Pirie. The virgin appendices, the immaculate gall bladders, all in death, impaled on thin pink and blue slides, bore permanent witness to the white-haired surgeon's declining prowess. It seemed that Prout had decided to eliminate this Greek chorus of tragedy, those strident jurors of histological accusation. He ceased carrying out those operations that produced surgical specimens for pathologic review.

Simultaneous with this decision, a plethora of new operative techniques appeared on the canary-tinted sheets. There were now the Marshall-Marchetti or anterior colporrhaphy procedure, a fancy name to describe tucking a few catgut sutures near the neck of the bladder so that the female patient who wets her pants with every sigh or cough or sneeze would once again be socially acceptable. The presacral neurectomy, that exquisite, though dubious practice of scraping the backbone to reduce menstrual and pelvic pain. The nephropexy, that wondrous act of putting a stitch through the kidney so that it could not move, and in the process allegedly curing a myriad of complaints from back pain to unpaid taxes.

No one could question the indications or efficacy of these new Prout procedures, for the magnitude of the preoperative symptoms and long-term follow-ups were documented only by the surgeon himself, in his office records. Most critical of all, none of these procedures ever produced any diagnostic tissue. There was nothing at all to validate the necessity or prognosis of these operations. Nothing—except the surgeon's word—and his honor.

Abels knew all of this. He also knew what Prout had possibly not considered, if indeed this choreograph of deceit was premeditated. The American Institute of Surgery had established time-tested statistics for the numbers of such operations in the average surgeon's practice. Should a particular physician display a predilection for an increasing number of such unaccountable cases, then they were swift to swoop down and demolish the offender.

Finally, sprinkled throughout, from the very beginning, only more striking as the years passed, were those obscene maggots—the true tragedies. Not only Francis Hébert, but also others, with healthy limbs left gangrenous, wombs excised with the seed of life still extant, thyroid glands explored leaving in their wake paralyzed vocal cords, and dozens of other perverted, macerated clinical cases that, like sharp crystals of prussic acid, poisoned the whole mélange with a bitter and lethal flavor.

No, Prout was hooked. Hoisted by his own petard. With a pleasant feeling of satisfaction for the end of his long travail, to lift his spirits and to wash away his fatigue, Dr. Martin Abels left a polite note on the dispatched pile of charts, thanking Sister Margaret Immaculata for her help. He turned off all the lights. Clutching in his hand the thick crackling yellow paper-braided noose for Prout's patrician neck, he quietly closed the door behind him.

Chapter / TWENTY-NINE

IF SYLVIA EVER WONDERED AFTER STEPHEN'S DISCONCERTING decision to practice at the Millsite Clinic why her husband was so strangely silent, she kept her increasing anxiety to herself. She was certain that Samuel had not acceded to the *fait accompli*. If anything, the encounter with Christopher Amen only seemed to tighten his manner and make him more reclusive and taciturn than usual. Never once did he express anger or recrimination, or even self-pity. If he had cursed at Stephen's ingratitude, she would have felt relieved. He did nothing. He got up each morning, went to the hospital, and then to his office, and finally home, to repeat the

((195))

pattern, day after day. She saw the fixed set to his mouth, the busy cerebration camouflaged behind the blank expression that quickly covered his face whenever he caught his wife looking at him. She knew with dread that the family was yet to taste the full dregs of her husband's commitment and purpose.

Sylvia's puzzlement at her husband's absent affect was heightened one evening by a telephone call that, under any other circumstance, would have aroused a strong reaction. The call was short. She informed Samuel that the Chief of Surgery at Mercy had asked to visit their home that evening. Despite her insistence, he had refused to state the purpose of the intended meeting.

"Carl Lash? Him?" her husband replied, unperturbed by either the precipitous self-invitation or its undeclared motive. "I can assure you that Carl is not coming over here for a social visit."

"I know that," Sylvia said, with an unusual edge of bitterness to her words. "We have been in Cromwell thirty years and never once did the Lashes, before their divorce, or for that matter any of their friends, ever invite us to their homes."

"It is this clinic business in the Flats," Samuel said. "Amen applied for privileges at Mercy at the same time that Stephen did. If he doesn't get on the staff to take care of his sick patients in the hospital, he won't be able to open at Millsite."

"Can the hospital do that? I mean, can they actually keep him off the staff?"

Samuel took in her innocent look. "You don't know medical politics," he snorted. "Of course they can. Sure he can fight back, but . . . time . . . *time,* that is the real hooker. If they can drag it out long enough, they can throttle the clinic!"

"How can they do that, Sam?"

Sam sat down on the sofa next to his wife and, taking both her hands in his, started to explain. "Listen to what I am telling you, Sylvia. Amen knows as well as I do that he will need government money for at least three to five years before his clinic is self-supporting. Federal grants are on an annual basis. If the clinic doesn't start to produce within the next twelve months, even our blond Messiah with all his pull won't get funded for another year. He and his damn clinic are through!

"Despite what Stephen thinks of him, there are plenty of other Christopher Amens all over the country, sucking up to the Washington tit for money. Amen just got there first with the biggest bite, that's all. Remember, though, if he doesn't make a big splash in the first twelve months, he can't hold on. And he can't make it without being on the Mercy staff. And if *he* can't get on the staff, you can be pretty damn sure that none of the other young doctors he is busy recruiting will be able to get privileges. Anyway," he tossed off, "what physician coming out of residency and trying to go into practice would risk joining him under those circumstances?

"Sylvia," he advised, "a doctor in a community who doesn't have hospital admitting privileges is like a eunuch in a harem." He gave a coarse laugh. "All he can do is hand out Band-Aids."

Sylvia digested the explanation, trying hard to reject her husband's collusion in such a scheme. It hurt her to see the fierceness of his conviction. "But, Sam, how can they block his privileges, if he is really entitled to them?"

"Sylvia, you get a bunch of doctors together and you have as vicious a group of bastards as you can find anywhere. They are just as conniving and back-stabbing as politicians, or businessmen, or union organizers. We doctors are all consummate carpenters when it comes to nailing one of our own on a homemade cross."

His wife looked up at him, alarmed. "Does that include you, too, Sam?"

"I don't know, Sylvia. I honestly don't know." There was a long pause as he tried to introspect without emotion or personal prejudice. "I try to do my best. I am not a hypocrite. I am not an idealist, either. I don't think that being a doctor gives me any special privileges. Medicine is a job, a craft, not a divine mission.

"If you follow that thought through to its logical conclusion, there is no reason in the world why anyone should expect doctors

((197))

to be virtuous or pure. If they are made of the same dust and clay as the rest of the human race, why shouldn't they be entitled to all their vices—to cheat, and steal, and maim—like everyone else?

"I suppose," he added thoughtfully, "the mortal flaw, that hidden evil, is not that doctors commit crimes like everybody else, but that they subscribe to an inviolate article of faith, that they are superior to their fellow mortals. That is what will cast them from the Garden, the invisible sin of hypocrisy."

"What are you going to do?" Sylvia asked. The question hung there, sharp and glinting.

"I don't know," he said. "I am just one member of the Executive Committee. The other nine doctors can decide what is going to happen to Amen without my vote." In jest, he said, "Probably the best thing I could do is not show up for the meeting at all. I can always schedule an 'emergency' case at noon and come in when the action is over."

"Is that right, Sam? I mean, not to say anything?" His wife would not be deflected.

"What do you want me to say? Do you want me to get up and shout out, 'Why don't you allow Dr. Amen on the staff? Sure, gentlemen, he is opening up a clinic. So what? Are you afraid that he is going to dispense poor medicine? If he does, *then* censor him or suspend his privileges, but later, when you have proof. No, gentlemen. That is not the point at all, is it?' " He continued his play-acting. " 'You are not frightened at the thought he might be a lousy doctor. You won't even let him into town to find out. Why?' " He pointed his finger at his imaginary audience. " 'Because you are scared. Scared of what, you ask?

" 'You are scared of his being a good doctor, a damn good one. Of his having a rip-roaring success to compete with. A clinic that owes you no allegiance. A medical center that has a claim on the loyalties of patients in Cromwell by coming *to them* rather than by right of monopoly.

" 'If you could be guaranteed that he would be a quack, a charlatan, a butcher. If you could be assured that his clinic would be an abortion mill, an abattoir, a dope parlor, then . . . then . . . you would welcome him with open arms. That is the cancer that obliges you to sit here in a Star Chamber looking for pious ways to slit his throat.'

"No, Sylvia," he said, leaving his invisible audience. "I couldn't just sit there and eat up my chicken salad sandwich and be quiet. I am not built that way. And yet, what am I supposed to say to that group of pompous, smug, greedy, Jew-hating hypocrites?"

"But I thought you were against the clinic," she said. "I heard you and Stephen arguing about it."

"Sure," he grudgingly allowed, "my gut reaction *is* to fight it. I am too old to change after thirty years of private practice. Especially when the decision is forced upon me by some clerk from Washington punching my time card, giving me a paycheck each week. No . . . no . . . not at the age of sixty-five. No Syl . . . not now.

"And yet," he lowered his voice, "if I had to, I probably could accept it. Only five more good years, and then I am out anyway. What really rubs me *is* those five years, Sylvia." His eyes brimmed with tears. "I have had a dream. Stephen and me. A father and his son. It is even more than that. A partnership, a pact, from one generation to another. I am not leaving Stephen a lot of money. We live well, but I don't have a fortune with millions in a will like Abe Kupperman has. For my son, I can leave him a lifetime heritage of love and loyalty from the people I have helped. A legacy that will make the thirty years not wasted. My life—reborn in his."

His face lit up with the vision. His words issued forth crisp and clear. "That is what I intended to do, Syl. I want Stephen to seize it, devour it, to make it his. But, only Stephen—and no one else."

When finally Carl Lash and his companion arrived, Samuel Halpern barely acknowledged them.

Carl Lash was in his mid-fifties. His leonine face was chiseled with sharp, angular lines, eyes were deep blue and piercing, lips thin and waspish with a square chin. His bushy black eyebrows were laced with gray like the thick hair covering his head, which oddly seemed to accentuate his still-youthful cast. It was obvious, however, that Carl Lash did not like being in the Halpern home for whatever the reason that had brought him here.

Unlike his chaperon, the short florid man dancing after the surgeon was delighted to be inside the Halpern home. His fat face was pink with fine crinkly lines that crisscrossed the perpetual smile and circled around his bloodshot eyes. He shook Samuel's hand over and over, unwilling to surrender it for even a minute.

"Dr. and Mrs. Halpern. It was gracious for you to allow us here on such short notice. Carl . . . Dr. Lash, that is, said that he was coming over here to visit you. I took the liberty of inviting myself along." His speech was constantly interrupted by wheezes and loud puffing.

He turned to Mrs. Halpern. "I apologize for the lack of my advance warning."

Samuel watched the asinine pantomime, amused by the hypocritical prelude to the serious business he knew his two visitors had brought with them.

"Sylvia," he declared with gravity, "Mr. Ryan is a member of the Board of Trustees of Mercy Hospital—a very prominent man." The poorly concealed sarcasm did not stop the beneficiary from inflating his smile all the more and showering his pleasure on Mrs. Halpern.

"He is the 'son' in 'Ryan and Son, Contractors.' The new Mercy Hospital building, you know," he said, aside.

Samuel offered the builder his hand for a second shaking. "Mr. Ryan. You are very welcome in our home. Please don't apologize. It is an honor to have you here, and . . . also Dr. Lash." With labored courtesy, he asked, "Can I offer you a drink? Carl?"

"No, thank you," Lash deferred, shying away from the unctuous generosity of his host. Ryan's face, on the other hand, self-illuminated at the mention of liquor.

"No. Well, just a small libation. Scotch, with a tad of water, if that is not too much trouble. June is such a good month for Scotch," he offered, with a small laugh to Lash who remained totally immune to the humor.

"Have a seat, gentlemen." Samuel seated himself in his favorite wing chair, his back to the window. The light from the crystal lamp on the intaglioed side table threw his face into the shadow. Sylvia could see the somber look on his face telling her to leave the men to their affairs. She rose to make her excuses to leave.

"Mr. Ryan. Dr. Lash. It was pleasant meeting you both. I hope that we will have the pleasure of seeing you again."

They got up to shake her hand, and she quickly left the room.

"Sam," Lash started in, "I should have told you that I was bringing Jack Ryan. Jack is concerned about the new family clinic coming into Millsite and its effect on Mercy. He wanted to get your opinion as a member of the Executive Committee."

"Oh," replied Halpern, ingenuously. "This visit concerns Dr. Christopher Amen and his government clinic? In what way?"

"Damn it, Sam!" Lash retorted, angered by his host's flippant attitude, "let's not beat around the bush. Christopher Amen is applying for staff privileges. Without them, we have him by the short hairs. His bread-and-butter circus will abort down in the Flats."

"What do you want from me?" Samuel asked. "That is for the entire Executive Committee to decide on next week. I am not sure what business we even have to discuss this matter here, in front of Mr. Ryan. I don't see the relevancy of this meeting."

"You don't see the relevancy?" Lash's voice heated in anger. "Your son is applying for privileges along with Amen. Both of them are to be voted upon at the next meeting. You know, Sam," he leaned closer to the listener to emphasize his point, "your son isn't entirely detached from this Millsite Clinic business. I wonder whether your son is Amen's Trojan Horse. And, you ask me of the relevancy."

"Doctors," Ryan said, "hear me out. I may be a hospital board member, but I am at heart just a simple bricklayer, or at least the son of one. However," he stated with authority, "I can tell a problem when I see it, even if it is in a totally different field from mine.

"From what Carl tells me, this new doctor, this Amen fellow, is applying for privileges. The board sees lots of men applying to the staff each year. We can't tell if they are any good. How can I, a builder, or Fred Dearing, a lawyer, or even Lyman Bell decide if the applicant is qualified to practice medicine at Mercy? Sure," he patiently explained, "we must approve or disapprove the application to make it legal, but, you doctors," pointing to both of them, "make the actual decisions. The Executive Committee recommends and we rubber-stamp. During the eleven years that I have been on the board, we have unanimously accepted the recommendations of the Executive Committee. The system has worked well, as far as I am concerned. You gentlemen know your business, and we know ours. You have the ability to judge your peers, and we accept your verdict. Isn't that true, Carl?"

"Yes, Jack. The Board of Trustees has always supported the decision of the Executive Committee. There has never been any problem, until now."

"That's right, until now," Ryan concurred. "That is why, Dr. Halpern, we need your help."

"My help. How?"

Ryan glanced at Lash who gave his approval. "I can't judge a physician," the builder started, "but I can damn well read a balance sheet. Carl and Prynne have pointed out, and I must add, very effectively, that this new clinic business could bankrupt the hospital, or at least cripple it financially."

"Bankrupt the hospital? Carl," Samuel turned incredulously to face Lash. "What kind of garbage have you been feeding the board?"

Lash did not flinch a muscle. "Let Jack explain," he replied, his tone icy.

"You know the new North Medical Wing?" Ryan asked the urologist.

"Yes, it is a beautiful job. We have a lot to thank you and the other men on the board for."

"Yes, yes, but that is not the point. The board borrowed seven million dollars for that wing. Seven million dollars, cold cash, at eight and a half percent. That is six hundred thousand dollars in interest each year, let alone the amortization. That is our problem, you can say, and so it was, until now."

Samuel was unable to follow the thread of logic that Ryan was unrolling in front of him. The contractor hastened to explain.

"Why did we put up the new wing in the first place? What we really needed, or at least what the board originally wanted, was one hundred and fifty new beds. But no. You and Carl here, the whole damn medical staff, jumped on our back. You boys wanted a new special services building—new X-ray, new laboratories, physical rehabilitation, new blood bank, emergency ward. All that crap!" He shook his finger at the two physicians. "Not a single new bed for patients.

"If you don't remember, I can damn well recall it for you. What a bucket of shit we tripped over then. The newspaper. The American Legion. The women's club. Rotary. The whole goddamn lot of them jumped down our throats. Every mother's daughter with a lump in her breast. Every son of a bitch with a hemorrhoid or a varicose vein. They all complained that they had to wait a month to get a bed in the hospital and all the Board of Trustees does is put up a new brick building full of fancy instruments to do fancy tests that the doctors don't understand anyway."

Ryan faced the physicians squarely. "We didn't listen to the community, even though we took their money. We put up the new north wing for you doctors. We relied on your judgment. You complained that you needed new expensive equipment to keep up with all the modern tests you kept plaguing us with. So you got your goddamn new building. And now, along comes Dr. Amen. His clinic will do the X-rays, the blood tests, see the patients instead of our emergency ward. His doctors will decide whether the patients go to Mercy or are sent to Boston. What happens to the additional volume that we projected we need to pay off the mortgage? Who explains to the newspaper and the public when this goddamn white elephant is running half empty and everyone still has to wait a month to get a pimple removed from their ass? And, the unions, goddamn it! I'm not going to sit down with them at a hospital meeting to ask their permission to run Mercy."

He glared at Samuel, defying him to disagree. "Dr. Halpern, I may not be able to judge a doctor's credentials, but I can damn well understand a profit-and-loss sheet. Carl is dead right."

"I don't understand all those figures, Mr. Ryan," Samuel said. "Not, at least, as well as you and Dr. Lash. But even if it is all as bad as you say, what do you want from me? I can't pay off your mortgage."

"All I want is for the Executive Committee to understand the board's dilemma. Dr. Amen's application is coming up for you doctors to vote upon next week. I want you to give it extra careful consideration."

"I do that on every application, Mr. Ryan," Samuel replied, his righteous stance serving to irritate the two guests. "I have a vested interest in seeing that only well-qualified people come on the staff."

Ryan looked up helplessly at Lash, then quickly shed the distasteful task, stammering, "We—what I mean—well—Carl can explain it better than I can and I've got to be going." He looked at his watch and gave a reluctant inventory of the room. "Thank you," he said, as Samuel got up to escort him from the room. "Thank Mrs. Halpern for me." Samuel saw him to the door.

"All right," Samuel said directly on returning to the library. "What was that all about? Is the hospital really close to the line?"

"Well, yes and no. Sure the clinic will take patients away from the hospital. The new north wing might even lose a little money. But that's no problem. All Mercy has to do is raise the per diem room rate. You can go to Millsite for an X-ray or for a blood test. But, if you want your appendix out or to have a baby or your veins stripped, you will still have to come in to Mercy. Ryan doesn't know, but the patients aren't going to want to go to Boston, forty miles away, for surgery. So Mercy still has Cromwell where it wants it. Prynne will just jack up the room rate to cover any deficit in the north wing."

"Then what's all this nonsense with Ryan about?"

"Look, Sam," Lash struggled to talk in an easy voice, "I didn't come here on a social visit."

"No, not after ten years."

"I don't want Amen here and I don't want his goddamn clinic. And I don't have to tell you why."

"Tell me anyway."

"Look here, Sam. You are no baby. You and I may not drink together or play golf together, but we both came up the same hard way. I remember our early years, all the good cases going to the big boys, while we were struggling, in debt up to our ass, working for a two-dollar fee. Now the old fuckers are gone, except for a few hangers-on. Mercy is a good hospital . . . a damn good one. *We* are the ones who made it that way. You and I. Not the Ryans or the Prouts or the Bells. And not the Amens!"

Lash put his hand on Samuel's shoulder in as near to a gesture of friendship as he could conjure without the act seeming hypocritical.

"We don't need to race for house calls any longer. Patients come to *us*! We have given the community damn good medicine. Are we ready to give up everything to a bunch of thieves who come into our house in the middle of the night?"

"Is it the future of medicine in Cromwell or your own private practice that stimulates this sincere concern?" Samuel asked, his voice alive with sarcasm.

Lash answered, unflinching. "Both, the same as you, or should I say 'not the same as you'? You've got it both ways."

Samuel was startled by this last remark. "I don't understand."

"Oh, come on now. Don't you?" His voice lunged mean and vicious. "Every doctor on the staff knows that your son is going in with Amen this July. If the clinic succeeds, he's got his oar in there, *your* oar. Stephen can protect your practice and your income. If the clinic fails, he joins you like you have been telling every doctor in the county since he was in diapers. You have this town by the balls, Sam, in more ways than one."

"You make it sound like a sinister plot. Believe me."

"Believing has nothing to do with it. We have watched your son, and his buddy, Amen. It won't work, Sam. If Amen gets privileges, your son won't. If you want your son in town come July, you had better make damn certain that the clinic doesn't get off the ground!"

"Is that a threat?"

"I don't threaten, I just acquaint you with the alternatives. Amen's application will be disapproved by the Executive Committee at their next meeting, with or without your vote. I would hope for your sake, and that of your son's, that it will be with yours too."

Lash's warning had a disturbing effect on Halpern. For his own private reasons, he was in total sympathy with his guest's selfish goals, but he could not see the need for his involvement.

"If you can keep him off the staff, and you are telling me that you have the necessary votes to do exactly that without me, why do you need my help?"

"As Ryan told you, up to now the recommendations of the Executive Committee have always been rubber-stamped by the Board of Trustees. They have never questioned our actions in matters of peer competence."

"Yes. I heard him." Samuel waited for the other shoe to drop.

"Well, I'm afraid we have a problem with Abe Kupperman."

"Abe Kupperman?" Samuel asked puzzled.

"Kupperman is a trustee of the hospital. He represents Jewish money in Cromwell. More important, he wants the clinic set up for his workers. Don't ask me how I've learned, but Kupperman has figures that prove that the medical cost per assembly line worker in Detroit is twenty percent less than the equivalent care in Cromwell. The difference is a Permanente-type clinic with salaried doctors, the kind of program Amen is planning to bring here. Under his contract with the union, Kupperman must buy medical insurance for his three thousand workers and their families. He is convinced that he can save twenty percent a year and get the same if not better medical care from Amen and his prepaid clinic."

"So what? Kupperman can't outvote the entire board. Surely you and Ryan have all the trustees sewed up, just like the Executive Committee."

"Just about," Lash replied with grim satisfaction. "There will be the usual report from the Executive Committee to the board that his application be disapproved."

"On what grounds?"

"Does it really matter? His credentials are spotless. The Executive Committee will then vote out their recommendation to deny privileges. The board will approve the action of the Executive Committee. That's it. All wrapped up nice and neat. Except for one thing."

"What?"

"If you and Kupperman keep your mouths shut."

"You mean that if neither of us asks to see the evidence collected by the Executive Committee that proves beyond a shadow of a doubt that Christopher Amen is unworthy of a staff appointment."

"Should Amen ever take this to a lawyer and legal action be instituted to reverse the decision, it is vital that the collective action of the physicians in judging their peer be unanimous so as to prevent casting any doubt on their . . . 'high-minded wisdom.' "

Samuel kept his counsel for several minutes. He ran his eyes up and down his guest's lean body, weighing the alternatives. "If I refuse?"

Lash did not deign to answer.

"And Abraham Kupperman?"

"That," said Carl Lash, "is *your* baby."

"How?" Samuel asked. "What dossier can you give me to blackmail *him*?"

"You have your finger up his ass, plugging that hole so that his life doesn't leak out. Cancer of the prostate, isn't it? You are keeping him alive or so he thinks. He has told everyone in town that you walk on water. If anyone in his life, you can get him to change his mind. He respects you. You took his balls off, didn't you? The victim always respects the person who castrated him. Yes, Sam, there really should be no trouble there at all. And Sam, I have another thing to tell you before I go. I spoke to Brad Gill on the Nominating Committee. Your name is to be presented at the next annual meeting for president of the medical staff. Your son should be very proud of a father who will be the number-one physician in the community. Quite an honor for you and your wife."

Samuel was appalled by the patent mendacity of the offer from Lash. "The carrot and the stick."

The surgeon ignored the comment. He rose to leave. "Thank your wife for me, will you, Sam? And remember, it is a long way from Milan and from those four flights of stairs in the Flats to Samuel Halpern, Chief of Staff of, how do you say it, a 'goy' hospital?"

Samuel did not look up as his guest left. His thoughts were in turmoil over the events of the past hour. To capitulate to Lash would mean victory over Amen and full possession of his son. But —the price! The hypocrisy that would forever defy expunging from his conscience. He gritted his teeth and shivered at the loathesomeness of the inevitable choice.

Chapter / THIRTY

IF BEA WAS SURPRISED TO RECEIVE LANSING'S TELEPHONE CALL, a casual request for her to spend the day with him in Boston, she did not show it. He offered no advance explanation other than to gratify an old friend's whim. Bea knew well that the proud physician was not a casual person. It was unlikely that any move on his part, however seemingly innocent, was guileless. But, how could she refuse the harmless invitation?

The small, intimate art gallery was a hermetic cocoon, dusky and mute. The only illumination in the room was cast by spotlights focused on the smooth-flowing sculpted figures of bronze and stone.

((209))

Her eyes were drawn by the light that played over the stationary forms like an endless white thread, pulling her around and around, trapping her in the pathos of the creations.

The gaunt gray-haired nurse reached out to stroke gently, oh so gently, the concave thighs, to caress the flowing locks, the angular shoulder blades that contained the imprisoned life. She thought of Lansing, old and alone, and her own similar circumstances, realizing that they were both, by comparison with these inanimate lifeless objects, the more inanimate and lifeless.

"They *are* beautiful."

She looked up in surprise to feel Lansing's hand close over her own.

"She is an amazing artist. You almost forget that they are made out of hard harsh metals and minerals. They look more alive than we, don't they?"

He led her to a small solitary bronze entitled "Two Figures." A man consoling a woman whose head was nestled against his chest, her curved body bent and bowed against his rigid form that thrust upward, erect, angular, sharp. It was pity, joy, consolation, solace—all of these, and yet perhaps none of them at all. Bea stood in awe of the simple casting.

"It is yours," he said. "A gift from me to you."

She looked up at him, afraid to be the guardian of such a potent talisman, which could provoke long-dead emotions to churning in her weary static life. With an insight that vouched for her usual perspicacity, she asked, "Lance, why? Are you trying to bribe me?"

Noting her serious expression, Lancing gave a soft, ingenuous laugh. "Of course, Bea. Doesn't every man who buys an expensive gift for a lovely woman want something in return?"

Lansing reached up and placed his hands on either side of her face and lightly stroked her cheeks. How long was it? Thirty, forty years since he had done that to her?

Was it possible that this aging, tremulous man, who like her had lived alone and apart, passing through time as through an endless corridor, could at one time have actually possessed the flame of a young virile body, touching, writhing, tumescent, penetrating, without shame or inhibition? Could she recreate that lust of youth which so wonderfully masqueraded as love?

She tried to sharpen the focus of those elusive time-bleached memories. It was no good. All that remained was a faded negative, a fossilized depression in the storehouse of her memories. Fossils. Yes, that is what they both were now, two human beings who once had orgasms, but today lingered like empty seed pods. Bea saw the determined expression on his face and abandoned the ineffectual gesture of refusal.

During the ride back to Cromwell Lansing would cast an occasional glance at her, noting the distant expression on her face. She would respond with a smile that clung to him like an amulet of good luck for his future purpose.

There were times over the years when it was hard for him to think of her as anything more than a fixture in his medical life. And yet now, when his back was to the wall, why had he turned to her? Perhaps that instinctive fact signified that there existed a bond between the two of them that he would not have dared to countenance openly. Even if that were true, had he the right to ask her to betray herself in the name of that ancient artifact?

When they returned to Cromwell, Bea invited Lansing up to her apartment for a cup of coffee.

Bea moved to sit next to him and watched him drink the dark, hot liquid. It was obvious to her that her guest was deeply troubled.

Finally, Lansing asked, "Bea, you know that I came here today to ask something of you, don't you?"

"I do, Lance. It wasn't hard to come to that conclusion. We haven't spent a day together like this in so many years, I am ashamed I cannot even remember." She reached across to clasp his hand. "But, you know, Lansing, you didn't have to wine and dıne me and give me expensive gifts, if you needed my help." She shook her head slowly. "No, Lance, a long time ago, you gave me a gift that has always entitled you to a reciprocal claim."

Lansing's eyes narrowed as he tried to recall what he had given her.

Bea gave a soft, throaty laugh. "But tell me what I can do for you."

His words halting, his gestures hesitant, Lansing Prout told her of his fears for his future in Mercy. The rumors that a cabal was attempting to remove him from the staff. The steady undercurrent of innuendo and threat that this time was sufficient to alarm him.

"But, Lance," Bea said, "they tried to attack you before. I remember. When Dr. Lash first came to Cromwell. Nothing happened. Nothing at all."

"No, Bea, this time, this time it is different. There is something frightening going on. I wake up in the middle of the night shaking with fear, my heart pounding, covered with sweat because I do not know what it is."

"Lance, haven't you even a clue?"

"Not a one. I don't know. Believe me, I have tried to figure it out but I keep coming up against a stone wall. Bea, I'm scared. I know I am old. Maybe I should have retired years ago. But what else can I do if I can't get up each morning and come into the hospital to see my patients, to talk with the families, the nurses, the orderlies. To be needed. To be active. Alive. Take all that away, and what do I have?"

"I know, Lance, how you feel. Don't you think that is the reason I never took early retirement? What would I do? Sit here, constipated and arthritic, and water my plants? No, Lance. I, if anybody, know how much we both need Mercy."

"Bea, when the day comes I must leave, let me walk out on my own feet, voluntarily, with my head held high. Not thrown out by my tail like a dead rat."

Bea knew Lansing had appealed to her, knowing that nurses had access to channels of information denied the most powerful medical hierarchy. When he finally rose to leave, she promised that she would try to find out what he wanted to know.

It did not take Bea long the next day to ferret out the lethal forces gathering together to destroy the man who had asked her for help. She learned of Dr. Abels's clandestine nocturnal activity from a file clerk in the archives, and of his final report, a Xeroxed copy of which she obtained from the newest secretary in the Administrator's office. She could not resist that impulse to read and learn for herself, documented in morbid detail, the death of a surgeon.

When she had finished she laid the sheets down on the table and stared at them. Her features were ashen as she reached for the telephone to summon Lansing to her apartment. Yet something held her back from making the call. Was it loyalty to the profession whose garb she wore, whose tenets and ethics she had sworn to uphold and practice? Oh, Lance, she cried to herself, you can't continue to hurt and maim patients even if such actions are without malice or premeditation. Innocence alone cannot condone exercise of tarnished talent. How else to force you to recognize that painful fact?

But, to ask him to retire to potting plants? Yes, that was the true tragedy. Give up medicine, the skeletal framework of his life, and what was left? Even if she could have resolved that conflict, what about the other?

Could she turn her face away from Lansing who alone of all the people in her life had given her that precious gift, the memory of love? True, it was old and faded, but whatever its shape or form or weight or size, it existed and could not be extinguished until the moment of her death. Could she deny the donor now that he had returned after forty years for her help?

But if she forewarned him to take saving action, what then about her oath as a nurse and her responsibility to the patients she had sworn to help?

When Lansing finally came to her late that evening, he did not open the thick manila envelope Bea gave him. He could see from the nurse's drawn and anguished expression what her charitable act had cost. Even his impassioned thanks failed to evoke a reaction on her part.

He paused on the threshold and turned to face her. For an instant, Bea felt that he was going to reach out and kiss her. She held her breath, realizing that the impetuous act would perilously drain whatever remained of her composure and self-confidence. Instead, to her relief, he just whispered her name and left. She stood in the deserted doorway watching him make his unsteady way down the corridor until she could no longer hear his footsteps on the cement steps below.

In some unexplained way she felt suddenly free of Lansing. That she had paid him back, reciprocated in some mysterious fashion, for the favor he had once given her. A debt now stamped "paid in full" with forty years compound interest.

As she moved back into the apartment, she realized that the rooms felt empty. She was conscious of that stain on her code of honor—a painful burden she would have to bear to her dying day.

She saw with a terrible clarity that, in helping Prout, she had substituted for the bittersweet memory that had sustained her only a guilty void.

. . . And Bea cried, for she knew at that moment that she would always hate Lansing for having compelled her to make the unprofitable exchange.

Chapter / **THIRTY-ONE**

IN ITS LONGEST LABOR OF THE YEAR, THE EARTH HAD FINALLY tugged away from the sun and Cromwell lay in the cooling embrace of approaching night. Samuel Halpern excused himself to his two seated guests and opened wide the French doors leading to the garden. He stood in the threshold refreshed by the rustling breezes that fled by him. "It's not quite the same as the fire escape on Avenue C, is it, Sam?" a subdued voice asked.

"Did you know, Sylvia," Abe Kupperman said, "that Sam's family and mine lived on the same block on Avenue C in the East Side of New York? We never knew each other, of course. I was ten years older than Sam. By the time your husband entered P.S. 116 on Houston Street, I was already selling rags for Seiler and Son in Fall River."

"You are right, Abe." Samuel moved into the room to take his seat by his wife. "On nights like this, I find it hard to turn on the air-conditioner. I think of crawling out on the fire escape with only my underwear on to catch a breeze to sleep. It wasn't always like this. You remember, don't you, Abe?"

Abraham Kupperman nodded in agreement. He was a short, thin man in his seventies. His head was balding with a few gray and white strands plastered across the glistening top. His face was covered with a texture of close-shaven white whiskers and irregular wrinkles and crevasses. His expression was perceptive and friendly, but with sharp searching eyes. His manner quick, alert, and functional.

His wife, Jennie, was plump and cheerful, her hair bleached blonde. She sat close to her husband, holding hands with him like a teen-ager. Her face, round and smiling, contained a full measure of affection honed by the awful truth that his tenure by her side was a fragile one.

"How many years, Sam, have we sat together drinking coffee?" Abe asked.

"Now, Abe," Sylvia said, "please don't make it sound like we are getting old."

"Sylvia, we are getting old. I remember Stephen's briss. Now he's married and soon you will look forward to grandchildren." He shivered slightly. "As for Jennie and me—we can't even do that anymore." His eyes watered over. "Sam, I still can't accept it. David. Only one son I had. And he was shot in Korea. Why, Sam? Why? What did I do? I don't cheat. I help the poor. I am faithful to my wife. I treat my workers right. Ask them. Ask them. No son. Nobody to leave my life's work to. When Jennie and I . . . that is the end of everything."

"Abe," Sylvia said, "you know as long as Sam and I are here, you and Jennie will never be alone."

"Abe," Jennie said, "remember, we came over here to visit friends, not to make them cry."

"Yes, you are right, of course, Jennie. Sam, you said you had something to discuss with me. What was it? Does it concern Stephen?"

Before Sam could answer, Sylvia took Mrs. Kupperman by the hand. "Jennie, come," she nodded in the direction of the two seated men, "I think the big thinkers want to be alone." With a pat upon the knees of their respective husbands, the two women left the room.

Abe was the first of the two men to speak. "All right, Sammie, what do you want to talk about first? Christopher Amen and his clinic down at Millsite? Or," he gave his host a devilish grin, "his application for Mercy privileges, which is going to be squashed next week?"

"You old faker," Sam sad with a sigh of relief, "you know everything, don't you?"

"I don't have to be an Einstein to know what's going on. You would think that the whole town was going to vote on whether they wanted the Resurrection. You are the only one as far as I know who should be asking me, who hasn't." He settled back in his corner of the sofa, like a caliph interviewing a penitent. "Now, Sammie," he said, "it is your turn."

"I don't know what to say," Halpern said.

"I know what is going on. You doctors," Abe said disparagingly, "are suddenly faced with a little competition. You have some young Turks coming in with a new product. You don't like it. Maybe I wouldn't either, if I were you. Nobody likes competition. It is not profitable. The proper question is, should medicine *ever* be profitable? Should not a doctor give up the profit motive in return for his exalted status and special powers over his fellow man?" His brow wrinkled in thought. "Like . . . like . . . a priest gives up sex in return for the keys of heaven and hell? What do physicians give up in return? Nothing. You have your cake and eat it, too."

It seemed to Samuel that his friend was being deliberately provocative. He felt an increasing disquiet as Abe continued.

"Money. Position. Respect. Even more, the power of life and death. Sam, did you ever stop to realize that judges and doctors are the only people in our society who can take life with impunity? Even at Auschwitz, it was rare for an S.S. doctor to take the life of an *untermenschen* he was sworn to exterminate if he knew he was a fellow physician. What does your elite class give up in return for all of this?

"I have heard it all," Abe said, stopping Sam before he began to answer. "Four years of college. Four years of medical school. Years of internship and residency. Night after night without sleep. Marrying late. So what? Big deal! Who wouldn't give their right arm, sell their mothers into slavery, for such an opportunity? I cried because I had to leave school and get a job. What worker on my assembly line wouldn't give up his life of sweating in my plant to escape and become a doctor like you? Do they have a choice? Did they ever have the choice? I have counted all the tears of misery each successful doctor drops automatically like a dog at a fire hydrant. So what? You sons of bitches are lucky. God gave you the opportunity to work hard and struggle and succeed. He gave you the chance to sweat and learn. All of us sweat, but not all of us end up with golden sweat like you. And what do you doctors do? I went to a doctor, that bastard Prout, for nine months with my cancer spreading. All I got was pills. He told me I was overworked. Too much tension. I trusted him. I didn't ask for another opinion. *He was my doctor!* My life was in his hands! I wouldn't dare to question.

"Sure, Sam, *you* healed me. You are a physician, like Prout. How did you come to help? If you hadn't been in the Emergency Room when I came in unconscious, I might never have known the difference. You saw me in a coma. You diagnosed the cancer. The uremia. I still have the cancer, but I am alive. For how long? I don't know. You don't know. None of us do. I am alive for as long as your penis-drooping pills will work. What then? Should I praise you? To do that I must first damn Prout. Should I do that? Should I do neither?"

As he stood there, the inner conflicts played across his countenance like a flickering fire, seething inside as his personal tragedy rose to choke him.

"Now, you tell me what to do in this case, Sam. Should I go along with Ryan and his cover-up? Stab Amen in the back? Allow you to crucify him? You know we have a great reputation for crucifying those who have really come to help us. Or should I raise a stink, contact Amen and advise him to get a lawyer? Tell them to subpoena the records and blow the whole stinking mess sky-high? You tell me, Sam. I will do anything you say. Sam, you have a chit on me. Pull on it . . . hard . . . and I will cover."

"I . . . really . . ." Sam said, unable to answer his old friend. Kupperman, in his own way, had exposed the hypocrisy at the core of his being.

"No, Sam," Abe drove on. "No bullshit! Don't con me. I am not Ryan. Don't try to explain your motives. Just tell me what I should do. I will do it and never ask you why. I owe you, Sam. Collect! Damn it! Collect!"

Sam broke his silence. "I . . . I don't know what to say."

"I don't expect you to say anything, Sam," Abe replied. "I know what is eating at you. But do you know what is eating at me?" He did not wait for an answer. "The clinic. That's what. Do you realize how many of my workers can't get a doctor to come to their home when they are sick? All right, you say that house calls are obsolete. The doctor can do more if the patient comes to the hospital. So be it. Why, then, when they come to the Emergency Ward, do they have to wait for hours while some stupid clerk tries to find their family doctor who has signed out to his answering service and can't be found? Why can't the hospital doctor sitting right there take care

((219))

of the patient? I will tell you. I know why. I sit on the board. So that the private doctor won't lose control of his patient. They hold on to their patients like chattels—or serfs—or worse."

He waved Samuel back. "Forget the Emergency Ward for a minute. Do you know how long it takes to get an office appointment with one of you doctors in the Highlands? How many of them won't take on any new patients? How many new executives I have hired who have moved to Cromwell and can't get a doctor to take care of their families?

"And what have you done? Brought in new physicians? God, no!" he exclaimed. "You raised your fees. Take off Wednesday to play golf. Keep everybody else out of town who wants to come here to practice. Sure, the hospital is better than it was twenty years ago, and sure the patients get better treatment.

"But if you don't improve medicine, then who should? You deserve a gold medal for doing your job? We pay for it. And damn well! Answer me, Sam. I am your friend." He held out his hand, but the doctor kept his arms clenched tightly to his sides. "No, don't. Don't say anything. So Amen won't hold the patient's hand and pat him on the ass. But remember, his clinic will see anyone twenty-four hours a day, whether he can afford it or not."

"That's true, Abe, but answer me, who is going to foot the bill?"

"I will tell you. The taxpayer—as always. Hell. What's wrong with that? He pays for everything else in this world. Why shouldn't the taxpayer and the government pay for medical care? What is so sacred that the dollars should go only to the doctors and leave it up to them to decide how to disperse it? Sam, in the last analysis, the clinic is here because someone feels that there is a need you haven't fulfilled. If you had, Dr. Amen would never have dreamed of coming to Cromwell. Remember, Sam, he and his Millsite Clinic are here because of your deliberate and selfish neglect.

"Now, Sam," Abe paused in the threshold, potent and taunting, "tell me what I should do. How shall I vote next week? I don't want to die owing anything to any man on earth."

He took his two hands and pulled them viciously up into his crotch, giving his body a savage twist.

"You gave me life when you took off my testicles. Now, Sam, tell me. What do you want in return?"

Chapter / THIRTY-TWO

SAMUEL HALPERN FORCED AN ARTIFICIAL SMILE AS HE ADVANCED toward the frail recumbent figure on the hospital bed.

"How are you feeling today, Mrs. Dearing?"

She nodded wanly at him and held her hand out. He grasped it, startled when his fingers encountered the cold, hard metallic apparatus that had been installed on her right forearm. Partially concealed by a sterile gauze pad were the two polyethylene cannulae that penetrated the skin on the underside of her arm just above the wrist. Each tube was permanently inserted into her body, the red tagged tube into her radial artery and the blue tagged tube into the reciprocal vein. Both catheters ended in a stainless-steel plate with two projecting nipples. The whole apparatus was sutured to her flesh, as if the wasted human being it was coupled to was part of some bizarre scientific experiment. Patient and doctor tried hard not to break visual contact, fearful that the fragile gesture would somehow spill open a Pandora's box of questions.

Samuel sat down on the side of the bed and indicated his desire to inspect her recent incision. He slowly took down the dressing. The incision was still red and angry. He could see the two rows of pink puncture marks on each side of the surgical cut where the skin stitches had broken the surface.

Halpern ran his fingers up and down the length of the incision, pressing firmly. It was healing well. There were no blood clots, abscesses, or gaps where the underlying muscles might have pulled away from each other in the regenerative process. The pressure made the patient wince and the doctor apologized.

Samuel ran his eyes lower and checked the placement of the dark rubber nephrostomy tube that exited from a separate stab opening two inches below the surgical wound. The tube was sewn to the skin with heavy black silk thread that, despite the best care of the nurses, was encrusted with dried serum and blood and small blebs of purulent exudate. The catheter was about eight inches long and connected to a transparent plastic drainage tube that ran into a flat polyethylene bag clamped to the side rail of the bed. Samuel followed the path of the tubing to its final termination. Despite two weeks of use, the bag was clean, sparkling, and empty.

The nurse standing behind him watched the pantomime without making a sound. She had seen the urologist carry out this identical ritual every morning for two weeks with the same result. Nothing. The kidney still failing to produce any urine. She looked at the doctor with unspoken admiration. He wouldn't give up. How much longer could he keep coming into this room with his false bravado, knowing that the patient was fully aware of the lack of improvement? The slight woman resigned to another twenty-four hours of life granted to her by the artificial twin-coil kidney that purified her blood every third day. Her arm coupled to a large cold monster the size of a washing machine. A leech that sucked out the red blood of her body, defiled with poisons and waste products, only to regurgitate it, cleansed and pure, until another day's worth of life would pollute it once again.

And so it went. Day after day, with only hope, that ephemeral glue, to fasten the patient to her precarious existence. Dr. Halpern, each morning, cheerful and optimistic, until he had left and closed the door behind him. Each visit, the patient afraid to ask *the* question for fear of receiving *the* answer. Would she ever be a normal person without that umbilical attachment she bore on her right forearm, like a stigma of servitude, a brand of death?

Samuel reached behind him. He took a sterile plastic basin and filled it from the bottle of saline on the table. He opened up a second sterile package and removed what resembled a large kitchen basting syringe. He quickly drew up one ounce of saline. With his other hand, he uncoupled the red catheter from the drainage tubing and inserted the end of the syringe into the catheter. He injected about half an ounce of fluid through the catheter deep into the heart of the kidney. The sudden influx of fluid distended the kidney and caused a momentary cry of pain. He smiled to reassure her. She smiled back. Mirror reflections of two dissembling symbols.

Slowly . . . ever so slowly . . . he aspirated and withdrew the instilled fluid, letting it run back into the bulb. He bent his head down to see more clearly. Nothing. He held the syringe up to the light. Nothing. He lowered the syringe to compare against the white sheet of the bed. Nothing. The fluid that had returned was as transparent and crystalline as the fluid that he had injected.

Damn! He swore to himself. Then he quickly flashed another optimistic grin to the tremulous patient who was monitoring his expression, her breath held in anticipation. When would the fluid come back dirty? Tainted with the life-giving yellow of a functioning kidney? Sullied with the vile amber of excreta? Contaminated with the wondrous filth that each one of God's creatures must throw out into the world each day, to soil his environment, if he is to survive?

He replaced the syringe and reconnected the nephrostomy tube to the drainage bag once more. He drew the lightweight blue blanket up over the patient's waist. He reached for her hand again.

"Not yet, Laurie," he said. "Soon . . . soon. You know it takes a long time. Usually many weeks. Sometimes even months. Don't worry. Everything will be all right. Your incision has healed well. Your electrolytes are in good order. As soon as we can make arrangements for the outpatient dialysis, you will be able to go home."

Tears collected in the corners of her eyes.

"Now . . . now . . . everything is going to be all right." He stood up, realizing how futile any other gesture would be. He backed away from the bed and fled to the crowded corridor outside the room. He took the chart from the nurse's hand.

"Nothing?" he asked, as his eyes skimmed down the vital statistics tabulated on the daily output sheets.

"Nothing, Dr. Halpern. You have there the last three eight-hour reports. Nothing, except maybe five cc on the eleven-to-seven shift last night."

Samuel handed her back the chart. Five cc in eight hours. God! She should have been putting out that much in five minutes. He shook his head. Two weeks. What lies he had been feeding the poor woman.

The kidney had been dead for months, blocked by Flaherty's sutures. Never had he seen a kidney come back after even three weeks of total obstruction. Four months! How much longer could he keep up the charade? Who would be the first to blink, to break down and confess the futility of hope?

With that unanswered question drilling painfully through his subconscious, he took in a deep breath and quickened his pace. He had yet to complete the last and most difficult part of his daily ritual . . . Mr. Dearing.

Chapter / THIRTY-THREE

MR. DEARING WAS PACING, IMPATIENTLY, IN THE SMALL TREAT-ment room off the Ward Six nursing station. In contrast to his wife's sickly appearance, Frederick Dearing was imposing both in appearance and attitude.

He wasted no time. He stuck his hand out imperiously, then said, "Laurie. You have seen her this morning?" The question was more a statement of fact than one of inquiry. "Well? Any change?" He dared Samuel to respond.

"Nothing, Mr. Dearing. Five cc, maybe, the last shift. I doubt, though, whether it really means anything."

Mr. Dearing let his glasses slide down the thin, slightly crooked bridge of his nose, staring at the physician over the top of the lenses. "Then, Dr. Halpern, what do you do next?"

Samuel averted Dearing's piercing glance, hoping to deflect the urgency of that hostile question. He walked slowly around the table to take a chair in the corner of the cramped room. He sat back, his expression noncommittal, trying to maintain the pose of the clinically detached consultant. It was not his fault that Mrs. Dearing was dying. He was not the one who had sutured the ureter shut. Yet Dearing stood rigid and fixed in the center of the room, waiting for him to answer.

He could see the fateful words as clearly as if it was only yesterday. Simon Pirie's own words. Cold, impartial, impersonal. "Linear refractile bundles of collagen. Elements of transitional cell mucosa, muscularis and adventitial tissue surrounded by interspersed granulation tissue and fibrosis." Very fancy words for degenerating catgut suture, which Ralph Flaherty with his two ripening cataracts had placed in and on and around and through and over and under and every which way to occlude, mutilate, and destroy that right ureter, and, with it, Mrs. Dearing, now waiting in the next room, being prepared for her trip down to the subbasement for six long hours in a windowless room, seeing and hearing and smelling nothing but the sight and noise of her urine being sifted painlessly from her body's blood so that she could come back upstairs for dinner, to eat more food, to redeposit the foul urea back in her bloodstream. Samuel shuddered.

"Well?" Mr. Dearing said, his face twisted with hate. "What do you do next?"

"Just as I have told you, Mr. Dearing. There is nothing we can do. Nothing at all. Just wait." He stood up to face the husband. "What do you want me to do? Stop the dialysis? Disconnect the cannulae in her arm? Pull out the nephrostomy tube?" His voice rose higher in pitch, flinging the bloody gauntlet back at its unforgiving donor. He was angry. What did the bastard want? He couldn't give her another kidney. Did he want him to kill his wife?

Suddenly, overwhelmed by the vehemence of Samuel's attack, Mr. Dearing drew back. His shoulders drooped, caving in his chest. His face looked sickly and wet. His breathing was labored and heavy. He felt his way to a chair with clumsy steps and sat down. He looked up at the doctor, his eyes pleading for succor.

"It's been almost two weeks. Still nothing. How much longer can it last, Dr. Halpern? How much longer?"

Samuel felt a wave of pity flood over him. Was his private anger, his instinctive dislike for the husband, an expression of his own impotence, a feeling of inadequacy in seeing his patient slip toward death without his being able to arrest the relentless process? He rose and placed his arm around the man's shoulder to comfort him. "I don't know," he consoled. "I really don't know."

"Dr. Halpern, how could such a thing happen? I mean, isn't there, wasn't there something that Flaherty could have done to avoid tying off her right ureter during the hysterectomy?"

"I am not a gynecologist, Mr. Dearing. That is a hard question for me to answer. Sometimes in my own field, we run into severe bleeding during what should be a simple case. We put in stitches frantically, almost blindly, to stop the blood loss. I suppose it is possible for Dr. Flaherty to have tied off the ureter in all good faith and innocence in his attempt to control a life-threatening hemorrhage."

He paused to recall. "I read his operative note. Endometriosis can be a very bloody process. The uterus was plastered up against the ureter and other vital structures in the pelvis. It is possible to snare a ureter without knowing it."

"OK. OK," the man interrupted. "Maybe I can buy that. But, later . . ." He stared at the urologist. "What you did two weeks ago, removing the obstruction and reconnecting the ureter. What if that had been done right after the hysterectomy? You know, several days or even a week after the operation. The kidney wouldn't have been damaged." Samuel could see the signs of busy cerebration in the seated man. "Yes, why didn't you operate then?"

The question hung pregnant in the air. Samuel looked at the husband, admiring his perspicacity. Dearing was too smart not to have come upon that cropper sooner or later. The physician had wondered over the past two weeks when the husband or even the wife would have happened upon that very logical question—and asked for the answer. "We didn't know the ureter was compromised," was the guarded reply.

"But there were tests, the I.V.P. Why didn't Flaherty order a set of kidney X-rays after the hysterectomy?" he demanded. "Wouldn't it have shown the ureter to have been blocked off then and allowed you to operate?"

"Yes, Mr. Dearing. It would have. But," he protested, "there was no reason to order the films."

"No reason? The butcher strangled one of the kidneys. Wasn't that reason enough?" His face was red and belligerent.

"No, Mr. Dearing," Samuel replied, unruffled by the outburst, "your wife was still putting out urine. How was anyone to know that it was coming only from her left kidney? Kidneys are funny things. When one is obstructed or damaged, the other one automatically takes over the work of both. The patient may never know. Your wife's left kidney was doing the work of two organs. If, however, Dr. Flaherty had tied off both ureters, Laurie would not have put out any urine at all, and then . . ." he shrugged his shoulders helplessly, "we would have suspected."

"It's ironic, isn't it, Dr. Halpern? If Flaherty had blocked both kidneys, you would have been called in immediately to repair both sides and my wife would still be alive today."

"She is still alive, Mr. Dearing. Don't forget that."

"Alive? Being connected to a steel tank the rest of your life? You tell me. Is that what you would call being alive?"

Samuel could not deny the justice of the man's accusation. There was nothing he could say.

"Dr. Halpern, you claimed that there was no valid reason to order the kidney X-rays after the hysterectomy, even though you stated that the test would have easily demonstrated the obstruction." He groped for the right words. "If the surgeon had recognized that he was having trouble with bleeding and that controlling the hemorrhage might have resulted in an inadvertent stitch catching that urine tube, why then not get the I.V.P. *anyway* just to be safe? Isn't that ever done?"

Dearing was nobody's fool. Samuel made a mental note that the lawyer had an intuitive grasp of problems, even medical ones, replete with foreign terminology. If he ever needed a lawyer, Dearing was the man to hire.

"Yes, Mr. Dearing. I am sure that Dr. Flaherty thought of that." Like hell! Flaherty hadn't thought in years. "However, there is a serious risk to getting an I.V.P."

"What kind of a risk?"

"Death. To do an I.V.P. we must inject a chemical into the bloodstream. About two ounces of an iodinated organic compound. Some people are acutely sensitive to the dye. It can cause what we call anaphylactic shock. The person's heart and lungs will stop and the person will be dead within minutes."

"How high is the risk, Dr. Halpern?"

"Well, it is a low risk, of course. Hundreds of thousands, maybe even millions of I.V.P.'s get done each year in the United States. But there are deaths every day."

"Can't you test to see if the patient is allergic to the dye?"

"Yes, Mr. Dearing, you can test the patient to see if he or she is allergic to the drug by injecting a few drops of the chemical into the patient's bloodstream before giving the patient the main dose. However, just as many people go into anaphylactic shock and die from the test dose as from the I.V.P. itself." He spread his hands in front of him. "So, most places don't even test. They just give the dye—the full slug—and hope."

A poker face, Samuel thought. It was as if another Dearing was sitting behind the one he was talking to, taking notes and stacking ammunition.

"Let me understand, Dr. Halpern. You agree that the X-ray would have revealed the problem, but that there would have been a serious risk to order the study. Yet, not to order the X-rays has led, in this case, to certain death, anyway." He paused and leaned forward, resting his elbows on the table. "Aren't you really telling me that it is a question of weighing one risk against another?"

"Yes, Mr. Dearing, you could put it that way. It is a balance of risks."

"Then I would assume that the physician would have to sit down and weigh the risks impartially?"

"Yes, he would."

"I would assume, then, that it would behoove the doctor to search carefully, very carefully, for even the slightest information that would aid him in deciding which set of risks to pursue."

"Yes, it would," Samuel admitted reluctantly.

"Dr. Halpern. If there was some evidence, some clue that could have helped the physician to make that fatal decision whether or not to get the I.V.P. when the indications, up to then, were fifty-fifty, then the doctor should have relied upon that data, that minuscule fact, in his final decision? Am I correct?"

"Yes."

"And if such clinical evidence, a chance physical sign, a fleeting symptom, a laboratory number, was available and the doctor did not recognize it, or, recognizing it, did not act upon it and made the wrong decision, then, in your considered judgment, would he be in error?"

Samuel had followed the laborious question closely. He also knew with a sinking feeling in his stomach what the answer had to be. An answer that he was certain Dearing already possessed. A checkmate consummated irrevocably twenty moves in advance of the opening white pawn to king's four.

Samuel knew that somewhere, somehow, Ralph Flaherty must have missed some vital clue, one that Joe Brandon had found. The physician looked into the gray-green irises of his interrogator, a wave of nausea mounting in his throat.

"Yes, Mr. Dearing," he said. "He would be in error."

Chapter / **THIRTY-FOUR**

LYMAN BELL TRIED HARD NOT TO MOVE. ALTHOUGH HIS MAN-servant had placed his lawn chair to catch the shadows of the nearby Lombardy poplars, that futile gesture could not hold back the rivers of heat that flooded over him this transparent June morning.

He could hear the cacophony of insect legs and wings rasping as they signaled their urgency for a matinal mate, and in the distance, the steady synchrony of lawn mowers cutting his acres of verdure. He could smell the fertile scent of cut vegetation lying as a pungent blanket of green around him. The heat was oppressive.

Even his clothes at this early hour were wilting in the summer dampness.

How long had he been alone? Minutes? Days? He tried to recall his tenuous link with the past, so as to prove, by lineal progression, his existence in the present. But the fact of his wife's death, the existence of his two daughters, married, with children, living far apart, all seemed as alien to him as the smells in his nostrils and the pressures on his skin.

Had it always been like this? He could not tell. That would require a cognition he was not sanguine enough to conjure up this slow, weary day. He let out his breath with a long sigh and for the thousandth time, meticulously inventoried the tight dimensions of his claustrophobic and solitary world.

Lyman Bell was an old man. Everything about him argued that conclusion. He was small, not more than five feet six inches; his face was covered with a uniform etching of fine-patterned wrinkles. Both eyes, when he would open them, were watery and the edges of the eyelids swollen and reddened; the skin of his face hung loosely under his chin and neck, and fell away in pleats. Even his hands shared this degenerative stigma. The creases and folds were redundant and loose. The veins dilated, turgid, bulging out from under the translucent dry scaling skin, threatening at the slightest prick to flood his arms with rivers of dilute blue ink. Only his hair was striking, a stark white thicket that lay neatly parted to one side, dense, pure, and solid.

From his chair Bell could see the lawn flow away in successive terraces until, far beyond his field of vision, it terminated at the filigreed iron gates that announced the threshold of the Bell estate. Water cascaded downward in white flashes, from fountain to fountain, following the layered terraces.

The dogwood trees remained blurred patches of white and pink like two-dimensional smears of pastel chalk. The Bell house itself was an exact copy of Josephine's *Malmaison*. In his youth, Lyman had seen the original of his ancestral home and loved whatever had been the quirk or eccentricity of the second Bell of his heritage that had inspired its reproduction here, overlooking the polluted Quabbin River.

Lyman Bell sat there, eyes closed, savoring the delicate equilibrium between his soft, pink, wrinkled carapace and the gentle zephyrs that rippled the glassy surface of the air. He was suddenly aware of a cool double shadow that lay across him. He opened his eyes and smiled to see the standing frame of his lifelong friend and now one of his last remaining companions.

"Lyman," Lansing Prout greeted the peaceful figure. "It is good to see you again."

For a time, both men sat next to each other in silence, steeped in the invasive summer day. When finally they did speak, it was with gentle phrases to evoke wistful wisps of memorabilia, which lingered only long enough to leave a fragrant mental scent. Although their conversation gracefully pirouetted like a formal minuet, Lyman thought he could detect a note of tenseness.

"What is it, Lance?" Lyman asked. "Tell me what is troubling you."

Lansing relaxed a trifle. Those who from afar demeaned Lyman Bell as a senile has-been were so wrong. His mind, beneath his failing frame, was as alert as back in 1928, when he had sold the Bell Mills, thus preserving the family fortune from the ensuing bankruptcy of the textile industry in New England during the Depression.

"Lyman," he began hesitatingly, "they want to remove me from the Mercy staff."

"Why, Lance?" Bell asked, his voice reflecting both curiosity and concern. "Why would they want to do that?"

"Well, it all started when some patient, some old diabetic died during an emergency operation. Really, though, that had nothing to do with it. Nobody could have saved him. But that's not the issue. That is not the reason they are trying to throw me off the staff. It is just an excuse. A whole lot of nonsense. Why," he laughed weakly, "they can go over that case with a fine-tooth comb. Nobody could have helped that dissecting aneurysm. Nobody, not even La——" He stopped short, hoping that his host had not heard him too clearly.

Bell watched his companion, appraising his awkward, halting, inconsistent rambling discourse. A wave of pity spread over him. He didn't honestly understand all of what Lansing was trying to tell him. But did it really matter? Prout was old, just like him. He had done a good job, made his reputation. Time had come to visit and was standing over him, fidgeting and impatient.

"Lance, I am sure that nobody really blames you for the death of that patient, whoever he was." He looked innocently into his old friend's eyes. "Tell me, Lance. What do you *really* think is behind this unfortunate affair?"

"It is a plot, Lyman. Yes, it is a plot. Abels is behind it. He is the one responsible for the lies."

"Abels?" Bell asked. "I don't recall any doctor by that name. I thought I knew every physician who practiced in Cromwell. Who is this Dr. Abels?"

"He doesn't practice. I mean, he doesn't have an office. He is the anesthesiologist at Mercy. He works for the hospital. He has maliciously complained to the Executive Committee about me," Prout blurted out. "He is the one who is trying to get them to suspend my privileges."

"Now, now, Lance," Bell said. "You know that they cannot do that. Not as long as I am on the board. But what does this man have against you?"

"Lyman, I once called him a 'dirty Jew.' It was nothing important." He rushed to clean out the distasteful details. "He was harassing me several years ago when he first came to Mercy, and he just wouldn't let go . . . let go . . ."

Lyman gave an involuntary shudder at the slur. It was not that Bell was pro-Semitic, nor, for that matter, anti-Semitic. He had spent his entire life carefully nurturing a select position that would negate even the remotest exposure to any situation where he would be forced to be anti- or pro- anything.

However, as he looked at his unhappy, agitated friend of almost three quarters of a century, Lyman could not quell his feeling of outrage that Prout, despite his probable failing powers as a healer, should be attacked so viciously for what must, in the last analysis, be only a thoughtless, ill-advised comment. There were some things even an old man could do to help correct an obvious injustice.

He was the richest man in Cromwell. For fifty years he had acquired chits. Now perhaps he should redeem some of those obligations to help a close friend.

"Lance," Bell reassured, "do not worry. Let me see what I can do. We have been friends too long for anything that hurts you not to wound me, too. Why . . . why . . ." he asked fervently, "did you even hesitate to ask?"

Lyman rose from his chair to shake the hand of his guest. He watched the slowly departing figure of Lansing Prout climb the gentle terraces to the driveway. Then, with resurrected strength, Bell accurately registered the retreating shadows and moved his own chair the necessary two and a half feet into the cool shade.

Chapter / **THIRTY-FIVE**

THE WIND DIED ALL OF A SUDDEN. STEPHANIE SMILED TO SEE
Chris look up with alarm as the jib sheet fell loose in his hands.
The boat lost its acute heeling angle and snapped up, throwing
him into the cockpit. He pointed to the mast, indicating the lax
fluttering of the mainsail. Up until a moment ago its broad white
expanse had bulged with an invisible fifteen-knot wind that had
propelled the boat rapidly out of sight of land.

Stephanie looked about her. The surface of the water was now
smooth and glassy without even a single matte patch to fingerprint

a lonely breeze. The telltales hung limply against the shrouds. She held a hand out to help her companion scramble back onto his seat, then dropped the sails.

"The wind dies down about two o'clock," she explained. "I guess there is nothing to do but have lunch. If you will take the tiller for a minute, I will get out the food."

Chris rose to take her place as she maneuvered to let him toward the stern of the boat. As she passed he reached out and clasped her in a firm embrace. For an instant she stiffened at the raw physical contact. She could smell the lingering mixture of drying salt and sweat that clung to his body as her head grazed his neck.

He did not say anything, but held her immobile. She could not move, but waited, breathless. He pulled her higher, forcing her to stand on her tiptoes as he kissed her. Her lips opened wide, their tongues explored the interiors of their mouths as their bodies ground together, pelvis against pelvis.

It had been two weeks since that night she had wrenched herself free from his arms. Even now, she could not excuse that irrational act. It was more than just fear of starting an affair and then finding herself rejected. He had not tried again, although she could tell the longing in his eyes and the frustrating ache in his groin. All the following evenings, as they talked until dawn, exchanging memories and childhoods and adult lives and dreams, she would see his almost frantic compulsion to make love to her. She could visualize Chris alone in his motel room afterward, ashamed and angry, relieving his painful tumescence. But what could she do? She could not, *would* not start a relationship and hurt him as she had Barry.

Now he released her, allowing her passion to subside. Without a word, she continued her way to the cabin, to get their lunch.

The molten reflection of sun on water mirrored back into the boat, surrounding them with white heat. The backs of her shoulders began to pinch and itch as the beads of sweat gathered, coalesced, and ran down her arms. She could see the perspiration condense on the coarse hair of Chris's legs and chest. Suddenly Stephanie scrambled onto the deck and threw the anchor over the bow. She pointed to a small rise of land far off in the distance.

"Baker Island. Can you swim?" Her face was alive with deviltry. Chris stood up, game to her taunt.

"You're damn right, old girl," he laughed back. "How far?"

"Half a mile?" she answered, her voice containing the hint of a challenge.

"You're on," he cried as he leaped onto the deck to stand next to her.

She looked at him, her eyes mocking. She unbuttoned her pants and shirt and dropped them to the deck. Slithering out of her panties, she kicked them back into the cockpit. Naked, she stepped to the edge of the deck and balanced there, waiting, looking back over her shoulder at his astonished expression.

"Well . . . old fraidy cat," she needled. "Well . . . ?"

He held on to her taunt as he pulled off his shorts and underpants in one swift motion. He walked over to stand beside her. She could see at the base of his spine, where the skin was pale and soft, an odd patch of soft curly hair above his two lean hollowed buttocks. As he walked over to her his penis and testicles swung loose, slapping noisily against his muscular thighs. She could not help commenting to herself how all men really looked the same in what they considered to be their private escutcheon of individuality.

She gave him a grin and held her arms above her head, hands together, her body bent over the water, poised to dive. The back of her legs were tensed to hold her to the deck.

He placed himself next to her and assumed the same position.

"Ready, get set, go!"

He suddenly straightened up and stopped. She looked at him with surprise.

"No, Stephanie." Now it was his turn to tease her. "A prize. There *always* has to be a reward for the winner."

She was seized by the exhilaration of the game. She bit her lower lip.

"OK, big shot. You beat me, Tarzan, and I am yours."

The words came hurling back to him as she dove off the side of the boat. Her slim body silently sliced the thick silvered surface with barely a splash.

He waited until she resurfaced, then cupped his hands to call to her, a defying grin on his face.

"Oh, no, Jane," he shouted out as his body left the boat to cleave the water by her side, "I win, *you* fuck *me!*"

Chris looked at the tireless woman playing him like a fish on a baited line. She would swim alongside, then dart on ahead, wait, tread water, double back, and dive under him to bob up again shaming his labored efforts, laughing, clapping in false applause for his feeble attempts to chase her. She floated, did somersaults and backstands, breast, butterfly, and back strokes while he huffed and puffed in the only inelegant crawl he had learned one summer at Y Camp and had cherished ever since.

His muscles felt tired and tense and swollen. Whenever he would stop to rest, Stephanie would pop up next to him, just to spit water in his ear, pat him on the back, and scoot away if he so much as tried to catch her.

Somehow, Baker Island got closer. When he looked back, the boat seemed to retreat into the white haze blurring the demarcation of sea and sky. God help him when he had to swim back.

He forgot the girl lolling next to him. It was no longer just a game, a childish challenge. He could now feel every stroke, every painful contraction and relaxation of his thigh and leg and arm and shoulder and neck muscles. His eyes narrowed. His breath came out in labored gasps. He ground his arms into the resisting swells and clawed at the hostile, fluid mass. He focused his sight at the far breakers. The white surf crested and crashed on the low sandy shore beckoning him on. He no longer had eyes for Stephanie. Just one thing. To swim. To survive. To win!

The girl swimming by his side could now see the change in her companion. He was not responding to her playful antics. He did not smile at her any longer. This was no longer a game for him. She suddenly grew cold and shivered although the water was warm and with each stroke her body rose high into the dry air and caught the radiant heat of the sun above her. Her body straightened, aiming directly for the land like an arrow of naked flesh. Her legs flashed pink and white foam as her head dug in, emerging almost at the very last moment for each desperate gulp of air to exchange waste carbon dioxide for needed oxygen. Her arms rotated on her shoulder pivots, alternating like rotor blades. She raced.

Then something happened. With the shore looming up solid and dark ahead of her, she stopped and hung limp in the water. She waited, head low in the water, for Chris to pass. He did not see her. For the last few minutes he had not been aware of anything. Not her. Not himself. Not the island. Only one thought drove him on. To win. To scrape his skin against the rock and sand of the beach. To rip open his flesh on the gritty projectile of the land. To establish his supremacy.

With a cry of pain, his knees hit the solid mass. He lifted himself out of the water with a cry of exaltation and exhaustion, then flung himself down again, naked and panting on the warm dry sand. Gradually, his breathing became even and slower. His chest ceased its horrible heavy heaving. His heart reentered the pleural cavity. He could feel the erotic tingling of his muscles as they surrendered their lactic acid debt to the circulating oxygen.

His eyes focused clearly. He sat up, wincing at the burning ache. He turned and looked out to sea. Stephanie was walking slowly onto the beach. Once on solid ground her gait picked up. She walked over to him with rapid strides and sat down on the sand. She gave him a gleeful smile, about to offer him a victor's kiss of congratulation at his success.

He savagely turned on her and slapped her hard across the face. The pain was nothing next to the shock and dismay on the stricken woman's face. Bewildered, she raised her hand to touch her cheek where a red stain was emblazoned. She looked up at him, with more than just hurt in her eyes. Why? Why?

He did not deign to look at her, but rose to his feet, kicking sand over her prostrate form. With a contemptuous backward glance, he walked swiftly away, his solitary footprints burning into her sight.

She scrambled to her feet and raced after him. She caught him and tried to hold him back. He shrugged off her feeble efforts and knocked her down to the ground. She tried again, grabbing onto his feet until he stumbled and fell to the earth. She clung to him.

"Why . . . ? Why . . . ?" she pleaded, tears in her eyes.

"Stephanie, don't you ever do that again!" he snarled, his face twisted with rage. "You deliberately lost the race!"

She stared at him, dumb struck, trying to excuse that instinctive and, she thought, innocent, harmless action.

"That was a fucking awful thing to do!" he spit. "I am not Barry. I am not your husband. So I cannot swim as well as you can. Don't you think that I knew that before I started?" His expression softened for just a moment. "I raced you anyway. So what if I had lost? Who the hell cares? You did not have to let me win!"

He reached down and held her face between his two hands, dazzled with sudden insight. "That's the trouble, isn't it?" He searched her startled expression. "You think that you must lose. You are afraid to win. You still think that being on top will put a man down? No, Stephanie. You are wrong. Not every man."

She sucked in her breath. Her eyes were unable to see his face any longer. She had let him win. Why had she stopped in the water when she saw how much winning meant to him? Was she scared of his reaction if she beat him after he had set his heart on defeating her? She waited for Chris to speak, her heart pounding in her chest, her breath choked up in her throat.

"Your husband, Barry," he continued sternly. "Were you afraid after you became successful that you might lose him? Was that why you weren't good in bed any longer? And then, when he wanted a child and you refused. That certainly must have ripped you apart.

He asked you to trade your success for a badge of your femininity, a big belly, and you said no. How that must have torn you up inside. Oh, I suspect your husband was right. You probably didn't make love as well as you had when you were both struggling in school. Stephanie, grow up. Be proud of what you are. A doctor. A success. A woman. Don't denigrate yourself because that is what you thought he wanted. What the bastard let you believe."

He saw the tears gather in the corners of her eyes. He took the tips of his fingers and gently brushed them away. He bent his head and grazed the curly lashes with his lips. He could feel her body tremble next to his.

"Stephanie, I am not Barry. Sure, I wanted to beat you. Not because you were a woman, but just because I like to win. Most people want victories. Look at yourself. You have competed and won in almost everything. Why shouldn't I have the same right? It is not a question of sex that changes the ground rules. But for you somehow that difference was critical. You looked at your husband and let it make a difference. Somehow you let the rules he played by become wrong when they applied to you. And your husband, damn him, let it happen."

He relaxed his position and leaned forward, his arms locked around his knees. Stephanie sat in front of him, her body resting against his upright legs, her hair spilling over his lap. Chris let his hand rest on top of her head. Even now, the hot sun was drying the damp tresses. Without realizing what he was doing, his fingers gently spread the locks apart, separating them into individual strands.

"Stephanie, I couldn't give a damn in hell if you beat me fair and square. Did you think I would hold that defeat against you because you were a woman?

"I have known women who have been successful. Damn successful. I don't know why, but in most cases the same success that would have made a man euphoric and boastful seemed to depress and embitter the women. Why?"

He let the question linger as the young woman raised her head to search his face for the answer. Her pulse quickened. She felt poised on the brink of some precious yet perilous journey.

"Stephanie, some women *want to fail!*"

She heard the words, sharp and clear. She understood their meaning but something inside her rebelled at accepting them.

"Yes, Stephanie," he insisted, aware of her increasing disquiet. "They deliberately want to lose. They have a dread, a reflex fear of success as if that prize was poisoned and would somehow, simultaneous with the fruits of victory, deprive them of their sexuality." He shook his head, warding off her fervent protestations. "I know that sounds silly, but perhaps there is something to it."

He stroked her hair gently. "If it is true, Stephanie, then those women must suffer terribly for their superior natural talents. They have a perpetual conflict between wanting to succeed and being able to achieve victory by virtue of their drive and native ability and a horrible fear that such success will destroy their feminine identity. That is a cruel, harsh conflict. One that we, the men, have never had to face, but probably encourage to demoralize our female competitors and give us an unfair advantage.

"I feel sorry for such women. They are to be pitied and helped. Not scorned and divorced. They need even more compassion and understanding than those who never try to win in a man's world. What they deserve more than anything else in the world is for someone to understand that conflict and to respect and love them for it."

He gazed down into her eyes. "Oh, Stephanie, Stephanie." He lay back on the sand, pulling her down with him. "I love you so very much. Do not be afraid of losing me, ever, because of what you are. Never change. Trust me!"

She did not reply but clasped him in a tight embrace. Tears flowed from her eyes. They were not tears of unhappiness but of joy. The wetness gathered in the hollows of her upturned face.

Chris kissed her cheeks over and over, licking away the warm saltiness.

He rolled her over onto her back. His lips slowly traced a circuitous path down to in between her thighs. His body rotated on the sand, twisting around, as he reached out with his tongue to touch, oh so gently, the tiny pink bud nestled at the base of the triangle of blonde hair. He crushed his head eagerly against her pelvis. His whole mouth, hot and wet, sought her inner recesses, finding there warm sea water mixed with her sudden secretions.

Stephanie ran her fingers lightly along his smooth phallus, brushing off the adhering granules of dried sand. She caressed the satin texture of the rigid shaft with her lips, gliding them along the sensitive frenulum at the underside of the swollen head. Her fingers pressed the raised ridge bisecting his scrotum, which marked the division between the two sides of his body. She followed the perineal line down to the anal ring, which puckered and tightened at her touch. She moved her hands higher to cup his dependent testicles and lightly compress them even while her lips and tongue swirled and teased its captive, driving him to writhe with impatience.

They stopped and rested, their heads on each other's thighs, and reached across their tanned bodies to touch and interlock opposing fingers. They did not hurry.

The sun beat down on both of them, evoking a blanket of sweat that collected in the natural creases of their bodies. They did not feel.

Small sand crabs nervously scurried away from them as their bodies began to move in response to a magical metronome. They did not notice.

The tide was rising, the foamy inroads of sea coming closer to tickle at their feet, now inseparably intertwined as the man changed position to place himself between her parted thighs. They did not care.

A parade of tiny sandpipers goose-stepped at the interface of glistening sand and surf, as he rose onto his knees, throwing her legs back on his shoulders, raising her high off the ground as his straining organ slid into the slippery channel sucking him deeper. They were not aware.

A breeze came out of nowhere to rustle through the scraggly jack pines farther back on the beach, to evaporate the sticky sweat on their bodies as they cried out short incoherent noises, her hands raking his back, scratching the skin, her hands rubbing his hair, her lips seeking and meeting his as blood and saliva mixed from the animal bites of tongue and lips and face. It was too late to stop.

Faster and faster they moved, until the sun and sea and the wind and the sand crabs and the sandpipers and everything all good and beautiful and wonderful and happy married deep inside both of them. Oceans swelled and ebbed against her body. She rocked uncontrollably, throwing back the crashing waves, driving his impatient ejaculation into her flesh as if she would be rent in two.

They melted and mingled and merged until they were one. Their cries of happiness ascended to assault no ears, to frighten no hearts, to offend no deity, as they both lived and loved for the first time on that deserted island beach.

Chapter / THIRTY-SIX

LYMAN BELL DID NOT MAKE AN APPOINTMENT. HE HAD REALIZED early in his lifetime that the advantage of wealth permitted not only acquisition of tangibles, but also extended to such frivolous considerations as appointments. He would merely call the desired party and leave word as to his time of arrival, then he would show up at the precise time, with full expectation that his host would be present. Thus Morris Prynne sat in his office this busy Tuesday morning, awaiting with curiosity the arrival of the frail recluse who controlled the Board of Trustees.

"Mr. Bell," the short, rotund middle-aged bureaucrat eagerly greeted the figure whom his secretary led in exactly on time. "Please have a seat."

Lyman could feel the clammy layer of wetness imparted to him by the administrative handshake and surreptitiously wiped his palm on the vinyl upholstery, which just as resolutely refused to accept the distasteful offering. The trustee edged back in the farthest arm-chair and smiled at his host, without saying a word.

Prynne broke the silence. "Is there something, Mr. Bell, that I, that we, can do for you?"

"Yes. Thank you very much, Mr. Prynne. Thank you for asking. Yes, there is." Bell's manner was appropriately gracious.

Somehow, without knowing exactly how or why, Morris Prynne found himself readily complying with his visitor's innocent request to review the dossier prepared by Dr. Martin Abels against Dr. Lansing Prout. Prynne knew instinctively at the time, and certainly with more conviction later on, that the request was highly irregular. The document was privileged information, strictly within the juris-diction of the medical staff and certainly not for the eyes of a free-lance trustee. However, even in retrospect, Prynne could never really discover what he could have done other than to surrender the report. One did not say no to Lyman Bell.

Each time Prynne glanced over at the seated figure rustling the pages, Lyman would present him with a gratuitous smile and thank him profusely for his courteous deed. Prynne felt himself an in-truder in his own office and inquired if his visitor would like to be alone.

"Why, how considerate," Bell softly replied.

Finally alone, he began to read. Much of the medical data he was unable to assimilate. Cases, patients, operations, he found his comprehension blocked by a lack of familiarity with the language, the terms, the names. But, the critical intent of the report, its sinis-ter conclusion, was irrefutable, the evidence unmistakable. The steady disintegration of a fine talent.

Ten years! God. How much longer than that had it been going on? Thank Abels for one thing. That he had not gone back any further in time. It was all there. It was not the obscene racial slur. Oh, no. It was more than that. If only you had never uttered that remark, he cried, then maybe Abels, like all the rest of the doctors, would have looked the other way and hoped that time, a coronary, a stroke, or hopefully common sense, would have stayed your hand from the operating room. But, no. Perhaps it was fate. There it was, exposed for all to see. Lance . . . Lance . . . what can I do?

Morris Prynne responded to Bell's gracious invitation to return to his own office. He moored himself behind his desk and once again assumed the gravity of his title.

Lyman placed the report in front of Prynne and then seated himself to face the Administrator.

"Mr. Prynne, have you read this report?"

"Yes, Mr. Bell, I had to. It was given to me as Administrator."

"Who else has read it?" Lyman abruptly asked.

"Only Dr. Lash, as Chief of the Department of Surgery, and Dr. Pirie."

"Nobody else?" Bell persisted, his manner for the first time that morning aloof and demanding.

"No, Mr. Bell," Prynne hastened to explain, "Dr. Abels wanted the accusation turned over directly to the Executive Committee. Dr. Lash thought it would be more appropriate if he reviewed the charges first himself, in his official capacity as head of the Department of Surgery."

"And?" Bell held the question hostage.

"Nothing has been decided yet. Dr. Lash received the report only last week. I suspect, however, that he will finish his review in time to present his recommendations to the Executive Committee at their session next week."

"Then what will happen?"

"Unless there is some unforeseen complication, the Executive Committee will approve the report as presented."

"To suspend Dr. Prout from the staff?"

"If that is their recommendation. However," he explained, "only if they find the charges valid."

"After that?"

"The recommendation of the Executive Committee will go before the Board of Trustees for their approval."

"And then Dr. Prout will be suspended?"

"Only if the board considers the action of the Executive Committee bona fide."

"Mr. Prynne," Lyman's words were cold and forbidding, "can you conceive of any circumstances where the board, acting in good faith, would rule against the combined wisdom of ten physicians, especially in a matter of medical peer competence?"

There was a long pause. Prynne's tacit assent was all that Lyman needed to know.

"Dr. Lash I have met," he said in a matter-of-fact tone. "This Dr. Abels. Tell me about him."

"Dr. Martin Abels," Prynne asserted, "is one of the finest men we have on the staff. He is head of the Department of Anesthesiology. We have never, never had any serious trouble in his service since he took over seven years ago."

Bell cut him off. "No. That is not what I mean." He hunted for his next sentence. "Is he in practice here in Cromwell? I understand that he does not have an office in town."

"That is correct, Mr. Bell. Dr. Abels is a full-time physician." He saw the puzzled look on his visitor's face and hastened to elaborate, growing expansive in the opportunity to demonstrate his expertise.

"We have several departments at Mercy where the hospital itself bills for the physicians' services. Anesthesia is one. Radiology is another. Dr. Pirie's Department of Pathology is the third. We collect the fees and the doctors in question receive a weekly paycheck."

"Isn't that a rather . . . unusual . . . arrangement? Don't most physicians, shall we say, like to be 'in business' for themselves, instead of being on a payroll like a bookkeeper?"

Prynne gave a short laugh. "Not all doctors." He turned informative again. "Certain physicians like the arrangement. It relieves them of the necessity of running a collection agency and allows them to concentrate on what they really should be doing, taking care of patients."

"I would imagine," Bell said, "that these physicians must impose quite a responsibility upon the medical staff, what with all their other problems, to have to negotiate such complicated financial arrangements, too."

"Oh no, Mr. Bell, these salaried doctors are employees of the hospital. The conditions of their employment have nothing whatsoever to do with the medical staff. In fact," he said, "Dr. Abels's contract with the hospital, along with all the other full-time men, comes up for renewal before the Board of Trustees next Mon——" He stopped short, realizing he had jumped into a trap and that nothing could prevent his wily guest from full extrapolation of that seemingly benign statement.

"Thank you very much, Mr. Prynne, for your courtesy in allowing me your valuable time this morning." Lyman Bell rose to shake the Administrator's hand. "I do not feel that our innocuous meeting here today need be the topic of exogenous concern. Do you?"

And, as Prynne found himself nodding in agreement, the small wraithlike figure left the room.

Chapter / **THIRTY-SEVEN**

ALL THAT SAMUEL HALPERN KNEW THIS LAST FRIDAY OF THE month was that the Executive Committee meeting was going to be a "ball-breaker," a comment gratuitously offered by Bradford Gill as the short, husky, uncouth Chief of the Department of Medicine noisily entered the crowded room. Samuel had wavered as to whether or not he should attend the meeting up until the very last minute. He had taken the precaution of booking cystoscopies from eight o'clock in the morning right up through two-thirty in the afternoon. At the very last minute, his cloth cap stuck askew on his head, his face mask dangling at his neck, his pale blue-gray scrub suit jammed into a long white coat three sizes too small, he hurried to the Staff Conference Room with just a hint of trepidation in his gait.

He glanced around the room, accepting the recognition of his confreres. Picking a chair in the far corner of the table, he leaned back to wait for the late arrivals. Simon Pirie, always punctual, was already there, picking daintily at his tuna fish salad sandwich, having first spread out four layers of napkins in front of him to make a sterile island of white paper to hold his food.

Arnold Best, the pediatrician, sat next to Pirie.

As usual, Gill had seated himself next to Carl Lash. The surgeon caught Halpern's eyes and froze them with a warning glance for several seconds before turning away. Although he knew in advance what the scenario was likely to be, Samuel found himself increasingly disquieted as he continued his inventory of the room.

There was Morris Prynne and Walter Fallon, the elderly alcoholic Head of the Department of Radiology, whose chief claim to respect was the clever way in which, over the past twenty years, he single-handedly prevented the hospital from acquiring the newest pieces of diagnostic X-ray equipment, thus forcing patients to his superbly equipped private office where he could collect fee-for-service payments in addition to his fixed income from Mercy.

And Martin Abels. Somber, staring straight ahead, secure in the knowledge that he alone in the room was possessed of stern purpose.

Missing only were Victor Craig, who was attending an orthopedics meeting in Seattle, and Ralph Flaherty, whose absence as Chief of Obstetrics and Gynecology was frequent and, although attributed always to imminent motherhood, usually concealed a passion for the golf course.

"All right, gentlemen." Lash's voice broke through the assiduous gustatory activity. "Let's see if we can move along today."

The reading of the minutes of the last meeting and review of old business was quickly dispatched. Only when Lash asked for any new business did the room quiet down. Taking advantage of the pause, Martin Abels stood up and laid on the table in front of him the manila folder containing the data on Lansing Prout.

"All right, Carl, I would like to present before the committee the report I prepared and turned over to you."

Before he could continue, Lash interrupted him and commanded, "Sit down, Martin. You are out of order."

Abels was frozen in place. His face turned scarlet. He stared at Lash, bewildered by his unexpected hostile attitude. Samuel looked around the room, accurately detecting by their conflicting expression which physicians were privy to and which ones were completely ignorant of the background of this emotion-charged skirmish between the Chief of the Department of Surgery and the Chief of the Department of Anesthesiology. Flustered, Abels searched out Prynne, whose face was aimed at the space between his two shoes. Finally Abels stammered, "I don't understand, Carl. You—you read the report. This is the time and the place to bring it up." His manner grew more confident as he observed the heightened interest of those around the table whose curiosity had been aroused by his remark. "You agreed that it was time we did something to stop that butch——"

Lash banged his fist down on the table. "Enough, Martin!" He swept the room with his eyes. "As I started to say, your report is still in the hands of the Administrator. It will *not* be brought up this time!"

Abels looked helplessly around the room, seeking support. Fallon leaned over and asked Samuel what was going on, but Halpern was one of those caught completely by surprise. He shook his head and touched his lips with his index finger to caution silence, hoping that the surgeon would enlighten the audience. Patience was not one of Fallon's virtues. He stood up and demanded in a loud voice for someone to please tell him what the hell was going on. Lash stretched across the table and guided the older man back to his seat where the message finally penetrated the three before-luncheon bourbon-and-waters that whatever was going on was definitely not going to see the light of this particular day.

"But—but—" Abels stammered, waving the sheaf of documents. He sought out Samuel who could only shrug his shoulders. Cursing, Abels finally took his seat.

Satisfied of his tactical victory, Lash moved to reassure the curious.

"Dr. Abels has prepared a complaint against one of the physicians in the Department of Surgery. As chief of the department I have reviewed the allegations and I feel that the charges should be fully investigated prior to their being presented before this body."

He said nothing more but confidently counted the nods of agreement from the uninformed men and the informed in the room, both groups apparently content that the obviously distasteful problem would not be exposed to offend their delicate sensibilities this precious lunchtime.

The next few items of business were rapidly expedited, until—that time had to arrive sooner or later—the doctors leaned forward to hear the report of the Credentials Committee. Up to then nothing had either been said or even hinted about Millsite, the clinic, or Amen. However, the hypocritical deed could not be put off forever.

Samuel was impressed by how smoothly the execution was consummated. Aside from some routine additions to the Emergency Ward staff and an application for a new internist to join Gill, the report concluded by recommending, without any explanation, that the application of Dr. Christopher Amen for privileges be denied and that of Dr. Stephen Halpern be approved.

Almost immediately, Gill moved to accept the report as read and Arnold Best seconded it. Before a minute had passed, the vote was called for, counted and, unanimous or not, studiously recorded as such, and Samuel saw Prynne immediately on his feet with the last item on the agenda, the Administrator's Report. The whole affair had been almost anticlimactic. Bloodless, painless. Like a clean, sharp surgical incision. It hardly seemed worthy of all the sweat and tears that had been required to effect such an elegant performance.

Even Prynne's monotonous singsong recitation of the monthly housekeeping statistics seemed devoid too of any special significance, except for his closing comment, which passed by so quickly that it was gone almost before anyone had even realized that it had been presented.

"While it is officially outside the jurisdiction of the Medical Executive Committee," Samuel heard Prynne whine authoritatively, "the administration has received an application from a Dr. Lawrence Bainbridge."

The name meant nothing to Samuel. He was surprised, however, to see Lash, who had been relaxed and at ease since the earlier exchange with Martin Abels, suddenly sit up and cock his head at the statement. Strangely, Samuel thought that he also caught a flicker of interest by Abels who blinked his eyes as if he was trying to place the name firmly in his memory.

Prynne continued, "Dr. Bainbridge is presently Chief of the Department of Anesthesiology at the North Shore Hospital in Marblehead and is interested in relocating in this area so that his youngest child can attend the Markle School for the Deaf in Worcester."

Abels sat bolt upright and rigid in his seat.

"I hope that Dr. Bainbridge will have the opportunity to meet with members of the staff during his interview here next week." Then, appraising the blank expression on the faces in the room, with the exception of Abels and Lash, Prynne sat down.

Carl Lash stood up. "If there's nothing else, gentlemen . . ." he looked around the table at the stunned and bewildered doctors, "then the meeting is adjourned."

Chapter / **THIRTY-EIGHT**

IF MARTIN ABELS HAD EVER ENTERTAINED ANY THOUGHT THAT
Dr. Bainbridge's surfacing at Mercy was serendipitous, such doubts
were dispelled by the message waiting for him upon his return to
his office, after the tumultuous Executive Committee meeting. It
was a short but formal request for him to meet with the Administrator at four that very afternoon.

The Administrator rose from his desk when Abels entered, and
escorted the anesthesiologist over to the immaculately attired
elderly gentleman seated far back in the corner of the room. "Mr.
Bell, this is Dr. Abels." Then he turned to the physician and said,

((263))

"Mr. Lyman Bell. Chairman of the Board of Trustees of Mercy Hospital. I am certain that you have heard of Mr. Bell before this. He is——"

"I know who Mr. Bell is," Abels lashed out at Prynne. "What I do not understand is what he is doing here. If it involves," he sneered, "what I think it does, I deserve an explanation."

The Administrator ignored the outburst. He gave Abels a gracious smile and pointed to the chair.

"Please be seated, Martin. That is why I wanted you here today. We wish to discuss several items with you that concern not only the future of the hospital but," he added ominously, "your own as well."

Reluctantly, Abels sat down. He remained perched on the edge of the chair, with his hands pressing into the cushions on either side of him, coiled to spring up again at the first provocation.

"First, Mr. Bell is here in his official capacity as a member of the Board of Trustees. You are no doubt aware," he hammered the words out clearly, "that your position at Mercy lies within the jurisdiction of the administration and the board, and *not* with the medical staff. Let us get that understood right from he start." His words held a harsh overtone that Abels could not miss. "Dr. Bainbridge has been interviewed for Chief of the Department of Anesthesiology at Mercy to begin this July."

"But, my contract," Abels protested, alarmed.

"Your contract is over at the end of the month." Prynne looked over at Bell and smiled. "The board does not look favorably upon renewing it for another year."

"For what reason?" Abels demanded. "There have been no medical complications within the department that I know about. It can't be money. Goddamn it! Anesthesia is one of the biggest money-makers in the whole hospital. Even I know that."

Prynne glanced at Bell for encouragement. "The Department of Anesthesiology occupies a very," he groped for the correct word, "delicate position in the hospital. Yes, *delicate*. You must deal

((264))

every day with surgeons on the staff. You actually work in the same room with them. Almost, shall we say," he beamed at his poetic license, "live at the same table, operating table, of course."

Abels was disgusted. Goddamn Prynne! Why didn't the little prick come right out and say whatever he had to?

"The hospital doesn't think it is in the best interests of the patient to have a Chief of Anesthesiology . . . who is in direct conflict with the men he is working with."

Abels's eyes opened wide as the lethal edge of Prynne's words stabbed him. He leaped to his feet. "So it is the Prout business, isn't it, Prynne?" he shouted. "Why don't you open your fucking mouth and come right out and say so?" He flung his arm out at Bell. "That's why Bell is here, too, isn't it? So, you are all ganging up on me? To protect that senile incompetent hack. Come on now, Prynne. Prout is a butcher. Just read my report. You can't just sweep it all under the carpet. You can't."

For a long time nobody said anything. When Prynne broke the fragile silence, his unctuous tones seared Abels's composure.

"Martin, even you can see now how impossible it would be for you to continue working here. Having to give anesthesia for a doctor for whom you have such little respect——"

Martin interrupted him. "It won't work. I have the report. The facts, the figures, the dates, the operations. I will take them to the Active Staff meeting. To the newspaper." His face lit up with a malicious thought. "Perhaps even to the families of Prout's victims. Show them how he murdered their loved ones."

"Yes, Dr. Abels," Prynne interjected, with a broad smile. "You could do that. We considered the possibility. But, it would just be your word against the hospital's, the word of a disgruntled doctor who had to be fired for," his face lighting up with malevolent purpose, "sorry reasons that Mercy Hospital is too considerate to make public out of respect for the members of your family. Oh no, Dr. Abels. Your task will not be all that easy. And, don't forget, we hospital administrators have a very close, shall we say union.

It is not as if you had a private practice to fall back on."

Abels played his ace. "You are wrong, Mr. Prynne. You seem to have forgotten one thing. Dr. Lash. You forget that he has read the report. It won't be just my word against Prout's. Dr. Carl Lash is the Chief of the Department of Surgery at this very hospital."

"I doubt, Martin," Prynne said softly, "that Dr. Lash is apt to say anything unfavorable about his new partner."

Abels could not believe what he had just heard. He fell back, crushed, unable to redress the balance in the room that had so unexpectedly tilted against him.

By the time Samuel Halpern found Martin in the parking lot, ashen, his speech incoherent, and his actions unpatterned, Abels readily acceded to his friend's offer to drive him home. Several hours later, when Samuel had laboriously extracted the facts of the meeting, it was with strained assurance he comforted Martin's wife that everything would be all right, and to call him if there was any further problem that evening with the anesthesiologist.

When, later that night, Samuel lay in his bed, staring up at the ceiling, recounting to his wife the traumatic story, only then, from her shocked reaction, did he realize how truly incredible the entire episode had really been. "Sylvia," he said, "they made a real patsy out of Martin."

"I don't understand," Sylvia said. "What exactly did they do?"

"It was a real put-up job," he exclaimed. "Those bastards!" He stopped to think for a minute. "No. I take that back. Just one bastard. Lash!"

"Sam, please explain."

"Oh, it was all so simple, Sylvia. At the beginning Martin went to Lash with his report about Prout. Carl was very enthusiastic. It seemed like such a clean way to bounce Prout out of the hospital. Both surgeons take care of the same WASP group in Cromwell, but Prout has the older, richer practice. Instead of waiting another five years for Prout to die, Abels would administer the coup de grace and Lash would immediately inherit the clientele by default, once Prout was off the staff. It would kill two birds with one stone. Nice and sweet!" Samuel smiled at his wife. "It happens all the time, Sylvia. But things didn't go as planned. Lyman Bell entered the picture. Oh," he laughed, "Lansing undoubtedly went running straight to the old man like a spoiled little baby who hurt his finger. Bell probably kissed it and told him he would make it all better. You know there was talk a long time ago that those two were more than just good friends." He paused to conjecture. "Well, perhaps there is some truth to those rumors. Anyway, Lyman must have decided to leave his gilded cocoon and went right for Prynne.

"So they cooked up that fake deal with Bainbridge. To frighten Martin. At first he didn't scare because he figured that he had Lash on his side. God! They were clever! They really grabbed Martin where it hurt and squeezed hard. Lyman told Martin that Lash had made a deal to take in Prout as his partner."

Mrs. Halpern had been following the narrative with difficulty, trying to sort out the Byzantine logic. "Samuel," she interrupted, "Carl may not be your friend, nor Martin's, but he is not a fool. He is a good surgeon. Even you have told me that many times. How can he take in Dr. Prout as his partner if the man is incompetent, especially after reading Martin's report? After all, he has a good reputation to protect."

"Ah ha," her husband laughed. "I haven't finished yet, Sylvia. Now comes the good part."

He lectured her like a schoolteacher. "Lyman Bell must have persuaded Lansing to agree to give up his operating privileges in return for Abels's withdrawing the report. Bell is not stupid. Even he could see that Prout had to be curtained. But this way, nobody would ever know, and Lansing's reputation would stay lily white."

"I don't understand, Samuel."

"Don't you see?" he argued. "It is all so simple. The report is expunged. Prout remains on the Mercy Hospital staff, but just stops operating. Because surgical privileges are controlled strictly by the Chief of the Department of Surgery, nobody outside the surgery floor will ever know. Lash, being Prout's partner, will scrub with Lansing on all the surgical cases and actually do the operating himself. I suppose that the partnership agreement will arrange for a kickback to Prout every time Lash operates on one of his patients. But, who will ever know the difference? The damn patient is asleep. Lash is happy. He gets Prout's charisma and his practice years before the old hack would have stopped hanging on. To the outside world nothing has changed with Prout at all. In fact, knowing that wily old bastard, he will probably go around telling everybody in Cromwell that it is he who is taking in Lash," he mimicked Prout's condescending tone of voice, "in order to teach the young whippersnapper some surgery. Lyman Bell is happy, Prout is happy, and Lash is happy."

"But, Martin, poor Martin. What will he do?"

"Oh, nothing. Everything will go on just as before. That Bainbridge nonsense was just a ploy. They don't really want Abels to leave. Not with him holding that hot little report in his hands. What if he should turn it over someday to someone else with more guts than he has? Then the hospital could really be in a pickle. No. They want to keep him right where he is, but quiet and minding his own business. Besides, he's a very good doctor."

"But, Martin?" she pleaded. "Did he agree?"

"Did he have any other choice? After all, Bell did stop Prout from doing any more surgery, even if he still remains on the staff. Also, knowing Prynne, he would have made certain that Martin would starve before he ever got another job."

Samuel's manner saddened as he thought of his bested colleague. He sat down next to his wife and took her hand in his.

"You know, Sylvia, what really started the whole thing?" She shook her head. "Lansing, a long time ago, called Martin a 'dirty Jew.' And Martin never forgot it. He is the kind of man who nurses hate for years until he gets the chance for revenge. It is so tragic.

It didn't work. Martin should have known better. If we wasted life waiting to get back at everyone who calls us a 'dirty Jew,' we would never have any time for living."

"How awful, Sam. How awful," Sylvia said.

"And what irony. Everybody came up smelling like roses. Bell for having helped Prout. Prout with his neck intact. Lash, that's obvious. The good citizens of Cromwell not to have that butcher working on them any longer. Even that bastard Prynne now has a chit on the great Lyman Bell himself. But, poor little Martin Abels, he just came up smelling!"

"Poor Martin. What is he going to do?"

"Do, Sylvia?" her husband admonished, annoyed at her sentimentality. "I told him what to do before I left him tonight. I told him that he should start to keep a dossier on Carl Lash!"

Chapter / **THIRTY-NINE**

With bitter resignation, Joe Brandon watched the painful disintegration of the proud Millsite Family Clinic. Simultaneous with Christopher Amen's decision not to fight the Executive Committee ruling, life suddenly disappeared from the once vital entity that was to have revolutionized medicine in Cromwell. To Joe's way of thinking, it was a stillbirth, blighted, and the sooner buried, the better for its disappointed parents.

Despite his own personal feelings of abandonment, he could not honestly argue with Amen's decision to leave. A fight to tear the medical community apart could not have helped the clinic. Even if

((271))

sufficient pressure could have been exerted against the entrenched hierarchy, any victory would have been pyrrhic. It would have raised sincere doubts in the eyes of the public to see doctors squabbling among themselves. Even more, as Chris himself pointed out, time was of the essence, if the fragile combination of grants, loans, union commitments, employment contracts, was to survive long enough for the unit to be self-supporting.

Over the following hot July days, along with Brian Terris, Joe watched the dream self-destruct. The almost instantaneous appearance of the two officious men from Washington, still carrying their own attaché cases, busy canceling contracts, voiding purchases of equipment and material, settling penalty clauses for remodeling work already carried out, terminating the lease with Cardano. Marjorie Hollis, who, much to the surprise of all who had worked with her at Mercy, had agreed to become the nursing supervisor at Millsite, had to notify those whom she had tentatively hired to staff the facility. Letters had to be sent out to the potential patients who had signed up, advising them of the indefinite delay in opening the clinic and recommending they seek medical care elsewhere. Finally, there was the heartbreaking task each night of repacking into corrugated cartons the many patient charts that the various doctors had transferred from their Cromwell offices in anticipation of their new quarters at Millsite.

All during this harsh period, Joe said nothing. He went through the motions of practicing as if Amen had never appeared on the Cromwell scene. He grew morose, ill-tempered, and brusque with those about him. He seemed consumed by a sense of personal failure.

Connie Mercier and Brian Terris watched him load the last box of folders into the trunk of his car and wave good night.

"What is going to happen now, Brian?"

"I really don't know. We, all of us, had such high hopes." He waved toward the storefront facility, now in a state of disarray. "It's sort of like Alice in *Through the Looking Glass*. We ran and ran and ran. Now, we are all out of breath. We look around and find that we are right back where we started from.

"Oh, I guess Stephen will go into practice with his father. Leonard and Joe and I will continue on High Street, knocking our heads against the Medical Arts boys. And Chris, well, there are plenty of other towns and cities, not like Cromwell, just begging for the kind of medicine he can offer. He will have no trouble. You know, Connie, probably the only one who came out of this whole stinking mess with anything at all is Stephanie. She is in love with Chris. It is ironic. Stephanie. The one person who couldn't have given a damn whether or not there even was a Millsite Family Clinic."

He pointed through the window at the busy parking lot outside, bustling with late evening shoppers. His voice rose in pitch, his round face now flushed with anger.

"Connie, I will tell you what is so damn tragic. There are the thousands of people who could have just walked right in here for medical care. It is all gone now. Gone forever. And they will never know. A group of ten bastards sitting around a table in Mercy Hospital destroyed this whole thing. It is not fair. It is not fair at all! The hardest thing of all to bear is that nothing, nothing can be done about it."

Connie knew Brian was not a person of rancor. She put her arms around his waist and held him close in a warm embrace. His rapid breathing slowed and he took measure of her stance by his side. He was aware of what store she had placed in the success of the clinic. How she worried about their future, his practice and Joe's, now that they were again isolated and vulnerable. Brian managed a weak smile of confidence as he moved to turn off the lights and lock up the clinic for the evening.

Halfway across town, Dr. Joseph Brandon was also thinking about the demise of Millsite. He, too, had invested hope and energy in the rich promise of the project and the knowledge that it would break Flaherty's and Best's stranglehold on obstetric and pediatric patients in Cromwell.

Now, with its demise, the bonds that held his frustration—and ambition—in check, crumbled. He sat long hours in the semidarkness of his living room resisting the pleas of his wife to come to bed. Hour after hour, he chain-smoked in the gloom, weighing alternatives. He tried hard to persuade himself that what he was contemplating was not precipitous or unjustified. By the time the cool fresh dawn had bleached the Cromwell sky, Joe had made his commitment.

He rose to shave and change his clothes for the new day. He remembered an old saying of his father's. If you are going to kill a rattlesnake, you had better make damn sure that you step on his head and not on his tail. Ralph Flaherty had had his chance. Now it was too late for him to try again.

Chapter / **FORTY**

THE BOARD OF TRUSTEES' ANNUAL MEETING THAT SAW THE eighth renewal of Dr. Martin Abels's contract as Chief of the Department of Anesthesiology at Mercy, also witnessed the accession to the staff of Dr. Samuel Halpern's firstborn heir, as well as that august body's acceptance of the Medical Executive Committee's recommendation that Dr. Christopher Amen be denied staff membership. The barrage of congratulations from his peers on the long-anticipated union with Stephen in practice left the father somewhat perplexed.

He found that his happiness was dampened by a feeling of guilt for a crime against his son and for which, someday, he would be held accountable and punished. True, he had voted in accordance with the dictates of his goals, and also true that Kupperman swam quietly with the rest, and would not the same result have occurred even without Abe's and his assent? Nevertheless, Samuel had an uneasy, hard-to-define sense of alarm that tarnished what should have been his moment of joy and that initiated for him an uneasy concern for the future.

For the first weekend in months, Stephen did not return to Cromwell. The same held true the following weekend and the one after that. Sylvia worried out loud, her anxiety exacerbating her husband's disquiet. Unable to withstand her entreaties any further, he relented and permitted her to call their son in Brookline.

Ann was hesitant and evasive on the telephone, her tone of voice trying to communicate something of what she was going through. Realizing the anguish that her husband was callously causing the two old people, she revealed that Stephen was not planning to return to Cromwell. He was planning to move to Livermore Falls, Maine, where Chris had received an open invitation from the town fathers for the very facility that Cromwell had so summarily rejected.

Samuel treated the disconcerting news with a silent withdrawal. Sylvia could observe the pain concealed within the shell her husband presented to the world. What she did not anticipate was that it would be Christopher Amen who would appear to formalize the breach between father and son. Perhaps the ambassador was motivated by the hope that the older physician would relent and give his blessing to the new venture. However, had he entertained any such unfounded belief that Samuel Halpern would condone the burial of his own dream, he was to be disillusioned. The short visit to the Halpern home was a cold one, the atmosphere chilled, despite the emissary's obvious attempt to find some middle ground to bridge the gap between the father's bitterness and his son's private aspirations.

The two men sat across from each other, nursing their cups of coffee, staring at their laps. In desperation, Sylvia tried to break the rigid silence. "Ann tells me the community in Maine is trying hard to make you welcome. I am very happy for you and Dr. Crane."

"Are you really, Mrs. Halpern? I would have wagered that you and Dr. Halpern would be just the opposite."

Sylvia was taken aback by the sarcasm in his voice. Her remark had been intended in sincerity. In return, Amen had made her feel that she was demeaning him. "We are happy for *you*, Chris, but not for our son."

The young physician had already turned away from her to her husband.

"Tell me, Dr. Halpern," he asked, "why did you keep me out of Cromwell? I heard rumors that you were offered the Chief of Staff at Mercy. I understand that it will be the first time in the history of the hospital that a Jew will occupy that position." He shrugged his shoulders in disbelief.

Samuel gave his guest a loathing look, hurt by the inference that he could be bought so cheaply.

"You don't really believe that, Chris? Do you?"

Before Amen could answer, Sylvia had risen to her feet. She felt a compulsion to defend her husband, even if he remained mute to the verbal blow he had so unjustly received. Her glare was punishing the young doctor. "You have no right to say that to my husband. Samuel is a good man. Sure, he may not be a crusader like you. He didn't come to Cromwell armed with government grants to change the world. He crawled here thirty years ago on his knees to earn a living." Her eyes swept over the seated guest, scorning the favorable image they received. "He didn't have your blond hair and your short nose. That's all it took for you for doors to open.

"No, Sam had it hard. Medicine was not a mission for him. It was his living. He worked hard at it. Now he is respected. You

((277))

think it was easy to practice here at first? People wondering why he had to train in an Italian medical school. A Jew practicing surgery in a New England town. You think that country clubs are restricted? You should learn about the surgical staff in our proud local hospital."

Her accusation hung leaden, defying rebuttal. Amen tried to offer a gesture of sympathy, but anger at seeing her husband abused by this alien who had stolen and polluted his dream, drove her on.

"I don't think that Sam had much respect for himself when he first came here. He thought he was a failure as a husband as well as a provider. He couldn't even be a father for many years, because I had to work in his office. I never said anything to him when we were told that Stephen would have to be our only child because of my age." She went over and kissed her husband on the forehead.

"I felt pain for my husband then. I knew what was going through his mind, the sore that has festered there all these years. He has gotten older and grayer but at least he has respect for himself. Not every doctor can say that."

Oddly, her husband said nothing, seemingly reluctant to make common cause with her thesis.

Chris leaned forward, his voice gentle. "Is that true, Dr. Halpern? Do you respect yourself? Do you deserve my respect? No, better tell your wife there."

Still Samuel said nothing.

"Tell him!" she implored, misreading his sudden reticence as fear. "Don't be afraid of this . . ."

Her husband reached up, his harsh grip hurting her wrist. He did not know how to soften the blow.

"Sylvia . . . Sylvia, don't say anything. Please. Just don't speak." He looked straight into her eyes. "Chris is right. By *his* standards I don't deserve his respect. By *my* standards, I ask him to forgive me."

Chris laid his hand on the father's shoulders in a gesture of compassion.

((278))

"I did vote against you, Chris, but against *you,* not your clinic. I wasn't afraid of Millsite. What do I have?" He spread out his hands in a futile gesture. "Five years, maybe? You couldn't have hurt me. No, that was not the reason." He let out a short, dry laugh. "Putting Stephen in your clinic might have been the best possible thing for him. He is weak. He can never succeed by himself. If the clinic took off, he would be a success in spite of himself. If it failed, he would still be able to fall back on my practice in Cromwell long after you had folded your charity tents and stolen away. If you look at it dispassionately, it would have been the best of all possible worlds for him."

"Then why did you fight me?"

"It is a difficult thing to put into words. Maybe even I can't understand it. I am an ordinary man, Chris. An old man with white hair and bad teeth. A constipated man whose worn-out heart skips to an irregular rhythm—an old weary tune. You are the hero in this piece, Chris. It is not your blond hair, your foreskin, but your dream that made you my enemy."

"Everyone is entitled to have a dream," Chris countered. "My father died because he couldn't get a doctor. In some small way I would like to make sure that it never happens to others."

Sam's voice drifted to a distant whisper. "But, Chris, heroes are rare. They dream rare dreams—for others. Fathers are ordinary people and we have ordinary dreams—selfish ones—for ourselves and for our children." He sat down beside the young physician.

"Children are the immortality in the dreams of old men and menopausal women. We praise heroes, but we are afraid of their dreams. We despise such men because they *are* unselfish and reveal our private dreams as avaricious and petty. And what we can't understand, we kill. Chris, we crucify our gods and heroes so that their dreams will exist only as storybook legends and biblical tales."

"I *had* no ritual mutilation," Chris said. "Does that make me less entitled to what I want? I am not a father, but must a dream be only for one's *own* flesh and blood? Is it a crime to help others?"

He selected from his quiver the final arrow to level at his host.

"Suppose Stephen had come to Cromwell and gone into practice with someone else, or even by himself in another office. What would you have done then? Would you have allowed him that grace? Or would you fight him, destroy *his* dream, to draw him to you? And, if you failed, would you then destroy him, like me?"

"Yes, Chris, I am a very jealous father. But, never forget, Chris. My son was only part of your dream. You will have many Cromwells, Livermores, and more. You have youth. Stephen was all of mine. I am old. I have no other dreams. No other immortality. You and I. A crusader's visitation versus a father's mirage. Remember, I do not share dreams. I am not a man to settle for half a loaf when he starves for a whole one."

"I do understand you, Dr. Halpern. It has been a contest all this time. You and Millsite, both competing for a soul who by accident of birth shares half of your chromosomes. I am truly sorry that you have lost."

With that exchange there was nothing left to say. Chris left the room with a heavy heart, abandoning his host to the gathering fates who had congregated silently to stay his happiness.

Chapter / **FORTY-ONE**

ALTHOUGH JOE BRANDON HAD PRACTICED IN CROMWELL FOR two years before this morning, he had never once been inside the new Medical Arts condominium. Three stories high, the severe brick facade was sculpted into tall columns of light and dark, with spandrels of burnished copper. The complementary use of natural materials and textures continued in the interior where alternating vertical panels of walnut and satin stainless steel guided the visitor and patient to the elevator. The wide corridors were carpeted and, even at seven o'clock in the morning, soft music played harmonious, if vacuous, melodies from cleverly concealed loudspeakers.

((281))

Flaherty's suite of offices occupied a prized location on the first floor front corner where it faced Mercy Hospital across the bordering green lawn. Brandon paused for a moment before testing the door. The older obstetrician had arrived there before him and had left it open. The spacious waiting room was empty, lit by a single strip of ceiling sconces softly illuminating the rows of modular seating.

As Joe entered, a contact switch closed under the entry carpet from pressure of his foot. He was startled by the sudden chime, but could still see no one in sight.

"Come in, come in, young man." Flaherty's hearty voice boomed out from a side hall as the elderly physician emerged from his private office in response to the bell sound. He held out his hand, his face creased in happy smiles. Joe could not miss the deliberate attempt at camaraderie. He kept his own hands to his sides and returned the effusive greeting with an unfriendly stare that did not appear to bother his host in the least.

"Come right in, Joe. This way. Follow me." He clasped the younger man on the shoulder and escorted him through a long, dimly lit hall whose walls were festooned with thousands of pictures of patients collected over the years. The glossy cards had been gathered into a mural-like montage, arranged with countless Christmas, birthday, and anniversary cards, all documenting the love and affection that the delivered of Cromwell bore for him. Joe took in the impressive pictorial testimonial without saying a word.

Flaherty's office was a shock to Joe. It was in complete contrast to the earthy image the older physician had nurtured over the years. The room was starkly modern. The walls were covered in book-matched panels of Brazilian rosewood, the desk a sheet of Italian cremo marble on legs of polished steel.

Flaherty himself sat in a high-backed swivel chair of tan suede. One entire wall of the room was covered with tiers of hanging plants. Joe could see, concealed in the ceiling above the pots, a series of built-in lights focused to provide concentrated illumination for the thriving verdure.

"What do you think?" Flaherty asked, indicating with a wide sweep of his hand the controlled elegance of the room. "The rug," he excused, pointing to the floor, "is here on loan. I am not certain that it does anything for the room. What do you think?"

Brandon looked down at the expensive silk and wool hunting Tabriz upon which two-dimensional green and ivory Persian hunters were chasing unicorns and tigers into the four corners of the room. Light glinted on the gold thread interwoven into the embroidered armor of the courtiers as they stretched their weapons for the final kill.

"Never buy an Oriental carpet, Joe, without first putting it down on the floor and living with it for at least several months." He leaned forward to take the younger man into his confidence. "Take it from me. Don't let those shifty Armenians talk you out of it. If they won't let you take the rug on approval, do business with someone else." He stared at the floor, his brow wrinkled in serious contemplation. "I just . . . don't know . . . about this one." He looked up to see Brandon chewing his lower lip, controlling with difficulty his rising anger. "I don't suspect though that learning about Persian floor-coverings is what made you call me last night and insist on my meeting you here at this God-awful hour, is it, young man?"

Joe found it hard to speak. Last night, after loading the last of his office charts back into his station wagon and leaving Brian and Connie at Millsite, his intentions seemed so simple. Now he wondered if he had been foolish even to consider direct confrontation with the medical establishment.

Flaherty, his office, rich and flawless in design, like the Medical Arts Building itself, made him feel suddenly weak and impotent. Then he reminded himself of Flaherty's cruel mocking refusal to cover for him when he thought he would drop from exhaustion.

((283))

Of the crushing disappointment when his prospective partner's application died in the Credentials Committee and the man was forced to settle in Fall River instead of Cromwell. Of the illicit agreement between Best and Flaherty to control the flow of pediatric patients in Mercy. And finally, of that all-too-vivid blood-drenched debacle, Laurie Dearing's guts spilled out on the clean surgical field, while Samuel Halpern tried desperately to salvage Flaherty's blunder.

He was no longer in awe of the rosewood paneling nor the classic restrained modern decor, nor even the antique carpet whose perfection had taken three twelve-year-old girls in Nā'īn four years of sixteen-hour-a-day labor to complete. His eyes scanned the room, knowing that all this could be lost as easily as it had been gained. He found, to his pleasure, that he could stare back defiantly at the older man, unafraid to lock glances with him.

Flaherty saw this subtle change, Brandon's increasing flush of confidence. The older man's smile tightened on his face. What did he have to worry about? He had been around too long to panic at a Joe Brandon, despite what he might think he had on him. Hah! The bastard had lost with his intended partner. He had lost with his practice. He had lost for his brother-in-law. He could not get into the Medical Arts Building. He had failed at Millsite. Did he think he could damn well win with Laurie Dearing?

"No, Ralph," Brandon said, "I did not come to admire your interior design. I am here to discuss Mrs. Dearing."

Flaherty shifted his weight in his seat, but did not lose visual contact with his visitor.

"You are aware that Mr. Dearing brought me in on the case because he suspected you had killed his wife."

Flaherty jerked up, incensed by that inflammatory accusation.

"All right, Ralph. I won't quibble over a technicality with you. She is still alive, although existing hooked up to the dialysis machine is not exactly what her husband considers as living."

Joe could observe Flaherty edge his chair closer to the desk.

"It has been over two months. Mrs. Dearing has still not put out any urine. Sam is preparing to send her home any day now. She will be scheduled to come into Mercy three times a week for a run on the artificial kidney. Mr. Dearing is a very angry, very bitter man. He knows that you sutured the ureter shut. He has read Simon's report. I have talked with Mr. Dearing many times, and at great length. He is fully cognizant that you did not institute any diagnostic tests after the hysterectomy. Tests that he learned from Sam Halpern would have disclosed the threat to her kidney early enough in the game to have saved it."

Flaherty's face turned mean and vicious. "Say what you have to, young man," he snarled. "I did not get up this early in the morning to meet you in a deserted office just to listen to a textbook lecture of Mrs. Dearing's medical problems. I don't think that it is any of your goddamn business anyway, to be discussing it with me. *I* certainly have no desire to discuss it with you—now or at any other time! You had better leave my office. If you have any tales, tell them to Mr. Dearing." He pushed his face to within an inch of his listener's. "I know the law, Brandon, and damn well, too. You are threatening me with a court case. Mr. Dearing's suing me for malpractice. You may consider me stupid, Joe, but if you think hard about what has happened to you and to your brother-in-law since you both came to Cromwell, you should rapidly discover ample evidence to convince you otherwise."

He placed his hands on the edge of the desk, his fingers rubbing the polished convex nosing as he concluded, "Mrs. Dearing did not have an I.V.P. because I did not order one. There was *no* reason to order one." His voice slammed down hard on the words. "It is *not* customary nor routine nor accepted practice to order that test automatically on everyone after that particular surgical procedure. There is nothing that you, or Mr. Dearing, or anyone else can do to alter that fact or to convince a jury otherwise—if that is your game. So, unless you have something else to say to me, I must ask you to get the hell out of here!"

((285))

Joe waited out the tirade, pleased to see his opponent finally aroused. When Flaherty had finished, Joe said, "Very good, Ralph. Very good indeed. But I am not one of your patients. Your bluster, or bullshit, as you will, doesn't scare me. Because that is all it is!" He raised his voice. "Sit down, Goddamn it! And listen. Listen, for once in your fucking life. I won't repeat it a second time. You are wrong. Mrs. Dearing had every reason, every right, every indication to have had that I.V.P. ordered by you. Two weeks after she left the hospital she was seen by you for her routine post-hospital follow-up. Right here, in your office. Mr. Dearing has compiled a complete documentation of her convalescent course. At that visit, Mrs. Dearing told you of pain." Joe noticed Flaherty's sudden tenseness. "Not just ordinary pain. Not the pain that you would expect from the recent incision or in her pelvis from the adhesions. Not even the discomfort of having intercourse before the surgery had healed. But, flank pain. *Here,*" he placed his right hand behind him, to rest on his back under his right shoulder blade. "Yes, Ralph, right C.V.A. pain." Flaherty paled.

"Pain in her right costo-vertebral angle. Pain in her right kidney. Pain because the urine couldn't get out of the kidney you sutured shut from your stitch in the ureter. Oh . . . I know you can change your office records, if you even paid enough attention to her complaint to write it down. If you didn't, don't worry. You won't have to remember it. The jury will do it for you. You see, Ralph," he moved closer to the desk, "Mrs. Dearing was very concerned about the back pain. You told her to forget it and it would go away. It didn't, though. She did believe you, however, when you said that it had nothing to do with her operation. She took herself to Paillard. She wondered if she had hurt her back. She told Leonard about the pain and that you assured her that it was not related to her operation. He gave her a thorough orthopedic examination and could find nothing wrong. He even got spine and bone films at Mercy. The reports are on file there in the X-ray Department. They were all negative."

Flaherty's jaw fell open, his breathing was now heavy and labored.

"It is all written down. Lenny's office notes about you and Mrs. Dearing. Her having to seek medical help elsewhere because of the pain, the pain you told her was nothing. The pain of her right kidney destroying itself. Oh, no. I think that the jury will listen. And they will listen well. If I know Mr. Dearing, he will bring his wife in on a stretcher, her arm hooked to the big artificial kidney. What a grandstand play that will be in the courtroom. The young mother. The four weeping children by her side. The horrible mechanical monster holding her life in its rotating cellophane tubing and saline. The testimony of Paillard, of Halpern, and me!" Flaherty gasped, fearful of what other mortal blows his youthful avenger had yet to deliver.

But Joe had turned his back on the man. He walked over to the wall of plants and ran his fingers tantalizingly down the long feathery asparagus fern fronds. He peered closely at the sprays of purple and red and white gloxinias. He praised his host's horticultural prowess, the gesture insulting to the shaken obstetrician. Finally, Joe returned and stood in front of the seated figure.

"Yes, Ralph. In the last analysis, it all comes down to me. *My* testimony. Without it, it is still your word against the pathos of the situation. Sure, the woman is afflicted, is to be pitied. Sure, her husband is a consummate courtroom artist. But, to drive that wooden stake through your heart, one thing must be established beyond a shadow of a doubt. Did you or did you not treat Mrs. Dearing in conformity with the accepted medical standards in the community? If you adhered religiously to the accepted norm for this area, then you are innocent—even if she dies. If, on the other hand, you did not carry out the necessary diagnostic procedures, namely in this case to get an I.V.P. because of back pain after a hysterectomy, when I, a fellow physician in the same specialty would have done so in this very hospital, then you are damned. Nothing and no one can save you!"

He paused for emphasis. "So you see, your crucifixion is in my hands, and mine alone."

It took the older man a long time to answer. Once or twice he had been tempted to argue back, to refute the charges and proclaim his innocence, or at least his lack of malice and premeditation, yet at the very last minute something made him hold his tongue.

Something bothered him and it was not the degree of Brandon's vilification. Something wasn't quite right. Why hadn't he recognized it before? The man was as much of a hypocrite as he was. Sustained by the happy realization that he could negotiate with his tormentor in a mutually acceptable currency, Flaherty prepared to deal.

"All right, Dr. Brandon. I have heard your case. I must confess that it is a very tidy one. Too tidy for my liking. You are correct. I don't like it. I don't like it at all. It bothers me. Perhaps even frightens me." He looked over the edge of his rimless glasses. "However, you had a definite reason in coming here today. It was not just to give me a rehearsal of my day in court. That is not why you threw the gauntlet down. You want something, don't you? If it were only revenge, then you would not be stupid enough to reveal your hand. Instead, you would join forces with Mr. Dearing and keep your mouth shut until you could impale me in front of a jury. No, Joe. *You want something.* What is it?"

The old bastard was certainly not senile or stupid. Yes, he, Joe Brandon, wanted something for himself and for Brian. The dream of every young doctor starting to practice. He had hoped that Millsite would have given them that prize in an honest manner. But Millsite and its dream had failed miserably. Was he now to give up his two years of sweat in Cromwell and leave with his tail between his legs?

Joe reached into his jacket pocket and brought out two folded sheets of typewritten paper. He laid them on the desk in front of him. Flaherty looked at them, but did not offer to pick them up.

"Two things, Ralph," Joe demanded. "First, there is a letter recommending Dr. Kline for the Mercy staff as my new partner. Jules is unhappy in Fall River and still wants to come here and go into practice with me. You and Arnold Best will both sign the letter, testifying to your complete approval of the man and his credentials and supporting him for full Ob-Gyn privileges on the active staff."

Flaherty said nothing.

"The second is a nursery roster, listing Best and his two partners and Dr. Brian Terris in rotation. All uncommitted newborns are to be assigned to the pediatrician on call according to this list. You and your partners will propose this protocol to the Executive Committee and abide by it. This will guarantee Dr. Terris at least a quarter of the newborns and their families in Cromwell, from this time on."

"Is that all?"

"That's all."

"And, in return . . ."

Brandon did not flinch. "I do *not* routinely order I.V.P.'s on post-hysterectomy patients who come into my office two weeks after surgery complaining of pain. . . . Front, back or," he added sarcastically, "sideways."

Flaherty reached over and gently picked up the papers. He did not look at them but slid open a concealed drawer on his side of the desk and placed the sheets inside. He closed the drawer and folded his hands together in front of him. His face was smooth and free of anxiety.

"I will have to discuss this, of course, with my partners. And with Dr. Best."

"Of course," Brandon said. "I will give you one week. At the end of that time, Mr. Dearing will take a deposition from me."

Flaherty escorted Brandon from the room. "You know, Joe," he confessed, "I misjudged you."

Joe looked up in surprise.

Flaherty continued, "Yes, I really misjudged you. I thought that you were a threat, Joe. You were honest and competent. But it wasn't your superior skills or training that worried me. Patients don't know about such things. Referring physicians don't give a damn about them. No, Joe. It was your . . ." he groped for the proper word, "your purity. Your goddamn sanctity that frightened me. But I was wrong, Joe. You are not honest. You are not pure. You are just like me. You don't scare me anymore. Like the old joke, now we both know what you really are. And, this morning, we finally found out how much you charge. No, Joe," he said, squeezing his shoulder, "I think that you and I will get along just fine from now on. I like to deal with professional whores. Especially cheap ones!"

Joe stood outside in the hallway, the taste of victory souring in his mouth. He could not help but wonder whether what he had gained from Flaherty could ever compensate for what he had lost for himself.

Chapter / FORTY-TWO

IF CHRISTOPHER AMEN HAD PRESENTED SAMUEL HALPERN WITH his cup of hemlock, it was Abraham Kupperman who was to insure that the designated victim drain the bitter poison. The break in the normal social schedule with the Kuppermans had not gone unnoticed by Sylvia. However, her attempts to broach the topic to her husband met with feigned uninterest. It was with guarded emotion that Samuel learned of the old couple's overture to reestablish their weekly gathering.

"That was Abe and Jennie on the phone," Sylvia informed her seated husband. "They would like to come over this evening. I told

Jennie we would love to have them." Observing his dour expression, she said, "Wasn't that all right? I didn't think you had anything else planned."

"No," he reluctantly gave his assent. "That will be fine."

"You know, Sam, we haven't seen the Kuppermans for ages. It is very strange."

"What's so strange?" he snapped.

"I don't know, Sam, but something is wrong. I saw both of them at the temple meeting last week. Abe barely said hello. Jennie was cool. Has something happened between you and Abe?"

Her husband deflected her query. "Do you mean, has he got worse recently? No, he is doing well. How much longer his estrogens will keep his cancer in check, I don't know. But Abe knows the score. I have never lied to him. Jennie knows it as well. Abe tells her everything."

"No, that is not what I meant at all." She glowered at her husband, trying to decide if he really missed the import of her question or was adroitly sidestepping the issue. "Abe has always been more than just a patient. Now the both of them just act distant. I hope that nothing has happened."

"Don't be silly. Nothing has happened. Abe is still my patient and I am still his doctor."

"I know. But Sam, are you still his friend?"

"Sylvia, you are just imagining things. Go. Go. Get your crumb cake. Abe likes it. They will be here soon." He gently pushed her toward the kitchen.

At the outset it seemed as if Sylvia had worried in vain. Her two guests were affable, lighthearted. The quartet quickly resumed the traditional pattern of innocuous conversation long part of their weekly ritual. If anything, it was her husband who was tense and preoccupied.

"It is good to have you here again, Abe. You and Jennie," Sam said.

"Is there some reason that we shouldn't be here? Has something happened, Sam, that we are no longer welcome? Tell me, Sam. Aren't we still friends?"

"Sure, sure, Abe, I didn't mean it that way. I just . . ."

"Oh. What did you mean?"

"I meant with this Christopher Amen affair," Sam said. "You know that, Abe."

Abe swallowed hard to clear his throat. "Sam, I kept my mouth shut and my eyes closed while you and your pious friends crucified him. Is that why you thought it would be awkward? Why I might not want to come here again? Why, Sam," Abe drawled, "where can I get crumb cake like your Sylvia makes? I don't know how she does it."

"Abe, I wouldn't want you to feel that I influenced you. After all," Samuel said lamely, "even without you he wouldn't have made it. There was too much pressure to keep him out of Cromwell."

"Are you telling me that I am not guilty? That I shouldn't feel bad? That my conscience is clear?" His voice rose in timbre, his eyes blinking rapidly. "Sam. This is Abe you're talking to. I am as much of an expert on consciences as you are, and mine stinks! I did your dirty work for you with my eyes open. I am over twenty-one. I knew what I was doing. And it was wrong!" He picked up his cup of coffee. "So, please don't you tell me that my conscience is clean. It isn't."

"Abe," Samuel pleaded, "if you knew, why didn't you say no? I didn't twist your arm. You could have refused." He sought Sylvia for support but she had turned away from him.

Kupperman straightened his back as he faced his doctor. His voice was cold. "No, you didn't twist my arm. No, Sam, that is not where you operate. You have your own special route to get at my guts. It is much lower down than my arm. Refuse? I couldn't have refused you—and you damn well knew it.

"Sam, two years ago you had me by the balls. You cut them off. You left a scar and a heavy emptiness that makes Jennie cry out at night for my shame. A month ago, in this very room, you had

((293))

me by the same raw exposed nerve roots. Only then I cried out for *your* shame. The scar on your conscience, your soul. You cut me both times as my physician. The first time was to save my life. The second time it was for your son. You held the knife to me twice, but only once deserved.

Abe searched Samuel's face, hoping to discover there some trace of humility, perhaps a fleeting vestige of the guilt that had to be present.

"Did being a father justify your prostituting your profession? Did love for your son give you the right, as my doctor, to cut me to heal *your* sickness?" Abe's voice cracked. When he resumed, his tone was more compassionate.

"Sam, if you had come to me as a friend and asked for a favor, I would have said no. I honestly believed in Amen. This town needed his dream. I would have refused you. You would have understood as a friend and not asked again. But, no. You came to me cloaked in your invincible mantle as my physician. My chit in one hand and my check book in the other. Two years of my life for twenty years of your son's."

"Abe," Samuel tried to protest, his hypocrisy lying exposed for all to see, "I did not . . . actually . . . ask you."

His words flamed Kupperman's anger. His expression turned hostile and cruel. "Sam, I remember that evening. No, you did not come right out and say, 'Abe, close your eyes while we lynch Amen.' No, you didn't open your mouth. I did the asking for you." He turned his face away from his friend in disgust. "But, don't hide from yourself. What if I had not said anything? Just eaten my crumb cake until Jennie and I got up to leave? What then, Sam? Would you have stopped me, grabbed me by the sleeve, my coat, my hem, my leg—my empty sack? And then asked me that question, demanded that favor even while your other hand twisted my windpipe and throttled the life in my throat?"

Samuel shrank back in his chair, hiding from Kupperman's cruel accusation, which was searing his conscience.

"Yes, Sam, you would have asked, and damn loudly. But *how* would you have pleaded and begged? As a friend and risk my saying no? With your son hanging in the balance?

"I will tell you how. As my healer who traded my manhood for my life. Two testicles for two years. Just think, Sam, twelve months for each dried-up shriveled piece of flesh. It doesn't seem like very much and yet it seems like everything. Yes, Sam, that is what you did. Isn't it?

"If you had bargained with me for cash. So many dollars for each hour of life during those past two years, *that* I would have understood. You produce, you get paid. But to ask me, even to know that you possess such a lethal option, one that obliges me to betray myself because you saved my life—that is wrong! That is your crime, Sam!

"What gives you that cruel power over me? And me? Why did I obey that silent command? Did you know all along that I would jump to the tug of that invisible chain? I don't understand." He stopped, his forehead knotted in thought. "Maybe I do . . . a little. As long as there have been witch doctors, or priests, or prophets, or healers, or gods, we stand in awe of them and obey. You, Sam. Are you one of them? Tell me. Are you one of those heroes or just a frightened father? Abraham would have sacrificed his son for his God. You betrayed your profession for your immortality."

He shook his head at Samuel with pity. "No, Sam. If only you had come to me, not as my savior, not as my friend, not even as my doctor—but as a father. Then Sam, I would have done anything for you, gladly. I know better than you what a son is, what a son isn't, when a son isn't. That I can understand. If you had wanted to kill, to maim, to perjure for your son and needed my help, I would have given it proudly. One father to another father. But you didn't. You couldn't come right out and ask. Hypocrisy smothered your honesty—if you ever had any."

Kupperman walked over to his chair and slowly lowered himself into it, seeking the security of its enveloping warmth. The final words parted from him with difficulty.

"You didn't trust in friendship. You didn't trust in simply being a father. You came to me as my doctor, my god, expecting, demanding as your right my acquiescence in your sin. That I can never forgive, Sam. I don't think even you will ever forgive yourself." The sentence merged into an almost inaudible lament. "You had no right!"

Before Abe had finished, Samuel jumped to his feet. Whatever guilt or shame had possessed him earlier had now disappeared. He glanced with contempt at the aged and trembling man cushioned in the sheltering wing chair. "Had no right? Hell! I had every right. Friend. Father. Doctor. What the hell difference does it make? I acted as I had to. For my son, I had every right, the dream of every man for his immortality. Stephen was my future. When I die, I shall live again in him. For that *all* was permissible. All was justified."

He paused to suck in a deep breath. "You are wrong, my friend, my conscience is clean. I have no guilt. But you, Abe, what about you?" The seated figure did not know how to respond to the sudden outburst. He could not fathom this enigmatic man who could thwart death and strangle decency with seemingly equal detachment. He was unprepared for Halpern's next words.

"You would have helped me as a father?" he brutally challenged. "Give me my son when yours is dead, buried a thousand miles from your heart? You? How?

"No bitterness? No rancor? None, Abe? You are the perfect man? The Job who never complains, never questions? My son, here with me. My immortality, guaranteed. The seed of my testicles for me to touch, to caress until the instant of my death. You, no son, not even your balls. Still no anger?

"And hatred? What! No hatred toward the man who holds death in abeyance in a little white pill that you must take every morning for the rest of your life? Whose knife gave you hope? No hatred toward this man who eats and defecates like you, but who can give life to a stranger like garbage to a stray mongrel?

"No jealousy? You lost your manhood. Lost your son. You have lost your life. Still . . . still . . ." he flung the words at him with violent gestures, crying with the injustice and the torment he knew they evoked, but driven nevertheless to expel the loathsome truth. "Still, you haven't lost your love for your fellowman? What are you? Some kind of holy man, a saint? You of all people still can have faith, hope, and love.

"No, Abe. I don't buy that. Don't *you* be a hypocrite. Help me out of friendship?" The question laced with disbelief. "Yes, I agree with you there. I don't think that you would have.

"Help me as one father to another father? No. I don't have such faith in the perfection of man and certainly neither do you. No, Abe. You helped me because I am your doctor, and I made the deal with the angel of death to trade fifteen grams of warm bleeding tissue for two years of your life. You are right, Abe. That is how and why I asked you."

Abraham Kupperman took his wife's hand in his. When he spoke it was with tears in his eyes. Not just from the lancinating wounds his friend had flayed upon him, but with pity for the inflicter. "Sam, it is not only that you have no faith in your fellowman. You have no faith of any kind at all. Not even in yourself. I would have helped you—as a father. But you didn't take the gamble."

"Would you, Abe? I didn't gamble with a dream."

"I don't know, Sam," he replied to the lingering question as he rose to leave. "Maybe, maybe I wouldn't have either. I, we will never know. You, you Sam, maybe you didn't gamble. But did you win? Did you keep your son?" He smiled at the irony. "You got rid of Amen all right. That was easy. You had me to do your dirty work on the board. But, Stephen, that was different. That was a little harder. What grip did you have on his testicles? You cut off his foreskin. Do you have a mortgage on his manhood as well?

From what I hear in Cromwell, Stephen is not coming back here to practice with you, anyway."

Kupperman helped his wife to rise from the sofa. As they walked to the door Abe turned and said, "No, Sam, maybe you didn't gamble, but you lost anyway." The words hung brittle in the air. "You lost me. You lost your honor, if that ever meant anything to you. You lost your son."

Both of them said good-bye to Sylvia who had clung to the periphery of the scene, crying softly with muffled sobs. Even as the aging couple quietly left the room, they could see Sylvia still sitting there, paralyzed by the tragic drama, unable to intercede either for her husband's safety or solace.

Chapter / **FORTY-THREE**

THE GRAY DAMP AFTERNOON SEEMED TO SIGNAL THE END OF summer. Samuel sat depressed and withdrawn in the corner of the library, shrunken back into his armchair, staring morosely into the garden where the light drizzling rain was patterning the thin puddles on the flagstone patio. The furrows in his cheeks and jowls were heavily creased as his face hung forward. Since Stephen's decision to go to Maine, Sylvia had watched her husband slowly die. It was as if a lethal poison was silently corroding the stability of his life and extracting his faith in the future.

It was inevitable that Stephen would return to legitimize his break with Cromwell. Not even his instinctive dread of another encounter with his father could condone an evasion of what he knew to be his filial duty.

"Stephen," his father repeated for the dozenth time, "you realize that you do not have to leave for Maine with Chris. You received privileges to practice at Mercy as of July first. I still want you with me as badly as I did before."

"How do you expect me to stay?" Stephen asked, still angered by his father's persistent refusal to acknowledge his decision to leave. "You know how much the Millsite project meant to me. And, stabbing Chris in the back. How could you do it? Even worse, to stand by and let him go down the drain without even lifting a finger or saying a word?"

"You overestimate my importance, Stephen. There was a great deal of opposition to Millsite, not only among the doctors but also among the Board of Trustees. I am only one person."

"Like hell. I don't know the whole story. Someday I will, and . . ." His voice trailed behind a lightly veiled threat.

"I will tell you if you really want to know. Sure, I voted for you and against Chris. Tell me, my son, would you have done differently under the circumstances? Be honest."

"Yes, I would."

"Well, you are not a father," Samuel retorted as if that statement demolished all opposing viewpoints.

"No. I am not a father. However, would you expect me to remain here with you after what you did?"

"Tell me something, Stephen. For the sake of argument, let us assume that I died tomorrow. Would you still persist in not coming back to Cromwell to practice?"

"I don't understand."

"I think that you do. Are you leaving because of Christopher Amen and his clinic, or just to spite me?"

His son just stared at him with loathing. "You still don't understand that someone other than yourself can have a commitment to something? Do you? No! The hell with Cromwell!"

"Why, Stephen? Why should you follow Amen?"

"Because I believe in what he is doing. I am thirty-one years old. I have maybe twenty-five, thirty years to make something of myself. I don't want at the end of that time to look back and count my days only by a growing pile of patient charts in my office. Chris had an idea to use my skills to create something I could be proud of.

"The clinic is more to me than just a building. It is a break with a hundred years of rigid tradition. A place where doctors can put the needs of the patient ahead of their ledger cards. A place where incompetence cannot thrive by cult and prosper on blackmail. A chance for medicine to recapture the respect that people like you have destroyed. To me, Dad, it is something to aspire to, a dream, *my dream*."

"Easy . . . easy, my son. Sure, it is a dream." Sam's voice turned stern and piercing. "But it is Chris's dream, not yours. *He* is the father and the mother. He is the midwife. It is his conception, his seed, his gestation, his labor of childbirth and, in the final reckoning, it will be his success or failure. What in it is yours?"

Stephen looked up, scared, as if a toy balloon he was clutching had slipped his grasp and was in danger of drifting away.

"I believe in it just as much as he does."

"Stephen, a child can have only one father. Your dream, you say? Up to nine months ago, you didn't know a clinic from a hole in the ground. You couldn't have cared any more than the man in the moon about welfare patients, tuberculous Navajos, starving Chileans. Nine months ago, there were no righteous cries of indignation against doctors driving big new Cadillacs. If I recall, you couldn't wait to join them yourself.

"Now, all of a sudden, you have religion. You are like the convert—more pious, more zealous, more bigoted than those who converted you. Tell me, why are you a disciple of Amen's? What caused this sudden revelation after thirty-one years of starving in a spiritual desert? This divine vision that came to you in a cloud of fire by day and a burning bush by night?"

His son ignored the blatant sarcasm. "Dad, I look at you. You came here thirty years ago with holes in your pants, looked down upon because you couldn't go anywhere else. You hung on and worked and succeeded. You are respected, successful. The point is, that you did it all by yourself. You can look back on your life and feel proud.

"What can *I* say? What have *I* accomplished so far? You have paid the bills, filled out the forms, signed the checks, opened the doors, fixed my teeth, even cut off my foreskin. What part of me is me? It is all yours!

"And, after July first, it would have been the same thing all over again for another thirty years. Your town. Your hospital. Your practice. Your patients. Not *my* child, but Samuel Halpern's grandchild. You belittle the clinic. Tell me instead, what in all of Cromwell is more mine?"

"Shall I put the foreskin back on for you, Stephen? Give you back your buck teeth? Do you want to sign a promissory note for the hundred thousand dollars you have cost me—at interest—and pledge your next twenty years' income as collateral? Do you want to open up your office in Cromwell and have me bring in my own partner and strangle you like Flaherty and Best do to their competition? Tell me what you really want, and I will do it!

"I will tell you something, Stephen. I do know how you feel. It is true. Even though I cry the warm salty tears and wince with the sharp pain of those early years, I do feel proud when I look back and see from where I started and how far I have climbed. For a brief moment, I could almost fool myself into thinking, goddamn it, it *is* good to have those memories, even if they hurt. But," he shook his head vigorously, "God willing, only for a split second. I don't really want those scars I bear any more than I wanted the original pain that first seared my flesh and left those ugly marks there to remind me of my struggles. It hurt too much then, and it pains too much now. Especially when you're old and your tolerance for pain is low.

"Ask me. Would I rather have had it soft and easy and without the happiness of achieving against odds? Or would I have preferred the past mean, the outcome doubtful? No! Not on your life! God-damn it, I would have wanted the easy way, the guaranteed future. But I didn't have any choice. I had to take what I was given and fight to improve my lot. Remember, Stephen, life is short. There is no such thing as a hereafter."

"Dad," Stephen tried to speak.

"Just a minute, Stephen. Let me finish. You claim to disapprove of what I have given to you. You are discontent with the prognosis of your future. You want the hard harsh dream. Go to Livermore. Suffer! Or—you can come here, keep your mouth shut, and be grateful. You decide, but do not ask me for my blessing."

"Dad, even if everything you say is true, that doesn't make my wanting to go with Chris wrong. Suppose I leave with him. If I find, after a year, eighteen months, that it is the wrong thing for me, I will come back. I need that chance. Let me have it."

"No, Stephen. I have waited too long already. I am an impatient father. Don't I deserve to be? I might be dead in a year!"

"But, Dad, if it is the right thing for me, then I will have avoided a tragic mistake in coming back to Cromwell. If it turns out to be no good, then I can never accuse you of depriving me of a chance to do something on my own. Don't protect me all the time. Let me make my own mistakes."

"Why?" his father retorted, stung by his son's defiant stand. "One Halpern to bleed in this lifetime is enough.

"No, Stephen, you are my son. My sperm. My ejaculation. I cleaned your diaper, burped you, wrote your excuses from school, and kissed away your tears when you hurt yourself. I have advised you, coerced you, and nursed you. You are my tarnished immortality. All that I possess. I made you, Stephen. You belong to me."

"Not anymore," Stephen warned. "I am my own future, not yours. You still don't see. Chris told you. You have lost me. I am leaving. Let . . . me . . . go!"

His father rose to face him. His face was drawn, drained white. His facial muscles twitched with involuntary muscular contractions. Panicked, he reached out his hands to grab his son and hold him.

"No, Stephen," he pleaded, his voice tremulous, "you are mine, Stephen. Flawed, imperfect, but I love you. You cannot leave. You can't . . ."

Stephen started to rebut but one look at his father convinced him of the utter futility of that vain gesture. He clawed his father's hands from his body. "Damn you to hell!" he shouted and stalked out of the room.

Samuel stood immobile, ashen, his limbs quivering. Not until Sylvia entered and led him to a chair did he begin to regain his composure.

"Sylvia, I have lost. Nobody has won. We have all lost."

"Oh, Sam, it has been like a bad dream. What we wanted has turned out so badly, so wrong."

"Sylvia," he begged for an answer, "what kind of a family are we? What kind of a father am I?"

"You are a good husband, Sam," Sylvia tried to comfort him. "It was not your fault that Stephen didn't measure up to your dream."

"That was the trouble all along, Sylvia. My sin was wanting a dream to come alive like real flesh and blood."

"But Sam, dreams are good. They nourished hope for thirty years. They made the long nights bearable."

"Yes. That should have been their only function. The dreams of heroes live on. When ordinary men wake up, their dreams vanish and persist only as some vague formless recollection. It was wrong of me to expect my dream to outlast my sleep. But, I had too much pride. That is why I could not let go. Now, Sylvia, what are my nights to be filled with? Emptiness? Like Abe? No son? No hope?"

"No, Sam, you must dream again."

"I don't know if I can, Sylvia," Sam said in a voice breaking with fear. "It has been so long with only one dream. I am scared. What if there can be no more?"

"Let me help you, Sam."

"Oh God, I need you, Sylvia. How much I love you." He reached for her face and kissed it greedily, unwilling to surrender even for an instant that shared moment of warmth. They clung together awkwardly, two thickened old people. They clutched each other in desperation, with the broken fragments of flickering hope falling around them like fireflies dying in the early glow of another new day.

Chapter / **FORTY-FOUR**

"DR. LASH? DR. CARL LASH?" SAMUEL HALPERN WAS INCREDU-lous as he waved the new patient folder at his office nurse.

"Yes, Dr. Halpern," Judy, his office nurse, confirmed for the third time.

"You are sure that it is not a personal visit?" he asked again, still astonished to find the Chief of the Department of Surgery waiting for him as a patient.

"Yes, Dr. Halpern. I specifically asked him. Otherwise I would have put him right into your private office. He said that he wished to see you as a patient. He would not tell me what the problem

((307))

was, but there is a note on the front of the chart for you to call Dr. Bradford Gill before you see Dr. Lash."

Samuel looked down at the chart again, completely bewildered. "Did you at least . . ." and he nodded in the direction of the crowded waiting room.

"Yes," she smiled. "I put Dr. Lash into examining room four. I thought it would be better for him to wait inside for you, rather than out there." She pointed to the motley assemblage in the waiting room poised to descend upon her boss this busy afternoon.

"Thanks, Judy, you did the right thing. Please get Dr. Gill for me on the telephone."

As Samuel sat at his desk waiting for the call to be completed, he flipped through the virgin chart, wondering what could have brought the uncordial physician to his office as a patient. For an instant, a smile crossed his lips. The clap? Jesus! Even Lash could get a shot of penicillin without exposing his diagnosis, let alone the disease itself all over the small city of Cromwell. Sexual problems? For that Lash would go as far away as he could for relief. No, it would be a cold day in hell before Lash would come to Samuel Halpern's office with a penis that didn't behave.

Then what? And why Gill? If it were a routine problem like a kidney stone, or prostatitis, Lash would buttonhole him directly and not pussyfoot around with an internist as an intermediary. He pursed his lips gravely, convinced at last that it could not be a good omen if Carl Lash needed another physician to run interference for him.

"Sam," Gill's hoarse voice boomed in his ear. "I sent Carl over to see you. Believe me, it was like pulling teeth, but I insisted that we get a urologic opinion. I didn't want him to talk to you in the hospital . . . too many ears."

"Sure, Brad. What can I do for you—and Carl?"

Gill hesitated for a minute, his words halting. "I don't know," he apologized, "maybe I am making a mountain out of a molehill.

You know the blood profile that Pathology does every six months?"

Samuel knew all too well the semiannual bloodletting, done gratis by Mercy Hospital as a service to the nurses and doctors. Each time, his own cholesterol had shown a steady upward tilt, a fact Samuel had resigned himself to, acknowledging the ever-rising figure as a bastard offspring of both his Jewish genes and the god of inevitability.

"Well," Gill continued, "Lash's acid phosphatase came back abnormally high." Before Samuel could interrupt to inquire the figure, Gill added, "Two point one. Maybe it was nothing, but I checked it with Simon myself, and the normal for the lab is zero point nine. Well, I made up some phony excuse and got some more blood from Lash. Believe me, that's a harder job than getting a sperm count from that stud."

"It all depends upon who is doing the collecting."

"Well," Gill's voice grew slow and measured, "this time it came back two point seven. Now maybe it was higher because I got the specimen after I did a careful rectal exam and you know that massaging the prostate may release some of the enzyme into the bloodstream. Even so," he said, "I still think that it is too high."

"What did you tell Carl?"

"Just what I told you. He knows about the two values. He wouldn't go to see anybody. So, we diddled. We got an I.V.P. but Fallon says the kidneys are great and the bladder empties fine. We got a radioactive bone scan, which showed no evidence of any metastatic cancer spread. I even did a bone marrow, but it was completely negative."

"All right, Brad," Samuel said. "I will be glad to go over Carl. I will also make sure that I see the films and the scan. But, I might as well tell you right now what my feelings are about this before I see him, because if you don't agree, there is no sense in my even starting."

"Sure, Sam. Sure. Anything. Anything at all. And, Sam," he

((309))

added, almost as an afterthought, "his prostate felt normal to me." He snickered. "But you know me, Sam. All I feel up there anyway is shit."

"That's all right, Brad. All I hear whenever I use one of you boys' stethoscopes is noise."

Stern once again, Sam said, "Let me tell you what my usual procedure is in a case like this. If there is any chance at all, even the slightest possibility that we are dealing with cancer, and obviously that is the only reason this whole business has already gone this far, I will biopsy the gland. If the report is negative, I will do nothing but wait and rebiopsy it again in three to six months. If, on the other hand, the biopsy is positive, God forbid, then I will do a radical prostatectomy."

There was a gasp at the other end of the phone. Samuel could hear the exclamation of horror and dismay that Gill was poorly suppressing on behalf of his friend, colleague, and now patient.

"We have to, Brad. If there is no overt evidence of spread of the cancer, and, from what you have told me, there does not seem to be any so far, then the chance for a cure is one hundred percent if we can get the local tumor out early."

Samuel waited for some sign of agreement. Gill was silent but his heavy breathing at the other end testified to his presence.

"Listen, Brad," Samuel insisted, "what are you interested in? Sure, he will be impotent after the operation, but which is more important, his life or his screwing around? Even more," he drove the words home across the electronic gap hoping to imprint them so deeply that there would be no future equivocation or recrimination, "three to six weeks after the operation we will repeat the acid phosphatase. If it is back to normal, then we will know that the cancer cells in the removed prostate gland itself were responsible for the elevated enzyme. *But* if it still remains high or the pathology report on the extirpated tissue shows a high degree of malignancy, then . . . then we must assume that there are microscopic deposits of cancer spread throughout the body that we cannot detect." He waited a minute for Gill to digest that information. "Then," he said, "we will do a bilateral orchiectomy!"

Samuel knew, as Gill knew he knew, that the specter of Carl Lash's possible castration hung over them. *That* was the primary reason, that and the impotence, Gill had shunted the vain egocentric patient onto his fellow physician with more than just the usual feeling of need for an outside consultation. Two dangling testicles, with the sterile scalpel to slash them off—all oscillating loosely back and forth. Samuel could hear Gill's sigh of relief now that the fateful words had been uttered and by someone other than himself.

"You are right, Sam. Do whatever you have to do. Lash is not a baby. He knows the score. Talk to him. Tell him. I think he will understand."

"One thing more," Samuel said. "If you or Carl would like to have another opinion, please don't stand on ceremony. If you don't know anyone else, I will be glad to recommend someone at Mass. General or the Leahy Clinic. Don't feel that you or Carl are beholden to me."

"Oh, no," Gill replied. "We discussed that. Carl is perfectly content to have you take care of him. After all, it is no great mystery; if Simon says the biopsy is cancer—that's it. Carl will have to agree to let you do what you must to save his life." Halpern heard a frantic rustle of papers on the other end of the phone. "Thank you, Sam. I really have got to go. Thanks a lot."

When Samuel entered room four it seemed to him as if the seriousness of the diagnosis and the horrible stigmata of its cure had at least outwardly affected him far more than the potential victim. Lash was calm, at ease, and correct in manner. Indicating the folder in Samuel's hand, he asked, "Did you speak to Brad?"

"Yes, we just spoke. But I am sure——"

"Why don't we get on with it, Sam?" Lash said impatiently.

Lash disrobed, hanging his expensive tailored suit up carefully on the wall hook. He stripped completely, without shame, his expression impassive.

"Here?" Carl asked, indicating the examining table. Without another word, he climbed up on it and lay flat on his back, his eyes focused on the ceiling, his hands held loosely at his sides.

Samuel palpated his abdomen. He felt the large heavy testicles hanging limp between the long tanned thighs. He stripped back the redundant foreskin to inspect the head of the thick pendulous penis. He peered intently at the glistening meatus through which, over a lifetime, rivers of Lash sperm and urine had exited.

He propped Lash up on his hands and knees, with his head and shoulders pressed down to the table. Samuel put on a brown rubber glove and inserted his right index finger gently into the rectum. Over and over he swept the digit, methodically examining every square centimeter of the firm walnut-sized rubbery gland. He shook his head in frustration. He could feel no protrusion, no lump, no deep-seated nodule, no rocky-hard margin, to arouse his concern. Again he pressed, trying to evoke some evidence to mesh with the elevated cancer enzyme. Lash let out a stifled groan as the rigid finger worked too stiffly into the seminal vesicles that lay adjacent to the prostate.

Nothing! Damn it! Exasperated by his lack of success, Samuel let the surgeon up and helped him off the table. He sat at the small writing corral while Lash washed himself and dressed. Neither man said a word. His toilet completed, the patient reseated himself and waited for Samuel to begin.

"Nothing, Carl. Nothing," he reported, "except—" and he shrugged his shoulders in doubt, "unless . . . maybe the right lobe feels a little bit firmer than it should. God knows, I can't tell. All I can say is that it certainly isn't anything large or threatening." He looked into Lash's eyes, trying hard to convince him that he was telling the truth and not just issuing false reassurances. The surgeon still said nothing.

"I would recommend that you come into Mercy for a day and let us biopsy both lobes of the prostate. It won't take long. We will use the Silverman needle and you will never know the difference."

"Unless you find something," his tone sarcastic.

"That is why we are going in, Carl. You know that. How many women with lumps in their breasts do you sit by and idly watch without biopsying? How many of them do you biopsy time and time again, afraid that you might miss that last one that is not a cyst, but a malignancy?" He squeezed the surgeon's shoulder in a gesture of sincerity.

"Carl, if I honestly thought you had cancer, I would start preparing you for the worst. I will be very surprised if the biopsy comes back positive."

Lash stared at him for a minute, unflinching, weighing the decision carefully. He conceded, "All right, Sam. When do you want to do it?"

"Anytime that is convenient for you. On the way out, we will ask Judy to get the next earliest time. We will admit you as 'Mr. Smith.' I will book the case as just an ordinary cystoscopy. Not a biopsy of the prostate. There is no reason for everyone in God's creation to know what is going on. Especially when it is probably just gilding the lily."

"Fine, Sam," Lash agreed. As he stood up to leave, he said, "Is there anything else?"

God! The man was cool, Halpern thought. Never once did he challenge the diagnosis, nor allude to the emasculating therapy. If anyone, Lash, the philanderer, should have given just a slight hint of trepidation. But, no. One would have thought he was coming into the hospital to have a hemorrhoid fixed. Well, you can say that for the man, he really has balls. Even as that morbid pun flitted in and out of his mind, he could not help comparing the departing physician, suave and commanding, with the helpless naked spectacle of flesh, knees to his chest, speared through his asshole by an impaling finger just minutes before.

For some odd reason, Samuel felt angry. Lash should have given him a chance to console, to counter grief. He should have begged for mercy, shown a little fear, a touch of humility, instead of the blatant machismo. If only he had pleaded, implored, railed against the injustice of his fate, then the compassionate urologist was certain he would not have felt that sudden menacing trickle of cold fear pierce his consciousness. That deadly question that slithered so silently through the crevasses of his mind to threaten this brazen patient. What would this brave man be, he wondered, *without* his testicles?

Samuel trembled at that very moment, just a bit, for fear that the cruel jesting gods above might also wonder the same thing about the tall, arrogant son of a bitch who had just left his office.

Chapter / FORTY-FIVE

CARL LASH HAD ENTERED MERCY, HAD HIS BIOPSY TAKEN, AND was discharged almost before anybody knew that he had been a patient. During the week it required for the tissue to be processed, Samuel encountered the taciturn surgeon many times while making rounds and even once or twice in the Operating Suite Locker Room. Other than a perfunctory nod or some totally noncommittal conversation, neither of them ever broached the subject of incipient diagnosis or the radical steps that might be required to extirpate it.

Brad Gill was more direct and overtly concerned. In contrast to his patient's laconic comments, the internist buttonholed Samuel whenever he passed him in the hall, to trap him against some convenient deserted alcove or to drag him into an empty room, there to enquire in a loud tone the status of the tissue evaluation. Samuel could not refrain from expressing sympathy for Gill's worry. However, he explained that nothing could hasten the laborious process of rendering that sliver of Carl Lash into an irrevocable commitment of his future morbidity or mortality, whichever the case would turn out to be.

Those physicians on the staff who were aware that Lash had been admitted as a patient would sidle up to the urologist, attempting to glean the true story behind the mysterious admission. Samuel's stock answer was that certain genito-urinary diseases were "private" property, chuckling at the pun. His demeanor was calculated to suggest to the inquisitor that there were sexual overtones, leaving the inquiring physicians certainly no wiser, but satisfied in entertaining the thought that Cromwell's medical super stud—or at least his phallus—had finally been brought low.

It was with other than a lighthearted mood that Samuel responded to the belated call from Simon Pirie's office. It was obvious that the news was not favorable. Taking Samuel by the shoulder, the pathologist escorted him into his private study. His expression was grim, his carriage somber. Samuel could see how the man was suffering under the heavy responsibility of having to report the irrefutable evidence of malignancy waiting under the oil-immersion lens. He gestured toward the microscope, inviting the urologist to inspect for himself the slide nestling within its substage.

Samuel sat down and took off his eyeglasses. He adjusted the ocular lenses to accommodate the width of the bridge across his nose. Then, millimeters at a time, he turned the vernier-scaled knob to bring into sharp focus the sheets of purple tissue cells. Suddenly, he gasped. He moved the microscope up and down, unable to rid the field of the unmistakable signs of prostatic cancer. Pirie picked up the cardboard folder resting next to the microscope, opened it, and replaced the original slide with a second one from a different part of the biopsy tissue.

"They are all the same, Sam," he said in a low voice, choked with distress. "Here. Look." He pushed the docket into Samuel's hands. Samuel went through all six slides. Field after field of cancer dazzled his retina, making him blink from the brilliant light pouring through the vivid chromatic pigments.

"What can I say, Sam?" Pirie asked. "Every slide!" He slowly replaced the glass specimens in the cardboard folder again and tied the two sides together with the attached twine loop.

"If you want," he said, "I can send them to Boston to Iwanovici at the General, or to Soule at the Peter Bent Brigham, or——" Pirie's voice trembled.

"Please. Don't take it so hard, Simon. It isn't your fault. I will ask Carl and Brad. I am not quite sure what good that would do. It's cancer. It doesn't take a genius to make the diagnosis. It isn't as if he had some rare rhabdomyosarcoma or some exotic leukemia. Cancer of the prostate is cancer of the prostate."

"How old is Carl?" Simon asked.

Samuel knew full well the tragic import of that innocent question.

"In his early fifties. I know . . . I know . . . at that age the cancer is more malignant. Harder to control. At least we got to it early, or I hope early. Maybe, maybe there is still chance for a cure. There is certainly no evidence of any metastatic spread. The bone films and scan are completely negative. Brad's bone marrow also shows no tumor cells."

He looked quizzically at the short pathologist, his voice reflecting a persistent uncertainty. "You know, Simon, the only thing that I don't quite understand is the acid phosphatase. Only once before have I ever seen it so high without any overt evidence of spread. Oh, well, maybe it just means that the metastases are still microscopic but then . . ." he stammered, trying to make some sense out of the confusing and conflicting facts. "At least, thanks to your fancy test, we were alerted to investigate the possibility of cancer early and we got the biopsy. In a way, Carl may owe his life to you."

If Samuel thought that he detected a wry twist to the pathologist's thin tight lips, he would not have been mistaken. The fleeting gesture vanished as evanescently as it had appeared and the bland, concerned, sympathetic expression reasserted itself. Simon nodded his agreement with Samuel's appraisal, loudly blessing for Carl's sake those divinities who had been responsible for the lucky chain of events that had detected this mortal threat to Lash's life and initiated the appropriate steps, albeit radical, by which his life could now be preserved.

"Thanks again, Simon. I will let you know if we want the slides sent out." Samuel's departing words lingered behind him, "I have a terrible feeling that you will be getting a lot more tissue from Carl in the near future."

If that morbid prospect worried the urologist, it did the reverse for the middle-aged pathologist. His spirits were definitely lighter and his manner almost cheerful as he watched the retreating figure move down the hall. He thrust his two hands deep into his pockets, his fingers finding their way to his crotch. He fondled his penis and testicles, savoring their meaty resistance, the warmth of the responsive flesh, the sensuous pleasure of the sudden pressure against the semiturgid glans. Clutching protectively the engorged totems of his masculinity, he walked back into the office, repeating over and over again, this time out loud, though no one was there to hear, "You are right, Sam. Oh, how right you are."

Chapter / **FORTY-SIX**

SAMUEL CHECKED THE LARGE ELECTRIC CLOCK OVER THE PORCE-
lain washtub and shifted the coarse nylon bristle brush to his left
palm for another five-minute scrub of his right hand and arm. He
stood there, engrossed in the required preoperative task, his stout
body hidden within the billowing cheap cotton pajamalike surgical
pants and shirt. His head was covered by a cloth cap, his face
concealed by the disposable paper mask. Only his eyes, curtained
behind thick lenses, gave any idea as to what he was thinking.

Samuel, whose instincts about people were unusually perceptive,
had an intuitive feeling that Carl Lash was heading for disaster, a

tragedy completely separate from the prognosis of his cancer. It was obvious that the man had changed. Last night Samuel had visited Lash in his private suite at Mercy to prepare him for this morning's radical surgery. For an instant he thought he was in the wrong room, for although the patient had been admitted hours earlier that afternoon he still had not changed out of his street clothes and was sitting huddled in the corner of the darkened chamber.

Carl did not move when Samuel entered the room. He continued to sit motionless, staring straight ahead. He barely responded to Samuel's greeting. His hands gripped the arms of the wooden chair as if afraid to let go of the support. His feet were pressed firmly on the floor in front of him, his demeanor petrified with fear.

Samuel tried to break through the barrier, reaching over to clasp Lash on the shoulder. The man shrank back to avoid the human touch. Samuel was shaken by his inability to make contact with the terrified patient. He sat down next to him, hoping that gradually a communion would be established. As gently as he could, he started to explain the nature of the operation. Lash's only comment was a barely perceptible nod of his head to acknowledge his assent.

Samuel knew that his words blotted out forever any future hope of Lash's remaining a sexually normal male. However, the deed and its painful sequelae had to be faced openly. Samuel had hoped for some close bond so that he could interject words of assurance and contribute the ritual gestures and signs of compassion that were so necessary at times like this, even when the patient was a physician himself. But Lash refused to allow even a handshake and remained isolated, as Samuel narrated the risks and perils of the radical surgery now less than ten hours away.

"Carl," Samuel said, "you know that you will be impotent. There is no way of preventing that."

Just the brief motion of the head in response.

"That we cannot help. There is also a calculated risk that you will be incontinent." Samuel thought he heard a gasp.

"We must operate close to the valve. To do a good cancer operation, we have to sever the prostate from the external sphincter. If we injure the valve, if the cancer is stuck to it, if a retractor presses too hard on the sphincter, or sometimes for no good reason at all, you might end up incontinent of urine." He quickly added, "We can always try some of those new procedures to reconstruct the valve, but the operation may or may not be successful. And Carl," Sam said gently, hoping that the surgeon would relent and confide his fear, even if just for a minute, "if I injure the rectum in peeling it off the prostate, you will need a colostomy." Lash started from his chair, terror-stricken.

"Carl, it will only be for a short time. That complication, thank God, is temporary." He paused, happy that he finally had something of relative comfort to offer. But Lash had already retreated back into his shell, his gaze once more averted from his unwelcomed visitor.

Samuel stayed seated for several minutes more, wondering what else he could say. Finally he got up to shake Lash's hand in parting, to reassure him that the operation would be successful, that there was an excellent chance for a cure.

The surgeon's hand was cold and limp and fell back on his lap as soon as Samuel had relinquished it. Samuel cast one last forlorn look on the silent, tormented patient whose fierce emotions of fear and pride were trapped within. He left with a horrible foreboding for this vulnerable man who refused even at the very last possible moment either to cry or to pray.

Chapter / **FORTY-SEVEN**

HIS LIMBS TREMBLING, HIS BODY DRENCHED WITH SWEAT, SAMUEL Halpern peeled off the blood-soaked surgical scrub suit and kicked the crumpled stained garment into the corner of the locker room. His heart was still racing from the tension of the operation. His forehead was creased with deep linear furrows from the tight cap. He sank, exhausted, into the battered armchair in the corner. He permitted himself a well-deserved sigh of congratulation. At least the complicated surgery had gone well.

The postoperative course was uneventful. There was no need for a colostomy. No urinary incontinence. Not even a wound infection.

Unfortunately, the surgical success was pyrrhic only. The acid phosphatase did not fall as Samuel had confidently expected. Even more devastating was the Pathology report on the extirpated specimen.

"Carl," Samuel approached his apprehensive patient on the sixth postoperative day, "I just spoke with Simon. He claims that the cancer has invaded the veins, the arteries. It has infiltrated around the nerve bundles and even spilled over into the lymphatic channels. It doesn't look good."

The patient just stared at him, his expression blank. His face was gaunt, the normal thin contours now accentuated by his recent loss of weight, which Samuel knew was occasioned more by an increasing disinterest in food than by any valid medical reason. His complexion was pale with a greasy film over the yellow cast of his skin. When he moved, his feet dragged like an old man. When he spoke, frayed chips of half-dried saliva collected in the corners of his mouth. Without his being aware of it, his hands began to pick and scratch their way down to his scrotum, which lay exposed under the short hospital johnny. Samuel observed the pantomime with morbid fascination. Oblivious to the unconscious act, the patient slowly stroked his penis and rubbed the large heavy testicles hanging lax below. As he stared vacuously at Samuel, his hands continued to work away on their own as if they belonged to some other person.

Hypnotized, Samuel watched the steady kneading, the obscene massaging, unable to take his eyes off the regressive infantile behavior. Finally, he reached out and withdrew the surgeon's hands and rested them on his thighs where they fluttered limply for a moment or two before remaining still.

"We have to, Carl," he whispered softly. "We must do an orchiectomy. There is no other way."

For an instant, there was no response. Then, without warning, Lash began to cry. His head jerked back and forth as he uttered low-pitched sounds of pain, grief, terror, fright, and sorrow.

Samuel seized Carl's hands like one would a wounded child. He kept up a steady barrage of soft words to soothe the aroused patient. Just as he thought he had succeeded, Lash pulled himself away. He grabbed at his scrotum, trying to tear off his testicles and throw them bodily at the doctor. His nails tore into the flesh until it ripped and bled.

"Take them, you fucking bastard!" he cried. "Take them! Take them!" he screamed over and over again even as Samuel with two nurses and an orderly watched the powerful sedative take effect and drug the tormented patient into restful silence and slumber.

When Samuel returned the next day, Carl was calm again. He signed the operative permit for his castration with no more than a cursory glance. Samuel looked at the patient wondering whether it was better for the man to vent his emotions or to keep them locked within. Suddenly Lash laughed. It was a high-pitched, almost feminine laugh, one that made Samuel's flesh crawl. Carl pointed to his groin. "You know, Sam, while I am asleep, and you take off my balls, why don't you cut off the whole thing? You can make me a cunt. Swap my prick for a cunt . . . prick for a cunt . . ." he said unashamedly over and over again, until Samuel was forced to leave the room in embarrassment.

Even outside the room, Halpern could hear the surgeon repeating the singsong phrase without letup. Samuel let out his breath slowly. As he walked down the deserted hall, he made a mental note in the morning to ask Fels to drop by and talk to Carl, if it wasn't already too late.

Chapter / **FORTY-EIGHT**

THE CASTRATION WAS SWIFT AND UNCOMPLICATED. THE ENTIRE elapsed time was less than twenty minutes. With Lash anesthetized and supine on the table, Samuel bathed the shaven genitalia with the dark iodine antiseptic solution, thrusting and twisting the heavy amber-coated sponges deep into the limp corrugated sac. He draped the field with layers of sterile blue towels until all that one could see of the lanky physician was the long flaccid penis and the two large testes still intact within their mantle of skin and fascia.

Samuel seized the right testicle in his left hand, wrenching it to the surface of the skin, as if he was trying to pop out the contents.

((327))

When the organ was tensed under the severe pressure, he sliced through the skin overlying the round bulge. He cut deeper and deeper with a razor-sharp scalpel until he reached the glistening tunics that enveloped the slippery oval organ and allowed it free mobility in between the thin sheets of lubricated membrane.

He forced the testes through the bleeding incision, extruding the organ like toothpaste. With a long steel clamp, he crushed the pulsating cord of artery and vein and nerve that had pumped life into the vital tissue. A quick slash and the avulsed organ lay orphaned in the sterile sheets. Within minutes, the left testes joined its companion, to make a pair of lifeless dead white male eggs.

Even as the specimens were being transferred to a clear polyethylene bag for the trip down to the Pathology Department and the patient's name and hospital number coded on the attached tag, Samuel was already sewing up the two skin incisions with a rapidity inspired by an abhorrence for the procedure he had been forced to carry out.

However, his instinctive revulsion at the necessity of emasculating a fellow human being was nothing in comparison to his shock when he accidently looked up and saw Martin Abels staring down at the surgery with undisguised joy. Samuel stopped what he was doing, appalled by the anesthesiologist's expression and his loathesome desecration of the surgical procedure. Martin saw the horror on the urologist's face, but, in response to his silent entreaty, only increased his smile. Samuel motioned toward the nurses in the room, trying to warn Martin of the grotesqueness of the scene but to no avail.

Abels was triumphant, all his past humiliations washed away by the euphoria.

"Oh, no, Sam," he said. "You are not going to deprive me of this moment. I have been waiting a long time to see this cocksucker lose his balls. My only regret is that you can't cut everything off. The fucking prick!"

And despite all of Samuel's fervent pleas, for the remainder of the case Martin Abels hung over the surgical field, soaking up the sight of the mutilation. He knew that should he live to be a hundred, he would always remember that sweet delicious moment of revenge.

Chapter / **FORTY-NINE**

MARTIN ABELS WAS NOT THE ONLY MEMBER OF THE MERCY
Hospital medical staff relishing the definitive act of Carl Lash's
emasculation. Even more than the anesthesiologist, to Simon Pirie,
the genital extirpation being performed six floors above him was
the culmination of a long, carefully manipulated chain of events.
There were times when the fragile shimmering web of deceit had
seemed too delicate, too weak, too farfetched ever to entrap the
wily prey. Now, waiting in his office, reading over and over the
morning's mimeographed "Operating Room Schedule," knowing
that the "Mr. Smith" on the list was receiving full measure for the

blow to Simon's own manhood, the graying pathologist could no longer restrain the shivers of excitement that coursed through his flabby body.

How many times over the past several months had he bitten his tongue rather than reveal his knowledge of Abigail's continuing affair with the proud, condescending Chief of Surgery? The countless nights he lay awake next to her, staring at the darkened ceiling, knowing that her contented state was the direct product of another man's sexual manipulation. The mornings he ate his breakfast and then bid her good-bye, receiving the perfunctory kiss on the cheek, the thought rankling that before he returned home that evening, Lash sperm would be smeared in her vaginal vault.

The self-control, the rigid bland effect, the harsh restraint chaining his emotions, realizing that the slightest betrayal would scare away his quarry. And now—now—he felt like an avenging angel. Retribution was being delivered.

He looked up at the clock, impatiently glanced at the door, waiting, breathless, quivering with anticipation for the prize of victory, the still-warm, succulent trophies that even now were being delivered to him in a thin transparent polyethylene bag.

When Simon returned home that night he found it impossible to thwart the rising tide of exhilaration. Even three Scotch-and-sodas were not sufficient to dull the blazing emotion in his eyes nor to calm his agitated, jerky movements. If Abigail had wondered what produced this heightened sense of tension, it is unlikely she ever would have deciphered the true reason. All she knew was that Simon was unusually affectionate.

It had been months since her husband had made the initial ritualistic overtures for intercourse. Usually, it was she who had to extend the aggressive suggestion. Not this night, though. Simon stationed himself close to her, nuzzling her neck and breasts as he finished, in quick succession, the strong alcoholic potions he poured for himself. Whether it was due to the uniqueness of his carnal desire or, perhaps, to her own cumulative sexual needs unsatisfied since Carl Lash's recent hospitalization, Abigail happily, even gratefully, responded in kind.

She unbuttoned his shirt, then, unknotting his tie, laid it neatly on the sofa next to him. He could feel her cool fingertips as they stroked the skin of his chest in wide circular patterns, lightly pinching his nipples, coming to hook on the top of his belt. He lay back against the cushions, his body slightly askew, as she knelt on the floor at his feet, taking off his shoes and socks, and then uncoupling his belt and opening his fly.

His short, stubby penis was erect and sprang forward as she released the tight restraints of his garments. He elevated his buttocks as she gently slid off his trousers and his white undershorts, leaving him a pallid slug, naked on the sofa.

Her hands still roughly kneading his abdomen, she moved her head lower until it was buried in the dark hair below. She flicked at the tumescent glans with her tongue, watching it thrust up, alive, to meet the glancing erotic touch. The head, glistening, bounced back and forth rapidly. Her tongue kept darting out to trigger off the reflex action, again and again while he made a feeble gesture to hold his engorged organ still, to impale its teasing tormentor, but she held his hands firmly, spread-eagling him on the couch.

He moaned and shifted his pelvis back and forth, trying desperately to climax his rising frustration. Then, before he could stop her, she seized the necktie and wrapped it tightly around his penis and testicles, knotting the silken thong in a grip of pain and pleasure. He tried to rise up, but she was already ahead of him. Avoiding his grasp, she led him, a willing frantic captive, up the stairs, tugging, hurting, exciting him with her painful multicolored leash.

She pulled him up onto the bed, catching his right hand in the silk bonds as he struggled to free his entrapped organs. Abigail quickly shed her clothes, afraid to lose any of the sexual tension building in her aroused spouse.

"You bitch! You lovely bitch. Cocksucker! Suck!" he ordered, frenzied. She seized his two testicles. Her mouth probed eagerly for his phallus, which he thrust deep into her pharynx. With practiced skill she manipulated the pulsating shaft against the smooth corrugations of her mouth, wrapping her tongue in an erotic spiral.

He thrashed wildly. His penis violetaceous and throbbing, he fell upon her, kissing, biting her nipples, ears, nose, mouth. Her face became flushed and her knees bent back, her thighs opening and closing to fan the warm wetness that heated her groin. She pushed his head down. It was his turn to rasp and caress, simultaneously sending coarse waves of pleasure through her heaving body.

Her pelvis rose and fell. Her knees locked and unlocked around his head until she cried out frantically, "No more! No more!" as her hands pulled him up, nails scratching and slashing his back.

He lunged forward, stabbing blindly. In and out. In and out. She screamed in senseless animal noises, urging him on. Her head arched back. Her eyes were glazed, unseeing. She panted short harsh gasps, her mouth wide open.

Had she been able to tear through the closed curtain of sexual desire she would have seen Simon suddenly discard any lingering expression of passion. His eyes were now steeled with hatred. His lips thin and mean. His right hand grabbed her neck. His fingers crunched in the gap between her jaws, driving them open. She looked up at him, her eyes unfocused, her thoughts dilute and impossible to coalesce. She could not . . . it would have been impossible . . . to know . . . to stop him . . . even if in her most lucid moment she could have conceived of the horror to come. With a vicious scream that tore from his lips, he shoved into her gurgling orifice the decaying spoils of his triumph.

As his wife struggled to surface, to reason, to feel and accept the round slippery objects that he had choked back into her mouth, as her nostrils tested to identify the putrefying stench of rotting flesh, as her eyes strained to focus upon the slimy masses of tissue gagging her, all she knew for certain was that her husband, still holding her imprisoned, knees straddling her body, was crying out howls of vengeance.

When she rose to consciousness, sick with comprehension, not daring to believe the evidence of her eyes, he bent close to boast of what he had done, dropping into her ears the pellets of verbal poison that would forever sear her soul.

Then it was her turn to cry out in desperate shrieks of denial that mingled in a cacophony of her terror and his joy. And Simon, above her, methodically masturbated. With a final ejaculation, he smeared the jets of thick white pollution over her body, brutally forcing the essence of his potency and dominance into her mouth where it mixed with the last mortal bittersweet taste of Carl Lash.

Chapter / FIFTY

It was three o'clock in the morning when Samuel Halpern received the emergency call from Mercy Hospital reporting Carl Lash's disappearance. According to the alarmed message from the night nursing supervisor, the last time the surgeon had been seen after his castration was at eleven-fifteen that evening when the charge nurse administered seventy-five milligrams of Nembutal to help him fall asleep. Two hours later, when she went to check his postoperative vital signs, the room was empty. His street clothes and shoes were missing. His hospital gown lay crumpled on the floor by the side of the bed, along with the blood-drenched pressure dressings that had been taped to his groin at the termination of the surgery.

Samuel dressed and drove to the hospital along the darkened deserted Cromwell streets. He noted a slight chill in the air, a token of the shorter fall days. The hospital seemed lifeless at that time of night, with the corridors half lit, the paging system oddly mute, and the bustling traffic arteries now empty and quiet. Entering Lash's hospital room, Samuel could only shrug helplessly at the irrevocable evidence of his patient's precipitous action.

"Goddamn it!" he said to the nurses on the floor. "Didn't any of you have the slightest indication that he was going to do such a stupid thing?"

It was not necessary for the nurses to deny the unjust accusation. One quick glance at their somber faces, and Samuel realized too well that his patient had exhibited signs of mental instability long before this night and, if anyone was to blame, it certainly was not they. He lowered his eyes to the floor, ashamed of his outburst.

He sat down at the Nursing Station, his fingers drumming nervously on the crowded counter. The overhead fluorescent lights cast harsh shadows in front of him. He thought hard. Lash had no family. His ex-wife, Priscilla, was living in Seattle. His children had moved away years before. He had no close friends, other than his random sexual partners. The operation was the least thing to worry about. Lash was a good surgeon and certainly could take adequate care of the incision. That would heal despite him, and just as well at home as in the hospital.

Home. On the half-chance that Lash might have gone to the only place of permanence he possessed, Samuel dialed his house. After many rings the phone was finally answered, not by the surgeon, nor even by his German housekeeper, but by a strange female voice, her speech splintered with emotion and fright. All Samuel could get from her was that Lash was there and sleeping quietly. Then the connection was broken, leaving him no wiser as to the fate of his patient.

The nurses crowded around the urologist, their expressions wide with curiosity and concern. Samuel could only make some inane comment, then fled, leaving behind him a trail of dejection and worry. There was no possible way in the world that Halpern could have known the identity of the party he had just spoken with. Not any more than the Mercy switchboard operator who, an hour before, had relented and let the almost hysterical caller through to the room of the new castrate lying within, shocked and narcotized.

Chapter / FIFTY-ONE

IT SEEMED THAT THE SHORT RIDE TO WEST CROMWELL TOOK
hours as Abigail drove Carl Lash from the hospital to his own
home. He lay sprawled across the seat next to her, his head
slumped at her side, as he tried to fight off the effects of the numbing drugs. Not until Abigail had got him to bed and stripped off
his clothes did she realize the horrible extent of the mutilation.

Carl lay there, in a dazed state, unseeing and unhearing, as
Abigail dressed his wounds and washed his emasculated body.
He would occasionally thrash about, his voice shouting hoarse
cries of "No! No!" whenever her gentle hands would accidentally

jar the raw flesh between his legs. The convulsions were more in response to some evil memory than from pain caused by her soothing touch. Finally, the hideous torment he had suffered surfaced no longer, and his sleep was peaceful.

Abigail sat with him those long countless hours while his body compensated for the trauma, and the injured tissues began their slow task of healing. She could see the rapid scintillations of the temporal artery pulsating across his forehead, the thump of his heart striking his chest wall. Her eyes caressed the bony frame, the skin ashen and white, and pulled tight like a drum over his concave thorax and pelvis. The dim night table light accentuated the deep hollows of his buttocks and carved dark shadows on his face, rendering him a cold, stark marble form.

During that long vigil many was the time her hands would slowly sculpt him, her fingers tracing his facial planes, continuing from his chest onto the flat abdominal wall, stopping only to depress the darkly pigmented inverted umbilicus. She would run her fingers over the rough grating stubble of what was once tight-curled pubic hair, avoiding as best she could the avulsed scrotum. The digital odyssey would finally come to rest around his long, thick, limp penis.

She held this remaining vestige of his destroyed manhood in both hands, with a firm grip, as if her pressure and will and warmth could protect it from further injury. Carl would stir for a moment. A faint flicker of a smile would cross his lips as if a happy illusion had made its way into a dream of bitter recollection. Seeing his response, Abigail would kneel down and, raising his detumescent organ, kiss the skin-wrapped head with her cool lips before lowering it down gently again.

Over the following days, as Lash's body gradually mended, Abigail never left his side. She had grown thin and wan and anxious in her devotion, and in the process seemed to have acquired a determination and kind of plain beauty Carl had refused ever to countenance before in a woman. He would often watch her when she did not know it. He cherished this tender woman who never denigrated his empty sac and whose presence, if only for a brief time, made him feel whole again.

Those were the moments, few and fleeting, when hope was re-kindled, and, with it, faith that life, no matter how imperfect, was the preferable alternative. He felt possessed once again of the necessary courage and confidence to accept his blemish as the exacting price of survival.

Then there were the times when he thought he could see the future for what it really was. A lingering, painful death from metastatic cancer, rotting his organs, rendering him incontinent, disoriented, and paralyzed, his skin blanched white from anemia, his breath fetid with bile. Those nights he would dream of the scalpel and the inevitability of the medical maze, like a dark blind alley, into which he had been thrust, without warning, and from which there was no escape. And, always, racing toward him—from both sides—to crush him, the headlights of advancing behemoths. He would shiver, trapped, the instant before their cumulative impact.

It was during those vivid nightmares that Abigail would feel the pain herself. Her flesh burning from the cruel revenge her husband had meted out to him, on *her* behalf. Her tears would mix with his, and she would weep for their mutual shame.

Thus, Carl Lash hovered in a sort of limbo, suspended between the realization, as a physician, that his prognosis was grim, and a desperate dream of a future, a tenacious wish for life, any kind of a life, to justify his sacrifice. It was not difficult for Abigail to perceive the perilous road upon which the victim was now treading, fighting to maintain his balance and to preserve his shredding sanity.

Abigail was frightened for his future safety. She knew well the diseased mind that had humiliated her and delivered the loathsome brand on her lover's body. She felt with an intuitive dread that Simon's compulsion for revenge would not be satisfied without one final mortal blow. She lived in dread of that moment.

She had not long to wait. When Carl was strong once more, his mind clear and alert, suffused with hope for the future, Simon Pirie came to call.

"Please, Carl," Abigail beseeched. "Please . . . please . . . do not see him."

Carl had often wondered how he would react to the inevitable meeting with the cuckolded husband. He *had* seduced his wife. No man could countenance such a flagrant blow to his ego and manhood. Carl could not repress a feeling of guilt.

More confusing was the disturbing knowledge that without Simon's skill as a physician, his life might have been lost from spreading cancer, detected too late to institute any sort of cure, albeit radical. For that, Carl felt a measure of gratitude.

Finally, he knew that the wronged husband could not help but see in him a half-man, emasculated, impotent. No longer a threat to his wife, nor, for that matter, to any woman ever again. A once virile, potent lover, now reduced to the contemptible pitiable state of a eunuch. The knowledge filled him with shame.

Simon waited patiently for Carl. He forced an even breath and ordered his quivering limbs to quiet, as he anticipated the last step in his plan. Only by his flushed expression, the flaring of his nostrils, the cold sweat that exuded from his pores, might one detect the signs of exhilaration that accompanied his malignant purpose.

"Please, Simon. Don't!" Abigail threw herself at her husband, pleading, begging, her face twisted with anguish and fear. "You can't, Simon. Haven't you done enough? Please . . . please . . ." He shrugged off her clutching hold, throwing her to the floor where she clung around his legs, to immobilize his person and purpose.

"Please, Simon. I will do anything you say. I will leave Carl. Go where you want. Do anything you wish. Only leave him alone. Simon!" she screamed, her cries piercing his deafened ears.

"Haven't you punished him and me enough? What more do you want?"

Carl descended the steps, one foot at a time, fighting back the pain. Upon reaching the living room, he was dumb struck by the scene that greeted him. Simon's impassive stance, his expression hostile and implacable. Abigail on her knees, tears streaming from her eyes, crying out futilely to her husband.

"Carl. Go back." She rushed over to him, to prevent him from approaching her husband. "Please. Do not listen to him. Please . . . for your own sake."

"Simon," he asked, his voice tense, "what is going on? I don't understand. What is Abigail so afraid of?"

Simon drew close. "I would imagine that my wife has not told you. I keep no such secrets." He cast a look of contempt at his prostrate wife who was now sobbing softly in a huddle at his feet.

"Tell me what?" Carl demanded.

"I came here to return something of yours," Simon began with a smile on his face, his demeanor pleasant and disarming.

"Something of . . . mine?" Carl asked. He sought Abigail who was reliving the scene unfolding in front of her like some recurrent nightmare.

Carl stared at the thin polyethylene bag that Simon placed in his hand. He could feel the weight of the gangrenous mass of semi-solid material that swirled softly in the murky liquid. He could smell the odd foul purulent vapors that clung to the outer surface of the container. But, how could he, any more than Abigail before him, absorb the horror of that offering? He listened to what this little man was telling him. The words seemed as unreal as what he held in his hands. He looked around him quickly, but could see only blurred and shapeless figures. Carl gazed blankly at the particles of his flesh trapped in the plastic container, unable to prove their existence any easier than the empty space that surrounded him.

Suddenly, he knew what he had to do. He stood very still, locked in place, quiet. He held his breath. Silent . . . never a sound . . . not a quiver. Only his eyes darting from one corner to the other. Almost . . . almost. . . . One last thing and then he would be safe.

Simon watched the strange pantomime with a morbid fascination as Carl Lash drew around him like a sorcerer's circle, a catatonic denial of the world to salvage whatever of value was left.

Simon started to say something, but one look at his wife, who was staring at him with an indescribable loathing, ready to tear at his throat, and he fled as if the devil he had just released had turned to pursue him.

Later, in the sanctuary of his own home, Simon Pirie found to his surprise that he was a changed man. For the first time in many agonizing months, he oddly felt at peace with himself. Even more unusual, and he could not explain why, he discovered that his heart was finally cleansed of its heavy burden of hate for the unworthy pair who had once so cruelly wounded him.

Chapter / FIFTY-TWO

SAMUEL HALPERN HESITATED BEFORE THE CLOSED DOOR FOR A minute, his expression sober. The extensive abdominal and neurosurgical procedures were successfully completed and the Garys had both come to the hospital this early fall day to take their child home. Samuel had talked with Mrs. Gary many times since the genetic studies had come back confirming that the child was a boy. He had laid out before the mother his projected timetable for the multiple urologic operations required to convert the chromosomal male into an acceptable masculine figure.

"First, Mrs. Gary, we will bring the undescended testicles down into the scrotum. Hopefully, we can operate on both sides at the same time and create a new scrotal pouch to hold the organs. Second, we will free up the penis, which is still partially buried in the pubic tissue and cover it with the foreskin to give it length. Finally, we will create a new urethral channel so that urine will come out the end of the penis instead of from the abnormal opening near the rectum."

"When can you start?" the woman had asked, eager for his answer. "You know, my husband has still not accepted the child. Perhaps," her face lit up at the happy suggestion, "if he can actually see with his own eyes, before the baby goes home, that it looks like a boy, the son he has always wanted, then, maybe . . . he . . ." She could go no further, shaking her head at the improbability of his conversion.

Samuel had been forced to dash her hopes. "I am afraid surgery should not be started until the child is much larger, to reduce the surgical risk. Because the structures we have to work with are terribly small and delicate, it would be unwise to repair the anomaly until the child is at least a year old, if even then. It would not be fair to the child, to push the surgery up, just for Mr. Gary's sake," he concluded, saddened by her desperate stance.

"I know . . ." She nodded, resigned to the unhappy verdict. "I just thought . . ."

Samuel had come in contact with Mr. Gary several times over the summer. The man remained just as resolute in his rejection of the child and in his resentment toward his wife for allowing the surgical procedures to insure the child's viability, as Joe and Brian had warned him. Samuel wondered, what then had possessed him to try, on his own, to reason with the embittered father when all others had failed so miserably?

He stared at the shut door, appearing to him now as solid a barrier as Mr. Gary's hatred. He gave a slight shudder. He had especially asked to have the father come to the hospital to meet with him. He owed Mrs. Gary at least this one last attempt to transfer part of the burden of clinical responsibility from her shoulders to the father's. With a gesture of anticipatory failure, Samuel pushed open the door and prepared to meet Peter Gary.

The scene that greeted him was the same as it had been on countless other occasions. Mrs. Gary was sitting in the wooden rocking chair that the Pediatrics floor provided for visiting mothers. The baby was wrapped in a light blue blanket, testifying to its sexual identity. Only its face was exposed. Samuel could not help remarking to himself what a beautiful child it was. Even now, he could see the soft blond hair, a golden washing over the pink scalp. The baby's eyes were inquisitive, intelligent, darting around the room in response to every sound and change of light perception. Its face was smooth and round, the skin clear and shining.

The mother was looking at him expectantly. He could see the fervent hope in her eyes. How could this tiny woman possess such an endless fount of that ethereal quality when by all that was holy in God's Kingdom it should have been totally consumed months ago and replaced with the sterile gall of her husband?

Peter Gary was standing by the window, the strong rays of the sun silhouetting his short lean frame. He had come directly from work and wore a pair of paint-splattered khaki pants and a torn denim shirt. He stood staring out the window, his body rigid and withdrawn, refusing to look at his wife and child. He turned slightly when Samuel entered the room, but then, just as quickly, turned away again from the unwelcomed intruder.

Samuel walked over to Mrs. Gary and silently squeezed her hand. He moved to the window and stood alongside the tensed father.

"Mr. Gary, Peter . . ." he said, holding onto the gentle greeting until the young man, embarrassed, was forced to turn to face him. "Peter, come and sit down with me for a minute."

The young man's face was cold and mean. "So that you can give me more of the same bullshit the other doctors have been feeding my wife?" he said, his fists clenched tightly by his side. "Don't bother! I have heard it all before. That thing should have been killed or at least allowed to die, instead of butchering it to keep it alive!"

Samuel took him by the arm and led him to a chair. "Mr. Gary, I am not going to tell you that you are wrong. I am not a hypocrite. I think if I had a child like yours, I would also want it killed, or at least to let it die, with dignity. No, Peter," he looked straight into the incredulous eyes of the father, "I am the last person in the world to tell you that what you are saying, the hate that you have, the rage that makes you want to strike out and hurt, to maim like you yourself have been wounded, is wrong and unjustified. No, I cannot say that to you."

Peter Gary stared at him with disbelief. Was this graying old man sincere, or just another wily bastard with honeyed words like all the rest? How could he tell? Against his will, he sat down in the proffered chair. He wanted so much to believe. It had seemed forever since he had believed in anything. Without his realizing it, he uncoiled and relaxed.

Samuel watched the tension subside, but did not say anything. He took Peter's cold hand and held it between his own. Oddly, the young father seemed to relish the human contact in spite of himself.

"You are right, Mr. Gary, in everything you say. I have no answer for that, any more than I can answer why your son was born the way he was. Nobody can ever answer that. Not any more than they have the right to take away your desire to avenge this tragedy. No. That is not why I am here."

The father was puzzled. He searched the physician's face for an explanation for his presence.

"Peter, your wife and the baby will be leaving the hospital soon. Any instructions, any future surgical discussions, we can have later, in my office. I came here to see you today because I wanted to tell you a story."

Suddenly suspicious, the father started to rise from his chair, but

Samuel reassured him. "No, Peter, I am not going back on what I just said. I am not going to challenge your justification for what you feel. No. I just want to tell you a simple story. Please. Sit down and oblige an old man."

Against his will, Pete found himself resting back in his seat, trapped by the power of the urologist's simple sincerity.

"Peter, we Jews have lots of stories. Maybe it is because for many thousands of years we had so little else. When you are persecuted and driven from place to place, stories are just about the only thing that you can take with you. And we Jews have had six thousand years to tell stories. This is one that my father, may he rest in peace, told me and my brothers and sisters, years ago when we lived in New York, in the slums of the East Side.

"Living in our tenement was a boy with a clubfoot. He was, oh, maybe eight or nine years old. His parents were poor. They couldn't afford to have the twisted leg fixed. So they gave him one of those big ugly black built-up shoes for him to hobble around on. You can imagine what the children, including me at the time, would do. You know how cruel children can be, especially to one another. We would laugh and make fun of him, make him cry, even despise him for his misfortune. The grown-ups would chase us away whenever we hurt him too much. They would warn us to stop, threaten, even punish us by hitting, but nothing helped. Then, one day, my father, may he rest in peace, decided to stop the baiting.

"I can remember it like it was yesterday. He made all of us, everyone he could find on the block, come upstairs to our small flat. He and my brothers and sisters and our friends. He made us all sit down on the floor of the tiny crowded living room and he told us a story." Samuel laughed. "I know, Peter, another story. But, as I told you, we Jews have a lot of stories. But, wait. Listen to me. It won't be much longer."

He resumed his tale, his expression soft and caring. "He told us a story of a famous rabbi in Poland who lived hundreds of years ago. To the Jews of that time, Peter, a rabbi was not just like a

((351))

priest or a minister, but more. He was also a judge, policeman, teacher, prophet. All of these, and yet *still* more. He was like a piece of the original cross, to be enshrined by the faithful. Something sacred and respected, and valued above everything else in the poor farming community where he lived.

"The inhabitants of this impoverished rural ghetto worshiped their rabbi. He was the sun in whose reflected glory their miserable lives shone. His wisdom of the ancient books of Hebrew law had spread throughout the whole countryside. People would come from miles around just to see him, to touch his shabby coat, to kiss his long stringy beard, to ask him a question, and, if they were truly blessed, to get an answer.

"One day, the people in the village decided that their rabbi should take a wife. The ancient law tells us that having children is a commandment. In those days, Peter, it was considered an honor to be married to the wise man, that holy rabbi. For a family to have the destitute, but renowned scholar as a son-in-law was an ornament of value beyond price. You must also remember that, at that time, marriages were made without the consent of the young people themselves. So, the elders of the community picked a bride for him. They picked the most beautiful maiden in town.

"She was seventeen. Her skin was clear. Her eyes large and bright. Her long black hair streamed down her milky-white skin. She carried herself regally like a queen. Her beauty was as renowned as the fame of her husband-to-be. Even more, she was the daughter of the wealthiest merchant in town. As to be expected, she had many suitors, for not only was she rich and beautiful, but spirited and intelligent and sensitive.

"Oh yes, Peter. One thing I forgot to tell you. The rabbi was a hunchback. His spine was horribly deformed. His tortured body cruelly twisted into a contorted stance. He limped painfully and dragged one shortened leg behind him as he walked."

Peter Gary seemed hypnotized by the dulcet voice of the narrator. He caught himself nodding as Samuel unrolled the beguiling tale before him.

"The marriage ceremony took place with joyous celebration. That night, in the marriage chamber, the new virgin bride lifted her veil to see the rabbi's earthly shape, in all its tragic nakedness. We can imagine the horror, the shock, the fright on her young face. The rabbi must have appeared, unclothed, an unholy apparition, a diseased figure whose flesh she must touch and caress. She cried out in disappointment and terror. Pity struck deep into the gentle heart of her husband.

"He did not compel her to consummate the marriage. He dried off her tears. He clothed her again and drew her to their nuptial bed. He sat down next to her and held her close to quiet the quivering in her slender frame. He then told her a story."

Samuel gave a short chuckle and shifted his position on the chair.

"The young girl's name was Rebecca. The rabbi said, 'Rebecca, last night I could not sleep. I do not know whether it was from eagerness at being married the next day or from fear of knowing what would happen when you saw me as you did tonight. For long hours I tossed upon my thin mattress, sweating, my heart pounding at what I knew would be this night we are now sharing. Then, in the early hours of the morning, I fell into a long, labored rest. I had a very strange dream.' "

Samuel smiled at his listener's now rapt absorption.

" 'I dreamed something I have never dreamed before. I dreamed that I was in heaven before I was born. I was there, high above the earth, waiting for my turn to be sent into the world. And, Rebecca, I was not as you see me now. I was tall and handsome. My back was supple and straight. My limbs firm and well-proportioned. My head upright and covered with ringlets of shiny black hair. My calves were muscular and I walked with a spring to my step. Oh, Rebecca, I was as handsome as you are beautiful.

" 'As I waited to descend to my mother, my heart was pounding with eagerness. How much I wanted to be born, to live my life with the zest and promise that my endowments guaranteed. I was an impatient, virile youth. Then I heard a noise. A low-pitched plaintive lament. I turned around and saw a little figure huddled in the corner. It was a little child, a girl. She was weeping, and the tears flowed like water. I went over to her and raised her head to see why she wept so.

" 'Rebecca, it was not difficult to see the cause of her sadness. She was deformed as if the hand of the devil had blighted her flesh. She bore between her shoulder blades the mound of a hunchback. One leg was foreshortened and her back twisted. Her complexion was mean and pitted, her hair thin and straggly. She cried in pain for her future birth.

" 'Rebecca, as I stood there, hearing her sadness, my heart went out to her. I helped her up and held her close to my bosom, letting her salty tears stain my glistening golden tunic. For some unknown reason I, too, started to cry, and I wept for her pain and suffering.

" 'Then I lowered her to the ground again. I thought long about this child whose tears had burned into my soul. Finally, I went to see God. I knelt silently before Him. He saw me there and raised me high. I looked at Him and at all the angels who had gathered at His side. I could not help myself. I fell down at His feet. Holding my hands up to Him, I pleaded.

" ' "God," I begged, "spare that little child. Look at me. I do not need my two feet level, nor even a straight back, nor a fair countenance. All I wish in the world to come is to love You and to worship Your laws of man. Take these other superfluous things from me, these lovely earthly adornments and mortal treasures. Let me, let me have the hunchback of the child. Give me her crooked spine, her broken limbs, her ugly features. Gladly I will assume all of these, if only you spare that helpless child of your love."

" 'Rebecca, I looked into the face of that child, and it was you. Then, I woke up.'

"And, Peter, it is said, my father, may he rest in peace, told me, it is written that the rabbi and Rebecca lived a full and rich life together. She made him the most virtuous and loving of wives. They had many children and descendants who have carried that story of their love down through the ages. Perhaps now, even you and I are part of that continuum."

Samuel rose from his chair and walked over to the window. Then he turned to face the somber seated figure.

"Peter, I have never met the rest of your family. Your wife tells me that you have three lovely healthy girls, each one a Rebecca. You and your wife are both handsome strong people. There are the five of you. All who can walk and live and love—all pure and clean and perfect. And there," he walked over to the mother, "there is your son." He reached to pick up the child. "Your son. The one who is misshapen and crooked and malformed." He held the baby up in the air, higher and higher, as if he were preparing to dash it to the floor. "And . . . he," Samuel shook the child so that it began to tremble and cry, "he will not walk, while the five of you can. Think, Mr. Gary. Think. You can walk over to love your child, if you ever will. He will never be able to walk over to love you." His voice grew stronger as he implored. "Now, Peter, tell me. What will you do?"

Peter Gary rose slowly to his feet. His wife held her breath. Samuel teetered as the weight of the child pressed heavily on his arms. Without a word, the father strode to the physician's side.

The father held out his arms. Although unable to mouth the words, his very gesture pleaded for the baby's body. Samuel surrendered the son to its father. Peter Gary took the baby over to the bed and gently laid it down. He unwrapped the blanket. Then, with a ginger touch, almost afraid of bruising the delicate pale skin, he undid the diaper. The pacifier fell out of the baby's mouth, and it groped blindly for it. Peter retrieved the lost object and replaced it in the baby's mouth. The child greedily sucked on it, making soft sounds of gratification.

The father watched the baby move. He felt the smooth abdominal skin, avoiding the scar that the colostomy had once penetrated. He shaped his hand lightly over the head, caressing the soft fuzz growing there. He flicked lightly at the everted umbilicus and gave a slight grin.

He turned the baby over to inspect its back. He could see only the still-red surgical incision through which Crowther had removed the deformity. The skin was otherwise smooth and intact. He ran his fingers up and down the now-intact spine. It was still sensitive and the baby gave a faint cry.

He tried to replace the diaper but fumbled with the tabs. His wife saw his clumsy efforts and went over to help him. He moved out of the way to let her complete the pinning. Then he came close again and carefully rewrapped the child in the blanket.

The baby began to make soft sweet cooing noises. Peter bent closer. One small hand grazed the stubble on his chin. He leaned even closer. The arms, now strong, adhered to each side of his face, the minuscule uncut fingernails sticking into his skin.

Then, unexpectedly, Gary drew back. He looked at the child with an expression that had never appeared before on his face. He raised his head high to see the urologist and his wife attentive to his actions. With a compulsion he could not account for, his head fell down on the bed next to his son. A piercing howl of anguish tore from his lips. It swirled around the room, seeking the forgiveness it knew it might never find. Then, the tears. The ever-flowing stream of sorrow for the pain he had caused. Helen Gary reached out her arms to pull him close to her. It was her tears of happiness, of thanks for a faith not misplaced that mixed with those of her husband.

Samuel tiptoed quietly from the room and closed the door behind him. Back in the hall, his demeanor changed once again to that of the dispassionate clinician. However, much as he would try, he could not erase that poignant tableau, which remained vivid in his heart for long moments afterward.

Chapter / FIFTY-THREE

THERE WAS NO REASON AT ALL WHY SAMUEL HALPERN SHOULD have recognized the soft, cultured, but persistent male voice that awakened him at seven o'clock on a Sunday morning. Politely, but firmly, it asked him to come to Carl Lash's home as soon as he possibly could. All Samuel could remember by the time he managed to sweep away the clinging cobwebs of sleep was that the matter was serious, could not wait, and could not be discussed over the telephone. Several times, during the two weeks since Carl Lash had fled Mercy Hospital, Samuel had tried to make contact with his patient. When he called by telephone, Lash's elderly housekeeper refused to put him through. When he drove by the house

((359))

on two occasions, he was denied admission. Concerned for the welfare of his patient, and alarmed by the unusual request, the physician rapidly dressed for the unexpected house call.

Lash's home was a large fieldstone and stucco Tudor dwelling set far back from the road with a circular driveway neatly bordered by a sinuous hedge of meticulously shaped yew trees. The house itself seemed quiet and empty, with shades and curtains drawn tight to hold in whatever secret it sequestered. What Samuel could not understand was the presence of the large, highly polished silver and gray Rolls-Royce sedan parked sedately in front of the pillared portico. The black uniformed chauffeur was slouched in the corner of the driver's seat, his cap tipped over his face. Samuel walked up the flagstone path, and with a mixture of foreboding and curiosity, approached the recessed door, prepared to answer the mysterious summons.

There was no reply to his repeated rings so he tried the knob. The door was open.

He entered the spacious foyer, but no one was there to receive him. He called out softly, "Carl, Carl," but there was no answer. The hallway was dark. As he walked farther into the empty living room he could see beyond a sliver of brightness outlining a partially opened door to the far library. He knocked lightly and then entered, to be brutally shocked by the horrible scene that lay poised within, waiting to pounce and tear at his sensibilities.

The surgeon lay slumped over his desk, his unshaven face accentuated by the deadly white color of his forehead that lay exposed within the crook of his arm. He wore nothing under his wrinkled bathrobe, which had pulled open, exposing his mutilated genitalia.

And—the stench! Samuel bent close to the inert form and sniffed the sour sewerage odor. It made him gag and he was forced to breathe through his mouth for relief. Lash was dead, and in his agonal moment he had evacuated his bladder and rectum. Even now, solid rivulets of yellow-brown feces slurried on the floor at his feet, staining the naked legs and feet.

Samuel lifted the head, a dead weight. The eyes were open. The pupils dilated. The mouth, dry and parched, jaws widely separated as if to say something in parting, but callously stopped in the process. Instinctively, Samuel slipped his right hand around Lash's cold neck to feel for the carotid artery. He pressed, harder and harder. Nothing.

Samuel stopped suddenly, his eye catching something he had not noticed before. Hanging from the wrought-iron sconce on the wall behind the lifeless form was a glass-liter bottle of intravenous saline. Running from it to Lash's right wrist, concealed under his fallen head, was a thin, transparent plastic tube, which terminated in a needle inserted into a vein on the dorsum of the hand and securely anchored to the pale skin with neatly cut strips of adhesive tape. Samuel examined the intravenous setup. The bottle and tubing were empty, full of air, and yet he could see there had been fluid in them from the residue of clear liquid left in the bend of the tubing where gravity had held onto it.

Samuel tilted the metal shade of the green tole desk lamp. The incandescent rays glinted off an assemblage of small glass bottles, hypodermic syringes, and needles scattered over the surface of the tooled-leather desk. The labels were identical—morphine sulfate. Samuel counted the vials. At least a dozen. He calculated quickly. There had been ten cc of potent narcotic solution in each bottle. At a strength of sixty milligrams per cubic centimeter, each vial had held, at one time, six hundred milligrams. Six hundred times twelve—God! He looked down at the dead man. Lash had run into his body a thousand times the normal dose of morphine for an adult male.

In a methodical manner, he disconnected the tubing and took down the large bottle. He straightened the cold figure, propping him up in the chair. He closed the eyelids and covered Lash with his robe. Then he picked up all the vials and gathered them neatly in a corner of the desk, the compulsive activity somehow relieving his emotional strain.

"Do you really think that is necessary?"

Samuel looked up in horror. For an instant he had the crazy thought that Lash was still alive. His heart raced. His palms flooded with sweat. He gasped as he leaned closer to reexamine the inert figure.

"No," the voice softly continued, "he *is* really dead."

Samuel turned, his eyes searching out the recesses of the room until they picked up the small white-suited figure, which raised itself up from the wing chair and walked slowly over to meet him. "Mr. Bell," the voice said, "Mr. *Lyman* Bell."

Samuel stammered his own name in reply, stumbling over the simple words.

"Yes, Dr. Halpern, I know who you are. *I* was the one who called you."

Bell led him away from the desk to the sofa on the other side of the room. Then, with much physical effort, he managed to move a velvet cushioned chair to face the urologist and seated himself opposite the shaken man. He could see the physician make a slow inventory of the room, his face always returning, magnetized, to the desk where Lash remained, an unwanted interloper in his own house.

Bell reached into his inside jacket pocket and withdrew a thin white envelope. He placed it in Samuel's hand and leaned back in his chair. "Read this, Dr. Halpern."

Samuel took out a folded sheet and read it through rapidly. Then, again, more slowly. There was silence. Once or twice Samuel looked up at Bell, his expression pale and frightened. He started to shake the paper at him, to beg him to cooperate in a mutual denial of the painful facts documented within. Bell did not move. Finally, Samuel reinserted the paper in the envelope and gave it back to Bell.

"Apparently, last night," Bell said, "Dr. Lash gave his housekeeper the evening off. He instructed her to deliver this letter to me this morning. You have read it? All of it?"

Samuel weakly nodded his assent.

"Then, tell me, Dr. Halpern. You are, or rather should I say have been, Dr. Lash's personal physician. I understand that you operated on him more than once. Tell me, is what Dr. Lash claims in the letter possible?"

Halpern remained as in a trance, staring at his interrogator, either unwilling or unable to voice the indescribable.

"Dr. Halpern, is it humanly possible for Dr. Pirie to have done that?" Bell said. "Could Dr. Lash in any conceivable way be telling the truth? Dr. Halpern! Could such a thing actually happen?"

"Yes! Yes! Damn it! Yes!" Samuel shouted. "Yes, it could." He looked over at Lash. "And it probably has."

"What do you mean 'probably'? Can't you tell?" Bell asked, disquieted by Halpern's equivocal and emotional reaction.

"Mr. Bell, everything that Carl Lash has written could have happened. But there is no way you, or I, or anybody, will ever know for certain. If Simon Pirie was clever enough to set up this whole unholy plot, he was certainly smart enough to cover his traces. Besides, whose word do you have? Mrs. Pirie, who was unfaithful to her hard-working husband? Who would believe her? The victim? What can *he* say? And I? The one who cut and mutilated and scarred?" His voice quivered. "I, who held the knife and led the poor bastard to do all this? What else can I say? I do these operations a hundred, no, a thousand times a year. I rely entirely on Pirie's word." He pointed to the letter concealed within Bell's jacket. "In fact, without this letter, I would have to do the same thing to Lash all over again."

"Dr. Halpern, in his letter, Dr. Lash commended me, as Chairman of the Board of Trustees, to pursue this matter. To see that justice is done. To punish the guilty. Therefore, I have a moral obligation to bring you into this unfortunate situation."

Samuel weighed Lyman Bell's words. Lash had made a dying man's request, pledged by his own life. It was a cry for retribution —revenge—for justice.

"Mr. Bell," he promised, "you have my help. It is not right for Pirie to escape unpunished. We'll take this letter to the authorities, expose this sordid affair, arouse the public——"

Lyman interrupted him. His face was darkened in a scowl. It was obvious that he disapproved of the decision. "Why, Dr. Halpern? Carl Lash was a philanderer, an adulterer. In a biblical sense, he deserved to be castrated. An eye . . . for an eye."

"These are not ancient times, Mr. Bell. Castrated. To be tortured like this? To be driven to suicide? No! No! It is not fair. Lash may have been an adulterer, but his murder was an injustice."

Lyman Bell cocked his head affectedly at Halpern's words. "Justice? Is that what I heard you say? Are we now talking about equity? Fairness? Is it a fight you want, Dr. Halpern? You and right— against Pirie and evil? I would have thought you would have had enough of fights."

Samuel looked quizzically at Bell. How much did this old fossil really know? Was he really a devil to see into men's souls? Yet, he was right. Did he really want another battle? He felt tired, exhausted. He was an old man. The future was a precious, fleeting currency. He stopped short to ponder how it should best be spent.

Lyman Bell sensed the urologist's doubt.

"Dr. Halpern, must we always fight? We human beings should have learned long ago that we can never win. It is not for us to rail against the injustice meted out by those in control of our destinies. The Greeks were proud, always fighting with their gods, disputing their fate. They were invariably defeated for their presumption. You Hebrews, too. Perpetually fighting with yourselves, like we Christians with the devil. You always lose, as do we. We have our hell in the next world for the fallen vanquished, while you have your purgatory in this life."

He paused, waiting for the words to imprint in Samuel's consciousness. "Do you still want to fight, to seek vengeance on Dr. Pirie whose only crime was to exact retribution?"

"But if we don't," Samuel objected, "then what purpose is life? If we just accept wrong without a protest, a struggle?"

"I may be an old man in Cromwell," Bell said, "laughed at by most, respected by a few. But, I have lived longer than you and most other people in this community. I have watched this garden of earthly paradise for many years. How many victories do you think that I have seen in my lifetime, Dr. Halpern? Do you delude yourself into believing you'd have been a victor if you had trapped your son into staying in Cromwell or kept out some poor innocent like Christopher Amen? These are such minuscule skirmishes. The fact that each of us is born to die is the final, consummate defeat, meted out simultaneously with the fact of man's conception. Tell me, haven't you had enough? How far did your friend Dr. Abels get? And poor Carl Lash. Where are *his* laurels?"

Bell stopped. He reached inside his jacket and withdrew the letter for the second time. He held it between his fingers, lightly, delicately like a butterfly to float off at the first suggestion of a breeze.

As much as Samuel tried to avoid it, he found himself drawn to the white letter. Should he accept the challenge? His thoughts fled to distant memories that surfaced and blurred and coalesced like a turning kaleidoscope far out of reach. He thought of Christopher Amen . . . and Kupperman and his son, David . . . and Martin Abels . . . and Simon Pirie . . . and Carl Lash. Then, his own son, Stephen, branded with hate on his forehead, like the mark of Cain.

"Mr. Bell, what you say may be true." Samuel's words bore the taint of reproach. "Perhaps dragging this terrible affair into the public eye would be most unsatisfactory. There is no guarantee that we could prove Simon Pirie's culpability, let alone legally punish him for this vile deed. Certainly, all we can be certain of is that dishonor would fall upon Mercy Hospital and all those in high places liable for the actions of its employees.

"But," Samuel continued, "it is clear that Dr. Pirie cannot continue to fill a position that weighs the values of life and death, of pain and mutilation. The man is sick and requires psychiatric help, if not judicial retribution. Even you can see that."

"I agree, Dr. Halpern. I will personally guarantee that Dr. Pirie is removed from the staff and placed in the custody of the proper physicians. He will never again assume a position of medical responsibility. Maybe in time some research post somewhere. Yes," his voice became assertive, "you have my promise. But," he added quickly, "let me handle Dr. Pirie in my own way . . . quietly, privately. Will that satisfy you?"

The urologist stared at the aged figure, a wondering expression on his face. He thought of his buried dream. Thirty years of the same sterile vision, gone now.

He remembered back to that angry evening in the empty store, the walls dark and forbidding, yet sheltering the nascent dreams of others in Cromwell, young and hopeful as he once was. Their dreams perished, too, like his own.

The confusing images suddenly cleared. He knew what he must do. He felt endowed once again with a sense of commitment long since interred by the gall of passing years. He plucked free from the outstretched hand the thin white crackling paper gauntlet and held it hostage.

"Yes, Mr. Bell. That will satisfy me. However," he added, tapping the white paper envelope against his palm, "there is one more thing."

Lyman listened well to the unexpected request. He agreed to the private bargain. His words gladdened the heart of the physician. "Then, Dr. Halpern, Samuel, we are agreed."

Without hesitating for a moment, Samuel ripped the paper into a thousand shreds and defiant, joyful, blew them, swirling and twisting to the floor like worthless day-old confetti. He knew now that the long nights to come would never be empty again.

Chapter / **FIFTY-FOUR**

"HOW CAN I EVER PAY YOU BACK?"

Samuel Halpern thought to himself that he had never seen Frederick Dearing smile. During the long months while he had impatiently watched Laurie Dearing for the slightest evidence that her right kidney was regaining function, her husband's threatening countenance had never varied. Now, seeing him in the small consulting room while he waited for his wife to complete her weekly battery of biochemistry tests, he seemed a completely different person.

All through summer and early fall there had been no improvement. Samuel would see the patient in his office every two weeks. He carefully checked the placement of the nephrostomy tube that still perforated her flank to drain out the urine that never came. Mrs. Dearing would pull out the small spiral notebook in which she kept a record of the kidney's output. The two or three cc each day seemed to mock her meticulous entries.

Each week stapled to her chart on his desk in his office was the most recent report from the laboratory testifying to the ever-increasing level of blood urea nitrogen that normal kidneys would have automatically extracted from the circulating serum.

Samuel would often pass her coming in or out of the Dialysis Unit where three times a week the artificial kidney purged from her system the lethal effluvia of life. He admired this frail woman whose ability to cope with the psychological and physical trauma of her tenuous bond with life never ceased to amaze him. She had adjusted the routine of caring for home and children to accommodate the critical hours spent in the cellar of Mercy Hospital. If she did complain, the rare lament was always coupled with concern as to what her affliction was costing her family, not only in financial terms, but also in denying them the undivided strength of a healthy mother and wife.

When the kidney finally opened up, the change was so silent, so barely perceptible, that at first Mrs. Dearing failed to recognize its salutary hallmark.

"I don't know if it means anything," she reported during one of her semimonthly office visits, "but, some days, it seems like there is more urine coming out."

Samuel examined her figures. The increments were small, but steady, and increasing. Ten cc a day. Then twenty, fifty, two hundred, until . . . until that memorable day when Mrs. Dearing was forced to measure the output by the hour, so rapidly did the precious fluid pour out of the tube to fill and overflow the plastic leg bag she had strapped to her thigh, empty and unsullied these long, patient months.

And the waste urea. It stopped its relentless rise and held steady. One perverse day it rose, but just as quickly lowered itself again before the tears had even a chance to gather. Then . . . it fell . . . and fell . . . and fell!

The dialysis. Those painful hours seeing her blood washing in an inert machine. The sessions grew shorter. Then less frequent, until that glorious morning when the two stainless-steel and plastic cannulae were removed from her wrist, leaving only a thin red scar to mark the site of the man-made umbilicus.

One last task. The nephrostomy tube was withdrawn almost simultaneous with a heartfelt hug and kiss, which embarrassed the urologist by its spontaneity and joy. He blushed, something Judy had never thought her boss capable of doing in all the years she had worked for him.

Now, looking up at the unbridled gratitude of Frederick Dearing, Samuel heard again those fateful words, "How can I ever pay you back?"

Samuel did not immediately answer. He glanced over the rims of his glasses at the happy husband. Samuel hesitated. Did he dare speak? Would this man understand the passion of his request?

Dearing observed his silence. He knew the dedicated care this Jewish physician had rendered his wife over the months. The doctor had unselfishly given him that necessary support, never begrudging that faith during those long months when it appeared that his wife would remain a renal cripple for life.

"Dr. Halpern, Laurie and I owe you so much. Without you she would not be alive today."

Samuel tried to protest, but Dearing held him back.

"I know what you are going to tell me. That you did the surgery and God restored the kidney. I know all that. I am not basically a religious person. If God gave her life again, it was through your hands and skill."

He looked straight at the doctor, his gaze burning deeply. "I have only one prayer for you, Dr. Halpern. That your skills never fade away, or, if they do, that God gives you knowledge of their failure and the wisdom to accept that fact with grace. Not like Flaherty!" Dearing's face suddenly darkened but the scowl was only a momentary one. "Did you know that Ralph delivered Laurie?"

Samuel could only shake his head, puzzled at the strange question.

"Yes, he delivered Laurie and her two brothers. If you ever go into Ralph's office, there is a Christmas card on the wall from Laurie's mother and father, blessing their Dr. Ralph as if he was the Second Coming. Even more, Dr. Halpern, there are four cards from us, from Laurie and me. One for each of our four children, two boys and two girls. Ralph delivered every one of them. Seven children he brought into the world. Every one of them perfect. I know that he didn't make them healthy, but somehow you have a special affection and respect for the man who actually severs the umbilical cord as if that act, in itself, is the definitive Creation.

"Our last one, Eric, was not an easy delivery. Laurie had a terrible time, bleeding throughout the pregnancy. There was a possibility that Laurie would lose the baby or, God forbid, the baby would be brain-damaged from lack of oxygen. Ralph worked miracles. He kept the pregnancy going. Then, at the last minute, he induced labor and delivered Eric—perfect.

"Oh, I know how angry and bitter I was these past months. I wanted to strike out and hurt, even kill Flaherty for what he did to my wife. Maybe, maybe," his voice drifted lower, "if Laurie had not gotten better, I still would have persisted. I don't know. Thank God I will never find out. But now, it is different. I cannot bring myself to seek revenge against Ralph. I have a wife who will live, thanks to God and to you. I have four healthy children. That should be my full cup of happiness. Perhaps I am afraid that if I seek revenge, and act as a lawyer and judge and executioner, God will strike me down for presuming beyond my measure. I know what I am saying sounds superstitious but I feel that I have no right to act vindictive. If one could weigh on a scale the good and evil that Flaherty has done, it might actually balance out over his lifetime. Oh . . . I don't know . . ." He sat down heavily and lowered his head to the table.

Samuel reached over to touch his arm in a gesture of understanding. After a moment, Dearing straightened up. He withdrew an envelope from his jacket pocket. He laid it on the table between them. He watched the doctor with a quizzical expression on his face.

"Dr. Halpern, even if I can excuse, though never forgive, what Ralph did to my wife, how can I possibly condone this?" He reached for the envelope and ripped it open, extracting a sheaf of papers. He waved a page at Halpern. "This is from Dr. Brandon. Yes," he repeated, in response to Samuel's startled expression. "Here it is. Blackmail!" He could see the urologist shaking his head, to protest what he was hearing.

"Your hard-working, sweet and innocent Joe Brandon. Oscar Brandon's son. Cromwell's own All-American. The pitiful underdog. Here it is. Blackmailing Ralph Flaherty to get what he wants for himself and for Dr. Brian Terris."

He laid the paper down again.

"Don't get me wrong. I am not the pious hypocrite. I am not saying his demands are unjustified. Quite the contrary. I am on the Board of Trustees at Mercy. I live in Cromwell. I know very well what Flaherty and Best have been doing to those two young doctors. But, that's life. It happens in business, in politics—even in law. It is the American way of life. But, that is not even the issue here. What is, is that Joe Brandon was blackmailing Ralph Flaherty —using my wife!"

Samuel started to rise. His eyes sought the door, desperately wishing he could escape.

"No, listen," Dearing commanded, "there is more. Ralph came to see me. He brought me Brandon's demands. He told me what Brandon had done, what he threatened, what he knew about my wife's case. Ralph offered to resign from the staff, to do anything else I wanted. He said he would not contest any legal action over Laurie that I instituted. He said that he would retire from active practice rather than spend the rest of his days fearing Brandon's hold over him. Dr. Halpern, he was an old, broken man. I told him to do nothing but just to sit and wait. That I would do nothing.

"Then, within a week, Joe Brandon came to me, offering to serve as my expert witness in a malpractice suit against Flaherty. He volunteered a deposition. Here it is." He picked up the second sheaf of papers. "All of it. A violent condemnation of Ralph Flaherty by none other than our healer in white. He did not know Ralph had been to see me. I did not tell him. I took his deposition and thanked him."

Dearing spread the pages out on the table in front of him where they made an asymmetric patchwork of white on the black Formica.

"Tell me, Dr. Halpern, what should I do with them? Who is the more guilty? If you can reduce people to a metric scale, which of the two is more deserving of punishment? Both? Or neither? If I condemn one, I exonerate the other. Flaherty, who has seen his skills disappear and, without malice or premeditation, has mortally wounded an innocent, a man who has had a legacy of trust and devotion as well as unethical conduct toward his competing medical peers. Joe Brandon. Smart. Skilled. Persecuted unjustly by the above defendant. Seeking only to redress that wrong. His *modus operandi*, blackmail. The weapon itself, not of his making, but discovered by his superior training and another's incompetence. His amoral or immoral commitment to correct an injustice at the cost of hiding his colleague's ineptitude. An ineptitude that would have cost Laurie her life if it had not been for you." He looked again at the silent man, remembering in the process, by a sudden intuition, his other earlier dilemma.

"And you, who saved my wife. What can I do—for you?"

((372))

Chapter / FIFTY-FIVE

IT WAS A DAY OF TRIUMPH FOR ALEX CARDANO. FOR DAYS HE HAD attended to the myriad of details for the opening of the Bell Memorial Family Clinic with a degree of personal commitment and energy that astonished even his closest associates at the Millsite Shopping Center who were already inured to his customary frantic pace. With a worried scowl, he looked up at the clouding sky and crossed himself, that blessing, like the preceding dozen, embellished from his limitless supply of ancestral saints.

The weather report for this gray November Sunday afternoon was unfavorable. A thick layer of dark clouds lay close and heavy above him, rolling down across the Highlands and blotting out the sun. He licked his finger and held it in the slight breeze. A northwest wind was blowing. He shivered as an errant pawn of arctic chill pierced through the last defense of Indian summer. He gave one last glance at the heavens. "Please, Holy Mary, keep away the rain!" he prayed, and then scurried in the direction of the parking lot where attendants were cursing at the avalanche of cars still trying to enter the packed five-acre site.

Marjorie Hollis and Bea Wharton had arrived early and were sitting at the head of the broad promenade of seats. Rented folding chairs stretched all the way from the platform in front of the clinic entrance to the high chain link fence at the opposite end of the asphalt pavement. Every few minutes, Marjorie would stand up on some pretext or other to adjust her clothes. She would sneak a fast look at the hundreds of seated people, most of whom were workers from the Flats with their families.

Bea watched her friend with bemused tolerance. She could not really blame her for acting so excited. The unexpected resurrection of the Millsite facility had caught her, like everyone else in Cromwell, by complete surprise.

Marge had reapplied for her former position and been immediately accepted back. She had carried out her job of recruitment with such zeal that Prynne, who saw many of his best staff resigning, told her with a wink of his eyes that she was his biggest competitor, figuratively as well as literally.

"You know, Bea," Marge said upon reseating herself, "I never thought I would see the day when those bastards in the Highlands would come to the Flats. Some of them haven't been down here since visiting their bootlegger during prohibition.

"Well, anyway, there goes your theory about the ladder," Marge teased. "There they all are. Flaherty and Best and Terris and Brandon, and the others. All sitting together like bosom buddies."

"I know . . . I know . . . I hate to admit I was wrong. It all goes to show that there is no accounting for people." Bea's face grew thoughtful.

"I wonder if there is something we don't know behind it all," she mused out loud, then leaned forward to hear better the third in the series of orators extolling the virtues of Cromwell's ruling hierarchy.

From his vantage point on the far end of the dais, Jack Ryan looked over the assemblage with a warm glow of satisfaction, fanned by five rapid shots of Jack Daniels taken in advance to fortify himself against the beginning of winter. This momentary effusion of happiness was heightened by the more permanent and tangible knowledge that all those people spread out before him in the audience, now so mercifully blurred and fuzzy, would soon be pouring through the doors of Mercy from its satellite facility in the Flats.

No longer would he have to worry about the new north wing, the deficits, and the complaints of those who faulted the Board of Trustees for their decision to build it.

Yes, he beamed at the man seated next to him, things were decidedly looking up. He smiled again at the receding crowd and nodded softly as he drifted off into a welcomed ethanolic reverie.

Morris Prynne knew well the reason for his contractor-trustee's boundless joy at the opening of the clinic in the Flats. He, too, shared the enthusiastic reaction. It was hard enough to keep the hospital budget balanced with costs rising daily to shame even his most expansive twelve-month projections. As the prime sponsor of the Bell Clinic, Mercy Hospital would be guaranteed all the admissions and would handle all the laboratory and X-ray tests. Thanks to Lyman Bell's largesse, there had been no need for any government handout, and, with it, the inevitable piper to pay. There was no longer any fear of interference in the affairs of Mercy from the labor unions, consumer groups, Washington bleeding-heart agencies.

He puffed out his chest with deserved pride as he looked over his audience, trying to pick out people he knew he should wave to, the wives of the trustees, generous donors, and the random priests and nuns who ran the diocesan office. The Flats got what they wanted. A walk-in clinic, sound, inexpensive, and in their own backyard. Mercy, as usual, would still continue to rule from the heights. Yes, it had all worked out so well. He nodded happily to himself and to the ancient man by his side who had made it all possible.

The sights and sounds of the celebration were muted and muffled to this reserved man. He had heard his name mentioned more this long weary afternoon than he had imagined it had been uttered all the years that preceded it. Countless times, some finger was pointed in his direction by the minions of idolators who paraded up to the microphone. How many more disturbing claps of applause before the tiresome procession would finally terminate?

He was aware that others, for varied reasons, were pleased with the afternoon's events. Was he satisfied with what he had done? Yes, he was that. Over one hundred years ago, the first Bell had walked on the very spot upon which his frail form now rested. Now there was a new Bell heritage started. A very private legacy. One of his doing—alone. At the very end of his life, almost too late, he had helped to create something that was his very own, untainted by the heavy hand of the Bells deceased. On the very soil of the first Bell Mill, the wealth that it generated from the sweat of its workers was returning to the source. He felt content. He had lived long enough to close the ring of the Bells. He was the very last of that name. The mills were gone. Now, here, he could see the beginning of another cycle. He looked far out over the audience with pride. Who there, he wondered, would be alive to see the end of this new one?

Lyman Bell was not the only person gathered in Cardano's real-estate bonanza this chilled November day to be preoccupied with his all-too-brief mortality. Samuel Halpern had promised Sylvia that he would not dwell upon the painful absence of his firstborn and heir. However, from his raised position, searching vainly through the audience for the familiar figure of his wife, he could not dispel the hurt that lingered. Without being aware of it, his fists clenched tightly in his lap until the knuckles showed white.

The attractive blonde woman sitting next to him could see this visible sign of distress. She laid her hand over his and squeezed it in a gesture of compassion. "Don't, Sam," Stephanie murmured softly so that no one around them could hear. "Instead—be *proud!*"

Samuel was quick to decipher her cryptic comment. He relaxed and took her hand in his. "You are right, Stephanie. I know I should. I guess it will just take time."

Time. He thought of the popular expression physicians use in the treatment of disease. "Tincture of Time." That magic medicine when you assured the patient that if he or she would wait long enough, everything would heal. Such a simple phrase. Yet he'd used it so often he'd forgotten what it meant.

Time. That is what he had told Laurie Dearing when her life was suspended by a water-bathed cellophane tube. What he told Frederick Dearing when he had no other answer to his beseeching questions about his wife's prognosis. Time had healed, or was it a miracle? What difference did it really make? He located Mrs. Dearing in the second row of the audience, looking up respectfully as her husband finished his speech.

Samuel wondered if Mr. Dearing had known what he was getting in for when he had asked him for his bill. Before replying, Samuel could not refrain from telling the lawyer the story of the rich man whose only son was dying, choking to death on a bone caught in his throat. After the doctor had extracted the foreign object, the father thanked the physician, asking him what he wished for a reward. The doctor sagely observed his potential benefactor. "Give me only half of what you would have given five minutes ago."

Dearing had laughed heartily at the Jewish physician's tale, but still persisted. Frederick Dearing had pledged his word and he had performed admirably. He had turned out to be every bit as smart and crafty as Samuel had predicted. Amen was happy to turn over to the lawyer the blueprints, the black-and-white schematics, the flow sheets, the protocols of what was once to have been his own. It had taken Dearing only five days in Livermore Falls to absorb and assimilate the data. Then, under his aegis, Prynne's bureaucratic expertise, and Lyman Bell's money, the clinic was reborn.

He could see the Garys, far back, the father standing out in the aisle with his new son in his arms. He could not make out Peter Gary's face, but it was not necessary. Time had helped there, or was it him? He laughed. How could a silly story wash away such hate and bitterness? Maybe it was just that the time was ripe.

Time. But he was sixty-five, with a cholesterol count of twice normal.

Would time heal the mortal wounds between Flaherty and Brandon? He had forced acceptance of Joe's two demands through the Executive Committee. Despite their malicious origins, the recommendations to help Terris and to let Jules Kline on the staff were honest requests. What about the two obstetricians? Both men would now have to face each other the rest of their lives, knowing that each possessed the secret of the other's crime. He sighed. What more appropriate punishment or hell than that? Well, perhaps they will learn to recognize in each other their own faults and vices. At the very least, it would certainly make them both more cautious and humble.

And Simon Pirie? It seemed that he had disappeared off the face of the earth, silently and without warning. It was rumored that he was suffering from overwork and nervous exhaustion and had been committed to a private hospital outside of Boston. His wife, Abigail, had taken an apartment in Cromwell and had filed for divorce. Samuel shook his head. How ironic that Simon Pirie had vanquished Carl Lash. But at what a price.

Time. That is what Stephanie said she needed when he asked

about her personal life. Chris was too busy to leave Maine and she had come to the opening of the Bell Clinic in his place. She reminded Samuel that she had been married once before, and divorced. Perhaps she was still too scared. She and Chris loved each other. As for the rest, wait and see was all she said.

Ann was pregnant, she reported. Stephen was very happy and enthusiastic in setting up the clinic. But, something was missing. Stephanie found it hard to put into words.

"A part of Stephen is here, in Cromwell, Sam. I know what has happened between you and Stephen. I feel, though, that someday Stephen will return. According to Chris, the clinic should be running smoothly in about two years. I believe that when Stephen has something proud to look back upon, something he has achieved by himself to show you, then he will be ready to come home."

Stephanie could see the deepening lines in the man's face. The yellowing of his teeth. The mottling of age staining the bald areas of his scalp. His back, rounded and slumped despite a vain attempt to hold himself erect.

"Two years, Sam. I know that it seems like a long time. You have already waited thirty years. It is only a hope. I can't guarantee that he will return, but this is his home. It is just that as *your son* he could not come back to you without first accomplishing something to make you proud of him. Now, he has."

Stephanie was right. He had never really been proud of anything Stephen had done during his whole lifetime. He had always belittled his son's successes as products of his own intervention and active assistance.

They say that mothers hold onto their children, he thought to himself. But fathers can be just as bad. Why had he held on to Stephen so? Just to fulfill a selfish dream of his own immortality? But was that really just an excuse to prevent the new generation from going out and competing with the aging parents? In the wild, when the young lion is ready to hunt and kill, the father deliberately drives it from the lair, to force it to seek a life of its own. Do we not deserve a child's vengeance, its sharp claw and tooth, if we pervert this natural evolution?

Samuel stretched his vision far out beyond the darkened hills sawtoothing the horizon. For the first time, he felt proud of his son for standing up to him and turning his back on everything he had been brought up to treasure, all that his father had taught him to revere. Pride. But, also—pain. Pain of that bloody vicious parting, the sign of his son's majority.

Pride and pain. What was it that Stephen once said to him? It is essential that a person should suffer and endure. He gave a mocking laugh. Since when, at the age of sixty-five, did he have to learn wisdom from the lips of a child? Maybe that, too, was part of living.

Pride—and pain.

His son.

Time—and healing.

He looked at the clinic sign over his head, suddenly realizing how much of its reality was his own creation. He could not repress the flush of pride in his accomplishment. Stephen was right. Monuments are even more important to the living than to the dead. Stephen, too, needed his own token of manhood.

He broke off from that twisted trail of reflection as Stephanie nudged his arm. He raised his head to hear his name calling out from a thousand loudspeakers, like synchronous echoes.

He slowly rose to his feet. He could not see individual faces, but was aware only of collective memories. He could not understand the rivers of praise and thanks and affection that poured over him, anointing him from every space. He could not comprehend the multitude who were on their feet, clapping, applauding, as Lyman Bell and Frederick Dearing moved closer to take him by the arm.

The sunlight streamed through a crevasse in the dark clouds to dazzle the path in front of him.

Enthusiasm gave wings to his feet. Hope gave strength to his heart. He knew not how many years were to come, nor what kind of years they would be. He no longer had any fear.

A doctor, a healer, a husband, but, most of all, a proud father, he stepped forward—to meet what remained of his life.